Last Chance
AT THE
Lost and Found

MARCIA FINICAL

Ann Arbor
2008

Bywater Books, Inc.
PO Box 3671
Ann Arbor MI 48106-3671
www.bywaterbooks.com

Printed in the United States of America on acid-free
paper.

Bywater Books First Edition: October 2008

Cover designer: Bonnie Liss (Phoenix Graphics)

ISBN 978-1-932859-28-7

This novel is a work of fiction. All persons, places,
and events were created by the imagination of the
author.

Mixed Sources
Product group from well-managed
forests and other controlled sources
www.fsc.org Cert no. SW-COC-002283
© 1996 Forest Stewardship Council
FSC

Acknowledgments

I would like to thank the following people for their help in bringing Bunny to life: Dale Atkinson, Judy Avila, Jeff Campbell, Colleen Conlisk, Dan Czaran, Marsha LaBounty, Betty Levin, Marianne K. Martin, Ruth Mondlick, Lynn Paskind, Paula Paul, Kelly Smith, Peggy Sullivan, and Kelly Williams. I apologize to anyone I've unintentionally forgotten.

And finally, I would like to thank my high school English teacher, Larry Sutton, for teaching me how to write a sentence. A little knowledge is a dangerous thing.

Prologue

Long, long ago, in a mythical time known as The 1950s, a man and his wife lived in a small cottage on a dirt road near the edge of town. The man worked as an auto mechanic and his wife, contrary to the mores of the time, did not stay home like a good wife should, but worked as a barmaid in a local saloon. Soon a little girl covered with soft downy hair was born to them. The man laughed and called her "Bunny," but his wife thought the baby was a pain in the neck.

They would have lived happily ever after, there at the end of a dead end street, on the wrong side of the tracks, but something snapped inside the man's wife. She screamed, "Take your 'I Like Ike' button and shove it!" at the man, packed her bags, and left for parts unknown.

Chapter 1

Born To Be Wild

I love to kiss. So when Cheryl Hoffman, head cheerleader for the Marysville Indians, planted one on my lips, I nearly swooned. True, I had just come first in the girls' district cross-country meet, but Cheryl Hoffman? She was Miss Teen Queen: rich, popular, pert, and perky with a '65 red Mustang that beat every modified rod on the street.

Still, I must have looked dazed when Cheryl wrapped her arm around my waist and led me behind the bus barn. She plastered me against the corrugated steel, took my face in her hands, and kissed me like there was no tomorrow—hot, passionate kisses that inflamed my senses, sweet, soft kisses that left me wanting more. Holy shit! She kissed so well I wanted to cry.

Cheryl pulled up my T-shirt and pushed my bra off my left breast. "It gets better," she said with a wink. She traced her finger over my nipple, down my stomach, past the elasticized waistband of my running shorts. "I'll pick you up at eight tonight. Be ready!"

She turned and ran back to the squad, her lacquered hair not moving a fraction of an inch in the stiff breeze.

She was right. It did get better.

That night, we drove to her father's sand and gravel

pit out on Highway 65. The grounds looked deserted—abandoned truck bodies backed up to massive piles of dirt, front-end loaders down, their buckets at rest. Once we got beyond the lights of the office, it was perfectly dark except for millions of stars twinkling in the heavens. We drove to the far side of the yard, where the rockcrusher stood. "Just to be safe," she said.

Cheryl shut off the engine but kept the radio on. The Righteous Brothers crooned "Unchained Melody." "Just a minute. I gotta get something." Quicker than you could say, "love, dove, peace," she jumped out of the car and ran around to the trunk, where she pulled out a six-pack of beer and a blanket. "Here, help me with these."

Obligingly, I opened the door and took the beer. As I reached for the blanket, she pulled me close and laid another soft one on my lips. I was hooked! Cheryl kissed better than Rick Sturgess, my current boyfriend, and certainly was prettier to look at. We climbed into the back seat of her Mustang and chugged our beers. With a prickling sense of anticipation, we unbuttoned each other's blouse and unhooked each other's bra. I had never "done it" with a girl before, so this was totally new territory for me. Sure, ol' Rick had tried to feel me up dozens of times, but it was never this exciting. I sat there for a moment, my heart pounding wildly, unsure of what to do. Finally, I pulled her close and kissed her to relieve the tension. Within no time, our heavy breathing steamed up the windows.

Cheryl rubbed her perky little breasts against my larger ones. "Oh God, Bunny, I've always wanted to rub up against you!" She pulled at my zipper. "Please," she begged, "I want to do it with you!"

Christ, I'd never been so hot in my life! I still couldn't believe Miss America Junior grabbed my ass and wanted

4

my breasts. I managed to take her pants off, no small feat in her backseat, and guided her on top of me. She looked star-struck as she reached out to fondle my breasts. With increasing urgency, she kneaded them in the palms of her hands until I couldn't stand it anymore.

"Cheryl, please, do it now!"

Her eyes blazing, she slid her fingers along my pussy, teasing and tickling my clit until I exploded in a way I never dreamed possible. Cheryl was an angel and I was in heaven.

"Oh, baby, I knew you'd be like this," she said between mouthfuls of boob. "You are sooooooooo good."

My grades improved that semester, mostly because I studied at her house so we could be together. At night, we'd take "study breaks" and cruise out to the gravel pit for more fun. No one ever figured out that we were lovers, although we hung out together as much as a girl/boy pair. Her friends couldn't figure out what a great girl like Cheryl—Student Council, Honor Society, captain of the cheerleading squad—was doing with a poor kid like me. Mismatched or not, all I knew was that I liked fucking Cheryl.

She graduated with the Class of '68 and managed to ditch her drunken friends for one last night with me before she was off to Europe for six weeks. "Oh Bunny," she said, looking up from between my legs, "I'm gonna miss you."

"I'm gonna miss you, too," I said as I arched my back to keep in contact with her mouth.

"Will you come visit me at Arizona State?" She probed farther with her tongue, tickling my inner lips.

"Yes, yes, yes, yes, YES!" I screamed as I thrashed about wildly in her backseat.

It was quite a send-off.

♦♦♦

Two years later, I graduated with the Class of '70, singing "All we are saying, is give peace a chance," swaying back and forth on the risers, stoned to the gills. I always felt cheated that I didn't graduate with the Class of '69. Cheryl said I was a natural. And true to my word, I was outta Marysville before the ink was dry on my diploma.

I packed all of the belongings I could fit into my Jeep and headed south to Los Angeles with my dad's blessing. Being a bum at heart, the first place I drove to was the beach. I got a job at In-N-Out, a local burger joint that paid my rent and provided both of my meals for the day. When I wasn't flipping burgers or going to the bars (thanks to my fake ID), I lived at the beach. Ah, sun, sun, glorious sun! I was the color of the Coppertone girl, with long straight blond hair that reached below my shoulders. Both guys and girls hit on me, but by the time I turned twenty-one I had ditched any remaining notions about being bisexual. Bring on the babes! Curvaceous babes, Chicana babes, Afro-American babes, blond babes, Oriental babes, white babes, tan babes. Softness and roundness mixed with an attitude—I wanted it all!

One night, I wandered into a place in Van Nuys, looking for some fun. I elbowed my way to the bar and ordered a drink.

"Draft, please."

A boozy floozy wrapped her arm around my waist and cuddled tight. "Hi, I'm Wendy. Wanna come to my house?"

I stared over Wendy's shoulder into the glaring eyes of a serious-looking butch. There was no way I was going to get between those two.

"Uh, no thanks," I said and dodged to the left. Wendy pursued. I stepped backward until I was up against the bar, my exit blocked in all directions.

"She's with me," said a man to my right. He put his arm around me and pulled me next to him.

Wendy looked deflated and slunk back to the protective arms of her butch.

I turned to thank my would-be rescuer and stared into the eyes of a drop-dead gorgeous man. He wore a black T-shirt stretched across his well-muscled torso and Levi 501's.

"I doubt that either one of them is your type," he said.

"Uh, yeah."

He held out his hand. "I'm Peter, and you are ...?"

Peter is right, I thought as I glanced at his basket. "I'm Bunny."

"Bunny?" Peter cracked up. "Bunny, let me buy you a drink. Here, stand by me and people will think we're a couple."

"You're not straight, are you?"

"Absolutely not. But we make a great-looking couple, and I do love to fuck with people's heads."

What the hell? He was gorgeous and I was almost broke. If he wanted to buy me drinks, who was I to spoil his fun? I offered him a smoke.

"No thanks. I got something better than that." He dug into his pocket and pulled out a small bottle. "Here," he said as he unscrewed the lid, "take a hit off this."

I looked at the innocuous bottle he held. "What is it?"

"Poppers."

I plugged one nostril and inhaled deeply.

"Slow down, hotshot," he said. "I have plenty."

About four seconds later, my entire body felt like it was going to explode. I'm having a heart attack! "What a rush," I said, finally.

He grinned. "I know. It's great for when you're having sex, too."

7

"I bet. A little too much for me, though." I handed him the bottle. It felt too creepy.

Peter and I partied together the rest of the night, each of us trying to outdo the other in a libidinal attempt to pick someone up. By the end of the evening, neither of us had scored and only the seriously sloshed were left.

"Last call." The bartender cast a weary eye over the remaining customers.

"Fuck. I'm too drunk to drive," I mumbled.

Peter put my arm around his shoulder and half carried, half dragged me out. The fresh air hit me like a freight train and I puked on the sidewalk.

"You're coming home with me," he slurred.

I was in no shape to argue. Peter poured me into his car and we headed for some distant neighborhood.

The next morning, I awoke in an apartment I didn't recognize, sprawled on a couch that wasn't my own. Where the hell am I? I heard coffee-making sounds coming from what I supposed was the kitchen.

"Mornin'." The same gorgeous man from the night before, Peter, greeted me, clad only in his Jockey shorts.

I stared at his body. It was every bit as good as I remembered.

"Thanks," he said as he wiggled his ass at me. "Would you like some coffee?"

"Yeah." I sat down at the kitchen table. On the wall hung a picture of a man in a Marine Corps uniform that looked to be Peter's twin. I glanced between Peter and the picture.

"Sergeant Michael Avelino Sena, United States Marine Corps, MA'AM!" He executed a perfect salute. Even his dick stood at attention.

"Who?"

He laughed. "My name's Michael Sena. I go by 'Peter' at the bars."

"So what do you do, Michael, when you're not getting drunk and picking up women in gay bars?"

"I do not pick up women," he said haughtily. "I merely rescue damsels in distress who are about to be pounded into a pulp by the bouncer."

"That woman was the bouncer?"

"And Wendy is her girlfriend who's always hitting on the prettiest young thing that comes in."

"Thanks, Michael."

"I wish I had something more to offer you than coffee, but I haven't gone shopping lately," he said apologetically.

"That's okay," I assured him. "Look, if you can give me a lift back to my Jeep, we can stop at In-N-Out for a burger."

"Mmmmmm. In and out. I love it!"

I wasn't quite sure what he meant by that comment. "Let's go."

Michael grabbed his keys and we climbed into his '62 Chevy Impala. The engine would not catch when he turned the key. "Shit!"

He tried starting it three more times with no success. "I think the battery is dead."

"Mind if I have a look?"

He gave me a strange glance and released the hood latch. "Sure."

I lifted the hood, braced it, and immediately saw the problem. "You got a wire brush? Your terminals are corroded."

"Huh?"

"Look here." I pointed to the hard white buildup on both of his battery terminals. "I bet if we got this off, your engine would turn over."

"Sorry. No wire brush." He shrugged.

"How about baking soda. Do you have any baking soda?"

"I don't bake."

"Didn't I see a can of Coke in your fridge? That'll fix it."

Michael looked at me blankly. "What?"

"Just get me the Coke."

He disappeared into his apartment and reappeared a minute later with a Coke.

"Now. Watch and learn." I popped the top and poured half of the contents on each terminal. Immediately the buildup started to dissolve. I helped matters along by scraping off what I could with a stick I found on the ground. "Try it now," I said when the white gunk was mostly gone.

Michael tried the key again and the engine roared to life.

"Thanks," he said, as I slid into the passenger's seat. "You know, you don't look butch."

"You know, I thought you'd be butcher, being a Marine and all."

He laughed. "Okay, okay. I get your point."

"You come to the beach often?" this old guy in his thirties asked before I even had time to get out of my Jeep.

"You oughta know, you've seen me here dozens of times."

He chuckled. "Hey, I gotta proposition for you."

I cranked up Aretha's "Chain of Fools" louder. "I don't do guys," I said and pointedly looked toward the ocean.

"Fuckin' dyke. I know you 'don't do guys,' " he said with a grin. "I can make you rich."

I turned and squinted at him. "I don't hook and I don't sell drugs either, at least not to people I don't know."

"Would you fuckin' shut up for a minute? You've got a fuckin' hot body. You know, the real classic type—long legs, big tits, nice ass, a face you wouldn't have to put a paper bag over. I'm a photographer for Franklin's of Beverly Hills and you're the type of girl we pay big bucks for. You know, the real 'party girl' look."

"Yeah, right." I looked toward the ocean again.

"Stupid bitch." He dug into his pocket and handed me a card. "Look, here's my card. If you're interested, call me." He turned to leave, then stopped. "Better yet, I'm doin' a shoot here tomorrow at four. Come down and take a look. You can talk to the girls, but you don't get to fuckin' touch 'em. Understand?"

"Yeah." I shrugged and stuck his card into my back pocket.

Mr. Photographer adjusted the strap on the heavy bag he was carrying and walked toward the beach.

After he was gone, I pulled his card from my pocket. It had the familiar "Franklin's of Beverly Hills" logo with his name, "Angel Ortiz, Photographer," printed on the bottom. Okay, so the guy had some cards printed. So what? On the other hand, I had seen him a number of times with some of the hottest-lookin' babes on the beach. What did I have to lose? I'd be off work by four tomorrow and come see what was happening.

I was very familiar with Franklin's of Beverly Hills, although I didn't own one lace-up corset or one pair of crotchless panties. I grew up with Franklin's panties and stocking and bras, all black or red or lace, draped over the shower rod, strewn across the living room, or heaped carelessly on the kitchen counter. My dad liked "uninhibited" women as he called them. They stayed with us for a few weeks or a few months until he got tired of them and sent them packing, or they left in disgust because of his drinking. Some of them tried to play "Mom" to me, you know, do the 1950s housewife thing—bake cookies, take me to the zoo, fix up the house. I think some of them thought I was some kind of living doll that talked, and all they wanted to do was dress

11

me up and play "house." God! Garter belts galore, seamed or seamless hose, push-up bras, bikini swimsuits before bikini swimsuits were acceptable, lacy see-through underthings, all those things that screamed Jump my bones! I just didn't have the money to buy that shit.

I met up with Angel the next day. He had three girls in various stages of undress, who tried to look sexy while they turned blue in the frigid water.

"You couldn't stay away, could you?" Angel smiled at me.

"I wanted to check it out."

"Well, check it out. Girls," he said to the models, "this is ..." he turned to me.

"Bunny," I said.

He rolled his eyes. "Bunny. Perfect."

"Hi, Bunny," one girl squealed. "I'm Gloria."

"I'm Rapunzel," said the tall one with the long red hair.

"I'm Aphrodite," said the brunette whose lips were an alarming shade of blue.

Angel turned to me. "Let's get some shots of you ..." his voice trailed off. "I know. Next to your Jeep. You've got the perfect 'bad girl' look. Rapunzel," he said to the redhead, "take off your top and give it to Bunny. I want a lot of cleavage here."

Quicker than you could say "naked lady," Rapunzel whipped off her top and handed it to me, a lascivious smile on her lips. One of the other girls gave Rapunzel a towel to cover herself. Rapunzel stared at me with a look of pure lust.

"Bunny, undo the top button on your jeans. That's right. Now stick your hands in your pockets and give me the best 'I can kick your ass' look. Too smiley! That's better. You're one hot lookin' dyke, honey. Now lean towards the Jeep and let me see a little of your butt cheek. That's right! Perfect!

12

Bunny, you're a natural! Wait 'til Arthur sees these shots. He'll hire you on the spot!"

We shot 'til the sun was too low to give the right light. Rapunzel kept giving me her best 'Come hither' looks and took great care to make sure my bikini top rode as low as possible. When it got too cold, she graciously offered to warm me up.

"You're somethin'," she said. "So what's your real name?"

"Bunny LaRue."

"No. I mean your real name."

"Bunny LaRue."

She looked at me incredulously. "Your real name is Bunny LaRue? That's not made up?"

"My real name is Margaret Donnette LaRue, but everyone calls me Bunny."

"Well, no one calls me Rapunzel except Angel and Mr. Stiff. You can call me Mary."

I smiled. "I like Mary, but 'Rapunzel' kinda suits you."

"I was christened 'Mary Elizabeth Christina Vincente.'"

"Where are you from? Not here I bet."

"Brazil, Indiana, by way of Taos, New Mexico, Phoenix, Arizona, and Blythe, California."

"Blythe? What's in Blythe?"

"My boyfriend was stationed there, then we split." Mary shrugged. "I always wanted to model, so I came to LA and met Mr. Stiff through Angel."

"Mr. Stiff?"

"Franklin's Art Director. His real name is Arthur Spires, but we call him 'Mr. Stiff' behind his back. Be careful around him, Bunny. He's kinda freaky." She shivered.

"Why do you call him Mr. Stiff?"

Rapunzel rolled her eyes. "Well, he's real stiff around us girls, especially when we're doing an in-house shoot. You

13

know, like he's too turned on by us and has this gigantic hard-on."

"Mr. Stiff," I mused. I pictured a gold chain wearing, Elvis-type who wore polyester jumpsuits, gold chains, and dark glasses—a real sleazeball.

"Avoid him at all costs, Bunny."

Angel was right. Mr. Stiff did hire me on the spot. And after meeting him, I fully understood why the other models called him Mr. Stiff. Somehow his posture seemed both unnaturally controlled and sleazy at the same time. He gave me the chills.

"Guess what?" I fairly shouted into the pay phone after leaving that freakshow of his office.

"What? You get busted for pot?" Michael teased.

"Very funny. No, I got offered a job as a model with Franklin's of Beverly Hills."

I heard a gasp at the other end of the line. "No shit! What are you going to model? Corsets? Bustiers? Shit like that? God, I'd die for one of those Franklin's harem outfits." Michael sounded as excited as I felt.

"I didn't peg you for a drag queen."

"I do gender fuck. I love the contrast between satin gowns with elbow length gloves over my hairy arms and chest. It's the best of both worlds." He chuckled. "Hey you freakin' model, you wanna go out and celebrate your new career? Half-price tequila shots at Mimi's on Saturday night."

"Sounds great, bro."

Four months later, when I was making decent money modeling for Franklin's, Michael and I rented a townhouse apartment together. Our landlady, Mrs. Caldecott, a sixtyish busybody with bright orange hair didn't trust same-sex roommates.

"I know you young people don't have the same values we had growing up, but I'm glad you're not like Phil and Terry, those homos in 112."

I was about to protest, but Michael silenced me with a glance.

"Yes, ma'am," he said.

"And your two bedrooms will give you lots of room when you start having babies." She took me aside and whispered, "He's so handsome! You'll make beautiful babies!"

"Uh, yeah."

Mrs. Caldecott handed Michael the keys. "Now don't you two worry about anything. You'll fit in just fine here!"

"Yes, ma'am," Michael said, shutting the door behind her. "Especially with those 'homos' in 112! Welcome home, baby!" He lifted me up and twirled around à la Baryshnikov.

Not missing a beat, we went out and partied that night, me with Rapunzel, and Michael with whomever.

Chapter 2

Long, Cool Woman

"Hi honey, I'm home!" I said in my best June Cleaver voice. Michael was in the kitchen, cutting up vegetables. "How was your day?"

"Okay. Mr. Stiff is acting weird again, but that's not new."

"How so?"

"Well," I took a bite of carrot, "he's got his favorites like Lucinda, the one who only does bra shots, and Rapunzel. He rides them a lot and neither one of them says anything. I don't get it."

"Rapunzel? Our Rapunzel? That doesn't seem like the Rapunzel I know."

"I know. That's what's so weird about it. By the way, we're going away for the weekend. Hopefully, if I ply her with enough weed, she'll talk about it." I stood there for a moment and watched him work. "Hey! Quit fondling the zucchini!"

Michael stuck his tongue out at me. "You're just jealous of my many talents. And, by the way," he pointed his knife at me, "why am I the only one who cooks around here?"

"Because, darling," I said as I lit a joint, "you hate my cooking."

"That's because the only things you ever cook are hamburgers, spaghetti out of a can, frozen TV dinners, or that weird rice stuff—what do you call it?"

"'Speckled Puppy' isn't weird, it's dessert—rice, brown sugar, and raisins. And if we're talking 'weird,' what about that sorry-looking teddy bear you have dressed up in a yellow satin swimsuit with a Miss America sash across his chest?"

"Bruno's celebrating the 1975 crowning of Miss Texas as Miss America."

"What?"

Michael laughed. "He's my teddy bear from when I was a kid. Sometimes I dress him up like a hippie with a tie-dyed T-shirt and bellbottoms, then midway through the year we switch to Miss America. Every year, I make him a new gown, or this year, it was a satin swimsuit. You wouldn't believe the price they wanted for lamé."

I imagined introducing Michael to a friend: This is my roommate, Michael, and his cross-dressing teddy bear, Bruno. I must be stoned.

"You're turning the conversation away from the fact that you never cook, you know." Michael arched his eyebrow.

I shrugged. "I hate to cook. My dad said I was the only person he knew who could burn water."

He rolled his eyes. "Give me a break."

"It's true!"

"Yeah, like you never learned a thing from your mother."

"My mother left when I was three. My father cooked hamburgers, TV dinners, spaghetti out of a can, Speckled Puppy, and macaroni and cheese out of a box. To this day, I can't stand macaroni and cheese out of a box."

Michael turned to me. "You're serious, aren't you." It was a statement, not a question. "My mother was a terrific cook. Even with six kids she made empanadas, chorizo, arroz con pollo, sucres, stuff that would melt in your mouth. I learned how to cook in self-defense, or you'd be calling me 'Gordos' now."

A sudden pain shot through me. "It must have been nice growing up in a big family."

"Yeah." Michael was quiet for a minute. "Yeah," he said bitterly, "it was great until they found out their son was queer. You know what my mother said to me?" His voice cranked up an octave. "'There's no such thing as a queer Chicano!' Then they turned their backs on me." Michael slammed the knife into the cutting board.

I hugged him hard. Although we were both gay, that's where our similarities ended. I was the single child of a single father in the fifties, decades before single parenting was acceptable. My father, bless his soul, tried to give me everything his auto mechanic's salary would allow—new clothes from J C Penney, vacations at the beach every summer, and a fire-engine red Jeep Wrangler he rebuilt when I was a junior in high school. He seemed to understand my heartache when Cheryl graduated. I can't say he was thrilled at the prospect of having a gay daughter, but he didn't love me any the less because of it.

Payday and the weekend beckoned. Rapunzel was chafing to get out of the city to find a new bar where she could reinvent herself again. I wanted new scenery because every time I turned around Mr. Stiff was hassling her over some inconsequential matter. As we drove to the coast, I asked the question that nagged at me for months.

"What's between you and Mr. Stiff, honey? He treats you like dirt."

"Nothing." She seemed an ice age away as she stared out the window.

18

Something was bugging her, that was for sure. I didn't want to wallow in the weird place she was, so I reached into my bag and offered her a joint. "Try some of this new weed—it's great."

She turned and smiled. "Thanks."

We found an overpriced motel in Laguna Beach with a view of the ocean and a complimentary bottle of bubble bath. Rapunzel immediately coked up and sat back in her chair, more at ease than I had seen her in weeks. I wanted to know what was going on, but I didn't want to know.

"Where do you want to go?" she asked.

"Michael said there's a men's bar here that's really nice."

"Great. I need to change." She dashed into the bathroom and reappeared as her favorite bar persona, "Rachel the biker," complete with leather pants and vest with a navy blue headwrap tied around her hair.

"I need a drink. Let's go," I said.

We were ready for another disco bar, the kind of place Michael liked to frequent, but this place was quiet and relaxed. We ordered our drinks and watched the fish swim inches below in the salt-water aquarium, which was also the bar. The boys around us bought our drinks or lit our cigarettes and slyly or not so slyly checked out Rachel's leather accouterments. Once again, Rachel was a hit.

An attractive dark-haired woman got up from a nearby table and approached us. "Hi, I'm Ronda. Mind if I have a seat?" She sat on the barstool to my right.

"I'm Rachel and this is Bunny." Rachel reached across and shook her hand.

"You guys new here?" Ronda looked us over carefully.

"We just drove in from Hollywood. You live around here?" Rachel asked.

"No. I'm visiting my brother," she indicated a man at the

table where she had been sitting. "This place is my getaway when I'm tired of the city. I get so bored going to girl's bars."

I don't know why, but I pictured Ronda as a suddenly single woman who came here to lick her wounds until her next conquest.

Ronda tapped out a cigarette from her pack and held it up expectantly. Rachel reached over and lit it for her. "So," Ronda said in a cloud of smoke, "what do you two do?"

Hook.

My radar was up and I knew she was homing in on Rachel. "We're models for Franklin's of Beverly Hills," I said.

Ronda looked genuinely surprised. "I thought I recognized you both. Don't you do the patterned hose shots?" she asked Rachel.

Line.

Rachel's face lit up. "Yeah, that's me!"

"And aren't you Franklin's latest bad girl?" Ronda looked briefly at me.

Thank you, God, for some recognition. "Yeah. How'd you know?"

"I work at Fox Studios in the Costume Department. We buy a lot of stuff from Franklin's." She looked across at Rachel. "It seems to me they have the two of you mixed up."

And sinker.

I could feel Rachel's ego expanding at the speed of light. If I ever needed to fear for our not-quite relationship, this was the time. Ronda was good-looking, flattering, and had direct ties to show biz. Rachel/Rapunzel/Mary was good-looking, insecure, and had major starlet fantasies.

"I have a headache, darling," I said to Rachel. "I'd like to go now."

"Sure, Bunny, go ahead." Rachel stared at Ronda, practically drooling.

I leaned into Rachel's line of vision. "No. I meant us."

Rachel got up and took Ronda's hand. "Don't worry about me, Bunny. I'll get a ride back."

Christ! It happened right before my eyes! "Fuck you, Rachel!" I screamed and stomped out the door.

I don't know how Rachel got home that weekend, but it wasn't with me.

Monday morning, Mr. Stiff called me into his office. I was batting 1.000. No one ever wanted to be alone with him. Arthur Spires was the dirty old man your mother warned you about. To him, women were breasts and cunts and asses—sexual playthings for a man's pleasure. But Arthur Spires was also Mr. Franklin's right-hand man. He instinctively knew what would appeal to every testosterone-laden male with a three-inch dick—leather and lace, sugar 'n spice and everything naughty, illusions of grandeur tied up with a pretty pink bow. He fancied himself a "ladies' man," but the only "ladies" he got were the ones whose insecurities were greater than his own.

My stomach did flip-flops as I walked into his office. His walls were plastered with shots that were unsuitable for the catalog: embarrassing, overly suggestive photos that showed too much boob or too much crotch. Arthur Spires was like the photos that hung on his walls—too much. His greasy hair was too long for a balding man in his 40s; he drank too much; and even with a beer gut he dressed in tight clothes like some young stud in his twenties. Arthur Spires was a nightmare acid trip come to life.

"Bunny," he began, "I'm very pleased with your work. You shoot well and we've been getting positive feedback on your 'look.' You're the 'baddest' girl I've hired in some time and our readers are eating it up. I want more of the 'you-can't-have-me' expressions you do so well. You know—more attitude."

More attitude? Already my poses bordered on "Bitch Goddess Supreme." On the other hand, Franklin's paid me well for what I did. "Okay, Arthur, I'd be happy to work on it." I glanced at his crotch. Sure enough, he had a hard-on. Time to leave. I started for the door.

"Oh, and Bunny, one more thing." His smile made my blood run cold. "I want you to stop seeing Rapunzel. It's interfering with her work."

"What? Rapunzel's work is fine! If anything, it's better than mine. She gets here in plenty of time for her shoots."

Arthur's smile turned to a snarl. "I didn't ask you. I'm telling you. Understand?" There was malice in his voice.

"Fuck you," I mumbled as I walked out. Not that there was anything between Rapunzel and me anymore, but he didn't have the right to ask us to stop seeing each other. What a prick!

Either because of guilt or divine intervention, Rapunzel and I didn't run into each other for the next couple of weeks. It was only when I dropped into Personnel to pick up my paycheck that I found she had been calling in sick the entire time. I realized then something major was going on that had nothing to do with me.

Late the next Friday afternoon, I was in the dressing room, gathering the items I needed for a lingerie shoot the next week. Try as they might, the photographer's assistants never seemed to find the right sizes for us. Most of us gathered our own clothing so the shoots wouldn't take forever.

"Hi, Bunny."

I turned to see Rapunzel nervously jingling her keys. My heart melted at the sight of her. "How've you been, Rapunzel?"

22

She hung her head. "Not too good." She looked up, tears running down her face. "I'm sorry, Bunny. I was a real shit to you."

I wanted to hug her and comfort her right then, but my pride wouldn't let me. Part of me wanted her to suffer.

She looked at the floor. "I came in to get my things. I thought everybody'd be gone by now."

The ball's in your court, LaRue. You can't be an asshole forever. "I've got everything I need. Let me help you, then. Let's get outta here."

She put her hand on my arm. "Bunny? I need to tell you something."

"What, baby?" Finally!

"It took me a long while to decide." She hesitated, then said, "I'm leaving for good."

"What?"

Rapunzel shook her head. "I have to. I can't stand it anymore."

"Stand what?"

"Mr. Stiff."

In some strange way, that answer satisfied me.

She smoothed my hair. "I'm sorry. It has nothing to do with you."

"What's he doing to you?"

Rapunzel shook her head and remained silent.

"Are you going to be all right?"

"Yeah," she said distractedly, "I'll be all right." She was gone. Although she stood four inches from me, she was already gone.

"Will you keep in touch?"

"Yeah." By the flatness in her voice, I knew I'd never hear from her again.

At her car, I buried my head between her breasts and cried. There was nothing I could do to keep her.

23

She held me for a long time. "Be good, Bunny." She got into her car and drove off without a backward look.

The following Tuesday, Mr. Stiff dragged me into his office. "Okay, where is she?"

"I don't know." I was numb. I had no idea where Rapunzel was.

"Her apartment is empty and she left no forwarding address. Where is she, Bunny?" He shook my shoulders.

"Take your fucking hands off me, you slime." Something inside me turned ice cold.

Mr. Stiff turned a shade of red I thought was the precursor to a heart attack. "Get out of here. I don't want to see you for a long time!"

No problem, asshole. My extended weekend lasted three weeks.

Chapter 3

You Are The Sunshine Of My Life

My love life with Rapunzel was ancient history when I decided to go to the "Take Back the Night" march. You know, meet some chicks, as well as do the socially responsible thing. Okay, really, just to meet some chicks.

There were over 300 people, mostly women, milling around when I got to the rally, although the paper later reported "between 60 and 80 demonstrators." Some held hand-painted signs with slogans like "Hands off my body!" and "The night belongs to women too!" Others practiced karate kicks at imaginary opponents. I wandered over to where a nice-looking woman with her hair pulled back preached to the crowd.

"Hear me, sisters! White capitalist pigs have oppressed us for too long. For too long we have been men's chattels, their bitches and their whores! For too long we've been chained to an impossible ideal of what a woman should look like: long blond hair, an unnaturally thin body. For too long we have been judged on our physical attributes, our boobs, our cunts, and our asses!"

She was describing me.

"We must rise above our oppressors and claim the power and dignity we have as women! No longer shall we let men define who we are! No longer shall we submit to socially oppressive roles—housewife, caretaker of men's needs, unpaid domestic laborer, mistress, or prostitute!"

A number of women called out, "Right on!" and "Tell it like it is, sister!"

I could tell her speech had been going on for a while—the crowd stood mesmerized by the rise and fall of her voice. Soon the climax would come. She would issue a challenge, and the crowd, swept up in the fervor of righteous social change, would rally behind her.

She strode up and down the podium, microphone in hand. "Tonight let us take back the night so we can walk down these streets with no fear of rape!"

"Yes! Yes!" Voices from the crowd called out.

"No fear of assault!" Her knuckles strained white around the microphone.

"You got it!"

"No fear of reprisal!" The speaker's eyes blazed.

"Hallelujah, sister!" A woman swayed back and forth, her hands above her head.

The speaker leaned toward the crowd. "Tonight let us create a community where Hispanics and Blacks and Whites can all live without fear of each other! Where housing is available to all, and where children go to sleep with food in their stomachs!"

"Yes, sister, yes!" The crowd frothed at the mouth. Mob mentality was setting in.

Her voice rose to a crescendo. "Join with me, sisters and brothers! Let us all join hands and Take Back the Night!"

Screams of "Yes! Yes!" and "Right on!" rang through the crowd.

"Let us begin!" The speaker joined hands with the woman on either side of her and marched up the street singing, "We shall overcome, we shall overcome, we shall overcome some daaaaaay ..."

Sounded good to me.

I joined hands with a Black woman—when did they stop being Afro-Americans?—and a six-foot drag queen who wore a platinum blond wig, sequined top, and white vinyl miniskirt. We would do it! We would take back the night and build a society where peace and justice abounded. These were my brothers and sisters, Black and White. And Hispanic? When did they stop being Chicanos?

The drag queen stumbled. "Bitch! I broke a heel!" He held up a former five-inch gold lamé spike.

The Black woman rolled her eyes. "I never could walk in those things."

He pitched the broken shoe to the sidewalk and bravely hobbled forward. "Piece of crap shoes."

We swept up the street full of love and good cheer, which was momentarily interrupted by a car full of young rednecks, who yelled "Queers!", " Dykes!", "Cunts!" Instead of quashing our spirits, their taunts fanned the flames of our determination. We surrounded their car and sang in their faces.

Despite their long hair, they looked more like four scared teenage boys who got more than they bargained for. After several minutes of intense brotherly love, we let them drive off—older, wiser, and totally freaked out.

When the march was completed and the rally disbanded, I saw the speaker duck into a nearby coffeehouse. She was nice-looking, but her pulled back hippie hair was all wrong. I wondered if she was good in bed, so I followed her inside. She sat with her friends near the front of the coffeehouse, which displaced other customers, who muttered about the inconvenience of it all and moved to the back of the room.

When I pulled up a chair on the fringe of the speaker's group, she flashed me a radiant smile. There was no way to get to her directly, so I kicked back and drank coffee, smoked cigs, and listened to her and her friends discuss the finer points of feminism and social responsibility. Occasionally she would look at me over the top of her coffee cup, a wicked smile on her lips.

Finally, the group broke up. The speaker walked directly to me and held out her hand. "Hi, I'm Sunshine Lindstrom." She radiated good vibes.

"I'm Bunny LaRue."

"Bunny, would you like to come over to my house, have a drink, some coffee," her face clouded, "or is it too late?"

I glanced at my watch; it was 11:45. I had a 7:00 a.m. makeup session and an all-day shoot, but I wasn't worried. It wasn't like I was going to come in hungover or anything. "No, it's not too late. I'd love to."

"Great. Can you give me a ride home?" She gave directions to a seedy section of town I normally wouldn't go into day or night. The neighborhood had a reputation for drugs, pimps, prostitutes, and poor people.

I looked at Sunshine, alarmed. She seemed to read my mind. "Cheap rent," she said, as she jumped out of the Jeep. She grabbed my hand and pulled me through the gate of a two-story house with broken front steps, an overgrown yard, and a boarded-up window on the second floor. It looked like the house hadn't seen a coat of paint since the Depression.

"Welcome to my humble abode," she said as she unlocked the front door.

I looked around at the Goodwill couch, bricks and boards bookcase, framed picture of Susan B. Anthony, and various handmade or castaway pieces of furniture. A kickass stereo system was playing songs from Joni Mitchell's *Court and Spark* album.

Still holding my hand, she dragged me into the kitchen. In the center of the room sat a red formica table edged in chrome and four matching chairs with their stuffing falling out. I didn't know whether to laugh or cry. It looked just like our kitchen table back home in Marysville. At the table sat a shorthaired woman surrounded by notebooks and pencils, her nose buried in Karl Marx's *The Communist Manifesto*.

Sunshine cleared her throat. "Evelyn, this is Bunny."

Evelyn looked up and scowled. "What kind of name is 'Bunny'? Are you a lesbian or one of those bisexual women who thinks it's fun to play with lesbians, then runs back to her man to enjoy the bennies of straight life?"

"It's a pleasure to meet you too, Evelyn," I said, holding out my hand. Bitch.

"Bah!" She picked up her notebooks, pencils, and book and unceremoniously tromped upstairs.

"Don't mind Evelyn." Sunshine shrugged. "She's going to school and trying to work and fight the system at the same time."

"Oh."

"What would you like to drink? I've got coffee, herbal teas, sodas," she looked in the refrigerator, "beer, and Jack Daniels."

I brightened. "Jack Daniels, please."

Sunshine rummaged through the dirty dishes in the sink, extracted two glasses, and rinsed them out while I pulled out my cigs. She poured the Jack Daniels and lifted her glass. "To a long and beautiful friendship."

"Salud!" I was hoping for something more than friendship.

Sunshine lit a cigarette. "Tell me about yourself, Bunny."

29

She settled back into her chair, her eyes aglow. "What do you do?"

"I'm a model for Franklin's of Beverly Hills."

She looked stunned. "You're kidding me, right?"

"No. In fact, I have a photo shoot tomorrow."

By the look on her face, Sunshine clearly did not know what to make of this. "How ..." she faltered. "How can you do that?"

"What?"

"Be a model! We're fighting against the objectification of women and you're a model for Franklin's of Beverly Hills."

"Hey, I make way more money as a model than I ever did working for In-N-Out Burgers."

"Is that what it is for you? Making money? Exploiting the poor working classes slaving in overseas sweatshops to make frilly underthings so women can play into the hands of heterosexual men? Bunny, you can't do that!"

I was taken aback. Nobody at the bars minded that I was a model. In fact, some of the girls confided to me that they had copies of Franklin's catalogs so they could lust over me.

"Hey, I'm a feminist—I'm for equal rights and all that."

"'All that'?" Her anger was unmistakable. "I'm fighting for the rights of all women to live safe from the dangers of men, to give them a place where they can live in peace and security with their children." The color rose in her face. "I want a world where we are free from the ravages of racism and classism and lookism and ageism!"

"You want a perfect world."

"I do want a perfect world. What's wrong with that? I'm a lesbian/feminist/separatist/socialist, that's socialist with a small 's' ..."

"Small 's'?"

Sunshine shrugged. "I'm not a party member. I don't

believe in any political party except the Socialists, and I don't believe their stance on women's rights goes far enough."

I had no idea what the Socialists stance on women's rights was, but I bet that Sunshine would be more than happy to educate me on the issue. I didn't ask.

She turned her great, passionate blue eyes on me. "Bunny, what about the proliferation of nuclear arms, the high interest rates that are forcing low-income people out of the housing market, the fact that we are six percent of the world's population and we are consuming fifty percent of the world's natural resources? What about air pollution?"

I freaked. In five minutes, I had become responsible for all the world's problems. "I'd better leave." I picked up my cigs and walked to the front door.

There was a mixture of anger and passion and something else I couldn't identify on Sunshine's face when I left. I breathed a sigh of relief when I stepped into the night. That was the shortest, long and beautiful friendship I ever experienced.

Something nagged at me. As I drove home, I realized that all during her tirade she had locked eyes with me and didn't stare at my boobs like so many other lesbians did.

Michael and I were watching *Starsky and Hutch* when the phone rang. Michael leaned across the couch and picked up the receiver.

"Hello?" Silence, then, "It's for you, Hutch." He handed me the phone.

"Who is it?" I mouthed, my hand over the receiver.

He shrugged. "I dunno. Some girl asking for you."

That was a big help. "Hello?"

"Is this Bunny LaRue?"

I recognized the voice immediately. "Sunshine?"

"Yeah, it's me. Can we talk? I mean, is it OK?" Her voice sounded tight.

"Yeah, sure. What's up?" I figured I'd never hear from her again.

"Well, um, I was kinda wondering, I mean, if you're not mad at me, maybe we could, uhhh ..."

"Just say it, Sunshine."

"I'dreallyliketoseeyouagain."

There was a long moment of silence.

Come again? Wasn't this the woman who reamed me the week before?

"How'd you get my number?" I asked, stalling for time.

"Well, I ..." she hesitated. "I looked you up in the Franklin's catalog just to make sure you weren't pulling my leg."

"Which one?" I asked. "The Spring Special? That one's my favorite."

"I don't know." She sounded exasperated. Doggedly she went on. "Then I looked you up in the phone book." She paused. "Is your name really Bunny LaRue? It's not your professional name?"

"My real name is Margaret Donnette LaRue, but I've been 'Bunny' all my life." I hesitated for a moment. "Yeah, sure, let's go out—do something." Why not? It wasn't like my phone was ringing off the hook and celibacy was wearing real thin. Besides, Sunshine was interesting and passionate. Maybe I could get her to wear her hair down.

"Great! What would you like to do?" She sounded all smiles.

"I dunno. Got any suggestions?"

"Yeah! Planned Parenthood is having a rally for women's reproductive rights at the Courthouse on Saturday."

Ye Gods! A woman with a plan! "Uh, I was hoping we could go dancing, maybe kick back, go for a walk on the beach, you know, get to know each other ..."

There was silence on the line. "Yeah, you're right. Have some fun. I can always go to the nuclear disarmament demonstration in San Diego on Sunday."

I mentally breathed a sigh of relief. "Pick you up at eight?"

"I'd love it!"

"And Sunshine?"

"Yeah?"

"Would you do me a favor? Would you wear your hair down?" Mentally I braced for a "no."

There was a peal of laughter at the other end. "Sure."

My heart raced after I hung up. I hadn't felt this high without drugs in ages. I turned to see Michael sitting up expectantly.

"Well?" He arched his brow dramatically.

"I got a date with Sunshine Saturday night."

"Ms. Perfect? Honey, do you know what you're doing? She could corrupt you. You might end up with morals or something."

"Not likely," I said as I took a long toke off a joint he offered.

Michael smiled broadly. "That's my girl."

"Sex, drugs, and rock and roll will be part of my life forever!" If there was one thing I was absolutely sure of, that was it.

He rolled off the couch, laughing hysterically. I couldn't tell if it was the weed or my witty remarks that sent him into fits. Or it could have been the fact I shook my tits in his face.

♦♦♦

Sunshine met me at the door, her long dark hair hanging in waves below her shoulders.

Her eyes sparkled as I managed to say, "Your hair ..." I couldn't quite finish the sentence.

"You like?" She turned around for me to inspect.

"I like very much."

We burst into laughter.

"Come in. I want you to meet my housemates." She ushered me inside.

Her four housemates snapped to attention as soon as I set foot in the living room. I was on display, scrutinized from all sides.

"Everyone, this is Bunny LaRue."

I smiled. "Hi."

"Sunshine tells us you're a model for Franklin's of Beverly Hills," said a woman in a plaid shirt, Levi 501's, and Frye boots.

This was the Inquisition and I was the Heretic. "Yes, but I also recycle!"

"Oh, God!" Sunshine covered her face with her hands.

There were snickers around the room.

"Let's go!" Sunshine grabbed my hand and dragged me toward the door.

"Nice to meet all of you," I said in my best Miss Congeniality voice.

The door slammed behind us.

Sunshine looked at me like I'd lost my mind. "I can't believe you said that!"

"It's true. Michael and I turn in all our bottles and cans."

Her eyes blazed. "You...!" She looked down at the porch then up again. Her eyes had softened. "Let's go." She slid her hand into mine, a decidedly feminine gesture.

I could barely breathe when I sat next to Sunshine in my

Jeep. Unprepared for our first minutes together, I pulled out into traffic and said the first thing that popped into my head. "Is your name really 'Sunshine'?"

She cocked her head and smiled. Sunshine flirted with such confidence that I almost drove into the car next to us. The driver laid on the horn and flipped me off as he sped by.

"Gotta keep my eyes on the road," I said lamely.

She laughed. "My name's really Suzanne Lindstrom but all my friends call me 'Sunshine.' "

"How do you get 'Sunshine' out of 'Suzanne'?"

She looked down at her lap and blushed. "Well," she hesitated, "it's from years ago. Someone once said it was like sunshine when I walked into a room. The name stuck."

"Well it certainly fits you. So did you grow up around here?"

"No." She grabbed the rollbar as we whipped around a corner.

Cool it. You don't want to kill her on your first date. I eased up on the accelerator. "No? Then where are you from?"

"Seattle. After high school, I worked for a food coop and a rape crisis center until the rain got to me and I moved to LA."

"Do you like it here?"

"I love it," she beamed. "Everything's happening here— progressive politics, the women's movement, antinuclear stuff. I find it so liberating to live where I can make a difference in women's lives without having to deal with men, you know?"

"What do you have against men?"

Silence.

Out of the corner of my eye I could see that Sunshine looked at me like I'd asked why Adolf Hitler couldn't be President.

"You're kidding, right? I can never tell if you're kidding or not."

"No, I'm not kidding. What do you have against men?"

There was another long moment of silence between us. Uh oh, here we go again. Before Sunshine could respond, I jumped in. "Let's go to Sunset Beach, where we can talk and I won't get us into a wreck, okay?"

Sunshine nodded.

Five minutes later, I pulled into a space that overlooked the ocean—a highly romantic spot under other circumstances.

Finally she said, "How can you be a lesbian and like men?"

"I've got nothing against men. I just don't sleep with them, that's all."

She sat sideways in her seat to face me. "But don't you see how women have been oppressed by men for centuries? It's criminal! Women are defined by their relationships to men—either they're some man's daughter or some man's wife. My God! Women still give up their names to become a man's wife! It's like transferring the title of a car from one owner to another. Men have held economic and religious power for centuries, killing, enslaving, and raping women to meet their needs. Women need to be freed from the chains of slavery to men!"

God, she was beautiful when she was angry! Her face flushed with passion as her words poured forth. I was totally captivated. After a long moment, I realized that she expected a response. "So you've been hurt by a man?"

"Christ! You haven't heard a word I've said, have you?" She glared at me.

Well, yes and no. I was too busy enjoying the fireworks to debate her point for point. They were the same old arguments and I'd heard that record before.

I tried to explain. "Sunshine, I don't live my life based on what's happened centuries before. I try to deal with men and women how they are now—how they treat me." I had a sudden brainstorm. "How would you feel if all the Blacks decided they didn't want to be a part of our white world? You know, they wanted to live together in separate neighborhoods, have Black-only jobs."

"That's segregation and I'm not racist." She folded her arms across her chest.

"But isn't that what you want for women? To be segregated from men? Doesn't that lead to lower wages for women because we aren't participating equally?"

Sunshine regarded me with a hint of a smile. "So you do have a brain, after all. It's just hidden in that hot body of yours." She smiled the same wicked smile as the night we met in the coffee shop.

With an invitation like that, how could I resist? I pulled her to me and kissed her. Sunshine responded in kind and soon we were in a makeout session that surpassed anything I'd ever seen on Beach Blanket Bingo, although I wasn't sure who was Frankie or who was Annette.

Michael and a friend were in the kitchen, making breakfast when I sat down at the table the next morning.

"Mornin'," I said as I lit a cigarette.

"Mornin'," Michael called back.

His friend stared at me.

"Hi, I'm Bunny." I held my hand out to Michael's friend. He looked over at Michael as if to ask, "Who's she?"

"Jeff, this is Bunny, my roommate. Bunny, Jeff." Michael indicated back and forth with his spatula.

"Nice to meet you, Bunny," Jeff said, blushing deeply. He covered his dick with both hands.

37

I laughed. "Don't worry. I've seen it all before."

Jeff turned to Michael. "I just assumed when you said 'roommate' you meant a guy. Excuse me," he said and headed for Michael's bedroom.

"Who's he?" I indicated to the naked man whose bare buns bounced up the stairs.

"A guy I met last night at the bar."

"And ...?"

"He's dynamite in bed. Pretty, too." Michael winked at me as Jeff reappeared in his shorts.

"Nothing personal you understand," Jeff said, still blushing.

I smiled. "Absolutely not."

"So where's Sunshine?" Michael asked.

"At home, I suppose." I distributed the silverware around the table.

"Didn't work out, huh?" Michael reached into the refrigerator and brought out butter and syrup.

"Actually, the night went really well. We went to Sunset Beach and talked 'till it got too cold, then we went to Mama's Diner and had something to eat."

"And then ..." Michael twirled his spatula in the air.

Michael and I always prompted each other's stories. It started when we were smoking dope and talking. When whoever was talking left for never-never land, and the other one was left hanging mid-story, we'd prompt each other.

"And then I drove her home."

"What? You still haven't told me. Do you like her or not?" Michael flipped the pancakes on the grill.

"I like her a lot, but ..."

Michael turned to me. "But what? But she's too straight-laced? But secretly she's a fan of Marabel Morgan? What?"

I started to speak, then stopped. "I don't know," I said finally.

"Let me guess," Jeff said. "There's something about Sunshine that you don't understand and still you want to be with her. And you don't want to blow anything by sleeping with her this early in the relationship."

"What's that say about us?" Michael looked pointedly at Jeff.

"You're my first, last, and forever, darling." Jeff smiled like a cherub.

Michael turned back to the stove. "Right."

"I do want to sleep with her, but not just yet."

"See?" Jeff looked vindicated.

Michael put the back of his hand against my forehead. "Honey, are you sick?"

I pushed Michael's hand aside. "Of course not! Can't I just see her for now?" God! Why this interest in me all of a sudden? Sunshine was ... I didn't know.

Maybe this was the beginning of a long and beautiful friendship.

Chapter 4

Take It To The Limit

The following weekend, Sunshine and I went to see *Alien*, the one movie we could both agree on because it featured a woman as the hero. It was the first time she could squeeze me into her schedule. Between the Low Income Housing Rights Coalition, the Ad Hoc Committee for the Equal Rights Amendment, the Committee to Save Mono Lake, and her work as union organizer, Sunshine had little time for socializing. Her life revolved around her work.

As we walked to my Jeep, I finally got the courage to ask, "Why do you work so hard?"

Sunshine concentrated on the sidewalk as she spoke, her hands stuffed in her jacket pockets. "Because if I don't, who will? This country is headed toward the polarization between the haves and the have-nots. Most people think I'm crazy. They think I'm over-extended with all the stuff I do." She looked up at me. "You probably think so, too."

I smiled. Yes.

"Unfortunately there's no guarantee that the good guys win. If there was, I'd be doing something else."

"Like what?"

Sunshine stopped in the middle of the sidewalk. "I don't know," she said blankly. "Anyhow," she resumed her pace,

"I like what I do—fighting for the underdog. It makes me feel like my life has a purpose."

"I guess my purpose is to have fun."

She laughed. "You seem to be doing an excellent job of it. But seriously, Bunny, what will you be doing in ten years? Still modeling for Franklin's?"

"Oh, probably modeling their latest geriatric line—you know, something sexy for the wheelchair and walker set."

Sunshine looked alarmed. "In ten years, you'll be thirty-seven. That's hardly geriatric."

"Yeah, but thirty-seven seems old to me. At thirty-seven, you should be driving a Buick or something. Don't you think it's old?"

"People at thirty-seven have more experience, they're more mature," Sunshine announced confidently.

"Yeah, and they have three kids and a dog and a mortgage. Not what I want to be doing at thirty-seven."

"I'd like to have kids," she said wistfully, "but I can't justify bringing them into this world when it's so messed up. There's too much poverty in this country and we're the richest nation in the world. We spend all of our tax dollars on bombs and to prop up governments whose abuses of human rights go against everything this country stands for. I'd want my kids to grow up where daycare has the same priority as the Pentagon. I don't see it happening in our lifetime." The corners of her mouth turned down.

Sunshine cared so much. I wanted to take her in my arms and kiss away all the hurt and worry that stuck to her like a bad hangover. Apart from the obvious sexual attraction, my feelings for her were growing. Sunshine listened when I talked. That afternoon, over cervezas, we discussed Jimmy Carter, the economy, religion, and the future of the human race—stuff that mattered. No one ever took me

41

seriously when they discovered I was a model for Franklin's.

Since Michael was away for the weekend with Robert, his latest fling, I decided to take advantage of his absence and invite Sunshine over for steaks. Between the movie that afternoon and the steaks, things were heating up.

"I found the wine. Would you like some?" Sunshine held up a bottle of Merlot and two glasses. She was the very picture of wholesome American girl: hair pulled back into a ponytail, sunburned shoulders peaking out from under her sleeveless shirt.

I turned away to catch my breath. I realized then, she wasn't another fling, a fun time until I found my next conquest. I was falling in love. "I'd love some," I whispered.

"Would you like me to put on some music?"

I nodded, suddenly too shy to speak.

Sunshine flipped through our albums and put Grover Washington's Inner City Blues on the turntable. She settled into a chaise lounge on the patio and lit a cigarette. "When's the last time you watered your petunias?"

I poked at the steaks sizzling over the graying charcoals. "You mean, Michael's flowers? I dunno—he waters them."

"Domesticity just isn't your thing, is it?" Sunshine let herself in through the slider and brought back a pitcher of water. She watered each pot and planter box and picked the dead flowers off each plant. "It makes them bloom more."

I wanted to make love with her right then—take her in my arms and softly stroke every secret place—let her know how much I loved her, lay down my life for her.

"Bunny, aren't the steaks burning?"

"Oh, God, they are!" I grabbed the fork and flipped them over to reveal nasty slabs of blackened T-bones. The smell of burned meat permeated the air. My world was falling apart at the speed of light. I had to get out of her presence before I melted into a puddle. "I gotta go make a salad!" I dashed into the kitchen and ripped up some Romaine. The physical distance between us made me feel slightly more in control, then I felt her hand on the small of my back.

"The steaks are done." She held out the platter of charred and medium-rare meat.

We stared at each other for a long moment. Finally, I set the platter of steaks on the counter, drew her to me, and kissed her. Minutes later, I took her hand and led her into my bedroom. I'd had the foresight to have candles in the room and clean sheets on the bed. Just in case.

Sunshine sat on the edge of the bed while I lit the candles. I sat next to her and ran my fingers through her hair, down her temples, and along the edge of her jaw. I held her face in my hand and brushed my lips across hers. We kissed tentatively, my lips lingering on hers, my tongue tasting hers.

She seemed to melt in my arms. I laid her on the bed and studied her face in the candlelight. She was altogether soft and feminine. Her assertive, combative side was gone, if only for the moment. I could worship this woman.

Sunshine opened her eyes and quickly closed them.

"Are you okay?"

"I ..."she faltered. "Sometimes I feel so vulnerable around you."

I smoothed her hair and kissed her hand. "You can trust me."

She took a ragged breath. "I do."

I unbuttoned her shirt and unfastened her bra. Her breasts spilled out and I brushed each one in turn, slowly exploring their contours, feeling their fullness. Sunshine's breath was shallow when I took each nipple softly between my thumb and forefinger.

"Oh!" she gasped.

I lingered over her breasts for a long time, rubbing my face against them, circling her nipples with my tongue. Finally my curiosity got the better of me, so I undid the top button of her shorts and unzipped them. She lifted her hips so I could slide off her shorts and panties.

I pulled her into a sitting position so I could remove her shirt and bra, then eased her back down onto the bed. "Roll over." I wanted to caress her ass. Sunshine was a marvel to behold. Her hair lay across her shoulders, the candlelight reflecting strands of auburn and gold among the brown. A brown line ran along her thighs where her shorts ended and her tan began. I ran my fingertips along the fullness of her hips and kneaded her cheeks until she moaned softly. "Turn over again, darling."

Sunshine opened her eyes; her shyness replaced by a look of—I don't know—undoneness. Her soul was opened to me and I silently vowed never to betray her trust.

My fingers found a wetness that I followed to its source. I slowly stroked her labia, then circled her clit with my finger, careful not to touch it.

"Omigod, Bunny!" Her hips moved with an increasing urgency. "Please go in me," she begged.

"Not yet, darling."

The womanizer in me wanted to take her now, watch her thrash all over, scream, ride my hand like a bucking bronco until she exploded into one colossal orgasm. But the lover in me wanted to prolong her pleasure until she swallowed my hand whole and collapsed from sheer ecstasy.

Slowly, I entered her with two fingers. Her pussy felt like soft velvet, wet and swollen, responsive to everywhere I touched. I stroked her softly at first, then harder until she gripped my fingers, riding them like we'd done this a thousand times before. I wanted this to last forever, but Sunshine clearly wanted more. I teased her nipple with my tongue, upping the ante as I put three, then four fingers inside her. She dug her fingernails into my back as her hips moved with greater urgency.

"Oh God, yes!" she whispered.

I matched my rhythm to hers, careful not to touch the place that would send her over the edge.

"Don't stop!" she pleaded.

I gripped her tightly to me, my hand moving faster and faster inside her. Locked in that embrace, she thrashed wildly, biting my shoulder. I could feel the tension building inside of her until she was past the point of no return. There was only one place left to go. I curved my fingers until I could feel that soft, spongy place and teased it until she exploded, sending wetness down my hand and onto the sheets.

She lay panting next to me for a minute, shuddering with aftershocks, until she could finally speak. "Omigod, Bunny. That was ... that was," she didn't finish her sentence.

It was amazing for me, too. I'd never been in sync with a woman like that before. Together, we had something fantastic. I took her in my arms, grinning from ear to ear.

"Wanna go again?" I whispered into her ear.

She rolled over and stared at me like a lioness surveying her prey. "In a bit. Now," she said, her voice a growl, "you're mine!"

She pulled me to a sitting position and took off my tank top. Her eyes blazed as she stared at my breasts. I was used to men zoning in on my tits or my ass, but early in life I learned to tune out that kind of attention. Even the women at the bars, the ones I spent one or several weekends with, I always managed to keep a safe psychological distance from.

But I was way past that point. Sunshine was treading on territory unknown even to me.

"I know you," she said. "You're used to women climbing all over you, all hands and hot breath. Well," she spoke each word slowly and distinctly, "I want you in perpetual, exquisite agony."

How does she know? I lay back on the bed, speechless.

She covered my mouth with hers and I forgot for a moment I was on my way to total surrender. She unfastened my bra and laid it open, then nuzzled her face between my breasts.

I don't know how long this lasted. Several minutes? An hour? It was exquisite agony and I couldn't get enough of her. My pussy throbbed before she had even relieved me of my shorts.

"Oh, please, baby, do it now," I begged.

Sunshine looked at me tenderly. "But darling," she said sweetly, "we've only started. There's so much more I have planned for you."

"Oh, fuck!"

She stifled a smile. "Yes. That too." She leaned back and watched me for a minute.

"I didn't mean for you to stop!" I trembled in anticipation, knowing it wouldn't take much to push me over the edge.

Finally, she reached down and unzipped my shorts. She casually pulled them off and dropped them to the floor, then trailed her fingers along the inside of my thigh. Sunshine lay on top of me and we kissed again. It was heaven, the feeling of her skin on mine, softness on softness. I ran my hands down her back and pressed her hips into my hips, my need growing more insistent by the moment.

Sunshine rolled off and propped herself up on her elbow. "What do you think you're doing?"

I couldn't speak.

She brushed my pubic mound with her fingertips, teasing me slowly. After what seemed like an eternity, she entered my pussy.

I think I screamed, lost in wave after wave of burning pleasure that flooded my entire being. Sometime later, I woke to find Sunshine asleep, snuggled against me. For a long time, I lay there and gazed at her sleeping. I blew out the candles and pulled the comforter over us. You've found your match, Bunny.

Michael was practicing the cha-cha to Donna Summer's "Love To Love You Baby" when I got home from work. I sloughed off my bag and joined him.

"Nice weekend?" I asked, backing up in time to the music.

"The best!" He backed me up against the wall, grinding his hips in something other than the cha-cha.

I never met anyone, male or female, who could wiggle their ass like Michael. If I'd been straight, Michael may not have escaped with his virtue intact. "Wedding bells anytime in your future?" I asked.

He turned and danced back to the middle of the living room, his hands over his head. "Maybe. How about you?"

"Oh, Michael, I love her!" I threw my arms around him, picked him off the floor, and shook him like a dog shakes a bone.

He camped it up. "I just love it when you're butch."

I dropped him to the floor. "I'm not kidding. My heart feels like it could hold the whole universe and still love her infinity times infinity."

"So what are you doing here?"

"Gotta take a shower!" I ran towards the downstairs bathroom, shedding clothes along the way.

He turned the volume down. "Does this mean I'm not going to be seeing much of you from now on?"

"Guess not," I said as I prepared to shave my legs.

"Well! Would you mind if Robert spent more time here?" By the tone of his voice, I could tell Michael was grinning from ear to ear.

"Go for it! You like him that much?" I turned on the shower.

"Yeah. He's a white boy from Peoria who's got one of those Third-World complexes. He thinks I'm exotic."

"Oh, God!"

"He's practicing his Spanish on me. 'Me nombre es Roberto.'" he mimicked. "I hate to tell him the only Spanish I know I learned in high school. It'd ruin the party!"

I laughed so hard I would have peed my pants, if I'd been wearing any.

"Meanwhile, I get to fuck his brains out." Michael gave a couple quick pelvic thrusts in time to the music.

"Whatever turns you on." Five minutes later, I jumped into a clean pair of jeans, loose sweatshirt, and sandals. "Happy partying, loverboy." I gave Michael a quick peck on the cheek and raced out the door, my hair still wet.

"Why don't you come inside, Bunny?" Evelyn called from the front porch. "It's not safe out there."

"Great. Thanks." I bounded up the stairs, thankful that I wouldn't have to sit in my Jeep for hours until Sunshine returned. She had a board meeting that probably wouldn't end until after 10. My feelings of relief were tempered when I saw Angie. As far as I could tell, Angie's mission in life was to convert everyone to her narrow little agenda. Just for fun, I threw out something I knew would get under her skin. "Sunshine sent me a dozen long-stemmed roses for no reason at all. Did she tell you?"

Flummoxed, Angie sputtered, "What a waste! She could have given that money to a homeless shelter."

"They were beautiful," I said, rubbing it in.

"I got roses once," Evelyn said dreamily.

"Weren't they from that woman who worked for Lockheed as an electrical engineer? Warmonger!" Angie pronounced judgment.

Evelyn looked uncomfortable.

"Well, I think it's lovely," I said pointedly. "Whatever happened to her?"

"She stopped seeing her, of course!" Angie interjected. "Evelyn couldn't be seen with someone whose livelihood depended on spreading death and destruction, now could she?" Angie stared at Evelyn.

"She was working on their space program," Evelyn said weakly.

"Someday they will come up with a way to put weapons in space. You mark my words." Angie turned and left the room in a huff.

"Thanks, Bunny." Evelyn looked at me like I was some kind of hero.

Three hours to go, I thought wearily. It must be love, otherwise I wouldn't put up with this shit.

Sunshine had been working without a day off for over three weeks. I wanted to take her out for dinner, but she didn't have time to prepare for her next crusade and dinner, so I came up with Plan B. "How does fast food sound?"

Sunshine let out a long sigh. "Yeah. Let's get some take-out from Eng's and go home. I'm exhausted."

"You wouldn't mind if we stopped for some beer would you?"

She rubbed her forehead with the back of her hand. "Sometimes I worry about your drinking, Bunny. I don't think it's healthy for you."

"One six-pack isn't going to kill me."

"Yeah, okay," she said wearily.

As we pulled into Eng's parking lot, I saw Gloria pulling away. I honked and waived, but she didn't stop.

"Who's that?"

"I'm pretty sure that was Gloria. She models for Franklin's, too." I hopped out of the Jeep.

"She works with you? Why don't you ask her to come to our neighborhood meeting next Friday?" Always the reformer, Sunshine seized every opportunity to promote her latest cause. She climbed slowly out of the Jeep.

"Okay," I said as I scanned the menu posted outside the door.

The following Monday, I hung around Payroll until I saw Gloria. "Hey, didn't I see you at Eng's last week?" I matched strides with her as she walked through the front door towards her car.

"Eng's?" She stopped and looked at me in disbelief. "What were you doing there? That's kind of a rough neighborhood."

"Sunshine lives south of Chamberlin, just east of the Mini Mart."

"She's got more guts than I do. As soon as I graduated from high school, I got out of there. My grandparents still live there, though. They're the ones who raised me. I stopped at Eng's to pick up some szechuan beef and noodles for my abuelita. It's her favorite."

"Your grandparents live there? Would they be interested in going to a community meeting on Friday night to get a bus line through that area? Sunshine is organizing a meeting to drum up support."

"Kinda short notice, but I'll ask them. See ya later, Bunny." Gloria walked across the parking lot to her car, her Cerritos College bag slung over her shoulder.

That Friday night, I went with Sunshine and her housemates to the Joint Committee to Promote Mass Transit meeting with the City of Los Angeles. Unlike most causes they championed, this issue did directly affect their lives. Between the five of them, they had two cars that ran and a junker that even the gangs wouldn't strip. Like everyone else in the neighborhood, they needed reliable transportation. Besides, I was tired of being the stay-at-home girlfriend, patiently waiting for my lover to arrive. I wanted to see Sunshine do what she did best, kick some pompous ass.

I saw Gloria and her grandparents arrive shortly before the meeting began. Abuelita was right! The woman was all of 4'8", if that. Several gang members got to their feet and moved toward the center of the row so Gloria and her grandparents could sit next to the aisle. Gloria waved to me, then settled in the listen to the proceedings.

Once people were seated, Sunshine stepped to the microphone. "I'm Sunshine Lindstrom from United Women Against Racism, the group responsible for organizing this meeting. To my left is the Reverend Thomas Sullivan, from the Prosser Street AME Church, and to his left ..." Sunshine proceeded to introduce the other eleven groups in attendance. "We're here tonight to tell the City of Los Angeles that as tax-paying citizens we want the same bus availability that other residents of the City enjoy."

51

People in the audience nodded.

"It's a matter of self-sufficiency and economic survival," Sunshine continued. "We need a reliable transportation to get from Point A to Point B."

The City of Los Angeles was represented by a fat pig in a silk suit, whose sole purpose was to divide the various factions in attendance, thus quashing the need for action and saving the city money. Silk Suit stepped up to the microphone. "Hmmm," he pondered. "United Women Against Racism. Why, don't those initials spell UWAR?" he said in his Texas drawl. He chuckled to himself, then continued. "Your opinion is noted but what we need here is clear thinkin', not emotional ploys by women who'd give away the store."

If there was one thing Sunshine detested, it was patronizing men. Silk Suit was the incarnation of everything she hated—the ultimate good ol' boy—a rich, white man who looked after his own or his boss' needs and treated anyone different from him like dirt. I knew her heart was pounding when she grabbed the microphone. "I am not here to 'give away the store!'" she said indignantly. "Everyone in this room is looking for work, maybe with the exception of you," she said to Silk Suit. "No work, no taxes." She pointed a shaky finger at him. "No taxes, no big raises for you!"

There was scattered applause around the room.

"Sunshine, darlin' ..." He smiled to himself. "I like that name, 'Sunshine'. Darlin', you can't run transit routes through areas which are largely industrial by day. Your ridership needs transportation for two hours in the mornin' and two hours in the afternoon. It's ridiculous to talk about turning this neighborhood into an urban route to serve the imagined needs of a few families livin' here. You're just gettin' hysterical over nothin'."

"Mentiroso! Liar!" Abuelita shouted. About half the audience nodded.

"Sometime our members can't rely on their family or friends to get them to the VA Hospital, so they miss their appointments," said the man from the Disabled American Veterans, getting to his feet. "We're good enough to fight for our country but 'Screw you, find your own damned transportation'—is that what you're saying?" The Reverend Sullivan stood up and put a gentle, but firm hand on his shoulder, forcing him back onto his seat.

Silk Suit sat undisturbed, surrounded by aides who carried official documents that proved the City's point. The decision had already been made, long before this meeting ever convened. Tonight was an exercise in democracy, a chance to give the whiners a voice.

A man from the NAACP stood up to speak. "There are over seven thousand permanent residents in this area, not 'a few families' as the city suggests. I think the tax base is large enough to support transit through this neighborhood."

Yells of encouragement followed applause from the crowd.

A school guidance counselor from Eldorado High School spoke next. "You're dooming our students to a life of poverty if they can't leave this neighborhood. Most of the families that live here can't afford transportation to places where the good-paying jobs are. Our kids have talent beyond the carwash and oil change jobs they typically get."

I was impressed. These residents really did care about the future of their neighborhood. Angry murmurs reverberated through the crowd as the room heated up.

Mr. Eng stood. "Need transportation to town. No fresh food, very bad!" he said in halting English. In a predominantly black and Hispanic neighborhood, Eng's Restaurant

53

was the great leveler. Everyone ate at Eng's: the Blacks, the Hispanics, even the Anglos who lived outside the neighborhood. Eng's was the best eats around, bar none.

It felt eerily familiar; large frothing crowd that chafed against injustice, just like the first time I laid eyes on Sunshine. I slipped out of my folding chair and was heading outside for a smoke when Silk Suit tried to regain control of the meeting.

"Can we please be reasonable? Your requests are being reviewed by the City Planning Department. It takes months, sometimes years, before studies are completed. You know, all those pesky environmental studies, population density studies, Air Quality Control studies. These things don't happen overnight."

Translation: "Fuck off!"

The crowd snarled. They were out for blood.

Silk Suit was used to playing to sympathetic crowds and misjudged this audience by a mile. Quickly he realized his tenuous position and scanned the room for his usual constituency, conservative white men and women who voted in fear of The Other. In his blindness, he identified me as one of his own. "Excuse me, Ma'am," he said into the microphone. "Wouldn't you agree that these speakers aren't representative of the majority of the residents of this area?"

Big mistake. I turned to him. "How would you know? You don't live here."

The crowd exploded with laughter and applause. Silk Suit stood with his mouth open, not used to his minority position.

A gang member grabbed the microphone from Silk Suit's hands and shouted, "Let's let this guy walk back to town and see how far he gets!" He pushed Silk Suit against the podium. "Here! Want to say the Rosary before you go, man?" He pulled his Rosary from beneath his shirt and dangled it in front of Silk Suit's eyes.

The color drained from Silk Suit's face. "I will not be intimidated by gang members who rule the streets by violence. I have a right to be free from intimidation!"

A man in the audience shouted, "So do I! So give us the fuckin' transit!"

Silk Suit hurried towards the door, his cool blown by homies he never met in his MBA program. The gang member elbowed Silk Suit in the gut as he pushed past. Not above hysterics himself, Silk Suit wailed, "He hit an unarmed man!"

There was nothing I could do. I stepped outside with the other smokers and lit my cigarette. We were a group of five: Mr. Eng's wife, a drug dealer who specialized in speed, a hooker who frequented the corner of Apache and El Rincon, a teenaged boy with a "Crips" tattoo on his shoulder, and me. We exchanged pleasantries over our cigarettes while the meeting deteriorated into a barroom brawl.

The teenage boy bummed a cigarette from me when we heard the cop cars. "Thanks, man."

"No problem." At least he was polite.

Sirens wailing, they pulled up to the front of the building. The Riot Squad, dressed in camouflage gear, stormed the building and dragged out "the instigators": the gang member, the man from the Disabled American Veterans, the school guidance counselor, Mr. Eng, Sunshine, and, much to my surprise, Gloria. Interestingly, Silk Suit was not among those arrested.

Two hours later, I had bail money for Sunshine and Gloria. Abuelita and her husband angrily denounced the City officials and jailers in the kind of Spanish I learned in the street. Together with Sunshine's housemates, they

55

eagerly contributed what little cash they had towards bail. I supplied the rest. Gloria and Sunshine were bona fide heroes.

"Pigs!" Sunshine spat when we got back to her house. The Righteous Sisters sat in a circle around Sunshine and nodded in agreement. She was just warming to her topic. "Forget it if you're female or not white in this neighborhood. God forbid that the resources of LA be used on the poor who can't speak English. Who do we think we are, a nation of immigrants?"

She ranted and raved the rest of the evening. Dutiful girl-friend that I was, I listened and agreed with her.

Not suprisingly, our lovemaking was especially passionate that night.

When I walked into Franklin's on Monday, I was greeted with both giggles and looks of disdain. But the dressing room was positively abuzz.

"Damn girl! You know how to create a scene." Aphrodite said. "Gloria told us about the meeting and you bailing her outta jail."

"What's jail like?" asked Regina. Although she was a natural brunette, everyone called her "BB," short for "Blond Bimbo," behind her back.

"Um, I dunno, I wasn't actually in jail," I said, the color rising in my cheeks. I wasn't used to being a hero.

"I think what you did was very brave," Lucinda said shyly.

"It sounds like the city should have thrown you all in jail," Juliet sneered.

"What would you know? You weren't there," Gloria snapped.

"Whaddya expect? It's one of the worst neighborhoods in LA, according to The Observer." Juliet's voice was cold.

"Ai, watch what you say, white girl. That neighborhood is where I grew up." Gloria took a step towards Juliet.

Angel poked his head into the dressing room. "Girls, girls. Save the cat fights for later." He pointed to me. "Bunny, Arthur wants to see you right away."

I had a sickening feeling I knew what this was going to be about.

"Bitch!" I heard Juliet mutter under her breath.

Gloria took another step towards Juliet.

When I reached his office, Mr. Stiff was pacing the length of the room. He glanced at me, then slammed his office door shut behind me.

"You fuckin' liberal meddler! You couldn't leave it alone with Rapunzel and now you're stirring up Gloria. What the hell do you think you're doing, inviting Gloria to some women's lib meeting?" His face was inches from mine. "That's just what I need, all of our models listening to that 'I am woman, hear me roar' crap."

"It wasn't a women's lib meeting, it was a neighborhood meeting with the city to get a bus line through the neighborhood," I offered.

"And Gloria got thrown in jail because she assaulted a police officer? Why weren't you arrested?" The veins bulged in his neck.

"I was outside having a smoke." Just to piss him off, I fished in my pocket, pulled out a cig, and lit up. "And Gloria was in jail was because she was defending her grandmother from the cops, who were trying to keep a four-foot old lady away from a six-foot cowboy in a silk suit." I just wished I hadn't been outside when the fracas broke out. According to Sunshine, Abuelita stormed up to Silk Suit and cursed him up one side and down the other before the police descended on her.

Mr. Stiff shook his head in frustration. "You don't get it, do you? I don't want my models in jail because they're listening to whatever you're peddling. I don't want them to think for themselves. I want them to take orders."

"I'm sure you do." Asshole! I blew smoke in his face when I stood up and walked out of his office.

The dressing room chatter subsided when I returned.

"Let me guess," Gloria said. "Mr. Stiff chewed you out for inviting me to the meeting."

"Yeah. But he thought it was some kind of feminist rally. You think he might have a guilty conscience?" I sat on the bench and removed my shoes.

"I'm sure he thinks modeling lingerie and being a feminist are antithetical," said Gail, the English major.

"Well, aren't they?" A puzzled Juliet asked from the other side of the room.

"Hell, no! I wear this stuff to remind my boyfriend that I am a woman, not just some convenient housekeeper who does his laundry. I tell him if he wants some, he has to help out." Gail chuckled.

Juliet looked surprised. "Does he?"

"He does now." Gail continued, "It's the old Lysistrata thing."

"The what?" Gloria voiced the question that was on everyone's mind.

"Lysistrata is a Greek comedy by Aristophanes. It's about when the women of Athens and Sparta wouldn't have sex with their husbands until the men agreed to stop the war."

"I don't get it," BB said. "What's stopping a war got to do with your boyfriend's laundry?"

Gail pulled her hair into a ponytail. "The men of Athens and Sparta were at war," Gail explained, "but the women of both cities talked to each other and came to their own decision about what to do, without consulting with their husbands or boyfriends. And that is feminism, pure and simple—women taking charge of their own destinies."

"If Ron is pissing me off, I tell him no," volunteered Lucinda. "Haven't you ever told your boyfriend no, Juliet?"

"Once. He ..." Juliet turned toward her locker without finishing her sentence.

A hush fell over the room.

"Is that how it is, Juliet? He uses you for a punching bag anytime he doesn't get what he wants?" Gail's eyes bore a hole through Juliet's back.

"He's hardly ever like that," Juliet stammered. "He always buys me flowers when ..." her voice trailed off.

"You don't have to put up with that," Gail said quietly.

Juliet turned and faced the room. "You don't understand." Tears streaked her cheeks.

"I think we all understand too well, Juliet," Lucinda offered.

An angry Juliet pointed her finger at me. "This is all your fault, Bunny! If you hadn't invited Gloria to that rally, this never would have happened."

"It was a neighborhood meeting," I protested.

"Shut up!" She turned back to her locker and wiped away the tears.

Chapter 5

The Letter

I don't remember one shot of me smiling the entire time I worked for Franklin's. It was the "Fuck you!" or "Come get me!" or "You can't tame me!" looks that made me famous. The guys ate up my pouty, wild girl look. I got as much fan mail as the prettier girls, although my letters tended to be heavier in male conquest fantasies.

The letter came to our townhouse in a nondescript white envelope, the kind you buy at the drugstore for fifty cents a box. Michael and I were smoking weed and drinking beer that night when I opened it.

"Oh shit!"

Michael looked up. "What's the matter, Bunny? You're white as a ghost!"

I handed him the letter.

He scanned the letter, jumped off the couch, and assumed his full height. "Oh, shit is right! That fucker! If he so much as comes within a hundred yards of here, I'll kill him!" Michael paced the room, grinding his fist into his hand.

In my THC-induced haze, I picked up the hastily scrawled letter and re-read it:

You Fucking Dyke,

I used to hold a picture of you in one hand and stroke my ten inches with the other, imagining what a good fuck you'd be. Then I found out your a goddamn dyke who'd rather eat pussy. Your the worst kind of pervert! I've made a room for your re-education equipped with handcuffs, collar, nipple clamps, gag, blindfold, and lots of dildos in every size. I'm going to make a real woman out of you. Watch out. Don't expect that fag you live with or the security gate to keep me out. When you least expect it, your Daddy will take you home.

It was a hundred times worse than the first time I read it. I ran to the bathroom and puked until there was nothing left in my stomach. I was way beyond scared. Every major demon in the universe gnawed at me, threatening to swallow me whole. This sicko could be right outside the door, waiting to shanghai me when I got into my Jeep. Michael helped me back to the couch where I collapsed in a heap.

I looked at the envelope that bore no return address. It was postmarked Victorville, CA. "Where the hell is Victorville?" My voice sounded tight and screechy.

"Uh, high desert, a hundred miles from here."

"He's a hundred miles from here? Oh God, Michael, what am I going to do?" I hugged a pillow to my chest, my knuckles white.

"First off, you're going to show this letter to Mr. Stiff and see what he can do." Michael's voice sounded reassuring.

"I'm never leaving this apartment again! Can't we call the police or something?" My heart beat a thousand miles an hour.

The police were no help. A bored 911 operator took my

report and said someone would get back to me. In the meantime, I was on my own. I stuffed a kitchen chair under the front doorknob and locked the deadbolt. I dragged the kitchen table to where it blocked the slider and loaded pots and pans on it and under it so any intruder would make enough noise to give me time to lock myself in my bedroom while I called the police.

I thought about escaping to Sunshine's place, but I wasn't sure I could count on any sympathy from Evelyn, et al. Despite my attempts at being the perfect guest, we were seriously getting on each others' nerves. And Sunshine, unfortunately, was sequestered that evening, putting out a newsletter for the Low Income Housing Rights Coalition, and wouldn't be home for hours. On the second floor of our townhouse, locked inside Michael's bedroom, I spent the night huddled under the covers in Michael's arms, alternately crying and shaking. I didn't sleep a wink, imagining the sounds of some hairy, six foot seven, four hundred pound sex fiend breaking in and tearing our place apart until he found me.

Wrung out and exhausted, I waved the letter under Mr. Stiff's nose at 8:07 the following morning. "What are you going to do about this?" I paced up and down, smoking cigs as if my life depended on it.

"Do about what?" He scanned the letter, sat down heavily, loosened his tie, and re-read it. "Put that thing out and sit down." He pulled out a handkerchief and mopped his brow. "Do you have any idea who might have sent you this? Some redneck you brushed off? Where would you have run into this character? A bar? The grocery store?"

"Christ, Arthur! I'm a fuckin' Franklin's model! My pictures are plastered all over dozens of catalogs, or have you forgotten?" With shaking hands, I lit another cigarette.

"Calm down," he ordered. "Most of the time, nothing ever comes of these letters. They're usually some guy's whack-off fantasy he got the nerve to stick into the mail, although this guy is in another league altogether ..."

In another league altogether. I thought my heart was going to stop. "So what are you going to do?"

His eyes blazed. "We don't like our models in this position. Why don't you take the day off, go the beach?"

"I'm never going to the beach again!"

"Okay, go see Sunshine. But you have to get a hold of yourself, Bunny. Get outta here. I'll see what I can do." He flipped through his Rolodex and picked up the phone.

I stuck my head out the backdoor of the studio, scanned the parking lot for suspicious looking characters, then broke my own fifty-yard dash record running to my Jeep. Once I got on the 101, I took a ragged breath. Deep in the middle of morning LA commuter traffic, I felt safe.

If anyone could save me, it would be Sunshine. I drove directly to her office, then circled the block for twenty minutes, looking for anything out of the ordinary. But what was I looking for? I didn't know. My other option was to keep driving until I ran out of gas or out of smokes, and I was fast running out of smokes.

I hung around Sunshine's cramped office, glad I had seven doors between myself and the outside of the building. The Creep would have a hard time dragging a screaming woman through the halls and lobby without someone noticing. Twenty minutes later, Sunshine trudged in, carrying two heavy-looking boxes. I threw myself on her as soon as she set the boxes down.

"Bunny, what's wrong?"

I sobbed and shook all over.

She held me until I stopped crying. "What's the matter, baby?"

Still shaking, I thrust the letter into her hand.

Her face turned white as she read it. "Omigod! When did you get this?"

"Last night." I was tired of holding up well and collapsed into the orange plastic molded chair across from her desk. "I'm really scared. Can we go somewhere for a few days?"

"Well, uh, yeah, I guess." She hesitated. "I'd have to rearrange my schedule. Do we have to go this minute?"

Was I wrong, or was she putting me off? Christ, if Sunshine, the love of my life didn't get it, who would? "Please," I begged.

Sunshine pulled me close and stroked my hair. There was something magical about her—if something was wrong, Sunshine could fix it. She was as dependable as the sun that rose every morning to banish the darkness.

"Let's go," she said.

I would never be wrong with her.

We stopped briefly at my apartment, grabbed some clothes, and left a message for Michael saying where we'd be. Strangely enough, I felt safer in Sunshine's neighborhood than my own—the gangs in her neighborhood didn't allow outsiders to cause trouble. But even Sunshine's neighborhood felt too close to The Creep. I wanted to put some distance between myself and him. The Mojave Desert was about the right size.

Two hours north of LA, I began to feel better. My plan was to drive to Marysville and spend a couple days with my dad. Many times, I thought about bringing Sunshine home and introducing her as my lover/partner/greatest woman in the world, but we never could find the time to get away. I knew it would be a couple hours before my dad got home, so we took the back road into town. Marysville was prime agricultural land that grew rice, grapes, and plums, the perfect laboratory for the Ag folks at UC Davis. By the time we reached Marysville, Sunshine had stopped strategizing her next seven battles. It was nice to see her relaxed. She admitted that taking time off was something she didn't do often enough.

Marysville still looked the same—one main road where high school kids wracked up thousands of miles every year cruising through town, looking for action. On an impulse, I pulled into the Dairy Queen.

"Bunny, how are you?" a woman I went to high school with asked eagerly.

"Good. And you?" I couldn't remember her name.

"Oh, you know, married. But you got out and became a model! I think every time my husband opens a Franklin's catalog he wishes he'd married you instead."

I smiled weakly.

"What can I get for you?" she asked.

"Root-beer float, please."

Sunshine shook her head. "Nothing for me, thanks."

As we pulled out of the Dairy Queen, Sunshine smiled. "I bet they all love you."

"Who?" I slurped my root-beer float, thankful that some things never change.

"Everyone in Marysville." She squeezed my hand on the stick shift.

"Why?"

"You know, local girl makes good in the competitive world of professional modeling," she teased.

Sunshine said, "professional modeling" not "Franklin's of Beverly Hills." Maybe that meant she was getting used to the idea.

"I certainly love you," she added. "In fact, I was just

thinking about how I'd like to love you, how long, where ..."

The five minutes it took to drive home seemed like an eternity. Six hours sitting next to my heart's desire had made me horny as hell. I pulled into the driveway and parked alongside the garage where I'd spent the greater portion of my childhood. In lieu of a traditional upbringing, my dad taught me everything he knew about cars. Together we rebuilt a '29 Model A Ford, '35 Ford Cabriolet Street Rod, '46 Chevy Fleetline Aero Sedan, and a '49 Packard. On the weekends, we worked on his friends' cars—tune-ups, brake jobs, exhaust systems (with or without glass packs), carburetor rebuilds, and solenoid replacements. "Everyone needs a trade," he often told me. When I was eight, I wanted to own a Mobil gas station with a big red Pegasus over it when I grew up.

I took Sunshine's hand and dragged her behind the house, beyond the prying eyes of the neighbors. My intent was to ravish her, explore all of her curves and secret places, but what I saw stopped me dead in my tracks.

Until that moment, I hadn't realized what, besides women and cars, was my father's passion. Don LaRue had painstakingly planned, plotted, and planted his own private Garden of Eden. Pampas grass well over seven feet tall grew on the north side of the lot that was bisected by a murky creek. To the west, an old laurel hedge four feet wide and twelve feet high grew in a tangled mass. I'd whacked out hiding places and made forts in it when I was a kid. A stone barbecue stretched twenty feet on the east side of the property to soak up the sun's rays. He built it stone by stone, carefully adding a niche here and a long bench there, and set pots of geraniums and pansies on it to give it color. Along the creek, bamboo that required severe pruning every year grew unchecked. The expanse of grass, bordered by small swales and raised beds of flowering trees and shrubs, was sculpted down to the water. The entire backyard was surrounded by a living wall of wild and domestic vegetation, the perfect visual and sound barrier for his many outdoor trysts. The man was a genius.

Sunshine was dazzled by the azaleas, climbing roses, and semi-dwarf cherry and peach trees. "This is beautiful, Bunny! You never told me your father liked to garden."

"Yeah, well ..." How could I tell her I hadn't seen the Big Picture, I was too busy digging up runaway bamboo before it took over the yard?

There were several hours of sunlight left, so I chose the most romantic spot in the yard, a grassy knoll under the cherry tree. We spent an hour reacquainting ourselves when we heard my dad's truck.

"Damn!" I fell away from Sunshine and stared into the cherry blossoms that dangled a few feet above us.

Sunshine giggled. She covered my mouth with hers and fondled my breasts until I was so ready I could have screamed. She knew it, too. "I like it when you want it bad." She wore a wicked smile.

Damn her and her perpetual, exquisite agony. I wanted her now! I threw on my shorts and sweatshirt while Sunshine struggled with her skirt and blouse. "Dad!" I shouted, heading him off before he could see what was going on in his backyard.

"Bunny!" He threw his arms around me in a bear hug and lifted me off the ground. "It's so good to see you! How come you didn't call your old man and tell him you were coming?"

"It's a long story. First, I want you to meet the love of my life, Sunshine Lindstrom."

It was an awkward moment for both of them. I'd never brought home any girl, much less called her "the love of my life." And Sunshine was still buttoning and tucking, trying not to look like she had just been ravished.

"It's a pleasure to meet you, Sunshine." Dad held out his hand. "Bunny has told me so many wonderful things about you."

Forthright feminist, righter of wrongs, brave David to the Goliaths of the world, Sunshine squeaked, "The pleasure's mine." Her face flushed crimson.

"How long are you here for?" He threw his arm over my shoulder as we walked toward the house, leaving Sunshine to pull herself together in private.

"A couple of days if that's all right with you."

"It's fine. Say, how about if I take you two girls, I mean women," he said hastily, "out to Potter's tonight?"

"Oh, yeah!" Potter's was our favorite pizza joint: ugly wooden booths, cracked linoleum floors, dim lighting, and out-of-date music with the best pesto pizza around. Potter's was our home away from home. I'd spent many nights there, happy to be with my dad and his latest girlfriend. Now I was the one with the girlfriend and he wanted to join the party. Life took strange turns.

"Is he always so ... accepting?" Sunshine whispered in my ear as we sat in the narrow booth.

I filled everyone's glass with beer while he ordered pizza at the counter. "Pretty much. He's always been a 'do your own thing' kind of parent. My dad never let me join Brownies or any of those 'turn-you-into-a-cookie-cutter-type-of-girl' organizations, as he used to call them. He told me he didn't want me to be just like everyone else. Now I know it was because he didn't have the money for it."

I drained my glass and refilled it. "He told me he loved me even when I pulled stupid shit, like when I got busted for

68

drinking at fourteen. He said only God and that skinny, ugly, stringy-haired girl on the other side of the mirror had the right to judge me."

"He told you that? I can't believe it!" She giggled.

"He let me do my own thing, whatever it happened to be at the time. For a while, I was Annie Oakley. I galloped around the house on an old stick horse and wore a red straw cowboy hat and cowboy boots. Next I was Amelia Earhart. Dad got me one of those old leather pilot's helmets and goggles that were way too big for me and threw a towel around my neck like a muffler. Later I had a major crush on Emma Peel. She defined what a woman was for me: smart, sexy, and able to take care of herself. God, she was hot."

"And she looked dynamite in those jumpsuits!" Sunshine added breathlessly.

"I went through a jumpsuit stage, myself."

Sunshine laughed until tears ran down her cheeks. "I love you! I wish I could be more like you."

I shrugged. "What's the big deal? I do what I want. People either like me or they don't."

Sunshine let out a long sigh. "I worry about what everyone thinks of me! Whether I smile at the clerk in the grocery store so they have a positive image of a lesbian, stuff like that. I know it's crazy, but I can't stop."

"The only people whose opinion matters to me is you, my dad, and Michael."

Sunshine shut her eyes. "Sometimes I'm overwhelmed by what I feel for you. It almost scares me."

I looked at her, alarmed. "What?"

"It's almost too much. I've never loved anyone this way before. You are so ... you!" Her eyes glowed.

"And that's good?"

"Oh, baby, it's very good!" She squeezed my hand under

the table. "We grew up so differently! I grew up with a list of rights and wrongs: it was wrong to drink, dance, play cards, or even think about sex before marriage. I could never take you home to meet my parents. They refuse to admit I'm gay. Every time I go home, they insist on setting me up with some eligible guy my dad works with. Consequently, I never go home anymore. They hate everything I am—a gay, socialist, feminist. They're standoffish Norwegians who never learned how to show love or affection."

"You never talked about your parents before."

"I don't know what to do about them." She looked exasperated. "I was their best hope of us three kids. My sister shacked up with her boyfriend without the benefit of marriage right out of high school, and my brother became a truck driver when he was supposed to follow in my father's footsteps and work for the Lazy B."

"'The Lazy B?'"

"Boeing. My father's a lifer at Boeing."

"What were you supposed to do?"

"Go to college, become a teacher, get married. In general, behave like the good, middle-class white girl they hoped they raised. Obviously, that went out the window when I left home." Sunshine let out a long sigh.

"I imagined you came from a happy, 50s type family. You know, dad-who-wore-a-hat and stay-at-home-mom."

"God! I wish! My father and I were always getting into fights. And I couldn't respect my mother because she was so passive around him. My parents were constantly on the verge of divorce, although divorce wasn't something you did in the '60s. They had their 'image' to maintain."

"If they were so miserable, why didn't they split?"

"You don't understand, Bunny," she said, impatiently. "You're always supposed to do the 'right thing,' even if it

70

means sacrificing your own happiness or the happiness of your family. My father was a church elder and it wouldn't have looked good if they got a divorce. He left us the first time when I was nine years old. Even then, I knew something pretty shitty was going on. My father always threatened to leave and my mother always begged him not to go. I decided then I never would be dependent on a man like my mother was. So what did my mother finally do? Went out and had affairs of her own, which caused him to be absent even more. A good portion of the time, I was left in charge of my brother and sister. I couldn't wait to leave home!"

"You ran away?"

"No." She took a long gulp of beer. "I turned down a scholarship to the University of Washington because it was for tuition only, not room and board. I identified as part of the proletariat, so I went to work fighting against everything my parents held dear: the military-industrial complex and the Committee to Re-elect the President. I was one of Spiro Agnew's 'nattering nabobs of negativity.' Besides," she wiped her mouth with the back of her hand, "there was so much important stuff going on: the Vietnam War, women's consciousness raising groups. I couldn't see myself teaching history to some middle class white kids whose only experience with Blacks was the one James Brown album they owned. It was ridiculous!"

We both laughed.

As my dad approached, carrying the pizza, Sunshine whispered, "I can't wait 'til we get back to your dad's house. I'm going to finish what we started." She slid her hand down the back of my pants, her activity hidden under the tabletop.

"Are you ready for the best you'll ever eat?" Dad asked.

"I'm starved. Bunny hasn't let me eat a thing since we left LA hours ago," she said with a straight face.

71

It was one of the happiest moments of my life: sitting in Potter's drinking beer and eating pizza with my girlfriend and my dad, while Jerry Vale sang "Volare" in the background. Perpetual, exquisite agony never felt so good.

My dad was sitting at the kitchen table, reading the morning paper, when I poured myself a cup of coffee. "You're up early," he said. "I figured you'd be sleeping in today, after last night."

"Huh?"

He smiled. "You were ... enthusiastic, to say the least."

"Sorry."

"Probably pay back time for your old man. Like father, like daughter." He let out a laugh that let me know everything was cool.

My dad, Don LaRue, the original live-and-let-live guy. I gave him a big hug and a kiss.

"I got the impression that there was something you wanted to talk about, Bunny. What's on your mind?" He folded the paper and laid it aside.

The ominous, gray cloud that I pushed aside the last twelve hours settled in once again. "I got this letter ..." I went to my old bedroom, where Sunshine still lay asleep on my twin bed. Careful not to wake her, I rummaged through my bag, took the letter back to the kitchen, and laid it on the table.

He read it once, examined the envelope, then read it again. He let out a long sigh. "This is bad."

All of a sudden, I felt eight years old again, running to daddy to protect me. "What do you think I should do?"

"Jesus, Bunny ..." He lit a cigarette and read the letter again. "You are so high profile, it was bound to bring some creep out of the woodwork."

Hearing my own dad say this made even Marysville feel unsafe.

"I think she should quit Franklin's and find another job." Sunshine stood in the doorway to the kitchen, dressed in one of my old Marysville High School T-shirts and shorts. She crossed the room, poured herself some coffee, and sat at the table with us.

"But that won't solve the problem," I protested.

My dad looked puzzled. "Why not?"

"Because he sent the letter to my home, so he knows where I live."

A frown creased his brow. "How did he get your address?"

"She's in the phone book. That's how I found her." Sunshine looked squarely at me, anger simmering just below the surface.

I felt nauseated once again. "Mr. Stiff thinks nothing will come of this. What do you think?" Talking about it made it feel more real, and I was trying very hard to avoid the reality of this thing.

"Have you received any strange phone calls?" he asked.

"No."

"Well, you could fight it." Dad sipped his coffee.

"What?!" Sunshine seemed taken off guard by this suggestion.

"How?" I asked.

"Go on with your life as if nothing happened. Make him think you didn't get the letter. Maybe Mr. Stiff is right. Maybe he won't bother you anymore."

"Can you trust what Mr. Stiff says?" Sunshine looked pointedly at me. "I think you ought to quit Franklin's and lay low for a while."

"Mr. Stiff is trying to protect me." It felt odd defending a man whose sole contribution to the human race was the fact that he couldn't contribute to the human race. Arthur Spires was a neut: he shot blanks. He not so subtly paraded this fact to every new girl he hired. Because of his position, many new girls felt pressured to sleep with him. His victims said he was lousy in bed. Big surprise. When he put the heat on me, I told him I wasn't interested and suggested he become best friends with his right hand. He was more than a little peeved by my rejection.

"Do you want to quit?" my dad asked.

"No. I like what I do."

Sunshine folded her arms across her chest and looked grim.

"This was never supposed to happen. I like modeling because it's fun and it pays great. There was never supposed to be some wacko guy who took my shots seriously." Nervously, I lit a cigarette.

"But, Bunny, someone does take your pictures seriously." Sunshine looked pointedly at me.

My dad leaned back in his chair. "I think Mr. Stiff is right. I doubt that you'll hear from him again."

I looked between the two people I loved the most, Sunshine and my dad. If it was a bright sunny day, Sunshine would point out the cloud on the horizon. My dad, though his life had not been easy, lived each day by looking on the bright side. The darkness from where Sunshine spoke scared the hell out of me. I wanted to live where hope was still possible, so I sided with my dad.

"Sunshine, you're always talking about how we shouldn't live in fear. I'm not going to quit. If anything else happens, I'll deal with it."

"We will deal with it," she said, angrily.

Dad stood up to leave. "I gotta go to work. Will you two be okay?"

I smiled. "Yeah, we'll be okay." I put my arm around Sunshine and squeezed her. I could tell her anger was already fading. Perhaps one more day of rest would do us both good.

"See you tonight?" he asked.

I looked at Sunshine.

"Yeah," she said.

Chapter 6

Lay Down Sally

I'm sure The Creep would have cringed to know his letter made me want to act out all of my lesbian fantasies. Now that I was back in LA, his threats were a kick in the butt to get me seriously thinking about making a life with Sunshine. She was everything I wanted in a woman: bright, funny, and warm, with a heart of gold. I was tired of doing the LA commuter thing. We managed to get through our second, twenty-second, and eighty-fourth date without a U-Haul in sight, but now it was time to commit.

I held Sunshine as we lay on her couch and listened to my Barry White album. She squirmed and tried to break free from my grasp when I nibbled on her neck. I held on tighter. She was half determined to wiggle away, so I locked my legs around her. "Don't you think it's time for us to live together?" I nibbled her earlobes.

Instantly she tightened. "I ... I don't know," she said softly.

"What?" Confused, I relaxed my grip on her.

"I've thought about it a lot. I even asked my housemates how they felt about you moving in."

"And?"

"The only one who said it was okay was Evelyn. Phyllis

and Connie weren't too keen on it. Angie said flat out, 'No.'"
She spoke barely above a whisper.

That figured. Phyllis, Connie, and Angie were so bent on saving the world that any distraction meant they weren't totally committed to "The Cause," whichever cause it happened to be at the moment. And Evelyn wanted to get laid. Preferably by me.

I was shaken, but not undone. "Okay, so how about you move in with Michael and me?"

"No! I will never live in the same space with a man."

There was no arguing that. I knew how much she disliked men. "Well, then, let's get our own place." I resumed nuzzling her neck.

Sunshine lay stiff as a board. "I can't."

"Why not?" I didn't know whether to be angry or hurt. "Sunshine, I love you!"

She turned to me. "I love you, too, but ..." Her voice trailed off.

"But what?" Suddenly it dawned on me. "It's because I model for Franklin's, isn't it?"

She played with a button on her shirt. "Not exactly."

"Then what is it?"

"Bunny, you make a lot more money than I do."

"So? We can live comfortably on what we make together."

"I can't." There was something absolute in her statement.

"Why not?" I heard my voice rise an octave.

"Because I'd feel like a kept woman."

"Oh, for Chrissakes! That's not what I'm proposing." This didn't feel right, but I couldn't put my finger on what was wrong.

Sunshine didn't say a word.

"WHAT?" I finally asked in frustration.

"How do I know that I'm not just another one of your

77

conquests—that you won't move on to someone new next week or next year?"

"What are you talking about? Next year? According to your timetable, the world is going to self-destruct in a year, anyhow." My mind reeled from her twisted logic. I tried again. "All I know is that I love you and I want to live with you!"

"You have all the answers, don't you?" She sounded like a petulant child.

This is bullshit! "Why are you picking a fight with me? Why can't we just live together like a normal couple?"

"What's so special about being normal? My family looked normal, but my dad and mom were constantly on the verge of divorce."

"Your dad and mom? What do they have to do with us living together?"

"It's all about power, Bunny. Everything is always about power," she huffed. "My dad always threatened to leave us, which put my mom in a totally powerless position. You're the one with the power here—your looks and your money. You could leave at anytime. I'd just be another of your exes!"

I'm in the Twilight Zone and this is Mrs. Rod Serling. "Damn it, Sunshine, I want to live with you! I want to get up and have you there in the morning. I want to go grocery shopping with you when you buy eggplant and tofu and all that other stuff. I want to take trips with you and grow old with you. This last year has been the best year of my life."

"But I'd still feel like a kept woman. That wouldn't change."

"Please, baby, I love you!" Sunshine, don't do this to me! We sat on the couch not speaking, not touching.

As if on cue, Angie leaned into the room and announced,

"Remember, there's a Neighborhood Revitalization Committee meeting at seven tonight. You said you wanted to go."

Sunshine straightened her shirt.

"Sunshine?" I pleaded.

She wouldn't look at me. "They need me. I told them I'd be there."

"I need you!"

"I'm sorry, Bunny." She kissed me on the cheek. "I'll call you later." She turned and walked up the stairs, clutching herself tightly.

Angie leaned against the doorway, her arms folded across her chest. "Maybe you should start thinking about something larger than yourself, Bunny," she said smugly.

Tears burned my eyes as I ran to the front door. I wanted to scream, "Go fuck yourself, Angie!" but the words got stuck behind a large lump in my throat.

I felt singed, nuked, burnt to a crisp, blasted by the one person who meant more to me than life. I smoked a lot of dope and drank the remainder of a fifth of Yukon Jack that night, knowing that I didn't have to go into work for three days. How could I make it okay for Sunshine to live with me? Quit Franklin's? But then what would I do? Bimbo-of-the-Month calendar shots for Al's Truck Stop? Being a Franklin's model was a dicey proposition. Some girls, a few girls, went on to the next level—Penthouse, Playboy, and the like. The rest of Mr. Franklin's stable fell into the "out of sight, out of mind" category. Franklin's of Beverly Hills equaled sex. There was no way I could segue into modeling for an Orvis or a LL Bean without someone, a lot of someones, noticing.

Any change of career meant a drastic change in my lifestyle. It wasn't my fault that I made tons of money doing nothing to improve the world while Sunshine toiled under-paid and underappreciated as she fought for the rights of the downtrodden. If I was in charge of the world, things would be different. But I wasn't in charge of the world, and worse yet, I didn't know what to do.

Finally, after several days of not returning my calls, Sunshine answered the phone.

My heart pounded like crazy. "I've missed you."

"I've missed you, too," she said softly.

"Would you like to go out to dinner Friday?"

"Bunny, we need to talk." She sounded tired.

"I know. That's why I want to take you to dinner."

"Don't make it anywhere special or expensive, okay? Let's go somewhere like Mama's."

"I'll pick you up at seven, and Mama's is perfect!" I wanted to take her to a romantic, intimate little restaurant we found in Claremont, but this situation called for major sucking up. Let Sunshine pick the restaurant, I was just glad to be with her. Besides, I could dress for seduction. Sunshine was so distracted by my white mini dress that we never stayed out for more than an hour or two before she wanted to undress me. It was a shameless ploy, but it worked. Every time.

I spent the next three days tanning by the pool and plan-ning our evening: I would arrive wearing my white dress, no panties and no hose, lightly scented with lavender, my hair tousled. We would drive the twenty minutes to Mama's Diner, where Sunshine would order a veggie burger and I would have a shrimp salad. I would rub my leg against hers while looking longingly into her eyes, whereupon she would insist upon leaving Mama's immediately and heading to my place where we would make mad, passionate love into the wee hours of the morning. By the end of the weekend, between interludes of sexual ecstasy and intimate conversations, we would devise a way of living together that would respect her boundaries and my profession of choice. It was perfect.

When I arrived at Sunshine's house, Angie's car was parked in front. Damn! That meant Connie, Phyllis, Angie, and Evelyn were all home, probably doing some post workweek desensitization training so they could focus their energies on the next crisis du jour. Suddenly I felt overdressed, or underdressed as it were, for this self-righteous group.

"Come in, Bunny," Angie said, not smiling.

The group turned their collective eyes on me. It was June in Southern California. The temperature had been hovering around eighty-six degrees all day, but it felt down right frosty in their living room. The term "cold war" took on new meaning. Evelyn noticeably reacted to my dress, but immediately buried her head in a book. I caught her furtively staring at me when the others weren't looking.

"We don't think it's appropriate for you and Sunshine to live together," Angie said.

"Lucky for us, we don't need your approval." I couldn't keep the sarcasm out of my voice. Those self-appointed guardians of the public welfare were getting on my nerves. If I had my way, Sunshine would move out tonight.

"Hi, Bunny." Sunshine looked tense as she entered the room. She wore a "Save the Whales" T-shirt, baggy shorts, and sandals. Together we looked like the "Odd Couple."

"Remember what we talked about," Angie called out as we climbed into the Jeep.

Sunshine was uncharacteristically quiet as we drove to Mama's. As much as I wanted to take her in my arms and kiss her, my plan called for Sunshine coming on to me. Just to be friendly, I held her hand.

81

Sunshine looked down. "Bunny, I don't know what to do." She traced her finger over the back of my hand.

"What do you mean?"

"You know I love you, but there are so many things I want to do before I settle down. I forget about everything when I'm with you." Her voice sounded strained.

Oh God. I had to be very careful what I said. "Sunshine, from my perspective you spend too much time working for people who don't appreciate what you're doing."

She looked up, her eyes bright. "That's just it. If I spent more time working, I'd have a better chance accomplishing things."

Oh God!

She took a deep breath. "We were talking last night."

"Who is 'we'?"

"Evelyn, me, Connie ...."

"I know, Phyllis and Angie, the Righteous Sisters."

"... about what direction we want to go next."

I pulled her toward me. "I want you to come in my direction."

Sunshine started to laugh. Soon tears were rolling down her cheeks and she leaned over and kissed me. "What would I do without you?"

"Crash and burn. Live a miserable, narrow life and have no fun at all," I teased.

"I grew up in the Lutheran Church. I'm sure the Lutherans would think you're the Devil Incarnate in that dress. I know Phyllis, Connie, Angie, and Evelyn think you are."

"Not Evelyn."

"Especially Evelyn." Her eyes narrowed. "What's with you and Evelyn anyway? Anything I need to know about?"

I decided to see how far I could push her. "Evelyn and I

have been carrying on an affair behind your back for months. I wore this dress for her tonight."

Her face flushed. "You better not have! I thought you bought that dress for me!"

"Yeah, but I never get to wear it for very long when I'm with you." I felt gratified to know I still held her interest. My plan was working.

Sunshine slid her hand up my thigh. "And you're not going to be wearing it much longer."

"Really?"

"You seem to have forgotten that you're my lover." She was acting downright possessive. The old Sunshine I knew was back—flirting, teasing, laying claim to me again. We never made it to Mama's, but drove directly to my place. As I predicted, we made love and talked the entire weekend, to the chagrin, no doubt, of her housemates. Sunshine agreed that it was time for us to live together.

The cold war was over and the Righteous Sisters had lost.

Chapter 7

I'll Be Good To You

We spent the next three weekends looking for a suitable apartment. Sunshine objected when the apartments were too expensive and I objected when the neighborhood jeopardized our lives. We were determined to find something that suited us both, but lower rent and a decent neighborhood put us in Riverside County, down the hill from The Creep.

We'd just finished a leisurely breakfast of Pop Tarts and leftover pizza when Sunshine looked at the clock. "It's 9:45. We'd better get going."

As I was already dressed, I went out to the mailbox to pick up the paper while Sunshine got ready. Attached to the Sunday LA Times was a handwritten note scrawled on a manila envelope that read "See Bunny. See Bunny run. Run, Bunny, run."

My heart was in my throat when I opened the envelope. In it was a grainy black and white photo of a nude woman with a picture of my head pasted on it. She/I was tied sitting down to some sort of BDSM frame, her/my legs spread wide exposed to the camera, her/my hands tied above our head, and a devilish looking knife, the kind you find in a hunting magazine, pointed at her/my cunt. A hand-tinted pool of blood lay between her/my legs, the exclamation point to the photo. His message was clear: you are dead meat. Ohmigod! I puked in the flowerbed, then collapsed on the sidewalk. I felt so dizzy, I was afraid I couldn't stand. I don't know how long I sat there until Sunshine came looking for me.

"Bunny, what's the matter? Are you okay?" She knelt down next to me.

I couldn't speak. How could I tell her she had been right, The Creep had struck again? And this time he was graphic and sadistic.

"It's him, isn't it? Give me that!" Sunshine grabbed for the picture.

"No." I clutched it to myself.

She was furious. "If you and I are going to live together, we can't keep secrets from each other, especially if it concerns you and The Creep. Give it to me!" The vein at her temple pounded.

Call it intuition or street smarts, but I knew if I showed her the picture our relationship would be over. Finito. Adios. Ciao, babe. And I wasn't about to let that happen. This was my shit. Sure, Sunshine's life revolved around the injustices one group of people inflicted on another, but this was different. There was an innocence to Sunshine I didn't want to violate, and this picture would do just that.

"You can't see this."

Although I didn't think the words "I told you so!" would fall from her lips, the intent, meaning, and implication certainly were there. She glared at me, her anger radiating ninety miles an hour. "Is this how it's going to be, then?"

Her words struck me like a blow. "Sunshine, you have to trust me."

"Trust you? How can I trust you? What else aren't you telling me?" Her voice cracked. "How often is this going to happen? Every month? Every week? Every day? I'm sup-

85

posed to ignore the fact that some crazed man is after you? That he can't distinguish fantasy from reality? I'm beginning to wonder if you can!" The color drained from her face. "Sometimes I look at you and wonder, 'What am I doing with her?" Bunny, you're tearing me apart! But worse than that, your life is in serious danger!" She burst into tears. "I can't stick around and watch you go under. Do your own thing, Bunny. It's over between us." Sunshine turned on her heel and walked toward the apartment.

Although my life was crashing around me, I needed to do one thing before I ran after her. I stumbled over to the dumpster and drew the cigarette lighter out of my pocket. I didn't want anyone to see this picture, not the kids in the neighborhood, not the vagrants who sometimes rummaged through the dumpsters, not the garbage men who emptied it. I lit the envelope and picture and watched them burn to ashes. The only trace of the picture would be forever seared in my memory.

Sunshine had already thrown her clothes into her overnight bag when I returned. She was on the phone, her back to me. "I don't care what you're doing! Come get me!"

"Sunshine," I pleaded, "let's talk."

"No!"

"I'll take you home," I offered.

She picked up her overnight bag and walked out the front door.

"I'll quit my job!" I said, racing after her.

"Do you really think that's going to stop him? Bunny, he knows where you live!" Her knuckles were white on her overnight bag.

"We could move somewhere he couldn't find us."

Her eyes opened wide in disbelief. "You still want to drag me into this!"

"I thought that was the plan, that we would live together!"

"That was the plan, until this! Where do you propose we move? Iowa?"

I'd never seen her so angry or so scared. I was sweating it big time. "I'll lay low for a while."

"Do whatever you like, but I refuse to be a part of this anymore!" She paced up and down the curb, chain-smoking as she looked for her ride.

I don't know whether it was from bravado or plain stupidity, but I decided to call her bluff. "You told me you loved me! If you loved me, you'd go anywhere with me!"

She stopped and turned, her cigarette halfway to her mouth. "You don't get it, do you? You want to go on as if nothing's wrong! You're as crazy as he is!" There was enough fear and hurt and anger on her face for ten people.

I wasn't ready to admit defeat yet. "OK, so I'll get an apartment away from here and when things calm down, we can live together."

"No!" There were tears in her eyes.

"Yes!"

"You haven't heard a word I've said!"

I had heard what she said, but my own logic dictated that Sunshine and I would spend the rest of forever together. We could work this out.

I babbled on for the next few minutes, digging a bigger hole for myself until Connie's yellow '62 Bug lurched to the curb with a coughing, sputtering halt. The bumper, which was attached by two coat hangers, came to a stop a second later. Angie jumped out, opened the front end, and threw in Sunshine's overnight bag.

"Sunshine, please don't go!" I begged.

Connie got out and glared at me as Sunshine climbed into the backseat. "Leave her alone. She doesn't need you."

Sunshine sat with her back to me, shaking as she lit another cigarette.

"Whatever you want, I'll do it!" I held on to the passenger's side window as if I could keep them from leaving.

Connie climbed back into the Bug and turned the key in the ignition. The engine backfired as it came to life, sending a cloud of black smoke into the air.

"Fuck off!" Angie yelled as they drove away.

The Bug lurched down the street and backfired again. When it rounded the corner, the driver's side coat hanger snapped. Amidst the spray of sparks, I could barely make out the bumper sticker that read: "One Nuclear Bomb Can Ruin Your Whole Day."

"You've got to stop him!" I screamed at Mr. Stiff.

"And good morning to you too, Bunny. I assume that because it's 7:40 on a Monday morning when you're not scheduled for a shoot means that your long-distance admirer has struck again. In fact," he thumbed through his calendar, "you're not scheduled 'til Thursday. It must be quite something. Tell me what happened. All of it." Contempt oozed from him like a leaky sewer pipe.

Exasperated, I sat on the chair across from his desk and lit a cigarette. "Yesterday morning, when I went to get the Sunday paper, there was an envelope attached to it."

He paused, as if waiting for more. "And? What did the envelope say?"

I could feel my heart pounding. "It said: 'See Bunny. See Bunny run. Run, Bunny, run.'"

He threw back his head and laughed. "That's it? Some guy quotes The Little Red Storybook and you come unglued? You're overreacting!"

"That's not all!"

He leaned across the desk. "Well then, what?" he taunted.

"There was a picture ..." I couldn't go on.

He frowned. "A picture? A picture of what?"

A wave of nausea broke over me. "A woman. Me. She ... I was bound. There was blood."

"What?"

"Christ, Arthur!" I screamed. "I was tied up! Ready for the slaughter!"

He gave me a lecherous smile. "Sounds to me like he's got some amusing plans for you."

"IT'S NOT FUNNY!" My heart beat a million miles an hour.

"Calm down. Don't be a drama queen like Rapunzel." He waved his hand dismissively.

"Rapunzel? What's she got to do with this?"

"This? Nothing," he sniffed. "Rapunzel was one of my charity cases who never could get her life in order."

I couldn't take his taunting or his contempt anymore. The man was filth. "Rapunzel was not your 'charity case.' She didn't need you to make her famous. You were just the opportunist who made her Franklin's vinyl queen."

"Oh, didn't she tell you?" His face contorted into a sneer. "Your darling Rapunzel was pregnant when she started modeling. I had to provide the, ahem, resources so she could continue working here."

"What the hell are you talking about?"

"You really are stupider than you look. Rapunzel had an abortion, rather late into her pregnancy as I recall. She was broke, but then she was always broke, and came to me for money for the abortion and a half-gram of cocaine.

"I gave her money for the abortion and for her rent, and enough cocaine to tide her over until payday. Of course, there's never enough cocaine until payday. She ran up quite a bill with me. So, being a businessman, I offered to set her up in business, selling coke. Nasty stuff, that cocaine. All of her profit went up her nose and she kept getting farther and farther into debt. What could I do?" He threw up his hands in a mock gesture of concern. "Rapunzel needed money quick, so I offered her a way out." He sat back in his chair, his fingers laced behind his head. "I have friends who are willing to pay substantial sums of money for Franklin's models to perform certain services ..."

I was horrified. "You slime!"

He cut me off. "Your naiveté appalls me. This is business. Rapunzel left owing me thousands of dollars. She would have paid, too, if it weren't for you."

"Me?"

"Unfortunately Rapunzel's attitude started to deteriorate after she met you. All of a sudden, she stopped taking direction and wanted to do things her own way. You're a disruptive element here and now Gloria is buying into it, too. I don't like that in a woman. I didn't like it in her and I don't like it in you."

Finally, I had something on this snake. "I think Mr. Franklin will be interested to know his art director is a major drug dealer who blackmails his models into white slavery."

"White slavery? Is that what you call it? It's pleasure, Bunny, pure and simple. It's the oldest occupation known to women, and men have always been willing to pay for it. If you were any kind of woman at all, you'd have some man paying for the pleasure of your company. So what do you do? Waste that beautiful face and pussy on some goddamn woman! You're the worst kind of pervert."

It was staring me in the face the entire time. "You're him! You're The Creep who wrote the letter and sent the picture.

It was you!" In my haste to get up, I knocked over the chair. Arthur Spires leaned back in his chair, a wicked smile on his face. "That's a crazy thing to accuse me of, when all I've done is help you. And Rapunzel," he added, his eyes gleaming. "You don't have the guts for this job. A real woman would understand that the letters and the pictures are the price you pay for success. You're just a two-bit cunt. And don't bother going to Mr. Franklin. Who do you think he's going to believe? Me or some damn dyke who disappears for weeks at a time? The same dyke who caused Rapunzel to have a nervous breakdown and leave in the first place."

"But I was ..." It hit me like lightning. I was screwed!

"Mr. Franklin knows I take special interest in models who are having financial difficulties. Mr. Franklin is a family man and wholeheartedly approves that I help out his family. You never were part of this family. And by the way, you're fired. Don't think you can walk into any agency and get a job. As far as the fashion industry is concerned, you're history." He put his feet on his desk, an evil grin on his face.

I backed out of the room, my heart pounding so fast my head was swimming. My only thought was to get away, as fast and as far from there as possible. Sunshine would believe me. I made it to her work in thirteen minutes flat.

"No." She shook her head. "It's over between us. I can't help you."

"Sunshine, please, you have to!"

"Bunny, I told you to get out when you got the first letter. It's not exactly like you didn't know this was coming." She looked weary.

"But it was Mr. Stiff the whole time! You can't leave me now! You have to help me nail him!"

"No, Bunny, I don't. I'm sorry you're in this predicament,

91

but I told you what to do. Go ahead, write a letter to Mr. Franklin, but don't expect him to do anything about Mr. Stiff. You backed yourself in a corner, and now you want me to bail you out of it."

"Please!"

She looked on the verge of tears. "Don't call me again. Don't come over and don't call. I don't want to see you."

Please, God, this can't be happening! I stumbled out of her building and ran for my car. Tears streamed down my face as I jammed the Jeep into fourth gear on the freeway. I felt completely adrift. Fuck this! Fuck this shit!

When I got home, I phoned Sunshine's work.

"She's out. I'll tell her you called," the receptionist said.

Fine. I dialed Sunshine's house.

"No, uh, Bunny, she's not here ..." Evelyn said softly.

I could hear Evelyn sweating over the phone.

Angie grabbed the receiver and shouted, "She's not here and don't call back!"

I heard an abrupt dial tone. I called back.

"Quit calling here! She doesn't want to see you," Angie screamed.

Another dial tone. I called back.

"Quit harassing us!" It sounded like Connie.

Another dial tone. I called back. The phone rang and rang and rang. I hung up and called back. I got a busy signal. I called the rest of the night and got a busy signal every time. Fine, I can wait this out. I sat on the couch and rolled a dozen joints. Between the dope and the Wild Turkey, I got pretty messed up, but what did I care? I had no job to go to anyway.

"Slow down," Michael cautioned.

"Fuck, Michael," I slurred, "she won't talk to me." I buried my head in my hands and sobbed until there were no tears left.

Michael picked me up off the couch, carried me into my bedroom, and laid me on the bed. I woke at nine the next morning in the same clothes that I wore the day before. The room swam in circles around my head when I phoned Sunshine again. The line was still busy.

"Fuck!" I showered and changed into some clean clothes. I would do anything to get her back—grovel at her feet, go work for the Salvation Army, join the drones in the typing pool. I drove, not to Sunshine's office, but to a boutique in Venice Beach we found in our happier days. It carried ultra-trendy, expensive items that would knock a hole in most people's budgets. On a lark, Sunshine had tried on a black leather miniskirt that hit her mid-thigh. She took two steps toward me, her eyes twinkling. "What do you think?"

I stared at her with my mouth open. That was the one and only time I had an inkling what guys were thinking when they looked at Franklin's models. "We'll take it!" I said to the salesclerk.

"Are you kidding? It's way too expensive and besides, where would I wear it?" She turned to the clerk, "We are not buying this."

Too bad! I knew she was right. She had her androgynous image to maintain. But it was nice to see her in something other than jeans and T-shirts. Now I knew how she felt about my white mini-dress.

They still had the skirt. I put it on my credit card and walked out of the store, humming. This was my ace in the hole. The game wasn't over yet. At her office, I pushed past the receptionist.

"She's not in."

Sunshine's door was ajar and I could see her at her desk.

I barged in and kissed her, my arms wrapped tightly around her so she couldn't get away.

"I told you I didn't want to see you!" Her face was flushed.

She was happy to see me.

The receptionist stuck her head into Sunshine's office. "Do you want me to call the police?"

"No. It's okay." Sunshine pushed the receptionist out and closed the door. "What are you doing here?"

"Visiting my girlfriend."

"I'm not your girlfriend."

"Yes, you are. Here, I bought you something." I laid the gift-wrapped box on her desk.

By the look on her face, I could tell she was torn between wanting to know what was in the box and wanting to kick me out. She hesitated, then sat down, drew the box to her and unwrapped it.

"Oh, Bunny." She stroked the leather with her fingertips.

I was right. I'd found her weakness.

"I can't," she said, tears streaming down her cheeks.

I brushed the hair out of her face.

She looked up at me. "I can't be around you anymore. I feel so much joy with you, and so much pain." She took a ragged breath. "I lose myself in you. My life has to have meaning beyond what I feel for you. I want to do some good in this world, Bunny, and I can't do it with you around." She turned to the wall and cried.

I'd never seen her look so defeated. "Sunshine?" I reached out and touched her shoulder.

She shoved my hand away. "Leave me alone. I never want to see you again."

"Sunshine?"

It was the tone of her voice that made me leave. I could

fight Phyllis, Connie, Angie, and Evelyn, those self-righteous twits. But I couldn't fight Sunshine; Sunshine who sobbed in the corner of her office, whose rejection pushed me to the outer limits of my sanity. It wasn't what I did she couldn't handle; it was who I was. No amount of gifts or attention or great sex would win her back. Sunshine had left me for good.

Chapter 8

Ladies Night

Tony Bennett may have left his heart in San Francisco, but I left mine in LA, a few years older, weary, and worldly wise. Now it was time for a new start. San Francisco—or The City, as it's known to the locals—was the perfect place to land. Besides being close to my Dad, The City offered cultural amenities offered nowhere else—The Fillmore, cable cars, and Candlestick Park. I'd see what kind of heart I could discover there.

The Castro District with its bars and boutiques was the gay heart of The City. Lesbians and gay men by the thousands lived their lives openly and with dignity in the company of like-minded people. I, too, wanted to live that dream. Visions of a benevolent landlady spreading peace, joy, and killer weed throughout her small queendom à la Armistead Maupin danced through my head. After four days of searching, however, The Chronicle yielded no such convivial paradise, so I settled for a third-story walkup on the edge of the Castro near Church Street.

I bought two six-packs and a T-shirt that read San Francisco, where the men are pretty and the women are strong, to wear while I moved in. I raised my bottle in a mock toast: "To a new life, a life without Sunshine." I downed the beer quickly and opened another one to take the edge off my day. I'd promised Michael I'd call him every week, so three days later, when my clothes were hung in the closets, new curtains graced my windows, and the telephone installer had just left, I called.

"Hey bro, I'm settled in."

"Yeah? Meet any girls yet?"

"For Chrissake, Michael, I just got here. Give me at least a week."

"You're slipping, Bunny. I figured you'd have slept with half the women in San Francisco by now." He chuckled.

"Check back with me in another week. I should be starting on the second half by then."

"You slut!"

"Hey, I learned it from the best."

"Why thank you, sweetheart. I'm glad to know that at least some of my sterling qualities have rubbed off on you."

Already I missed Michael, one of my few ties to sanity and my old life. I liked The City so far, but it was still new to me. I had no job, no girlfriend, and no prospects for either. I downed another beer. Welcome to The City.

It took a month to check out every gay haunt within a ten-mile radius of my apartment. Besides the gay restaurants and bookstores, there were gay counseling centers, gay B & B's, and gay churches that sponsored gay AA and NA meetings, one of which was around the corner from my apartment. The bar scene was like stepping into a Fellini movie: girls' bars, wimmin's bars, men's bars, leather bars, and glory holes. Like girls who looked like girls? Then put on your heels and head for Clementine's, where all the women dressed to the nines. Want to ease into sleaze? Try the rough trade bars in the Tenderloin district.

The City boasted a sexual smorgasbord where you could

find everything from double vanilla to extreme kink: dykes and drag queens, faggots and fairies, transvestites and transsexuals, Gays Against Brunch, Sisters of Perpetual Indulgence, top and bottom leathermen, gay accountants, attorneys, teachers, and construction workers; gay bureaucrats and auto mechanics, bisexual housewives and nellie waiters, men and women who passed for straight yet gambled their lives and their futures on passionate interludes with the same gender. If ever I was going to find myself, it would be in The City.

Summertime and the lovin' was easy. I particularly liked to cruise Valencia Street, where I had my pick of any nubile body I laid eyes on. With the sting of Sunshine's refusal still fresh in my mind, I was determined to exorcise her ghost at any cost. If the first woman I slept with wasn't Ms. Right ... well, there were others. I compared all of the women I dated to Sunshine. The farther they were from Sunshine, the more I drank. It didn't make them more like Sunshine, but I after a couple of drinks, I didn't care. My saving grace during those years was the one thing I damned loudly and often: my work involved traveling and working weekends, thus cutting short my headlong fall toward losing myself in a tangle of sweet woman flesh.

Hormones aside, I needed to find a job, fast. Bills were eating me alive, and I wasn't sure how long I could play one credit card company against another.

I walked into the big agencies—John Casablanca's, Queue, and Alpha—and couldn't get past the receptionist. Polite white women with Farrah Fawcett hair smiled professionally and promised to pass my portfolio and comp card along to the reigning queen of the agency. Not that it mattered what gender the head of the agency was; they were all queens. After a couple of weeks hanging around my apartment, waiting for calls that never came, I tried a couple smaller agencies. They didn't return my calls, either. Face it LaRue, you're not hot shit anymore. Or here's a thought: maybe you never were.

After six weeks of not working, when my savings account looked as pale as my ficus, I decided to lay in wait for Richard Adams. Head of Adams and Associates, he helped unknown models get their first assignments. I hung around his building long enough to know exactly when he left for lunch. Armed with my portfolio, comp card, and résumé, I shanghaied him in the elevator, going down.

"Hi Richard, I'm Bunny LaRue." I held out my hand. "I've left several messages with your receptionist. I guess you've been so busy you haven't had time to return my calls."

Richard Adams was a big-time leather queen who, I knew, frequented The Ambush. He looked up at me, startled. "Bunny ...?" he extended his hand.

"LaRue. I'm looking for work. I just got in from LA."

He looked me up and down critically. I'd charged a black leather mini skirt the day before to wear with my black leather jacket and tube top in hopes that my outfit would make him sit up and take notice.

"Who did you say you worked for?"

"Here's some shots, the usual." I handed him my port- folio in evening gown, sports attire, swimwear, and lastly, lingerie. I didn't want to let the cat out of the bag by telling him Mr. Stiff canned me.

The elevator door opened into the lobby.

"Very nice," he murmured. Richard lingered over the photos, looking at them carefully. He glanced up and smiled at a hot, hung, hunky blond who looked like he'd stepped out of the pages of Tom of Finland. "Where's a number I can reach you?"

"It's all in there. I can start immediately." Did I sound too anxious?

"I'll be in touch." Richard looked back at his trick. They walked through the lobby together, the blond's arm thrown over Richard's shoulder.

Score!

Suddenly, Richard stopped in his tracks and turned to me. "You're that troublemaker from Franklin's of Beverly Hills, aren't you?"

Shit! "What are you talking about?"

"The word on the street is you're major trouble—drugs, alcohol, don't show up on time, or don't show up at all." He handed me back my portfolio. "Sorry. There are some people even I won't fuck with."

Damn it! "I need the work!" Smooth move, Bunny. Why don't you tell him you're so broke you're considering selling dope, too?

"No one will hire you in this town. I'd like to help ..."

The trick glared at me, probably upset that Richard was being delayed.

"Are you absolutely set on modeling? Because if you're not, there is one thing I could suggest ..." Richard looked back at the blond. He was gone again, lost to the primal mating call. "I'll call you this afternoon." He stuck the business card I had just printed into his pocket, then waved to indicate our meeting was over. As they walked out of the lobby, I noticed a navy blue handkerchief peeking from the trick's left back pocket.

I jumped into my Jeep and raced back to my apartment. The clock read 12:47 p.m. when I got home. Maybe Richard's trick would be a quickie and he'd be back in his office in an hour. I wondered what his suggestion would be. Not another "personal service" gig. I didn't need a leather queen for a pimp. I got those kinds of offers on my own.

I calculated my bills: I was in the hole at least two thousand dollars. My savings bought groceries and paid the utilities with nothing to spare. By three-fifteen, Richard hadn't called. I decided not to smoke a joint to mellow out because I wanted to present an image of a responsible, professional model. By four thirty-two, Richard still hadn't called and I was on edge. At five-ten, I fired up my bong and took a couple hits. Fuck the mellow, I was too nervous to wait any longer. It's okay, it's okay, it's okay, he said he'd call with some work. By five-thirty, Richard still hadn't called. That fucker! See if I ever do business with him again!

My phone rang at six-twenty. Please, please, please let it be Richard!

"Hi, is this Bunny LaRue?"

It was Richard. Pull yourself together. "Yeah."

"Sorry I didn't get back to you earlier. I had an appointment that lasted all afternoon."

"No problem. You said you had something I might be interested in?"

"Yeah. You'd be doing some promotional modeling, you know, conventions, exhibitions, doing some sales and PR work."

"Selling what?"

He paused. "Auto parts."

"Auto parts?"

"Yeah. Look, I know it's probably not what you had in mind, but you've been blackballed and nobody will touch you with a ten-foot pole. If you're not interested, just say so." He sounded apologetic.

I took a deep breath. "Sure, I'm interested. Where do I go?"

I took down the information and thanked Richard for

the lead. From modeling for Franklin's of Beverly Hills to selling auto parts. My card would read: Bunny LaRue, Tires, Batteries, and Accessories.

Auto parts.

I breezed into Allied Distributing, looking more confident that I felt. The only trouble I could foresee was whether my looks would have any bearing on getting this job. Everyone knew that girls, especially pretty ones, were not mechanically inclined or willing to get dirty gapping a spark plug or changing the oil. I had almost crossed the line from concerned to desperate, so I turned on all the charm I could muster. My interview with the President and the Vice President of Allied lasted four hours, during which we swapped high school drag racing stories and put a major dent in a case of beer. I think the story that clinched the job was when I confessed to hot-wiring Cheryl Hoffman's father's brand new 1968 Lincoln Towncar. They liked my style. I liked their money.

Indeed, my card would read: Bunny LaRue, Sales Representative, Allied Distributing, Tires, Batteries, and Accessories.

Mr. and Mrs. Young Middle America stood arm in arm, inspecting the engine block of a '82 Ford at the Western Regional Automotive Aftermarket Expo in Las Vegas, Nevada. He shook his head at his wife and wiped his forehead with the back of his hand. "I don't think so, honey." He smiled weakly at her.

"Well, Dan, just ask one of the guys. They oughtta know."

As all of the "guys" were busy, I stepped forward. "Can I help you?"

"Well, maybe," Dan offered shyly. "I was wonderin' if I

could swap out my carburetor for this one." He pointed to the display.

Mrs. Young Middle America pushed in front of husband. "How the hell would she know? All she is, is a walking advertisement for tits and ass!" Her lip curled in a snarl.

I was in no mood for Mrs. Young Middle America. My head ached from last night's after-hours party, courtesy of the convention sponsors. I looked her up and down in one sour glance. She embodied Franklin's most sought-after customer: a woman who would spend any amount of money because secretly she believed herself to be not quite pretty enough, not quite thin enough to keep her man. Mrs. Young Middle America was sure her hubby would drop her as soon as I gave him the slightest encouragement.

I smiled wide and focused my attention on Mr. Young Middle America. "What are you drivin'?"

He smiled back. "A '72 Mustang Fastback."

Mrs. Young Middle America snorted.

I ignored her as I motioned him closer to the display. "This is our six-barrel, wide-throat carb. Actually, it was designed for the Ford after-market."

"Really?" he managed to choke out.

I leaned in close. "Should be no problem for your 'Stang."

When they left, I pushed behind the curtain and rummaged through my purse for the bottle of aspirin I carried. My forehead felt like a swarm of bees was setting up housekeeping. I slammed down four aspirin with a big gulp of soda.

"Don't you mind what that heifer said, Doll. She's the kind who would cheat with her best friend's husband!" The woman who spoke, looked to be another exhibitor.

"Excuse me?"

"My name's Barbara. I'm here with Rocky Mountain

Sheepskins. I liked the way ya handled that heifer. Somebody needs to kick that girl's ass!"

I took another sip of soda to keep from laughing. This woman, all five foot six of her, was poured into a dress that didn't leave much to the imagination. Her neckline plunged to reveal the South Rim of the Grand Canyon and her hemline was barely south of the border. Then there was her hair! I hadn't seen Big Hair like that since Valley of the Dolls. Whatever this woman was about, demure and unobtrusively feminine weren't part of the act.

"I'm Bunny LaRue. Nice to meet you." I offered my hand.

"Hey, Bunny! I saw ya at the party last night, but ya had so many men around I thought they were fixin' to crown ya Rodeo Queen."

"Rodeo Queen?" I burst out laughing.

"I'm sorry. Y'all must think all Texans are rude sons of bitches. I heard ya talkin' to that couple. It's nice to see a woman who's got a brain."

I couldn't tell if Barbara was flirting or not.

She grabbed my arm. "Hey, let's you'n me go find ourselves a little fun tonight, doll!"

Not your average date, LaRue! "Okay, as long as you don't call me a 'heifer.'"

Barbara looked me up and down. "Doll, ya ain't got one ounce of heifer in ya."

I'd been called a lot of things in my life: "bitch," "slut," "whore," "cunt," "pussy tease," "cock tease," "puta," "jota," "butch," "femme," "killer," "dumb blond," "airhead," "stoner"— the list went on ad nauseum, but "heifer" wasn't one of them. Barbara and I agreed to meet in the lobby at ten.

Amidst the clanging, ringing, sun-never-sets atmosphere of the casino, the patrons gulped free drinks and stared, glassy eyed, at the slots for hours on end. In this intensely focused world of gambling, when someone hit a jackpot, the other players would glance up and scowl, then go back to feeding the mechanical monsters in front of them, silently cursing Lady Luck for not tapping them on the shoulder. They spent little time making small talk, less time people-watching. But when Barbara strutted in, looking every inch the Rodeo Queen, heads turned in amazement. She wore skintight Rockies, Ropers, and a Dallas Cowboy jacket over a lace-edged blue camisole top. Balanced on top of her mile-high red hair rode a powder blue Stetson. Yeehaw! The cavalry had arrived!

We found a table next to a low wall, where we could sit and watch the gamblers on the floor below play Blackjack. A cocktail waitress, dressed in a tight black mini-skirt to not so subtly influence the amount of tips she received, took our drink orders.

"Cuba Libre," Barbara ordered.

"White Russian here."

"So where are y'all from?" Barbara reached over and lit my cigarette.

"The City. How 'bout you?"

"I'm from Amarilluh, Texas. Moved to Daly City, just south of Frisco six years ago with my husband, Dwight. He's a long haul driver who's outta town a lot." Barbara took a long drag on her cigarette.

I shoved a $20 toward the cocktail waitress when she returned.

"That's okay. Those guys over there already paid." The cocktail waitress nodded in the direction of the bar.

We turned to see three men sitting at a table across the room, smiling at us. "Mind if we join you?" The bald one was already on his feet, drink in hand, stumbling over to our table. His friends grabbed their drinks and a minute later the five of us were squeezed together pretending intimacy.

Where's a gay bar when you need one? Although Barbara was married, she'd still be more fun to drink with than the Three Stooges.

"So where y'all from?" Barbara turned on her Texas charm, batting her eyelashes at Curly, Larry, and Moe.

"Poughkeepsie," offered Curly.

"Columbus," said Larry with the ruddy cheeks and red nose.

"Pittsburgh," said Moe, the bald one. "We're here for the Shriner's Convention. How about y'all?" Moe was already three sheets to the wind, oblivious to how hokey he sounded.

Okay, so Barbara wanted to flirt with the boys—not my idea of a good time. I scanned the room for any diversion and quickly found one: a dark-haired woman in her twenties, playing blackjack at one of the two-dollar tables. I turned my chair slightly so I could get a better view of her without appearing obvious.

"Why, I'm from Amarilluh and my sister's here from Frisco, ain'tcha, sis?"

I choked on my drink as I came back to the conversation.

"Need some help?" Moe pounded my back.

"What's the matter, sis, can't hold yer likker?" Barbara eyes twinkled with mischief.

She has no more interest in these bozos than I do! "Sorry, wrong hole." I waved Moe away. As the dark-haired woman was oblivious to my interest, I decided to play along with Barbara.

She finished off her drink and set the glass down slowly on the table. "Hits the spot!" She eyed the glass and smiled.

"Here! Another round!" Curly waved frantically at the bartender.

A sly smile vanished as soon as it crossed Barbara's lips. Moe continued. "Can I get you anything? Water? Aspirin? Do you need a ride home?"

Barbara cut in. "My sister's had a rough time of it lately. She just lost her husband, didn'tcha, sweetie?"

Lost my husband? I choked again and this time tears rolled down my cheeks.

"Oooohhhhhhhhhhhh." Moe patted my back again, this time pausing to rub my neck. His hand drifted down my back until it came to rest on my hip.

"That bastard! I caught him with a checkout girl from Walgreens! He told me that inventory wasn't going well and he had to go down and 'supervise.' Well, he can discuss Miss Feminine Products, the house, the cars, and the boat with my lawyer!" I covered my face with my hands so they wouldn't see me laugh.

The cocktail waitress returned with our drinks. "Another round?"

Larry nodded, probably hoping to follow the time-honored tradition of getting them drunk, then seducing them.

We drank and chatted amicably until the next round came. Barbara asked about their jobs and civic responsibilities with such ease I knew her lines were practiced. I wondered if she had any tricks up her sleeve to get us out of this mess.

"We need to freshen up a bit, don't we, sis? Let's meet these boys in the lobby, say, fifteen minutes from now?"

The "boys" were drooling in anticipation of their big score. "Sure!" Larry said. He looked at his watch. "About eleven?"

"Eleven it is! Come on, sis." She pulled me up by the arm. "In the lobby. Fifteen minutes. Be there." She winked at them.

Barbara stumbled down the two stairs to the main floor

and pulled me along behind her. "Three drinks in forty minutes? Not bad, but we gotta get away from here before they find us!"

"Is this what you do at conventions? Con guys into buying you drinks, then splitting?"

"Them? Doll, by the time those boys get home, we'll have turned into two high-class hookers they took turns fucking all night!" Barbara led the way past the blackjack tables. "And show me who you've been lookin' at. I can't figure out which one he is."

I shook my head mysteriously. No sense making it difficult for her. After all, once the convention was over, we'd never see each other again.

"Oh, c'mon doll, give!"

Just then, we walked past the table where the dark-haired woman sat. She looked up, smiled, then turned back to her cards. My heart skipped a beat.

"Ohhhhhhhh. Herrrrrrrrrrr."

By the tone of Barbara's voice, I knew we'd crossed a threshold and there was no going back. She held my wrist tighter. "Hell, if I didn't like dick so much, I'd probably join ya. Sometimes the fuckers just ain't worth shit. Ya know what I mean?" Barbara's eyes were bright and her Texas accent was getting thicker by the minute. I figured the three drinks we had with "the boys" were not her first this evening.

"C'mon! We gotta get outta here, pronto!" She ran ahead, dragging me by the wrist.

We ran through the air-conditioned lobby into the furnace blast of night air and jumped into the first cab we saw.

"Where to, ladies?"

"Somewhere three middle-aged men going through mid-life crisis would never look for us," Barbara said.

He looked in his rearview mirror. "Big and glitzy, where they'll get lost or small-and-out-of-the-way, where they'll never find you?"

We looked at each other. "Small-and-out-of-the-way!" I said.

We drove to the far end of the Strip, where the mega-casinos were replaced by smaller, sleazier casinos; the perfect place to hide.

"I need a drink." Barbara pulled me through row after row of slot machines until we found a quiet area where we could play Keno and talk.

"You sure know how to show a girl a good time!" I teased.

The cocktail waitress approached. "A couple guys want to know if they can buy you drinks."

"Not again!" I moaned.

"Tell them boys thanks, but we're not interested. I'll have a Cuba Libre and doll here'll have a White Russian. Ain't that right?"

I nodded.

She winked at me as she lit her cigarette. "How about you, doll? Do you have a ..." she faltered.

"Girlfriend? Not at the moment." I didn't add, I had one but she dumped me.

Again, Barbara reached over and lit my cigarette. "Well, that girl at the blackjack table was kinda cute. Why don't cha go after her?"

I didn't want to get into Introduction to Lesbian/Gay Lifestyles 101 with her. Why did straight people assume one-night stands were our preferred mode of emotional and/or sexual interaction? I shrugged. "Probably not from The City anyway."

"Doll, I don't want you to miss anything because of me!"

I'd had enough to drink by now to tell her what I really

thought. "I don't want to stop you from jumpin' anyone's bones tonight either!"

"Those jokers? Hell, even if I did sleep around on Dwight, which I don't, I'd choose you over those pigs!" She slumped in her chair, her eyes unfocused. "Sometimes, I think he's sleeping around on me, but goddammit, I took those vows and I'm gonna keep 'em!"

The cocktail waitress returned and set our drinks on the table. "Too bad. I think one of them is some kinda rich Arab or something."

Barbara and I looked at each other and burst out laughing. "Well, ain't that the shits!"

The cocktail waitress shrugged and walked back to the bar.

Barbara took a long drag on her cigarette. "Ya know, all I ever wanted was a couple of kids and a ranch where we could have a few horses. I was pregnant when I married Dwight—we had to get married. Then two months after the wedding, I had a miscarriage. We've been trying to have kids ever since, but with him gone so much of the time, I can't seem to get pregnant. Sometimes I think God's punishing me for being pregnant before we were married!"

"I can't believe God would punish you for being pregnant."

Barbara took a sip of her drink. "Well, that's 'cuz you weren't raised a Southern Baptist, I'll bet!"

"No, I wasn't." And thank you, God, for small favors.

Her words slurred as she continued. "I hate Frisco! It's too big and too la-de-da for me. I want to see the sun rising on the desert, clouds that stretch across the horizon, the smell of dirt after a rain. Jesus! There ain't no life in that city!" Tears rolled down her cheeks, smearing her mascara.

Behind the Rodeo Queen I saw a troubled wife who longed for a life she understood: kids, dirt, and horses. I could picture Dwight in his cowboy hat and Wranglers, his slow Texas drawl charming the pants off every cowgirl wannabe this side of the Rio Grande. It was Barbara's insistence on her cowgirl identity that kept her from unraveling, drowning in the strip mall sameness that invaded every town big enough to claim two zip codes. I wanted to take Barbara in my arms and comfort her. Instead, I lit another cigarette. I didn't want her to think I was coming on to her.

"I wanna go home." Barbara buried her head in her hands and sobbed until I thought she would choke.

I didn't know if she meant home to her room, her home in the burbs, or home to Texas. "Let's catch a cab back to the hotel." I offered her my arm.

Barbara wiped her tears on the sleeve of her Cowboy's jacket. "I'm usually not like this, I just feel so lonely tonight."

I felt lonely too, but I knew anything between Barbara and me would be instant disaster. Never get involved with a married woman, a lesson several of my friends learned the hard way. "Let's go."

I helped Barbara stand and gather her purse. She leaned heavily on me as we walked through the aisles of slots, the tears streaming down her cheeks. Boy, she can't hold her liquor! We caught a cab back to the MGM Grand and prayed we wouldn't run into The Three Stooges.

Safely on the twelfth floor, Barbara fumbled with her room key.

"Let me get that for you," I offered.

She hung her head and slumped against the wall.

I opened the door and switched on the light.

"I didn't mean ..." Barbara looked up at me through large, teary eyes.

"It's okay. I know. Don't worry about it." I backed out

of her room and rode the elevator to the eighteenth floor. I stripped off my clothes and collapsed onto the bed, feeling ... what? Jesus, what a night! My mind was too muddy to make any sense out of it and I drifted into a dreamless sleep.

By 9:00 a.m. I was back at work—tired, shaky; in other words, normal. More aspirin and the promise of a short day made it bearable. If it had been up to me, I'd have stayed in my room, channel-surfing the whole day. It was a mystery where these conventioneers got their stamina. Between talking to people and taking orders, the day flew by. When I looked at my watch, it read 12:43, about three hours to go.

Someone tapped me on the shoulder. "Wanna smoke?" Barbara stood there dressed in her convention attire: low cut top, mini skirt, and four-inch heels.

If I hadn't looked closely into her eyes, I would have sworn I dreamt the night before, but there was a certain tentativeness I hadn't seen there yesterday.

My boss waved me away. "Go on. It's slowed down. We can manage."

"Let me get my purse." I rummaged behind the curtain for my purse and smokes.

We walked silently into the halls, where the incessant clanging of the machines muffled the uneasiness I felt growing between us. Barbara slid into a chair at one of the bars.

Ya know, Bunny, there can never be anything between us. I'm straight and I think you're, well frankly, I think you're misguided. I could hear it now.

"Bunny ..."

I pretended to look through my purse for my lighter. I looked up.

"I'm usually not like that. I had too much to drink last night." She paused. "I didn't want you to think I was coming on to you."

Coulda fooled me! "Don't worry, Barbara, you're not my type anyway." I felt safe enough to acknowledge she had been flirting with me.

The cocktail waitress walked up. "What can I get for you two?"

Barbara looked at her watch. "It's afternoon. Make mine a Bloody Mary."

Tomato juice would make me puke at this point, but a pick-me-up sounded good. "Screwdriver, please."

Barbara winked as she leaned over to light my cigarette. "This means nothing, ya know."

"Like hell it doesn't!" I smiled. By the way this was unfolding, I could see that we could flirt 'til the cows came home, and nothing would happen. We had passed that critical moment where sex was an option, and now we were free to play. "So where are you going after this convention?"

"Gonna go home, jump his bones, and think of you!" she teased. "I still think ya oughtta get that blackjack girl's number and give her a call. Ya never know."

"She can't hold a candle to you, Barbara—doesn't have your cleavage."

Barbara sat up straighter and thrust her bosom toward me. "Really?" She smiled the same "gotcha!" smile she gave the Three Stooges.

"You really need to do something about that attitude of yours. It's gonna get you in trouble someday."

"What do ya mean?" she asked innocently. "I'm just bein' friendly. Ask any of these boys." She waved her cigarette towards the gaming floor, where players stood or sat transfixed, oblivious to the world inches away from them.

Although in my head I wanted no part of a married woman, her physical presence exerted a powerful pull. I needed to get away quick before I made a big mistake. "Damn, Barbara! If you weren't married ..."

She blushed. "Ya know, you're the first gal I ever had feelings for."

"Sexual feelings?"

"Yeah. I figured those other gals just couldn't find a man or something."

"That's usually not the case." Alarm bells started going off in my head. Get out of here now! Don't get suckered into this conversation!

The cocktail waitress set our drinks down. "What else can I get for you?"

Breathing space! "Nothing for me, thanks."

"I'm fine. Thanks, hon." Barbara fidgeted with her celery stick. "Bunny ..." she stopped, not even midway through her thought.

Oh, God, no! This is not the time or place!

"I've never thought about being with a gal before. I mean, it's kinda sexy if you think about it. Ya'd pretty much know what the other gal was wantin', how she'd wanna be touched and all. Then there'd be all that kissin' ..." She stared into space before slurping her drink.

I didn't know what to say. "Damn right it's sexy!" or maybe, "It's better left to us pros." I didn't think "We've made our quota for this year. Otherwise I'd offer you a free trial" would be appropriate, so I said nothing.

There was a silence between us wide enough to drive two semi-trailers through. We both needed an out.

"Well, doll, it's been a pleasure meetin' ya, but I'd better be gettin' back." Barbara finished her drink and set her glass down on the small table.

"Yeah. Maybe we'll see each other at another convention."
Lame, LaRue, that was really lame.

Barbara stood and fixed me with a look I interpreted to mean, "another lifetime, perhaps."

I watched Barbara disappear into the Convention Hall, then stubbed out my cig and headed back to Allied's booth.

The rest of the convention was a blur. I remember packing our van, then settling in the backseat with a book to keep from having to join the conversation on the drive back to The City. The other guys seemed likewise subdued, lost in their own private heavens or hells, while the scenery rushed by at 70 mph. Whatever happened to my dream of living with Sunshine and changing the world with her? Making money is great, but I'd trade all my money to be happy with you, Sunshine.

Chapter 9

Bette Davis Eyes

The woman with the dark, curly hair pulled out every weapon in her arsenal—the pout, the looks across the smoky bar, the low cut dress, sucking on her fingers one by one as she stared at me. She was everything I pretended to be for Franklin's of Beverly Hills: the sexually insatiable woman. There was nothing coy about her; she walked directly up to me and laid the palm of her hand against my breast. Her eyes smoldered with such intensity and self-assuredness that I was hooked on the spot.

"Tell me you came here to find me," she said.

I'd had three beers while I stared across the room and planned how I would approach her, so her opening didn't strike me as odd.

She ran her hands down my arms, locked fingers with mine, and squeezed tight. "Have we met before? You look familiar."

"Maybe," I said, trying to sound casual as her fingernails dug into the back of my hands. I did look familiar to a lot of people—the occupational hazard of being a model. This woman seemed the type to have a couple of back issues of the Franklin's catalog stashed around her place.

"Ooooh, cool and silent! I like that." She stood on her

tiptoes and kissed me, her warm mouth engulfing mine.

Cool and silent, my ass! I was speechless, stunned by her boldness. Most women tended to trip over their tongues in their eagerness to come on to me. This woman with a bad attitude played like a pro. My heart racing, I circled her waist with both arms and pulled her close. Eleven weekends out of town without nookie had left me irritable and horny—there was no way I was going to let this babe get away tonight.

"Are you as good in bed as you are at kissing?" She pressed against me.

"Maybe." If she liked her lovers cool and silent, I could play that game. We stood in the middle of Amelia's, clutched tightly, and swayed to Donna Summer's "Last Dance."

She nibbled my neck. "Can we go someplace more private?"

My place was still trashed from being on the road so much, so I didn't want to take her there. "Your place?"

She scooped up her purse, hooked her fingers through my belt loop, and pulled me through the crowd to the door. Several women watched us intently; whether they were envious or interested, I couldn't tell. You still got it, LaRue. Her eyes lit up at the sight of my silver RX-7, which I had bought the week before to regain my sanity. The high-energy lifestyle of San Francisco killed my old Jeep and the thought of picking up women in my company car, a tan Ford Fairlane, was enough to make anyone puke.

"God, you've got it all, don't you—good looks and a hot car. I can tell we're going to have some fun times together." She pulled me close and we sucked face in the middle of the parking lot for all to see. She squeezed my ass with both hands, and then began unbuttoning my jeans. "Let's do it in your car."

Jesus! Doing it in my car was better fantasy than reality.

The back seat of Cheryl Hoffmann's Mustang had offered more room than my new car. Between the stick shift and the roof, I could barely stretch my 5'10" frame comfortably. Hot hands and mouth mixed with stick shift and steering wheel didn't seem conducive to a romantic encounter. Distraction was the plan. "I think your bed would be more comfortable for what I have in mind."

"You're gonna make me wait? You're bad!" She smiled one of her killer smiles as she ran her fingers through my hair.

"What's your name?" I peeled out of the parking lot, momentarily throwing us against our seats.

"Elizabeth Corbin. And yours?"

"Bunny LaRue." I tried one of Rapunzel's tricks—brought her hand to my mouth and licked her palm. She jumped like an electric shock coursed through her body.

"What do you do for a living?" she asked.

"I'm in sales. And you?"

She cupped my breast and squeezed hard, which caused me to steer dangerously close to a parked car. "I'd buy whatever you're selling. I'm in sales, too."

Try to sound like you're in control. "Oh? What do you sell?"

"Financial instruments."

"What?"

"You know—stocks, bonds, munies, mutual funds. You wouldn't happen to need a stockbroker, would you?"

Her suggestion took me by surprise. "Well, uh, yeah. I guess so."

"Never mind. We can talk about that later." She leaned over and bit me on the neck.

We needed to get to her house before I came unglued altogether. I sped though the deserted streets and ran every red light until we came to a stop in front of her house.

Elizabeth Corbin lived in a fashionable, upscale neighborhood, where every owner's second or third occupation included remodeling their Victorian home. Her place was half done—a sparkling new kitchen and living room with refinished hardwood floors, mixed with a torn-apart bathroom that featured a vintage-looking clawfoot tub. She obviously had money—cream leather couch and every conceivable kitchen gadget on her newly tiled countertops.

Elizabeth set two glasses on the bar. "What can I get for you?"

"Screwdriver, please."

She poured a Courvoisier for herself. "When I watched you across the room, I thought to myself, 'Who is that gorgeous new woman?'" Elizabeth downed her drink in one gulp.

"I don't get out on weekends much. In fact, this is the third time I've been out to the bars on a Saturday night in four years."

"Really? Well, then, I guess we'd better make this evening memorable." Her eyes glowed. She took my hand and led me through the living room into her bedroom. Her king-size waterbed sat in the middle of the room, opposite three large windows that faced the city skyline. Flokati rugs scattered on the floor underscored a large framed print of Georgia O'Keefe's Red Poppy. If this had been a man's apartment, you would have called it a "bachelor pad." In Elizabeth's hands, it was the perfect place to seduce a woman. I had no illusions I was her first, or for that matter, last conquest.

She pushed me against the wall, where she unbuttoned my jeans and slipped her hand down my pants.

I closed my eyes. Yes, this is where I want to be. Soon I was breathing heavy, the anticipation of a feast of the flesh reverberating through every nerve.

"Let me slip into something more comfortable." Her fingers lingered on my nipple for a second before she disappeared into the bathroom.

I pulled off my jeans, shirt, bra, and panties, then slipped between the sheets. Everything was perfect.

Elizabeth reappeared five minutes later, dressed in a Chinese red silk dressing gown with two more drinks in her hand. "Screwdriver, right?" She sat on the edge of the bed and sipped her drink.

I set my drink on her nightstand. There would be plenty of time to celebrate later. I pushed the dressing gown off her shoulders and admired the curve of her breasts.

She tipped back her glass and drained the remainder of her drink before she lay down next to me.

Soon my tongue tasted the hollow of her neck and traveled into the cleft between her breasts. As I ran my hand down her side, she let out a long sigh and closed her eyes. I wanted to linger between her breasts forever—luscious melons ripe for the taking. The sight, the smell, the velvet feel of her skin made me wet as hell and I ached for when Elizabeth would explore my skin with her hands and tongue. I reached down and lightly touched her thighs. No athlete thighs were these—no rigid, well defined muscle here. Elizabeth had the body of an office worker, soft forgiving woman flesh that conformed to my touch. I found that special place between her navel and the top of her pubic hair and I licked and kissed her until I was about to explode with desire.

She lay perfectly still, too still. I looked up and realized she had passed out, her head fallen to the side, snoring softly with her mouth wide open.

Damn! There was nothing to do except lay next to her and play with myself until I came with an annoyingly weak orgasm. I pulled the blanket over us, turned on my side away from Elizabeth, and fell into a drunken sleep.

The next morning, I felt Elizabeth's hand travel lightly down my side until she squeezed my ass.

"Good morning." She propped herself up on one elbow, leaned over, and kissed my shoulder and neck.

The feel of her mouth and hands made me weak. All of our pent-up desire from the night before returned full force and soon we were victims of each other's lust. Her bed quickly resembled a war zone—blankets on the floor, sheets tangled with legs and arms. We made love for two hours before another primal need got the better of us.

"I'm starved. Wanna go to a nice place for brunch? My treat." Elizabeth smoothed the sheets under her.

"Sure."

A shower and an hour later, we were seated at Cameron's, a trendy eatery not far from Elizabeth's house that catered to a largely gay clientele. Smiles and nods indicated the regulars, winks indicated new friends met the night before. Elizabeth got a lot of winks.

Along with the Crêpes St. Jacques, quiche, Brie, and fresh fruit, pitchers of mimosa lent the meal a civilized atmosphere.

"A toast," Elizabeth raised her champagne flute, "to one sexy woman."

"Thank you, and to you." I raised my glass to hers.

"When can I see you again?" Her eyes looked dreamy, possibly due to the mimosa.

I set my flute on the table and avoided her eyes. "That's a hard one. I travel out of town on business a lot."

She sighed and stared out the window. "Tell me about it. I'm a Big Sister for a fourteen-year-old girl named Tiffany, plus I check in on my Grandma every week. My schedule is impossible at times."

I expected Elizabeth to be like my other flings, women who dropped everything at a moment's notice to be with me. Evidently, Elizabeth had her own life, and I wouldn't be at the center of it.

"How about dinner this Thursday?"

She pulled out a well-worn appointment book and flipped through the pages. "No. I have a meeting with a potential client. Saturday night?"

"Definitely not. I'll be in Stockton."

"Week from Tuesday?" She shook her head. "No, I can't. It's Grandma's birthday." She made a note in her book.

"How old is she?"

"Ninety-two and still spittin' fire."

"Just like her granddaughter."

Elizabeth blushed.

"This is the pits. Here I am trying to get laid and you're not cooperating." I put my hand on the table, an open invitation to her.

"Do you have any plans for the rest of today?" She reached over and laid her hand over mine. "I thought," she looked at me with the same sultry glance from the night before, "you could come back to my place so we could ..."

"... get to know each other better? My pleasure."

She refilled our champagne flutes. "As the Bible says, 'Eat, drink, and be merry.'"

"Amen, Mary."

Between Elizabeth's and my schedule, we managed to catch one movie and meet for lunch five times during the first month. Three of those lunches turned into quickies, the sexual equivalent of grabbing a burger and fries on the way to somewhere else. It fed neither the body nor the soul, but I convinced myself it was better than nothing.

But to her credit, she did make good on her offer to help me make investment decisions and after five years at Allied I needed more than a savings account. I'm no financial genius, so I appreciated her advice. Like Sunshine, she suggested I squirrel away ten percent of my income into investments for the future, like for buying a house someday, and retirement. Retirement? I'd be 65 in 2017. Certifiably old. I smiled to myself to think of a time when I wouldn't have guessed I'd make it to age 25, much less 65. How many mornings had I woken up wondering how I'd driven home without killing myself or someone else after drinking the night away?

Too many to count.

"Okay, so who are you boinking now?" a familiar voice said when I picked up the phone.

"Hi, Michael. Please don't call it 'boinking.' I hate that term."

"Oh right, I forgot. With all those girl hormones, lesbians make love. It's just men who boink."

"God! You're incorrigible."

"So who are you, ahem, making love to now?"

"Her name's Elizabeth Corbin."

"Elizabeth? Not Beth or Liz? Kind of an upscale name for a dyke, doncha think?"

"Elizabeth's an upscale kind of dyke."

"Really? You mean she only works on Mercedes and Jaguars?"

"No, she's a stockbroker. Correction. She's my stockbroker."

"Wow, that's great, Bunny. I'd hate to think you're blowing all your hard-earned money on wine, women, and song."

"I'd love to blow more of my hard-earned money on wine and women, but I'm never in town on the weekends to do it."

"Bummer. What a dilemma, love or money. So how's work?"

I hesitated. "It ... it's okay," I said finally.

"What's the matter?" Michael's tone turned from good-natured kidding to genuine concern.

"I'm getting old. I'm almost thirty-three." How can I possibly be thirty-three? Only old people are thirty-three. What am I doing selling auto parts? Didn't I graduate from high school about a year ago?

"And I'm thirty-seven, you teenager. So what's the problem? You've got a job that pays you well, you're not living on the street, and you're getting laid." He paused. "Let me guess. Your life didn't turn out the way you thought it would? Welcome to adulthood."

"I'm lonely." Fortunately, work kept me busy, so I didn't have much time to obsess over Sunshine. Elizabeth was nice, charming even. And if I had to move on with my life, Elizabeth was a better bet than most. But Michael was right, my life hadn't turned out the way I thought it would. On top of that, I missed him hugely these five years I'd been gone from LA.

"Actually, that's what I'm calling about. How about if I come up for a visit in a week and we can do The City?"

"Oh, Michael, I'd love it!" Although Michael wasn't exactly a stranger to San Francisco, I knew of some places that he probably hadn't been since his last visit. This was the best news I'd had in months.

"And I can meet Eeeelizzzzzabeth."

"Yeah," I laughed harshly, "if she's available."

"What do you mean, 'if she's available?'"

"Never mind. Just get your ass up here. I need to see a friendly face."

♦♦♦

124

Michael arrived about 6:30. "God, I hate that drive! Bad enough I had to work half a day. It seems like half of LA commutes to The City. I shoulda been here by 5:30 at the latest." He threw his overnight bag on my couch and headed for my fridge. "All you've got is cottage cheese, beer, coffee, and milk? No wonder you never put on any weight." Michael opened the carton of milk and drained it in three long gulps. "I hate to rush you, but can we go? I'm starved."

"It's good to see you too, bro." I gave him a hug before I grabbed my jacket and my keys to the company car.

"That's okay, I'll drive." Michael took my keys and hung them back on the key rack.

As I climbed into his Accord, I filled him in on our plans for the night. "I thought we'd try a new place that's just opened—the Church Street Diner. It's close to here." I was more than a little curious about the place. According to a flyer I'd gotten the week before, their menu boasted "Steak and Fish are Our Specialities." As many of my meals came from restaurants, I'd wanted to try it as soon as the flyer came. If it was any good at all, I'd make the Church Street Diner part of my restaurant rotation.

When we pulled up in front of Elizabeth's house, Michael's mouth dropped open. "It's a Painted Lady!" he said, grinning from ear to ear.

"A what?"

"A Painted Lady. That's what they call these kinds of Victorian homes. I like Elizabeth already."

Elizabeth stood smiling down at us from her front window. "Welcome, Michael," she said when she opened the door. "Would you like to come in and see my house?"

"Absolutely!" He bounded up the front steps. "And here I thought only gay men had homes like this."

"Would you like a drink?" She poured a large Courvoisier for herself.

"No thanks. Not on an empty stomach." Michael said.

"A screwdriver, please." I wandered around behind them, drink in hand, while Elizabeth narrated the tour. Who knew that when many of these homes were originally built they had no indoor plumbing? I didn't. Twenty minutes later, Michael and Elizabeth were still discussing some of the more arcane details of Victorian architecture. "Anyone for dinner?" I prompted. All of this Martha Stewart attention to detail was fascinating, no doubt, but how long could you stand being around Martha Stewart?

Fifteen minutes later, we were seated in the newest Castro district restaurant. Already it was hugely popular, as evidenced by the number of mostly gay men who occupied the nearby tables. The waiter, a slight young man who was as big around as my wrist, approached out table. "Welcome to the Church Street Diner. Can I start you off with something to drink? We've got some vodka specials tonight." He indicated a multi-page drink menu sitting on our table.

Elizabeth picked up the menu and ran her finger down the long list of drinks. "God, look at all of these! What do you want to start with, Michael," she asked, "a Slow Comfortable Screw Against the Wall, Sex on the Beach, A Screaming Orgasm, or a Cum Shot?"

"Wha ...?" Michael grabbed the menu from her and continued to read. "Here's one for you and Bunny—2 Lesbians."

"That's a drink? " I asked.

"Yep. Cranberry juice, coconut rum, vodka, and a cherry," Michael read aloud.

"Gimme back the menu," Elizabeth grabbed the drink menu from his hands. "Let's be adventurous tonight." She paused. " I'll have the Slow Comfortable Screw Against the Wall, and Michael will have the Purple Penis," she said to our waiter.

"What the hell is that?" he asked, looking very concerned.

Elizabeth waved her hand dismissively. "Don't worry, you can handle it." She continued, "and Bunny will have a Dirty Girl Scout."

"Very good." The waiter went for our drinks.

I took the drink menu from Elizabeth. "Next round, Michael will have the Big Dick Kenny and Elizabeth can try the Bald Pussy. I'll have the Beaver In A Blender."

"Oh Christ!" Michael groaned. "I do want to live to see another day, you know."

We dissolved into laughter.

Minutes later, our waiter set our drinks on the table and handed us the dinner menus. "Tonight we've got a strip steak and tenderloin to die for. Or we have chicken if you like," he said with a straight face. "And for the ladies, we have a yummy grilled salmon with key lime butter or a nice grilled halibut with fennel, red onions, and oregano."

Michael sat back in his chair and looked the waiter up and down. "I'm always up for a good piece of meat. Give me your strip steak. Rare." He winked at our waiter.

"You have exquisite taste, sir," our waiter said, with the emphasis on the word "sir."

"I'll have the tenderloin." Tonight I could maximize my dining possibilities by trying both types of steak. I pushed for a three-fer. "Elizabeth, would you mind ordering the fish? That way I can try everyone's special."

"This has to do with you eating out every night, doesn't it?" she guessed. "Okay, I'll try the grilled halibut."

Our waiter smiled and headed back to the kitchen with our orders.

We raised our drinks in a toast. "To meat and fish!" Michael said.

"To exquisite taste!" Elizabeth added.

"To booze and sex!" I offered.

Michael perused the drink menu again. "Look Bunny, they named one after you—a Skip And Go Naked!"

"Damn! A couple more of these," I indicated my glass, "and I will skip and go naked. This thing is wicked." I could feel the buzz from the Crème de Menthe, Coffee Liqueur, Irish Crème, and vodka creeping up on me.

"Excuse me," Michael said as he stood up. "I need to go to the john." As he squeezed behind my chair, he leaned over and gave me a kiss on the top of my head.

Elizabeth stared after him. "What a nice guy he is. He sure loves you."

"Yeah." I smiled. "He kicks my butt when I need it and he's the one I go to when I want the unvarnished truth about anything. I don't know what I'd do without him."

"He's your best friend," Elizabeth said softly.

"Yeah, I guess he is." I felt my throat constrict. I wasn't ready to get all maudlin, so I finished off my drink. "Ready for another round?"

"That's what we're here for." She motioned to our waiter. "I'll try a Screaming Orgasm. What do you want, Bunny?"

"I'm always up for 2 Lesbians," I said.

"Do you want to order for Michael?"

"Yeah. Let's see if he can wrap his lips around a Big Dick Kenny," I said.

Pleasantly buzzed, we amused ourselves with the other suggestively named drinks on the menu: the Dirty Sherly, the Adios Mother Fucker, the Fuzzy Screw, the Ho-tini, the White Trash Martini, and the Purple Hooter.

"Ladies." Our waiter set our drinks on the table.

Elizabeth took a sip of her Screaming Orgasm. "Nice! And the caffeine in the Coffee Liqueur will keep me awake. How's that for a multi-purpose drink?"

I laughed. "Only you would think coffee liqueur could be a stimulant." Call me a party pooper, but I knew that the coffee in the coffee liqueur was just a ruse to get people to drink it.

She ignored my remark. "How about a Dirty Diaper?"

"Ewwww. No thanks. Christ! Who thought these up?" I wondered aloud.

Elizabeth chuckled to herself. "Drunk people like us."

"You'd have to be drunk to try some of these." I looked up and saw Michael weaving his way through the other tables. "There you are. I thought you got lost."

"Or got lucky," Elizabeth added, an alcoholic smile plastered on her face.

Michael rolled his eyes. "If I'd wanted to get lucky, I woulda stayed in LA. I have the company of the two loveliest women in The City and that's enough for me." He shook his head, then stared at the drink in front of him. "What's this?" he asked, eyeing the Big Dick Kenny.

"Your date for the night." Elizabeth said proudly.

"Oh, God," he muttered. "I think I'll pass on anything more to drink tonight." He wiped his forehead with the back of his hand.

"Oh, c'mon, Michael. You can't give up now. They've even named a drink after you. It's called the Fruity Bone!" Elizabeth laughed hysterically at her own joke.

Our waiter arrived with our entrées. Michael attacked his meal with such gusto it made me wonder when the last time was he'd eaten. My steak was a bit overdone, but I scarfed it down anyway. Elizabeth raved about her halibut. When I tasted it, I had to agree—it was delicious. I made a mental note to give this place another try.

"Who's ready for dessert?" our waiter asked when we'd finished our meals.

Michael shook his head. "I'm good."

"Hell, I'm not ready to give up yet," Elizabeth announced. "I'll have another Screaming Orgasm."

Not to be outdone I said, "I'll have another Dirty Girl Scout." Finally I'd found an all-purpose drink—both utilitarian (Coffee Liqueur, Irish Cream, and vodka) and dessert (Crème de Menthe). It hit all the right notes.

Michael lifted his water glass in a toast when our drinks came. "To Painted Ladies."

"To best friends," Elizabeth chimed in.

"To Martha Stewart," I volunteered.

"To Martha Stewart? Why Martha Stewart?" Michael looked confused.

"Never mind," I mumbled. Maybe I just thought I'd mentioned Martha Stewart earlier in the evening.

Our outing was a howling success. And after our well-lubricated dinner, we headed to Moby Dick's.

"Look, 2-for-1 margaritas." Elizabeth pointed to the overhead reader board when we entered. "You want anything, Michael?"

"Diet Coke."

She marched up to the bar and ordered our drinks. I noticed that Michael was getting the once-over from a number of men. One guy in particular, a scrawny blond with shoulder length hair, seemed to have his eyes glued to Michael. "Someone's got a big fan." I indicated in the direction of the aging hippie.

"Probably cruises all the new meat," he said offhandedly.

Elizabeth arrived with out drinks.

"Let's finish these and find somewhere we can dance," Michael suggested. "That guy is creeping me out."

I felt it too. The guy was creepy. I whispered to Elizabeth what was going on and we slammed down our drinks. Even as we left, the hippie's eyes never left Michael. The cool spring breeze made us walk faster, dodging the other patrons on the sidewalk. We didn't know where we were going and we didn't care. Some time later, we found ourselves in a noisy disco bar, the name of which I couldn't remember to save my life.

"This is more like it!" He grabbed Elizabeth's hand and pulled her out onto the dance floor. Miraculously, I found an unoccupied table near the front, which I guarded with my life. I wanted a place where I could sit and watch the other patrons while I enjoyed my buzz. After a few more tunes Michael led Elizabeth back to the table. "C'mon Bunny, let's shake it." He pulled me up from my chair and I staggered after him to the dance floor. Michael gave a signature performance, shaking his booty across the dance floor while I jerked erratically to the music. Either I needed another drink to keep going or I needed to collapse into bed. After another few minutes, I headed for the bar.

"Want anything?" I shouted to Michael as I pushed my way through the other dancers.

"No." A big bear of a guy danced into the space I'd just vacated and said something in Michael's ear.

I returned to our table with another margarita for each of us. "This is the most fun I've had in years," Elizabeth exclaimed, her eyes, half shut. "We gotta get Michael up here and do it again."

I nodded. The only thing missing tonight was Sunshine, but somehow I couldn't imagine her drinking like this. When it came to drinking, Elizabeth beat Sunshine hands down. I pushed that thought out of my mind.

Michael sat down next to me.

"I'm tellin' ya, you coulda scored tonight." I looked over the dance floor for the bear, but didn't spot him.

"Nah. He just wanted to sell me some coke." Michael looked bored. "I'm ready to go when you are."

"Yeah." At this point, it really didn't matter where I was— at a bar, at home, or on Venus. I had slipped into that blissed-out place where the world was one endless party and I was floating on its currents.

Michael led us to the car and poured Elizabeth into the front seat. I collapsed into the back seat and didn't come to until we got back to my apartment.

Michael was drinking coffee and reading the Sunday paper when I crawled out of bed around noon.

"Good morning, " he said brightly. "I got some bagels and cream cheese at the store. Want some?"

"Uhhhhhhhhh," was all I could manage to say.

We stayed in the rest of the afternoon and watched episodes of "Cheers" I'd taped.

"Boy, that Elizabeth can knock 'em back," Michael said as he packed his overnight bag that afternoon.

"She was just having a good time. Hell, I had as much to drink as she did."

"I know." Michael was about to say something, then stopped. "Bunny," he said gently, "I think you should lay off the booze for a while. It's not good for you."

"Don't go getting all superior to me, Mister I-Can-Score-Whenever-I-Want-To."

"I'm careful who I fuck, so I'm not worried. But booze will kill you if you drink enough."

"Thank you, Mother," I said sarcastically.

Michael held up his hands and backed away. "Okay, okay. I'm just showing a little brotherly concern, that's all."

"Apology accepted and your concern is duly noted. If I

ever think I have a drinking problem, believe me, you'll be the first to know." I changed the subject. "I'm worried about you driving back to LA so late."

Michael shrugged. "Better to start after dark. That way, I miss most of the traffic. I'd rather drive at night five hours straight through than sit in traffic for seven hours and sweat to death."

"Oh, all right. But promise you'll call me when you get home, okay?"

Michael kissed me on the cheek. "Sure, sweetheart."

The following month, Elizabeth failed to pick me up for a birthday party for a mutual friend. At 8:30 she knocked on my door, an apprehensive look on her face. "I'm really sorry. Forgive me?" she pleaded.

"No one's ever stood me up before. How could you?" I turned and stomped back to my kitchen, where I busied myself putting away dishes from the dish drainer. The nerve of this woman!

"I'm sorry. Our Big Sister picnic lasted three hours longer than we planned. I was head of the cleanup committee, so I couldn't very well leave."

"Sometimes I think you plan your life so you don't have to have any kind of relationship." I refused to look at her.

"What are you saying?"

"I'm saying that you surround yourself with so many things to do, you don't have time for me."

She took my hands in hers. "You know that I care for you."

I turned away. You're worth more than this. Tell her either she prioritizes you or you're outta here.

Elizabeth led me to the sofa and sat on my lap. "Let's plan a weekend for ourselves. We'll fly to LA, get a hotel, and take in a concert." She ran her fingers through my hair and down my neck to where the blood pulsed just below the surface.

Don't let her think she can buy you off this easily. "I don't know ..."

"Oh, c'mon," she coaxed. "When's the next weekend you'll be free? I'll make it worth your while." She nibbled my neck.

I unceremoniously dumped her off my lap and made a great show of getting out my Day Planner.

She smiled sweetly from the floor.

Christ! I was stunned to realize I'd worked every weekend since the middle of January. Not that I minded it much. All of those long, out-of-town weekends had translated into money in the bank for me. I hadn't met anyone worth staying in town for until Elizabeth had shown up. I could take some time off work to play with her. And Elizabeth was a stockbroker. My money plus Elizabeth's knowledge equaled a sense of security I hadn't had until now. Even Sunshine hadn't managed to give me that.

"I have the weekend of May 16 off."

"I'll make the reservations right now." She dashed into the kitchen, poured two vodka and grapefruit juices, then picked up the phone. "I'd like two reservations for May 16, round trip from San Francisco to LA, returning on Sunday, May 18." She handed me the drink.

I could see that whenever Elizabeth was "on," she could move mountains. It was finding the "on" switch that made my life difficult.

"Do you have some kind of package deal that includes a hotel room?" She nodded as she scribbled something on a notepad. "Yeah. Can you put it on my credit card?" Elizabeth motioned for me to get her purse. At heart,

Elizabeth was a fiscal conservative who knew exactly where every penny of her money went.

"You don't have to do this, you know." I came up behind her and nuzzled her ear, confident that as long as reservations were made, she'd be hard-pressed to flake on me.

"Done." She smiled triumphantly as she hung up the receiver. "Do you have any plans for the rest of the evening?"

"Not really." Let's see what happens.

"I do." She took my hand and led me to the bedroom, where she pulled my shirt over my head. "God, I love these," she said to my boobs. She unfastened my bra and laid me on the bed, then went into the living room and put "Flashdance" on the tape player. When she came back into the bedroom, she peeled off her clothes in a spontaneous strip tease to "What A Feeling." I could feel my clit throb.

"Uh-uh," she said as I reached for her. "You don't get to touch yet."

If her clients could only see her now.

Elizabeth was no stranger to sexual manipulation. She shook her booty just out of my reach, then ran back into the kitchen and whipped up two more vodka and grapefruit juices. She knew exactly what turned a woman on, including generous amounts of alcohol.

I could feel her heat as she danced in front of me. I sucked down the drink, then pulled her on top of me. We made love long and hard, then slow and tender as the months of sexual tension evaporated. After midnight, we collapsed from exhaustion and slept in each other's arms until my alarm rang at 7:30 a.m.

"How are you this morning?" I wrapped myself around her, spoon-style.

"Not good." Elizabeth sat up groggily and rubbed the sleep out of her eyes. She looked at the clock. "Damn! I've gotta go!" She leapt from my bed and scrambled into her clothes.

"What's the matter?"

"I've got an 8:30 meeting with a client. I'll call you later, okay?" She checked herself in the mirror and ran her fingers through her hair.

"Sure."

"God, I wish I brought something to change into. This'll have to do."

Indeed, her Big Sister sweatshirt and Levi's weren't the traditional uniform of the Financial District, but I had no doubt that Elizabeth would think up a good excuse by the time she arrived at work.

I spent my day on the phone and did paperwork, a trick I learned after one-too-many parties. Although I was on the road a lot, I could arrange my schedule any way that suited me when I was at home. Today it suited me to lay low. By four that afternoon, I felt good enough to go out. Elizabeth still hadn't called, so I called her at work.

"Hey, gorgeous, how about dinner tonight?"

Her voice sounded strained. "I'm sorry. I've got a lot of work to catch up on. Can we make it Thursday night?"

"Yeah. Sure." She's blowing you off. If she really cared for you, she'd have dinner with you tonight.

Her voice brightened. "Thanks, Bunny, I'll call you Wednesday."

"Yeah. Okay." I hung up the phone, not at all satisfied. If she didn't want to go out, then screw her. I'd party by myself. I wouldn't be driving, so there was no chance of anyone getting hurt. I headed for my liquor cabinet. I had a lot of drinking buddies—Jim Beam, Johnnie Walker, and his cousin Hiram Walker, and my Scottish friends the Glens: Glenlivet and Glenfiddich. And for flights of fancy I could always trust the old Grey Goose. Today the sting of Elizabeth's rejection made me head for my Absolut favorite, vodka. I unscrewed the cap and drank straight from the bottle. Without anything in my stomach, the buzz came on quickly. It helped push away the thought that one day, no matter how many promises she made, she'd stand me up again. What will you do then, Bunny?

Elizabeth made a last-minute upgrade to First Class—a "peace offering" she called it—to make amends for blowing dinner off that Monday night. On our way through the airport, we picked up an LA Times to check out who would be playing in town. We settled into our seats and watched the Coach Class file onto the plane while we drank our complimentary drinks. Our plane taxied down the runaway at 6:05 p.m. In a little over an hour, we would set down at Burbank Airport.

"Jeez, it looks like all of the big concerts will be Memorial Day Weekend. I'm sorry." She folded the paper on her lap.

"No problem. How about we play it by ear this weekend?" I laid the paper over our laps and then slipped my hand into hers.

"What do you propose we do?" Her eyes sparkled.

"Party. Hit the bars after we catch up on our sleep. How does that sound?" I suppressed a smile.

"Sleep?" She looked concerned.

"Yeah. Sleep." I rested both of our hands near her crotch and kneaded the inside of her thigh.

Elizabeth brightened. "Oh yeah, sleep." She poured a Seagram's miniature into my glass, then downed her drink and motioned to the Flight Attendant for another.

When we arrived in Burbank, neither of us was fit to

drive. We took a cab to the Hyatt in West Hollywood, the center of gay LA.

"Nice place." I threw my suitcase on the bed, popped it open, and changed into shorts, sandals, and a tight, black tank top.

"Wanna drink? I brought your favorites." Elizabeth produced a fifth of scotch and vodka and two rock glasses from her suitcase. "I'll get the ice." She dashed out the door.

I picked up the phone, got an outside line, and dialed Michael. "Hey! Guess who's in town?" I wanted to say when he answered, but there was no answer.

Within a minute, Elizabeth was back with a bucket of ice. "To a great weekend." She lifted her drink that was more liquid than rock.

"Hear, hear." I tossed back the scotch and held out my glass for a refill.

Elizabeth sat on the bed next to me. "So where are we going tonight?"

I pulled out my Damron's Guide and flipped through the pages until I came to Los Angeles. "Not much here I recognize—everything's changed since I moved. Why don't we go somewhere not too far away? That way, we're not on the road so much."

"You don't think we're going to drive this weekend?" Elizabeth looked shocked.

"No, but I don't want to spend all of our money on cabs, either." I leaned over and kissed her.

"Thank you, darling, but this weekend is your special treat. We're not worrying about money. What's the purpose of saving and investing if you never spent it on the things you love? If we have too much to drink, it's okay. We'll take a cab anywhere we want to go." She leaned in to kiss me and lost her balance. "I haven't had nearly enough to drink yet. Pour me another, please?"

I knew this would be one of those unforgettable weekends where we partied until we dropped. After dinner in the restaurant downstairs, we hopped a cab to a lesbian bar a few minutes away.

"You're not going in there are you?" The cabbie looked incredulous. "That's a dyke bar!"

"Yeah, and we're dykes." Elizabeth spun me around and planted a big, sloppy kiss on my lips for show.

"Jesus fuckin' Christ," he mumbled.

"Have a nice day!" Elizabeth waved to the cabbie as he drove off. She slipped her arm through mine to steady herself as we entered the bar.

I steered her through the crowds to the bar, where we ordered a couple beers. We found a table near the dance floor, where we could watch the girls. Soon Elizabeth was pressed up against me, lethargy already creeping into her body.

"Let's dance," I said. Sleep was not what I had in mind at the moment, so I pulled her onto the dance floor. When we returned to our table four songs later, two young women were perched on our stools.

"Sorry, did we take your seats?" the blond asked.

"Yeah." I reached for our beers.

"It's okay," Elizabeth said. "Let's find another bar." She finished her beer, then pulled me out the door.

"Taxi!" Elizabeth flagged down a passing cab. "Take us to the most popular gay bar you know."

The cabbie grunted and flipped on the meter. Fifteen minutes later, we found ourselves outside a western bar of mostly men. After I ordered our drinks, I scanned the room and hoped by some miracle I'd spot Michael.

"Who are you looking for?" she asked.

"Michael. I thought he might be here." There was no sign of him.

"Can we find someplace else? This isn't what I had in mind." She smiled at me, then laid her head against my breasts.

"Sure." We downed our drinks and made our way back out to the sidewalk. It was getting late and I was running out of places to take her. "Let's try some place closer to our hotel." We flagged down another cab.

"West Hollywood, please," I instructed the cabbie as we climbed into the back seat.

"Sunset or Santa Monica Boulevard?" His accent sounded middle-Eastern. "I know a place, very nice—lots of rich men."

"Not interested. Just drop us somewhere on Santa Monica."

The driver turned to us. "These men, they pay for you." The taxi lurched from the curb.

This cabbie obviously didn't have a clue. "Here," I said when we stopped at a stoplight somewhere along Santa Monica Boulevard. I threw a twenty-dollar bill at the man and hoped he would get the hint.

"Beeches!" the cabbie yelled at us as he drove off.

"Have a nice day!" I waved to him as he pulled away.

Elizabeth sagged against me as we stumbled down Santa Monica Boulevard. "Let's see what's happening here." The words were fuzzy in her mouth. Elizabeth pushed through the door of a noisy bar and dragged me after her. "Bartender, two beers!" We joined a table of four women who invited us to sit with them.

Despite the festive mood, I felt a deep ache inside—not an alcohol kind of ache, another kind. I missed LA, the

messiness, the absurdity of it all. The City might be cosmopolitan, but LA was alive in a way San Francisco could not
match. And I still missed Sunshine. Get real, LaRue. Did
you ever stop to think that maybe you didn't have what it
takes to keep her interested in you? That maybe you were
some kind of fling for her, not the other way around? Yeah,
you cared about her then. Now the only thing you care
about is your next drink because it's a sure thing.

"Another round, bartender." One of the women at our
table was celebrating her fortieth birthday. She wore a T-shirt
that read "Over The Hill" in ominous black lettering.

"Happy Birthday." We toasted the birthday girl and our
new friends in the warmth of alcohol-induced bliss.

"Last call." The bartender was overrun by drunks clamoring
to get their last drink.

I wasn't steady as I pulled an even shakier Elizabeth up
from the table. We kissed the birthday girl and made promises
to keep in touch—promises we wouldn't remember in the
morning.

We had an unspoken agreement that tonight we'd party,
tomorrow we'd play. I was barely able to get Elizabeth
undressed before she fell into bed and passed out. I passed
out ten seconds later. We woke at eight and made love slowly
until our bodies shut down from overuse, then snoozed
until noon. I didn't know about Elizabeth, but this much
drinking cost me dearly. Part of me knew that I couldn't
keep partying like this forever. I hated to think of how many
brain cells I'd killed over the years.

"Wanna go to the pier?" With no certain plan in mind, I
figured we could walk the beach and maybe have lunch at a
nearby restaurant I knew from years before.

"Sure." She turned to me. "Let's take it easy this afternoon. I'm feeling a little tired from last night."

Santa Monica Pier drew hundreds of people—tourists from out of town, skate boarders and punks, plus the usual contingent of gays and lesbians. Cruising was awesome. We descended to the beach after the crowds became too much and watched the waves roll onto the shore. Soon we took off our sandals and played in the ocean. The cool water quickly knocked the remaining grogginess out of us.

"Let me take you to a great place I know for lunch." If I didn't eat something soon, I knew I'd be out of commission for the rest of the afternoon.

"I was wondering when you were going to get hungry. Let's go." Elizabeth found our sandals and we walked along the sidewalk until we found the restaurant.

"They have the best seafood here." My mouth watered in anticipation.

Elizabeth scanned the menu. "Oh God, it all looks heavenly. I'll have the mussels in wine sauce and a bottle of Reisling," she said to the waiter.

"I'll have the snapper in a cream sauce." I wondered if it would taste as good as the last time I was here.

"Excellent choice, ladies," our gay waiter said. He brought us warm French bread to go with our wine. "Can I get you anything else?"

"No thanks." We turned our chairs so we could watch the ocean and the people who lay on the beach or walked along the water's edge. At dusk, the crowd would change—the tourists would leave and the lovers would arrive. I wanted to sit here until sunset and then watch the stars come out. I missed the beach. It was in my blood.

"It's not The City, but it'll do." Elizabeth teased.

"Spoken like a girl from Pocatello," I teased back. Although Elizabeth was a great drinking buddy and good in bed, I wanted to roll back time to when Sunshine and I walked this beach—a time when my life was simpler and my love wasn't colored by rejection and loss. I finished off my wine. "Let's order another bottle." I'd be damned if I was going to let some repressed memories ruin this weekend.

"Will that be all?" our waiter asked as he served our entrées.

I had a sudden thought. "Where's a good dance bar for women?"

He looked stricken. "I don't know. Let me ask one of our cooks. She'll know." He winked at us, then sashayed into the kitchen.

"One thing about being gay, there's always 'family' around you can ask for advice." Elizabeth chuckled.

He came back in a minute. "She says there's a new bar out in Pasadena. They're having their grand opening this weekend."

"Thanks, sweetie." Elizabeth gave him a pinch on his ass, then turned to me. "Wanna go later?"

"Yeah." We finished our meals and the bottle of wine, then caught a cab back to our hotel.

We arrived at the bar at 10:30 and found a long line of women that stretched from the door to the end of the block. Twenty minutes later, we finally made it through the door.

"Let's get a drink," I shouted to Elizabeth above the music. We pushed to the bar, where it took another five minutes to get the bartender's attention.

"There's no place to sit," Elizabeth shouted to me.

I nodded. The place was packed beyond capacity, the dance floor so crowded that if you lost your footing, you wouldn't hit the floor for fifteen minutes.

"This is perfect!" Elizabeth squeezed my hand.

I found a pillar to lean against and pulled Elizabeth into me so we could watch the goings on. I buried my head in her hair and smelled her sweet scent. It wasn't nearly enough. I wanted to run my hands all over her, undress her, tease her with my kisses until she turned around and let me have her. Instead, I squeezed her ass.

"You're bad," she said as she ground her hips into my hand.

"I'm not the only one." I gave her a quick pinch.

The music changed to a slower tempo and we pushed our way toward the dance floor. By the time we got there, the music changed back to the high-energy disco. The DJ knew how to keep the place hopping—INXS, Psychedelic Furs, Whitney Houston, Boy George and Culture Club, Tears For Fears, Prince, and every woman's current object of lust, Madonna.

On the verge of collapse several hours and many drinks later, we caught a cab back to our hotel.

"Thank you. Tonight was lovely." Elizabeth stretched out next to me, her soft skin pressed against mine.

I still wanted her. Despite the drinking and the dancing and the fact that I was ready to pass out, I still wanted to bring her to orgasm before she fell asleep. I petted the insides of her thighs, so soft and forgiving, then entered her pussy.

She took one sharp breath, tensed, then sighed.

I snuggled next to her, content.

Chapter 10

Life in the Fast Lane

A lesbian joke—Question: How many dykes does it take to make a relationship? Answer: About 50, give or take 20. The two women in the relationship, the 8 ex's who have turned into best friends (4 for each partner), their 2 therapists (one for each partner), plus assorted coworkers, friends, and relatives when the going gets tough. That's about 50.

I felt all alone. Where the other 49 people had gone, I didn't have a clue. And I wasn't laughing.

Elizabeth's answering machine picked up. "Hi, this is Elizabeth. I'm not in, but if you leave a message, I'll get right back to you. Have a nice day!" Her voice smiled.

"Hi, baby. Where are you?" My voice sounded choked. "I'm at Amelia's. You said you'd be here by noon." Reluctantly, I hung up. She better not stand me up! I sat at a table near the bar.

"The usual, Bunny?" Joann asked.

"Yeah." I put my feet on a chair and lit a cigarette.

Fredericka came over and dropped into the chair next to me. "Waiting for Elizabeth?"

I nodded.

"Wanna play some pool 'til she gets here?"

"Thanks, Fred, but my game's been off lately."

"Sure, another time." She squeezed my hand and walked back to the pool table.

I didn't want to tell Fred that it wasn't only my pool game that was off, but I felt like shit in general. What's the matter with me? I gulped half my White Russian down in one swallow. It seemed like I was drowning in slow motion, pulled down by an enormous undertow. Without thinking, I slammed the rest of my drink down and lit another cigarette. The damnable part was I couldn't blame this on Sunshine anymore. For years, I'd harbored fantasies that Sunshine would drive up to The City and beg me to come back. That fantasy lasted longer than our relationship and now even the fantasy had turned bittersweet.

"Joann, another one please." Everywhere I looked, smiling women happily drank, danced, played pool, or fell all over each other in love. I used to be one of those women. Shit!

"Hi, Bunny." Leanne slid into the chair next to me, all femmed to kill. "Buy me a drink?"

Leanne, forever the Come On Queen—all mind games and no action. I'm not that desperate! "Sorry. I'm waiting for Elizabeth."

She sighed dramatically. "Good luck. You'll be waiting the rest of your life." She leaned in closer. "You need someone who will appreciate you, someone who will take care of you, be your wife."

"Like you?"

"Of course like me, silly."

I'm drowning and every dumb fuck date I ever had is passing before my eyes. "Leanne, I'm not in the mood."

"Bunny, one day you're gonna regret not taking me up on my offer." She stood and walked away, her head held high.

I doubt it. I downed the second White Russian double-quick. Two dead soldiers. All of my life, women had been walking away from me. First my mother, next Rapunzel and Sunshine, then numbers four through I-shuddered-to-think-how-many. And Elizabeth hadn't even bothered to show up. My watch read 12:53 p.m. Was it something I said?

Every morning, I looked in the mirror for signs of aging: crows feet, little worry lines across my forehead, sagging skin. It was a race against time I was bound to lose. I laughed.

"What's so funny?" Joann asked.

"Getting old."

"Old? You're not old." Joann shook her head as if I was crazy.

I held up my empty glass and indicated for another. No, but I sure feel old! That happy woman in the mirror, the one I thought I knew so well, had turned frightened and hard-edged. I didn't like her much.

Joann set the drink down and looked closely at me. "You okay?"

"Yeah." I smiled and lit another cigarette. Never let them see you cry. My watch read 1:11. Elizabeth still hadn't arrived.

I walked to the payphone with my drink. Her answering machine picked up again. "Hey baby, where are you?" I hated it when Elizabeth stood me up. Of course, she'd have a plausible excuse for not being on time: she had to visit her brother in the hospital and the time got away from her; she and her mom had to shop for groceries for her grandmother; she and Tiffany picked up trash for a highway cleanup project. Elizabeth always did good for everyone except us. When we were together, she was too exhausted to make love or passed out all together. And today was the first Saturday in almost three months I wasn't working. Obviously you're not that important to her.

I looked down at my empty glass. Three dead soldiers. The sun was shining and I lived in San Francisco, the Gay Capital of the Universe. Bit by bit, my life was falling apart. My vicious side kicked in. *You're the best-looking woman here and still you've managed to fuck up your life. You ain't worth shit!*

Someone throw me a lifeline, please! "Gimme another drink, Joann." I slammed the money on the bar.

"Jeez, Bunny, take it easy!" Joann looked alarmed.

I strolled over to where Fredericka sat with her pool-playing friends and sat down next to her.

"... not if she's gonna be playing tonight. I think that woman Trish is gonna be playing against them."

"So how's Paula, Fred?" I feigned interest in their conversation. Maybe Fred would cheer me up.

"She's fine, Bunny." Fred turned to another woman at the table. "Trish has a wicked shot. I've seen her make a double combination off a bank shot."

I tried again. "You two want to go out with Elizabeth and me to dinner soon? There's a great Chinese place in Sausalito we like."

"Yeah, sure. We'll do it soon." Fred stood and chalked her cue.

You see? You're invisible! Nobody likes you! Fred doesn't like you and Elizabeth doesn't care enough to tell you to fuck off! Bunny, you're nobody! I gulped down my drink.

Shut up! My heart pounded in my ears. Maybe another White Russian would drown out that voice. My watch read 1:27 as I walked back to the bar. "Gimme another one, Joann! No. Make it a Blind Russian."

Joann looked up at me from beneath her dark bangs. "Don't do this, Bunny." Concern was written all over her face as she handed me the drink.

148

I was in no mood to listen to anyone. My heart ached and I wanted release from the pain. Alcohol was my comforter, my friend, and too often lately, my lover. Enough booze would take me to the place where it didn't hurt anymore. I was tired of the hurt and tired of the pain. You don't deserve love, Bunny. You're not good enough.

"Fuck!" I sat down with my back to the room and tried to light a cigarette, but my hands shook so badly I couldn't find the end of it. Tears streamed down my face. This is a hell of a way to live! You're better off dead!

Shut up!

See Bunny. See Bunny run. Run, Bunny, run!

They were back, all the demons, taking potshots at me from every side, and this time it wasn't Mr. Stiff who orchestrated their attack. These demons all had the same name: Bunny LaRue. I looked down at my empty glass. Five dead soldiers. Or is it six? Fuck, I can't even count anymore! I was dying. I wanted to go to a place where my demons were banished forever, where someone would love me.

I need to call Michael. RIGHT NOW. I dug into my jeans pocket, drew out a handful of change, and fed the payphone. Quickly I punched in his number. The phone rang and rang and rang. Shit! Just when I expected his answering machine to pick up, an unfamiliar voice answered.

"Hello?"

"Hi, is Michael there?" I could hear loud music in the background.

"Michael is gone for the weekend," replied a cold voice.

"Gone? Gone where?" I could feel the sweat pouring off me.

"I am not his secretary, nor do I inquire about his week-end activities."

"Who are you?" I usually found all of Michael friends to

be cordial, even the ones I hadn't met in person, but this guy was a jerk.

"Who are you?" he replied. "Michael doesn't waste his time with women, in case you didn't know."

Okay, he was an asshole. "Look, can you leave him a message to call Bunny?"

He let out a long sigh. "I suppose."

"And tell him it's very important, okay?"

"Anything else?" His irritation was unmistakable.

"Have a nice day." I hoped he caught my tone.

"Huh!" Asshole hung up the phone.

I felt slightly better and wondered how soon Michael would call.

I need another drink.

But first I had to pee. The tables and chairs steadied me as I stumbled to the restroom. I stood in line behind two women and hoped by some miracle that they would let me go first. A mirror on the wall revealed the essence of my life: wasted, empty. I looked away.

Two women emerged from one stall. They touched each other and kissed, only slightly embarrassed by their impromptu tryst. The first woman in line ran into the vacant stall.

Soon three women stood in line behind me. Long minutes passed. Obviously frustrated, the woman at the front of the line turned to me. "They'd better hurry up. I can't wait any longer."

I didn't respond. It was all I could do to stand upright.

Two doors opened and the woman ahead of me dashed towards the nearest vacancy. I swayed to the end stall, locked the latch, unbuttoned my jeans, and sat down. Mission complete, I laid my head against the wall for a moment's respite.

"HEY, YOU IN THERE! ARE YOU OKAY?" Someone pounded on the stall door.

I awoke with a jerk.

"I'm coming in!" she shouted.

Omigod, I passed out! I watched in humiliation as a red-haired woman stuck her head under the stall door and looked up at me sitting on the john.

"I'm fine. Really." I could feel my face turn crimson.

"Sorry. It's just that you've been in here for over ten minutes. I thought something was wrong," she said as she pulled herself back to the other side of the door. I waited until I was alone before I made myself presentable. A long line of women glared at me as I stumbled out of the restroom. Why don't you die of embarrassment right now and get it over with?

My last piece of gray matter, the smidgen that wasn't 100% pickled, screamed: Get out now! I weaved my way through the crowd, past the bar and pushed through the doorway, only to crash into two women who were coming in.

"Sorry," I mumbled.

"Are you okay?" one of them asked.

I heard the other woman say, "She's drunk."

The ground didn't hold steady as I stumbled down the street. People stared and gave me a wide berth on the sidewalk. I hugged the wall and headed toward home, the one place I knew I'd be okay. Around the corner from my apartment I knew of a brick church with cement stairs going down. Every burned out alcoholic and addict in The City knew the place. It was the ultimate jumpin' joint—last stop before Hell.

Twenty minutes later, I found the place and descended the stairs to the smiles and knowing looks of the smokers gathered outside. I sat down heavily in a folding chair near the back while the room spun around my head. People talked, but I couldn't follow their conversations.

A big, bad, butch woman in tight jeans and a 49ers jacket smiled as she lit my cigarette. "Go ahead, introduce yourself," she urged.

My universe constricted to a single point of light; everything else was darkness. I heard myself say, "Hi, my name is Bunny, and I'm an alcoholic."

"Where the hell have you been?" I paced the floor, sucking furiously on my cig. My nerves were stretched to the breaking point.

"Where have I been? Jesus, Bunny, calm down. I just talked to you a week ago."

"Why didn't you return my call? And who's the rude little fruitcake you had staying at your apartment?" God, I want a drink so bad!

"Shit! You mean Donny? That little fruitcake used to be my housekeeper until he had a party and trashed my apartment. You know that antique bentwood rocker I had? They demolished the cane seat and the back. Don't ask me how," Michael said through gritted teeth.

"Jeez, I'm sorry. I bet I called right in the middle of their party." In my me-centered state it was all I could do to slow down and listen to Michael's woes. I knew quitting drinking would be tough, but damn it! Did it have to be this tough?

"Actually, I called to give you good news." I paused. "I quit drinking four days ago."

There was silence on the line. Finally Michael said, "Are you shittin' me? Bunny, that's fabulous! And no," he sounded pissed again, "that rude little fruitcake didn't tell me you called. Normally I'd say, 'I'll come up and we can go out and celebrate,' but I guess that's out of the question."

"Come up anyway. We can celebrate without drinking. At least, that's what my AA group says. I miss you, bro." I wiped away the tears that suddenly appeared from nowhere.

Twenty-two sober days later, I sat in a lesbian AA meeting and wondered which was worse: being drunk or recovering from being drunk. The meeting dragged. It felt like the bottom of the fourth inning with no end in sight. By now, I had a few sober friends who struggled with the same issues I did: Why don't all my problems go away now that I'm sober? Who am I if I don't have alcohol? Would someone please tell me that being sober is something more than hanging on by my fingernails? Still, there were women whose problems made mine look pale by comparison. I thanked whoever was up in the sky that I had only my shit to deal with.

A woman named Sharon moderated this meeting. "Is there anyone here who had an overwhelming urge to drink today?"

Top of the fifth, Darcy spoke. "Hi, my name is Darcy and I'm an alcoholic-addict."

The group chimed, "Hi, Darcy."

Darcy pulled on her hair. "Well, my ex-girlfriend, Tina, called me yesterday and said she's still in love with me even though she has a new girlfriend and she's not sure if she loves her new girlfriend as much as she loves me and could we get together for sex some afternoon when her new girlfriend is at work and yes, she's still using but she's determined to turn her life around, but for now selling is the only way she's making any money and God knows, I've been trying to stay clean, but there's something really sexy about

Tina that makes me want her so badly and she's the one I always got my coke from and I knew that she'd have some coke if I went over to her apartment." Darcy twisted her hair into a tangled mass. "Somehow, I managed to tell Tina no."

The crowd applauded.

Thanks for sharing, Darcy.

"Thanks for sharing, Darcy." Sharon scanned the room for her next volunteer, then looked in my direction. "How about you, Bunny?"

I had dreaded this moment since I started coming to meetings. "Hi, my name's Bunny, and I'm an alcoholic."

"Hi, Bunny," the group intoned.

"Well ... I have a lot of friends who drink. I hung out at the bars whenever I could, looking for some fun, maybe a little ..."

A few women around the room nodded in agreement.

"I always found it easier to make friends when I drank. I guess you'd call it social drinking."

There were snickers around the room.

"I think the episode that pushed me to the edge was when the woman I was seeing and I planned a special weekend. You know, get away from The City, drive to the Russian River, stay at a bed and breakfast." Common courtesy dictated I not mention Elizabeth by name.

"An hour out of The City, her car stopped dead. We had it towed to Sebastopol and ended up spending the night in the only motel that had any vacancies, the El Matador. It was one of those places with cigarette burns on the carpet, silverfish in the tub, and a cracked sink in the bathroom."

"I know that place," a woman named Angela said, her face turned deep red.

"At first, it was funny. We bought some wine and a bottle of scotch and drank it while we watched reruns of 'Charlie's Angels' and 'The Love Boat'. During the commercials, we kinda fumbled on the bed, trying to make love, but we were both so drunk that it was awful. Finally she passed out. They weren't able to fix her car until Monday, so all we did was drink. No bed and breakfast, no walks through the woods, just stupid TV and drinking. Not social drinking. Desperation drinking. Drinking to keep reality somewhere out there."

I hesitated for a moment. I wasn't sure I was ready to let go of all my secrets. Slowly, I went on. "I had to take care of myself. I'm not the world's best person, but I knew I couldn't keep going like this—drinking to keep someone else company. I lived from one party to the next. My grasp on the rest of my life was eroding away so slowly I was barely aware of it. I didn't stop drinking then, that came later, but the sense that I was drinking myself to death took hold in the back of my mind. Unfortunately, it took another couple of months before I was ready to quit." I looked down at my hands because I couldn't face the women in the room. "I quit when I realized it was either live without booze or die. Even today, I had to stop myself from buying a bottle on my way here. Sometimes I'm afraid this shit will never end." Tears sprung from my eyes and I felt like a complete idiot. You're a pathetic loser, LaRue.

One woman reached over and hugged me.

"Thanks for sharing, Bunny. Everyone here is behind you." Sharon fixed me with a look that conveyed all the love and support she could muster.

Through my tears, I saw everyone smiling at me, nodding in agreement.

Sharon continued. "Is there anyone else who has something they want to share?"

My moment was over. I hadn't died of humiliation. And for some strange reason, I felt lighter.

After the meeting, everyone milled about the room, jostling for access to the old-timers.

Sharon turned to me. "Are you looking for a sponsor, Bunny? Because if you are, I know the perfect one."

"What do I need a sponsor for?" I hated to admit my ignorance.

"Someone to talk to when you're feeling the urge to drink, or when you're feeling overwhelmed in general. C'mon, let's go to Ko's for some Chinese. You can meet Ella."

My watch read 8:45 p.m. "Good thing I don't have a hot date tonight."

"C'mon." Sharon dragged me by the sleeve out the door, up the stairs, and down the sidewalk.

"We're not going to walk the whole way, are we?"

"It's only seven blocks. You're such a wimp, LaRue!"

I lit a cigarette.

Sharon raised an eyebrow. "Whatever you do, don't light up in front of Ella. She hates cigarettes!"

Fine. Sober and she doesn't smoke. "She must be quite the saint."

Sharon chuckled. "You don't get it, but you soon will."

"Huh?"

Sharon turned to me. "I'm doing you a favor, Ms. LaRue. Ella has sponsored a lot of women, but she's pretty much given it up. She has certain criteria for any women she sponsors. We're going to Ko's to see if she'll take you on."

"So what's her criteria?" Good looks? Hot body? Jeez, I wonder if I'll pass.

"Let's see. Too dumb to find her way outta a paper bag, the ability to chew gum and drive at the same time." Sharon laughed. "You'll have to ask her."

I could see where this was leading. "Ella" and I would be introduced, whereupon she would be first in line to jump my bones. Of course, the AA regulars would turn a blind eye to what was going on because she would be my sponsor. At times, even AA sucked.

Cutting across Market Street, Sharon advised, "Remember, no smoking."

I flicked my cigarette into the gutter.

When AA people get together to socialize, it's always at the type of place we avoided when we drank—family-style restaurants with good lighting and endless pots of coffee. This place was no different—lots of light, little décor, and instead of coffee, the alkies drank tea while they scarfed down pot stickers: camaraderie mixed with fortune cookies for the shit outta luck.

A few regulars I recognized from the meetings sat at a long table in the nonsmoking section. In the center of the group sat a dark skinned middle-aged woman whose looks wouldn't have merited a five on a scale of one to ten. I headed toward the end of the table, where I wouldn't be so conspicuous. Sharon grabbed my sleeve and pulled me to the middle of the table. "Ella, I want you to meet Bunny. She's the one I told you about."

"Nice to meet you, Ella." I offered my hand.

She looked up, took me in with one glance, and shook my hand. "Nice to meet you too, Bunny." Ella turned and resumed her conversation with a woman two chairs away.

I sat in a chair across from Ella, next to Sharon, and half-heartedly joined the conversation. It ranged from asshole bosses, a perennial favorite no matter what group anyone socialized with, to returning to school for the undergraduate and graduate students. Already I wanted a cigarette, but I wasn't about to blow my chances with Ella if she could help me stay sober. I drummed my fingers on the table until a waitress came by.

"Tea?" she asked.

I indicated my cup, thankful I finally had something to occupy my hands. While I sipped my tea, I studied the women at the table. One thing I noticed about alcoholism, it did not respect age, race, or socio-economic status—it knocked us all flat. Although I may never have met these women in a bar when I was drinking, their stories seemed strangely familiar.

"You seem quiet tonight." Ella spoke softly.

"I'm just tryin' to put it all together."

"How does it feel to be sober?"

"Well ..." I stopped. "It's like being on dry ground after being on a ship in the middle of a storm. I guess I haven't got my landlegs back yet."

She laughed. "What else?"

I ran my finger around the lip of my cup. "I'd like to say that it's great and I feel fine, but the fact of the matter is, I've been sober for three weeks and I feel like shit." I spoke so only Ella could hear. I didn't want everyone around me to know my life wasn't taking off like the rocket I thought it would.

"The first couple days I was on Cloud Nine. But that kinda ..."

"... disappeared?" Ella smiled kindly.

"Yeah! How'd you know?"

"It happens." She reached into her pocket and handed me a card. "Here's my number. If you need to talk, call me." Ella stood and hugged everyone at the table. The mood in the room changed as everyone said good-bye. In some invisible way, this group centered on her.

"Isn't she great?" Sharon enthused.

"Yeah, I guess."

"So is she going to be your sponsor?" There was a sly, half-grin on Sharon's face.

"I don't think so. She didn't mention it." I reached in my pocket for a cigarette lighter.

"Yeah, but what did she say?"

Sharon wanted a particular answer, but damned if I knew what it was. "She hardly said anything. She asked me how it felt to be sober, then she gave me her card. No big deal."

One of the women whose name I didn't know turned to me. "She gave you her card? Well!"

What's that supposed to mean?

Sharon laughed. "I thought you and she would hit it off. Ella must like you, or she wouldn't have given you her card."

"Nothing happened, we just talked." I felt like I was in a foreign country and couldn't understand the language. What was going on here?

I was dying for a cigarette, but grabbed a fortune cookie before I dashed out the door to light up. The fortune read: "Confucius say: Be careful what you ask for—you might get it." The only thing I wanted was to win Sunshine back. I had a feeling that fortune would read: "Confucius say: Snowball's chance in Hell." So if I couldn't have Sunshine what would I want? That was easy. At this point, a little peace of mind sounded like heaven.

Chapter 11

Tainted Love

Bewitching Hour began at five. We arrived via car, via cab, via shuttle bus, young and old alcoholics full of psychic twitches and cravings that still plagued us.

A greasy looking biker mumbled, "Just because I quit drinking don't mean I have to quit smoking."

"Amen, brother." A well-dressed woman in her late forties lit up in agreement.

Across the nation, AA was experiencing a split between the smokers and the non-smokers. But this was Las Vegas, where the smokers still outnumbered the non-smokers ten to one. For the moment, I was safe.

We filed into the building, cautious glances to the side, looking for familiar faces, faces we were glad to see, faces we didn't want to see in a million years. The moderator launched into his opening spiel, "This is a meeting of Alcoholics Anonymous ..."

I sat on a folding chair near the back of the room. About twenty other women and men sat scattered throughout the room. Some looked anxious, some bored. Years ago, thanks to countless sales meeting, I'd mastered the art of looking spellbound, a professional skill that saved my butt more times than I cared to admit. I could maintain a facade of interest while I examined my momentary crises or crushes. Today I felt edgy. I needed this meeting to keep me from walking into the nearest bar and slugging down an entire bottle of Stoli, hold the ice. Since I became sober, I dreaded trade shows, particularly the ones in Las Vegas and Reno. There were too many after-hours affairs where deals were struck under the influence of copious amounts of alcohol. Earlier today, I bowed out of yet another invitation to booze, schmooze, and sleep over.

"... can read Chapter Five ..." The speaker droned on.

Someone from behind tapped me on the shoulder. "Never in all of my born days did I expect to see you, doll."

I knew that Texas drawl. There, dressed to command the attention of every man within forty feet, sat the Rodeo Queen. "What are you doing here?"

Her eyes twinkled as she leaned provocatively towards me. "Tryin' to stay sober." Barbara gave me a dazzling smile. "How bout y'all?"

One of the women who sat close by, frowned.

"What are ya doin' after the meetin'?" she whispered.

"Going back to my hotel room. What do you have in mind?"

"Shhhhhhhhhh!" The woman gave us a dirty look.

"Let's get together afterward, okay?" Barbara sat back in her chair.

"Yeah, sure." I turned around and tried to pick up where the speaker left off. It was difficult because Barbara ran her foot across the small of my back. I could hardly breathe, let alone listen to the speaker. Good thing she's married, or I'd swear she's coming on to me. By the time the meeting was over, I wanted to tackle her and rip off her hot pink tube top and white short shorts. It wasn't only my sobriety I was hanging onto by a thread. I wanted to keep this light. "Come here often?" I asked as we walked outside.

"This is it, the last one." She winked at me.

"What do you mean?"

"No more conventions for me. I'm goin' home."

"I'm not following you." Surely she didn't mean what she was saying. Together we climbed into a cab.

She turned to me and laughed. "Too bad you ain't followin' me! I could use a friendly face there."

"Where is 'there'? You mean The City, don't you?"

"Nope. No more San Francisco for me. I'm quittin'. Goin' back to Amarilluh!"

A certain glee in her statement made me realize she wasn't pulling my leg.

Five minutes later, our cab pulled into the entrance of Bally's and deposited us at the front door.

"C'mon, Bunny. Let's go upstairs and I'll change. Then we can go out and eat." Barbara pulled me into the elevator.

Well ... it sounded good. My stomach had been telling me for some time that breakfast and lunch were long overdue. I looked at Barbara out of the corner of my eye. This elevator ride was different from our last one together—today we were both sober and in control. Although outwardly it appeared that we were strangers, there was a sexual tension between us that neither of us wanted to broach.

"It'll just take me a minute." Barbara disappeared into the bathroom.

"You're quitting and moving to Amarillo? What's in Amarillo, anyway?"

"Cattle, mostly. Trucks and horses. And family," she added.

"Is Dwight quitting his job, too?"

"THAT GODDAMN FUCKER CAN ROT IN HELL FOR ALL I CARE!"

"What? What happened?"

162

"Got one of his roadside chippies PG. Then came and told me he wanted a divorce!"

If Dwight had been in the room at the time, I think Barbara would have cut off his balls. Divorces, whether straight or gay, were messy affairs. I didn't want to get into this any farther, so I changed the subject. "Do you have any kind of work lined up?" It seemed incredible. How could she leave the glamour of The City to move to Amarillo, where every morning at 6 a.m. you woke to the Farm Report?

"Yep. Gonna be drivin' the school bus 'til something better turns up."

"Oh." School bus? Jesus! My stomach growled. Dinner with Barbara might turn out to be—what? Painful? The forerunner to another kind of empty feeling? She'd made all the right moves at our AA meeting and there we were again, teetering on the edge of temptation. Did I really want that? Sometimes the day-to-day struggle of living sober was hard enough without battling that seductive monster Lust.

On the other hand, maybe I imagined it all. Maybe months without sex led me to imagine every situation as sexual. Maybe this was Barbara's way of being friendly. Maybe ...

Barbara emerged from the bathroom dressed in a red satin charmeuse. She leaned against the door and smiled.

A wave of heat washed over me and settled between my legs. No need for an engraved invitation here. I walked over, locked her fingers in mine, pushed her against the bathroom door, and kissed her deeply. Not surprisingly, Barbara responded in kind. I pushed her onto the bed and climbed on top of her. This wouldn't be the first time I'd have dessert before the main course.

The minute I touched her breasts, I knew her to be the kind of woman who had a direct connection between her

163

breasts and her clit—the autobahn of sexual feelings with the throttle wide open. We moved in and out of each other in perfect step to a dance as old as the universe. I undressed her slowly, tasting and touching every secret place. Those spots that seemed most sensitive, I lingered over.

For a first-timer, Barbara seemed eager to explore. I'd gone without for so long that my body was on fire every place she touched.

"Oh, Bunny, I never woulda guessed." Barbara lifted her head from between my breasts. Her hand rested on the inside of my thigh.

"Don't stop!" This was no time for chitchat. The last thing I wanted was another conversation about sex. I'd had enough of those to last a lifetime.

Barbara's lip curled into a smile as she pressed her fingers deep inside me. We rocked together in a love embrace until the night sky was a blaze of neon. The clock read 2:20 a.m. when we emerged from her hotel room. We wandered down the strip until we spotted a restaurant with a $4.95 steak and eggs breakfast.

I don't know if I was lightheaded from lack of food or too much sex, but breakfast had a surreal quality to it.

"Damn! I'm hungry!" Barbara tore into the food like she hadn't eaten in days. She played footsie with me under the table and grinned like the Cheshire cat whenever she looked at me.

I picked at my breakfast and wondered how she bridged the gap from married Texas gal to fast-track Las Vegas lesbian lover.

"If you ain't hungry, I'll eat it." Barbara leaned over, stabbed half of my steak, and transferred it to her plate.

Thinking took more energy than I had at the moment, so I sat back and watched her devour my steak. Sex, food, divorce, black coffee, conventions, sex, drinking, sex, cattle, sex, sex, sex, sex. What was I doing here and where was my bra?

When we walked back to her hotel, I was acutely aware we would never see each other again. Part of me believed I was dreaming and when I woke up, this would be a figment of my libido.

The flashing lights and cacophony of sound filled my head as we walked into Bally's. Barbara grabbed my hand and pulled me into the gift shop, where a sleepy salesclerk flipped through a copy of People magazine.

"Can you get us in there?" Barbara motioned to the tonier Le Grand Jewel. The sign on the door read: Open 10 a.m. to 10 p.m.

The salesclerk shrugged. "Sure." She locked the gift shop and waved to one of the night managers. He unlocked the door and stood unobtrusively near the entrance while the salesclerk turned on the lights.

Barbara made a beeline to the most expensive jewelry case. "Those." She pointed to a pair of 2 carat, princess cut, diamond earrings set in 18-karat gold.

The salesclerk opened the case and handed Barbara the earrings.

"We'll take them." Barbara reached into her purse and laid her credit card on the counter.

"Shall I wrap them for you?" the salesclerk asked without blinking.

"No. Thanks." Barbara turned and presented them to me with a flourish. "For you."

I was dumbfounded. "I can't take these."

"Sure you can." She smiled brightly. "If that lowdown skunk of a husband can have a girlfriend, so can I."

"But they cost a fortune!"

"It's Dwight's credit card. He made me carry it for emergencies. Well, this is an emergency if I ever saw one." There was a look of devilish triumph on her face.

"Thank you," I mumbled, still in disbelief. "I feel like I ought to get you something."

"Nah," she said. Her voice softened. "I got what I wanted. Thanks for everything, doll."

"But I didn't give you anything."

"Yeah, ya did. Somethin' I'll never forget."

"What?"

"My freedom." She pushed me against the counter and laid a long, passionate kiss on my lips.

The night manager, long accustomed to wacky tourists, picked lint off his shirt. The salesclerk disappeared behind the counter.

"Because of you, I realized that I don't need a man in my life. Oh, I'll probably want one again, but in the meantime, my life is my own." There were tears in her eyes when she turned to go. "Call me if you ever get to Amarilluh, okay?" Barbara walked out of the shop and through the rows of slot machines until I couldn't see her anymore.

My heart felt like lead when I walked back to my room. This must be a dream. When I awoke the next morning, the earrings were on my nightstand and my bra was nowhere to be found.

Three weeks later, my life crashed when Allied's new Sales Manager tried to make my employment conditional upon sleeping with him. In my desperation, I contacted the Vice President, only to find out that the new Sales Manager was his brother-in-law. Omigod. I panicked and found myself in the liquor section of a grocery store with a bottle of Wild Turkey in my hand. Jesus, Bunny, what are you doing? My survival instinct kicked in and in less than a minute, I was outside on a payphone to Ella.

"Is this Ella?"

"Yeah."

"This is Bunny LaRue. I met you at Ko's."

"I remember you."

"Ummm, I was wondering if you had some time we could ..."

"You sound upset, Bunny. What's wrong?"

"My life is falling apart and I want a drink so bad!"

"Where are you?"

"At a grocery store, why?"

"In the liquor section?"

"Yeah. God, Ella, I feel like I'm going to explode."

"Would you like to come over?"

"Yeah!" That wasn't why I called, but it sounded good at the moment.

"Here's my address ..."

I took down her address and drove to a working-class neighborhood south of town. After I drove around for several minutes, I pulled up in front of the only house on the block not sliding into disrepair. A four-foot chain link fence surrounded a postage stamp-sized front yard. The grass was mowed and clumps of heather, euonymus japonica, and heavenly bamboo lined the foundation of the house. Two round planters of petunias and alyssum graced either side of the front stairs. Ella's house was the noticeable bright spot in a row of otherwise dreary tract homes.

As I knocked on the front door, I heard the loud snarling of a dog inside.

Ella opened the door a crack. "Hi. Let me get Cerberus into the bedroom. He's very affectionate once he gets to know you."

I could hear Cerberus being dragged against his will across the room. Ella reappeared in a minute. "Come in."

Her house was furnished modestly. On the couch lay a pile of work shirts and jeans that needed to be folded. Ella moved them into a wicker basket. "Have a seat."

I sat on the couch and noticed a "No Smoking" sign on the wall.

"Would you like a soda?"

"Yeah. Thanks." All of a sudden, my throat was dry.

Ella sat opposite me in her recliner. "Tell me what's going on," she said kindly.

"Well, uh ..." God, I wanted a cigarette! I held the glass to keep my hands from shaking. "My new boss has been pressuring me to sleep with him. So I reported him to the Vice President and then I find out it's his brother-in-law."

Ella shook her head. "So what did the Vice President do? Act as though you're making a big deal out of nothing?"

"So far, he hasn't done anything. But really," I added, "that's not the only reason I called. I called because ... when does the desire to drink end? Sometimes I feel so lost because I don't know what to do anymore."

"Let me guess, you feel like shit. And drinking used to take off the edge and now all you're feeling is the edge, multiplied by about a hundred times. And life seemed easier when you drank?"

"Yeah. Everything seemed easier when I drank." I could feel my heart pounding.

"Everything?" She smiled. "Even the hangovers?"

"No, not the hangovers. They seemed worse." I'm feeling the edge right now.

She gave me a small smile. "I know. Did you think people wouldn't like you as much if you didn't drink?"

"I don't know." Christ, I'm feeling the edge and I need a cigarette! My hands shook noticeably now.

"If you need to smoke, go outside and do it." She waved me toward the kitchen, where I spotted the backdoor.

"Thanks." Before I pulled a cigarette from the pack, I closed the door. I didn't want her to know how addicted to these things I was. Sharon was right. Ella was not the gung-ho rah-rah kind of sponsor I'd expected. She was more of a hand-holder, we-can-do-this-together type of sponsor. I liked that.

After I lit up, I glanced around. Along the south wall of the house grew tomatoes, onions, and carrots. What looked to be the former garage had sunk a foot behind the rest of the house. An amateur application of tarpaper and flashing connected it to the main house. Two bright eyes peeked from under the steps for a second, then scurried back into the darkness. My heart fluttered. It's a cat. I took one last drag before I stubbed out the cigarette in her trashcan and went inside.

"Feeling better?"

"Yeah, thanks."

"Those things'll kill ya."

"I know." Edge, edge, edge. One step at a time, Bunny. "How do I get there?"

She looked at me, puzzled. "Where is 'there'?"

"Happy. Content. Not thinking I'm going to collapse if I don't have a drink."

"It's not something you get like a VCR. It's something you grow into. I bet you didn't start out in life an alcoholic." Even her eyes were kind.

"No, but after listening to everyone's stories, I've been drinking like one from the beginning."

"Yeah." She smiled wryly. "So did I."

"So what was your drug of choice?"

Ella sat back in her chair and smiled. "José Cuervo." She sipped her soda. "Beer was fine, whiskey was better, but José ..." Her eyes sparkled. "I drank until the worm danced in my head, until it wasn't cactus juice anymore. Just pure energy that burned from the top of my head to the tips of my toes. José and I had an affair that landed me in the drunk tank many times. See this scar?" She pulled back her denim shirt to reveal a twelve-inch scar that cut from below her waist, across her middle, to just below her left breast.

My eyes grew wide. "What happened?"

"We were in a bar when my girlfriend decided she'd had enough of my drinking and got up to leave. Well, there was no damned way I was going to lose face in front of my friends, so I pulled a knife. When I lunged at her, she stepped aside and grabbed my wrist. I fell on my own knife and screamed, 'She tried to kill me! She tried to kill me!' They hauled my ass off to the hospital, and from there, to jail." She laughed. "Of course, I still didn't get it and was back drinkin' as soon as I got out."

She continued as she looked out the window. "All José did was bring me to my knees. At the end, I lived in my car, a '73 Chevy Suburban, and turned tricks to pay for my drinking. I hallucinated so badly that I was involuntarily committed to the County Hospital until I could dry out. I was so fucked up I couldn't remember my own name."

I didn't know what to say. "Tequila, huh?"

Her eyes blazed. "Dammit, Bunny, you're missing the point! Being sober is the beginning of your sobriety, not the end. Now you have the chance to create the life you want."

It was all there in her face—the pain, the struggle, the passion. I could see the out-of-control drunk inside of her, brain synapses firing at a staccato pace, screaming more!

170

more! more!, her life sucked away into a whirlpool of darkness from which there was no escape.

She pushed the hair out of her eyes. "But enough about me. What made you quit?"

"When I moved here, I decided to get to know a few women." I paused. "I wanted to feel wanted again."

She took a sip from her soda. "Running from someone?"

I hesitated for a moment. "I was running from Sunshine. She dumped me."

"Uh huh."

"She was everything to me. I wanted to spend the rest of my life with her." Why does this sound so insipid?

"Damn near killed you thinking about her, so you thought you'd ease the pain with another drink."

"Something like that." I hadn't planned on telling Ella, or anyone this. It went beyond hurt, it felt like failure, my own private, fucked-up failure. Sunshine, I loved you. I still love you! Soon I cried uncontrollably as the pain and humiliation of my failure reverberated throughout my being.

Ella got up from her chair and held me, like a mother comforting her child.

You've totally fucked up your chances with Ella now. She thinks you're a fucking, spoiled white girl who always got what she wanted.

"I had a lover like that, too. Said she couldn't see me when I was drinking my life away."

I wiped my hand across my face. "But you're sober now. Can't you call her?"

"She was killed in a car accident by a drunk driver. Isn't that ironic?" Ella fell back against the couch and buried her face in her hands as sobs wracked her body.

Now it was my turn to be the comforter. I took her in my arms and held her as she rocked back and forth on the couch.

After several minutes, she wiped the tears from her eyes. "I'm sorry. Sometimes it all comes back like an avalanche."

We were inside each other's soul, sharing the rawness and the pain. The boundaries between us were gone. Ella moved to the other end of the couch.

"Don't run away from the pain, it's all part of the recovery. It takes time, Bunny. Give yourself time. It's scary, but you can handle it." She wiped away her tears.

I recovered with a start. "Yeah, thanks."

She seemed more in control. "Call again if you want to talk."

As I drove home, I thought about my life. I wasn't the first woman whose boss had made an unwelcome pass at her. Women had been putting up with this shit since time immemorial. Nor was I the first woman who had been dumped by her lover. Pain—the universal human condition. The trick was to put my life together one day at a time, while I dealt with the pain.

Chapter 12

The Thrill Is Gone

It's probably a blessing that time tarries for no woman or man. I was no longer testing the waters of age with my big toe, but sinking to the deep end—Baby, you ain't gettin' any younger!

I remembered Marilyn, one of the older models used by Mr. Stiff. When I was sixteen, she was Mr. Franklin's latest ingénue. Seven years later, I was the hottest thing Franklin's had to offer; Marilyn, a tired-looking tart. Her only words, ever, to me were, "Just you wait!" The bright, smiling darling of Mr. Franklin had hardened into a bitch on heels, who turned on the charm only for the camera.

At work, I saw guys who used to stand in line to talk to me. Now they waited to talk to Chris, the new twenty-four year old sales rep, who could bullshit her way through anything. She had a photographic memory and in one night could read and memorize every torque spec, every piece of automotive trivia needed to sell the next line. Beneath her cuteness wasn't a girl grease monkey, but a brain that strategized every move. Her sales figures were climbing, and I knew she'd be breathing down my neck in a couple of months.

At thirty-five years old, I was the aging beauty queen of

a bygone era. Already my "look" was outdated. Younger models, thinner and more muscular, some who verged on athletic, smiled back at me from the pages of the catalog I once dominated. I was as passé as a mood ring—cute in its time, but ancient history now. But it wasn't just that; my anxiety was harder to pinpoint. I had done it all: gotten sober, made good money, and even managed to keep some of it without Sunshine's intervention. Something else was amiss that X number of lovers never put to right. My life wasn't what I wanted it to be. Maybe Ella will have some words of wisdom. I picked up the phone and called her.

"Sure. Why don't you come for dinner?"

An hour later, I pulled up to Ella's house. A black, short-haired cat, the one that peered out from under her house on my first visit, walked boldly across my path.

Ella indicated for me to come inside. "So, what's going on?"

"I'm not happy." I slouched onto the couch. Cerberus climbed up with me, laid his head in my lap, and gave a great, contented sigh.

Ella seemed unimpressed. "About what?"

"I don't know—my job, my life. I'm tired of traveling all the time. I think I need a new career."

"Like what?"

"Like, get a job in computers or something."

Ella shrugged. "I don't think jumping from one career to another will necessarily make you feel any better."

"Why not?"

Ella let out an exasperated sigh. "Because you're seeking novelty. You're seeking answers outside yourself."

"Isn't that what you did? Find a job that you liked? You found your answer outside yourself."

"That's not what I'm talking about," she snapped. "After

all my drinking and running away from my problems, look what line of work I ended up with: I'm a gardener, just like my mother before me. I like what I do. It gives me satisfaction to plant something and watch it grow." She wore a tired expression. "Don't look outside yourself to find solutions to problems that are inside of you. Find some line of work that gives you satisfaction. Use your brain instead of your body. I know you have one." She handed me the Sunday Chronicle. "Why don't you check the want ads and see what's out there. It's a start."

She's in a seriously pissy mood. I tried a different tack. "But sometimes a person needs a fresh start."

Ella laughed. "Oh, yeah. I forgot about Sunshine."

"What's Sunshine got to do with this?"

"You pulled a geographic."

"I did what?"

"You split. You moved. You left. You ran away so you didn't have to deal with your problems."

"I didn't!"

Ella smiled. "Oh, didn't you? Then why did you move here?"

"Because I wanted a change of scenery. I moved here to be closer to my dad. What's the matter, I'm not supposed to be happy about where I am?"

"Be an adult, Bunny. Make yourself happy with yourself. If a job is what it takes for you to get on with your life, then do it. Just don't bullshit yourself into believing that you left LA because you wanted to experience more of the world, when in reality you were running away from Sunshine."

"Are you saying that I have 'unresolved issues' over Sunshine? It's been eight years. Sunshine is history! I don't even think about her anymore." Liar.

175

She looked pointedly at me. "Everyone has unresolved issues. If they didn't, they'd be dead."

"Okay, Ms. Know-it-all. What's your solution to my situation?"

She laughed again. "My solution doesn't matter. Do what you want."

"Damn it, Ella, I'm asking for your advice!"

"Then this is my advice: follow your heart. Do what you have to do in order to get what you want."

Fighting with her was like shadow boxing—there was nothing to hit. Where did she come up with this stuff? "But what if I don't know what I want? What then?"

"Bunny, you know what you want. What I see is that you're afraid to go get it."

"How can I be afraid to find something when I don't even know what I'm looking for?"

She laughed. "Oh, Bunny. You are so you!"

"God, I hate that!"

"Hate what?"

"What you just said. 'You are so you!' What's that supposed to mean?"

"It's a compliment." She shook her head. "Did you ever wonder why I agreed to be your sponsor?"

"Yeah, why?"

"Because you have a good heart. I'll admit, at first I was leery of you. I'm sure your looks have gotten you places the rest of us had to work for in life. But the first time I met you, you didn't have to be the center of attention. You listened. You were trying hard to open yourself, not push away something new." She paused. "A long time ago, I learned not to waste my time on women who weren't serious about staying sober. You need to learn to make good choices for yourself, Bunny, just like I did. Ask yourself, 'What would make me happier than anything in the whole world?" That's your starting point."

I was dying for a cigarette, but I didn't want this conversation to end. "I've asked myself that question a thousand times."

"And?"

"The answer keeps changing."

"What did you expect? You're not the same person you were when you were with Sunshine. And in a couple of years, hell, a couple of weeks, you'll be different. Life is change. If you stop changing, you're dead even though you're still walking around."

This reminded me of the talks Michael and I had when we smoked pot. "I don't know what I want."

"Then look inside." She got up from her chair and walked into the kitchen.

"Arrgghh!" I got up from the couch and walked outside. My hands shook as I lit up. What did I want? I wanted Sunshine! I wanted to be something other than what I looked like! I wanted to prove to the world I had a brain too!

How did Ella do it? Of all the women I knew, she seemed the happiest. Sure, she was sober and didn't smoke. She was by no means rich. Her job as a gardener couldn't pay as much as I made. She had friends. No, more than that, she had friends who were devoted to her. All this without the benefit of a high school diploma or a flawless complexion. I walked into the kitchen and watched her make dinner. She winced when she cut herself as she chopped the tomatoes. She didn't have much in comparison to me, yet I would give everything I had for her serenity.

She looked up and smiled. "Dinner's ready." She indicated for me to sit at the table.

"It smells delicious." I was ravenous for something more substantial than the Pop Tarts I'd eaten six hours earlier.

"If I were still drinking, I'd offer you a glass of wine. This'll have to do." Ella walked into the living room, selected a CD, and hit play. A piano solo, more hauntingly beautiful than I'd ever heard, floated into the kitchen.

Dinner was magical. I couldn't help but gorge on this bounty of zucchini, onions, garlic, and tomatoes. Restaurant food had long since lost its appeal and cooking seemed as far removed from me as the man in the moon. In my opinion, women who cooked were one step away from God. As we ate, the music transported me to a place at once both tender and sad. I felt more open, more vulnerable than I had ever been. I looked at her, suddenly aware that this woman had everything I wanted. She was complete by herself. She didn't need anything or anyone, and I wanted a part of her. So what if she was almost 50? I reached across the table and took her hand in mine.

"No," she said softly. "We can't cross this line."

"But I love you."

She withdrew her hand. "I love you too, but there are reasons why we can't get involved. It fucks everything up."

I could feel my face turn deep red. "But I need you."

"Don't confuse love with sex, they're not the same." She looked down at the table.

It seemed like she struggled with the same feelings I had for her. I felt desperate. "Can't you for once give up your fuckin' principles and act like a woman?"

Her voice sounded choked. "It would destroy us both. I can't do this for you. I have to think of myself."

She's rejecting you. You had a good thing going with her and you blew it. Even sober, you're a fuck-up. "I'd better go." I got up from the table and walked into the living room to get my purse. My pride had been ground into a fine dust.

"Bunny, don't do this," she pleaded.

"I'll call you." Purse and cigarettes in hand, I crossed the living room to the front door. What is that music? I stole a quick glance at the coffee table where the CD case read: Ludwig Van Beethoven's "Moonlight Sonata." Without a backward glance, I shut the door behind me.

It was a month before I could think of Ella without feeling the humiliation of that night. She hates you. She never wants to see you again. In my heart, I knew that Ella did not hold grudges, yet I felt I needed some room, a longer passage of time, before I could face her again. I'll call her as soon as I can face her.

Interpersonal problems aside, Ella had some insightful things to say about my life. She managed to strip my problems down to the bare essentials: Don't like your job? Then find one that fits you. Girlfriend problems? Ella was right. I did move to The City to get away from Sunshine. Unresolved issues.

Over the next few months, I examined my life. My job with Allied was at a standstill. There was no room for advancement even after they fired the new Sales Manager for sexual harrassment. Regardless of the strides other women had made in cracking male-only occupations, the business of automobiles was still male-dominated. I had thirty years of automotive trade shows and sales calls to look forward to, thirty years of manifolds, gaskets, and air fresheners. No thank you. At one time, cars had been my passion. They promised, if not exactly sex, at least the illusion of unlimited power and pleasure, rolling venues where men and women played out their alter egos.

Being an adult sucked at times. The multitude of options

before me felt like a crushing weight. Find a new sales job or start a new career? Date a hundred new women? For that matter, if all options were on the table, did I want to remain in The City? If not, where would I want to live? Marysville? Women's land in rural Oregon? Belize?

Although I hadn't figured out what I wanted, I knew what I didn't want. Small towns and country living were definitely out. I remembered Barbara. She chucked every-thing, pulled up stakes, and started a new life. If she could do it, I could do it, too. I was a city girl through and through. I could picture myself living in only one other place after eight years in the most cosmopolitan city on the West Coast. The City of Angels beckoned. What LA lacked in refinement compared to The City, it more than made up for in sheer magnitude: more people, more jobs, more opportunities, more money. I wanted to go home.

I had another less rational motive for wanting to move out of The City. After years of reading stories in the Chronicle about gay men getting sick, it was quite apparent that San Francisco was in the middle of an AIDS epidemic. I quit reading the Medical Section when I didn't want to know any more.

When I read a small item in the Sunday fashion section, my decision to move back to LA crystallized:

> Richard Adams, head of Adams
> and Associates, died last night at
> San Francisco General Hospital
> of undiagnosed complications
> from pneumonia. Known as a
> maverick in the fashion world,
> Adams popularized a look that
> brought leather chic to the mass-

es. Dead at age 45, Adams is survived by his father William Adams, and mother, Francis Ruth Adams of Cedar Rapids, Iowa; his brother Lewis Adams, of Denver, Colorado, and sister Cecilia Adams Edgar, of Hayward, California.

I could read between the lines. I wanted to get away from this specter that haunted the San Francisco bathhouses. LA looked a lot safer than San Francisco, where this plague seemed to be centered. All I knew was that I wanted to get out fast, live somewhere this thing wouldn't follow me.

I picked up the phone and called Michael. "Hey, what would you think if I moved back to LA?"

"Well, it's about damned time," was his only reply.

Chapter 13

Don't Worry, Be Happy

The move from The City to LA lasted almost eleven hours. I planned to leave by 9 a.m., but by the time I got the last of my stuff in the U-Haul it was almost noon. The five-hour drive over that interminable ribbon of interstate lasted more than seven hours. I was supposed to be at Michael's no later than 5 p.m. He planned to make dinner for us and then we'd watch a couple movies to help me unwind from the drive. By the time I stopped for gas and waited while the CHP cleared a wreck outside of Gorman, I was two-and-a-half hours late. Tired and starved, I pulled up to Michael's house at 7:47 p.m.

"God, it's good to be here. I've missed you so much." I threw my arms around Michael's neck and hugged him.

"I've missed you too." Michael returned the hug, then escorted me into his kitchen. "Sit down. Everything is ready. It's a little overcooked, but it's better than nothing."

I smiled through the overdone teriyaki chicken breast, thankful that he hadn't steamed the asparagus until I arrived.

The phone rang halfway through our meal. Michael smiled as he spoke into the receiver. "Yeah, she got here. Finally. Nope, we're going to watch a couple movies, then hit the sack. Call you Monday?" Michael hung up the receiver and smiled at me.

"New lover?" I teased.

His eyes twinkled as he pulled a picture of his new boyfriend out of his wallet. "This is Brian."

A mustachioed young man in cut-offs and a black tank top sat astride a motorcycle, looking tan and lean.

"He's kinda young, isn't he? No offense, but I didn't think you went for chicken."

"Nah. I'm just showing him the ropes. I'm his first real male lover. And, he's my insurance," he added.

"Your insurance?"

"Yeah. I figured I should get a younger lover, someone who hasn't been fucking around for years like I have."

"So how old is he?"

"Twenty-two. He said he tried it with girls, but it wasn't right. You know, he visited the rest areas when he could, but he couldn't deny he was queer anymore, so he came to the bars as soon as he was old enough. He's young and innocent." Michael's casual demeanor vanished. "Better safe than sorry." He sat at the kitchen table, his hands clasped together so tightly his knuckles turned white. "I'm scared, Bunny. All of those AIDS risk factors? I'm at the top of the list."

Not you, too! "Are you HIV positive?" I blurted out.

His lip quivered in an attempt at a smile. "No, I'm not. At least, when I tested two months ago I wasn't." He moved uncomfortably. "I didn't believe in the AIDS thing at first. I figured it was something the government invented to shut down the bathhouses. But then my friends started getting sick." He held his breath for a minute and tensed all of his perfectly sculpted abs, pecs, and glutes as if by sheer force of will he could push away the pain. "Jesus, Bunny, I fucked most of them!" He put his head on the table and sobbed.

I handed him tissues and imagined him to be a Treblinka death camp resident, hoping the Allies would march in and put an end to the madness.

After a few minutes, Michael regained his composure. "Wanna move in with me?"

"Thanks, but at this point I'd rather live alone."

"Suit yourself. But remember, anytime you need a home, you're welcome to live here."

I smiled. "Thanks, bro."

"So, what did Ella think of you moving here?" Michael carried the plates to the dishwasher.

Inwardly I cringed. "I didn't tell her I was moving."

"You what?!"

"Hey, I'm planning on writing her a letter."

"Don't be an even bigger asshole, Bunny. Pick up the phone and call her right now." Michael stood with his hands on his hips and glared at me.

"Who are you—Miss Manners?" God! Michael could be such an obnoxious queen when he wanted to be. I didn't want to get into this now. Michael was right. Of course I should pick up the phone, call Ella, and apologize for walking out the door, then never calling or telling her I moved. As the weeks, then months, had passed, I'd felt an increasing sense of guilt that made me even more reluctant to pick up the phone. Yeah, I was a shithead. So what else was new? But I also knew that one day I would call or write her and tell her I was sorry for leaving her like that. But not today, and the way my schedule was booked, not tomorrow either.

The following day, I looked at eight apartments. Large complexes with swimming pools, exercise rooms, saunas, and play areas for kids didn't appeal to me, so I immediately wrote off five of them. I eliminated the ground floor apartment in a house owned by a retired couple because I didn't want anyone to monitor my comings and goings. A triplex located near the freeway didn't seem right, either. Finally, I found a group of twelve small garden apartments close to shopping and the freeways, tucked away in a cul-de-sac. I paid the deposit, first and last month's rent, bought a used refrigerator, four African violets, and a bucket of chicken. Ah, Home Sweet Home.

Finding a job wasn't as easy as finding an apartment. I read the classifieds for three weeks straight and mailed résumés to companies that never contacted me. As no offer of employment was forthcoming, I tried several employment agencies. When the headhunters looked at my résumé, I got offers of sales jobs left and right. It was tempting. I knew how to sell, but I wanted to try something new, and it didn't take a genius to see computers were the growth industry of the future.

I took a job with a big software corporation for one reason: they offered to pay for computer classes. To stay ahead of the game, the company needed people who could write code. Until now, most people's computer knowledge extended from PacMan to Pong. I soon found that learning a new language, whether it be French or dBase, was time-consuming and frustrating. On more than one occasion I longed for the old LA days, when I could arrive at In-N-Out Burgers, make it through a shift, then bake in the sun until I headed for the bars at night.

I worked ten hours a day, took classes three nights a week, and went to AA meetings the other four nights. I was determined to become an above average programmer, good enough to get put on interesting assignments but not geeky enough to write code in my head on coffee breaks. As I didn't have enough time or energy to go out and spend what

I made, I stuck my hard-earned money in my investment portfolio. For a year, my social life was non-existent.

Spring arrived with a monster heat wave that strained Southern California Edison's ability to deliver electricity to the power grid. My Beemer's air conditioner hadn't cooled the interior much lower than the 104° outside. I made a mental note to have the freon recharged. Tired, bored, and overheated, I desperately wanted to go home, cool off, and veg, but first I had to pick up a few things at the grocery store. Being in an air-conditioned building must have been on everyone's mind, I decided, as I surveyed the full lot. I found a spot on the far side and pulled in. I waited fifteen minutes in the checkout line, then lugged four plastic bags of frozen food through the maze of cars, got in my car, and headed home.

The stifling heat hit me in the face the minute I entered my apartment. I nudged the switch on the air conditioner and anticipated a cool breeze in a matter of minutes. There was no response, not even a click.

"Damn it!" I read the indoor thermometer: 98°.

If there had been enough room in my freezer, I would have climbed in with my groceries. Instead, I poured myself a glass of iced tea and pressed a carton of mocha chocolate chip ice cream against my forehead and arms to cool off.

The phone rang. I pulled away from the couch, not feeling the least bit sociable.

"Bunny?"

"Hey, Michael, what's new?" I asked unenthusiastically.

"Bunny ..." His voice faltered. "I need to talk."

By the tone of his voice, I knew something was horribly wrong. "Michael, what is it? What's the matter?" The hairs on the back of my neck stood up.

"I'm HIV positive," he said softly.

Oh my God! This can't be happening! "No, that can't be! Maybe your results are wrong. Maybe your test read a false positive."

"The test isn't wrong." His voice sounded choked.

"You want me to come over?"

"Oh, Bunny, would you, please? I'm so scared."

"I'll be right there." I grabbed my keys and jumped back into my car. HIV positive? I felt like I was swimming in slow motion under water. Emotionally I swayed to the right and to the left and soon I was swirling round and round, not knowing which way was up. My whole world was crumbling around me, smashing what sense of wholeness I'd achieved these years I remained sober. I drove toward his house on autopilot. As I rounded the corner toward the freeway onramp, a neon sign in a convenience store window caught my eye. "Budweiser—King of Beers." Hell, I didn't even like Budweiser. Sweat trickled down my sides, but I knew it didn't have much to do with the heat. I managed to get past the convenience store when up ahead loomed the Albertson's. Shaking, I pulled into the parking lot and sat there. Thirty yards to the north, beyond the floral arrangements and past the checkout counters, I would find liberation from the weight of the world. I couldn't handle Michael's illness. I just couldn't. One drink. One drink would give me the courage to go to him and hold his hand and tell him I'd be there no matter what. Please God!

Tears rolled down my cheeks. I cried for Michael and I cried for myself until I was too exhausted to cry any more. Michael didn't need a drunk right now, he needed me. I felt empty, weightless even. Looking in the mirror, I wiped away the tears and made myself presentable. I turned the key in the ignition once again and pulled back onto the street.

♦♦♦

Michael sat on the couch when I arrived, wrapped in Brian's arms. He disengaged himself from Brian and held me tight. "I'm so fuckin' scared!"

I held him and stroked his hair like he had done for me so many times. God, how handsome he is, I thought distractedly. He can't just waste away. Buff and beautiful, with a muscle tone that was never better. His hair was now cut short and he wore his International Male clothes with such elegance he looked like a model for Gentleman's Quarterly. "You can beat this," I urged. "They'll probably come out with a cure soon. All you have to do is keep fighting." God, my words sounded hollow even to me.

Michael nodded mutely. His face reflected the war inside his soul—hope against anguish that competed to the death.

One month later, I understood every aspect of AIDS— how it was transmitted, its incubation period, AZT and alternative treatments, prognosis for recovery. For eight months, Michael and I called each other every day. He brought me up to date on every headache, period of lethargy, ingrown toenail. I noticed his tone of voice and energy level—subtle cues he didn't realize he gave out.

"Fuck this!" Michael's voice boomed at the end of the receiver one winter evening.

An unusual amount of anger today. "Michael, what is it?" I asked in a well-modulated voice.

"I hate this! I'm going back to living like I used to."

Anger and denial in an attempt to recapture his days before he was HIV positive. "Do you think that's a good idea?"

"Stop it, Bunny. Just stop it."

"What?"

"Stop psychoanalyzing every move I make."

"What's the matter?" I felt the blood pound in my ears.

"This morning, I woke up to realize that I'm probably going to die of AIDS. But you know what? I could get run over by a bus tomorrow and be just as dead. I'm through with living like I'm ninety years old. I can still get it up. This fag ain't dead yet."

I didn't know whether to laugh or cry. Michael had been sounding like a curmudgeonly old bachelor, the kind who ate melba toast and applesauce promptly at 5:00 p.m. every night. "Aren't you scared?"

"Of course I'm scared. But I'll deal with this shit as it comes along. I'm through walking on eggs. I can't prevent this from taking a turn for the worse when it wants to."

"I see." My voice was tight.

"You don't sound convinced."

"Yeah, well, maybe I'm not."

"Bunny, life is for living and for the living. I'll die quicker if I sit here and worry about every time I cough or hiccup. Besides," the tone of his voice became smooth and sexy, "I have a reputation to maintain."

I could picture Michael brushing back his hair with his hand. He was right—so many men, so little time.

"Michael." I paused. What's he going to think of this? "Remember, safe sex, okay?"

"Are you kidding? There's no way I'm going to spread this around."

I felt a cascade of relief. "Thanks, Michael."

"Hey, sweetheart, have I ever told you that I love you?"

"No, you bastard."

"Well, I do."

I wanted to say, "I love you, too," but it got stuck behind a large lump in my throat.

189

Why work sucked so much emotional, physical, and psychic energy out of a person was beyond me. A few lucky people found employment that suited them. The rest of us got jobs and waited for the bills to come. Still, I felt better off than my co-workers. Many of them lived from one weekend to the next, or—the unlucky ones—one paycheck to the next. Whatever individuality or initiative they had when they arrived, soon got lost amidst concerns over incorrect time-card punches or whether the boss watched the clock as they walked to the water fountain. In this culture of conformity, the men tended to seek affairs to relieve their stress, while the women gossiped about their co-workers. If something wasn't a known fact, then by all means exaggerate, or hell, just make something up.

One day, Mrs. Loretta Stanley, a twenty-something redhead with mousy brown roots, walked into the lunchroom, where I ate lunch with two guys from our group. She pointedly turned her back to me and sat with two other women from her group. For some time, she had been making noises to her co-workers about having to work with a "known lesbian"—an odd complaint because not only did we work on different projects, we worked different shifts. Evidently I precipitated unresolved gender role issues for her. No one spoke for nearly five minutes.

Finally, when the tension became too great, Mrs. Stanley turned to me and screamed, "Why don't you people go back to where you came from? You make me sick!" Panic was written all over her face.

I slugged down a soda to keep myself from saying something nasty in return.

My co-worker, Jim, who fancied himself a liberal-minded

man, spoke up. "Didn't you move here from North Carolina, Mrs. Stanley? Why don't you move back there? I happen to know Bunny is from California." He winked at me.

Mrs. Loretta Stanley sputtered and fled from the room, her face red. Her co-workers shuffled their feet under the table.

"I don't think she's your type," he kidded me. "I'm more your type." He put his hands behind his head, leaned back in his chair, and thrust his pelvis toward me, his legs spread wide.

Liberal. Not perfect.

That night, I called Michael to bitch.

"You sound pretty low tonight. What's the matter?" Never one to mince words, Michael zeroed in on me.

"I don't know. I feel kinda flat."

"Why don't you see a lesbian therapist," he suggested.

"Is there any other kind?"

"Cynic. Maybe you need to address some of your issues— talk it out with someone."

"What issues? The fact that my job sucks and I can't get laid anymore to save my life?" I lit a cigarette.

"I thought you liked your job."

"I do—most of the time. Sometimes I get so frustrated, working for a company that doesn't recognize its employees might have something interesting to contribute. They seem to think they can dictate our lives in the name of making money. Like there may not be other ways to motivate us."

"Like what?"

"I don't know," I admitted.

"I do. You made your sales calls, did your convention work, and got the job done without anyone breathing down your neck. You were an independent adult, not a mindless clock puncher."

191

"Something like that. How'd you know?"

"Because for years I toyed with the idea of starting my own company, being my own boss. Now it's too late—I couldn't get insurance." Michael sighed. "If you ever get the chance, start your own company. You have the brains to do it."

"Thanks, bro." Great advice for someone who had the wherewithal to do it. But I was starting all over, learning a trade as my dad recommended. The world of computers was poised on the brink of a new era. Some hard-core geeks predicted that every home would have a computer by 2000. The ravings of wild-eyed visionaries or merely far-fetched? I didn't know. But no matter what the future brought, I wanted to be ready.

Smog lay over the San Fernando Valley like a greasy film. It permeated the red, pink, and white oleanders that lined the freeways, and which, contrary to their cheerful color, were as deadly as Socrates' hemlock. Hundreds of square miles of fertile land lay under ribbons of asphalt and concrete that crisscrossed Southern California like a crazy quilt. It was a small price to pay for affordable housing and the means to get from home to work. As long as the economy kept humming along, no one seemed to care.

When did life lose its zest? Reality assumed a new façade, worry covered by slick marketing campaigns. Ronald Reagan's "Morning in America" had turned into a prolonged wait at the loan shark's office, and the bills were piling up.

Why was I in such a foul mood? LA had changed imperceptibly during those years I lived in self-imposed exile in San Francisco. However, unlike LA, my internal landscape had changed completely. You're just another two-bit cunt, Bunny.

192

My appointment was for five o'clock. Dr. Carla Patterson came highly recommended, and if her rates were any indication of her proficiency as a therapist, she was good, damned good. Her office was in a suite of five mental health professionals, where one receptionist served the group. "I'm here to see Dr. Patterson."

The receptionist, a young woman in her twenties, smiled. When did women in their twenties become young?

"She said to have a seat in her office. She'll be a minute." The receptionist indicated down the hall. "Second door on the left."

Reluctantly, I entered her office and looked around for any indication of what Dr. Patterson was like. Behind her carefully appointed desk hung framed diplomas—RN, MSW, Ph.D.—enough letters to make alphabet soup. Her office was a showroom for the latest trend in interior design—lots of leafy green plants, soft soothing colors and fabrics, and a box of pastel tissues next to a clock perched unobtrusively on the polished cherry desk. Throughout this display of taste and education I saw no personal effects, no pictures of family, no sweater slung over her chair, no gum wrappers in the empty wastebasket. Does this woman exist?

The door opened. "You must be Bunny. I'm Carla Patterson. Pleased to meet you." Her eyes connected with mine a fraction of a second too long. She held out a perfectly manicured hand to shake mine.

Alarm bells started going off in my head. Dr. Carla Patterson was a very attractive woman, from the top of her Clairol highlighted hair, to the tips of her Gucci shoes. She looked as if she stepped right out of the pages of Talbot's—gray flannel trousers, gray-green linen shirt, and expensive-looking earrings. Her persona screamed tasteful.

How could she possibly relate to me—recovering alcoholic who had lost herself somewhere along the way?

She sat in the opposite chair. "Why are you here today?"

"I don't know where to begin, Dr. Patterson. My life is so outta whack."

"Please, call me Carla." She turned on her professional smile. "Tell me more about 'outta whack.' "

"I dunno—the usual shit. Recovering alcoholic, major career change. I feel like a deflated balloon, wondering what the hell happened to my life." Carla Patterson made my blood pressure rise. How could I tell her all my crap and not end up looking like an idiot?

"You seem nervous," she said.

"I am. I don't like to talk about these things."

"I know it's hard." Again she smiled to reassure me. "Tell me when it all started."

It started when Sunshine dumped me. I pushed the hair out of my eyes. "I used to be a model." I didn't add, "for Franklin's of Beverly Hills." "Ever since then my life has been disappointing."

Carla said nothing.

"Life was more fun when I drank and partied and had a girlfriend. No, not a girlfriend. When I had Sunshine."

"Who was Sunshine to you?"

I laughed, although nothing could be less funny. "Sunshine was the woman of my dreams. Sounds corny, I know. We played. We had fun. We were going to solve all of the world's problems together. She made me happier than any woman ever has."

Carla made a notation on her clipboard. "What else?"

Between the attraction I felt for Carla and the pain I felt talking about Sunshine, I couldn't look at her. I played with a loose thread on my slacks while I talked. "We fought about my career, about where we were going to live, about what was and wasn't okay. When I look back on it now, I should've given in to her. Finally, we broke up. I was devastated, to say the least." I looked up. "I suppose all of your clients think that."

Carla shrugged. "What matters is what you think. Tell me what happened."

"It went ... I went downhill from there—moved to San Francisco, slept around, found a new job, eventually got sober. A while ago, I moved back to LA. Now I write software and go to AA meetings. End of story." I gave the thread a tug. It ran through the seam into the body of the fabric and started a small hole. Damn!

Carla wrote another note on her clipboard. "And your current relationship is fine?"

"I'm not in a relationship. There's no one special."

For an instant, Carla's eyes burned with an intensity I hadn't seen in years. Her professional demeanor vanished and I could see "I want you!" written all over her face.

I knew better than to get involved with my therapist. It wasn't just a breach of professional ethics, it was more like incest, a convoluted closeness that left at least one of the people feeling fucked over.

She recovered quickly. "And your work ..."

"It's okay. Nothing exciting. It pays the bills."

"Overall, how would you describe your life right now?"

Boring, meaningless, still in love with Sunshine. "Let's just say I'd hoped for something more at 36."

"Like what?"

I held out my hands, exasperated. "God! If I only knew."

Carla remained silent.

"I guess I'm looking for ... meaning. Some kind of assurance that we're not cosmic hamsters running madly around

195

on exercise wheels, getting nowhere. I want my life to have meaning beyond eating and sleeping and working and dying, with magic moments of sex to break up the monotony."

Carla smiled, then put down her clipboard.

Was it my imagination or was the room getting hotter?

"I can't be your therapist," she said finally.

"Why not?" I could feel the color rise in my cheeks.

"Because I'm very attracted to you. I'll have to refer you to someone else." She played with her pencil.

"The least you could do is write me a script for Prozac or something."

"I'm not a psychiatrist. I can't write prescriptions." She sat forward on her chair, her eyes twinkling.

I got the distinct impression that Carla was teasing me. The tension between us filled the room. My heart pounded, but it wasn't anger that I felt. I felt aroused. "Does this mean you're not going to see me again?" Two can play this game.

"I've never done this before. I need to know you better to make a good referral. Do you have any plans for tonight? It's early, but I'd like to take you out to dinner." Carla sat with her hands folded neatly in her lap. She reminded me of a cat I once saw that waited an entire afternoon for a mouse to come out of its hole.

"None. None at all." So what if I blew off an AA meeting? They'd still be there when I needed them. And Carla was infinitely more interesting than the Big Book.

"Shall we?" Carla stood up and indicated for me to leave before her.

On our way out of her office, Carla stopped at the receptionist's desk. "Just a minute," she said. She lightly brushed her hand across the small of my back as she reached for a pencil. Carla flipped through the pages of the appointment book and erased two entries.

"What's that?" I peered over her shoulder.

"I had you penciled in for a couple more sessions. You won't be needing them."

"Why did you pencil me in?" I whispered. "You didn't even know me yet."

She smiled. "You were a potential customer."

"You pencil in appointments with clients you don't have?"

She shook her head. "It's no big deal. Let's go."

We took separate cars to a nondescript strip mall. Other than a bulletin board covered with brightly colored notices and announcements of lost pets, the place looked pretty bare.

"It's not much to look at, but the food's great." Carla pushed through the front door, picked up two menus, and headed toward the back of the restaurant.

The menu featured sandwiches of every kind imaginable—roasted red bell peppers and eggplant with basil leaves on a seven grain bun, thinly sliced Italian salami and watercress on sourdough, smoked turkey and stilton cheese on whole-wheat french bread, sliced plum tomatoes with kalamata olive spread and basil leaves in a pita pocket. Without a thought to the consequences, I chose the grilled Vidalia onion and arugula on a whole grain bun. I had inherited a taste for onion sandwiches from my father. "Food of the Gods," he called them. I understood why.

"You like?" Carla smiled a cat-who-ate-the-canary smile.

"Oh yeah." At that moment I realized the embarrassing position I put myself in. You can't kiss her with onion breath.

"Wait 'til you try dessert." Carla lifted a fork of radicchio and spinach leaves with house dressing to her mouth.

"I can't wait." Between the eye contact and the suggestive

masticating, dinner felt like the feasting scene from the movie Tom Jones.

We lingered over our lattés, our first-date chitchat exhausted.

"Can I call you? It's been wonderful." Carla positively glowed.

"I'd really like that. When?"

"Would you like to go to a party next Saturday night? Nothing fancy. I'd like you to meet some of my friends."

A party with a sexy woman? A chance to do something other than go to work, classes, and AA meetings? "Sure."

In the parking lot, Carla wrote her home phone number on the back of her business card. "Thanks for coming." She leaned over to kiss me.

I backed away, my face bright red. "I can't. Onion breath."

"You think that's gonna stop me?" She took me in her arms and laid her lips against mine, then kissed me again, a long passionate kiss that left me breathless.

I was on the edge of sensory overload—the food, the conversation, the woman, the kisses. "I'll call you, okay?"

"You'd better." She winked as she got in her car and drove off.

I got into my Beemer and drove the opposite direction. For the first time since coming to LA, I felt alive.

Chapter 14

What's Love Got To Do With It?

Carla arrived at 8:30 p.m. Saturday dressed anything but casually—green crepe cocktail dress, matching sandals, and gold earrings. She epitomized the emerging trend in hip dykes: the lipstick lesbian. My strategy was to dress conservatively—light yellow silk tank top with gray slacks and yellow and white striped espadrilles—until I became comfortable with her friends. Her face registered shock, or perhaps disappointment, at my attire.

"Do you think I should change?" I offered quickly.

"Well, um ..." Carla looked at the floor.

"I'll be right back." I dashed into my bedroom and pushed to the back of the closet, where my more festive dresses hung. At the very back, I found the white dress that had knocked Sunshine off her feet so many years before. No way. I pulled out three alternatives: a skintight red satin number that screamed, "I want to get laid"; a long sleeved knit teal dress that conveyed, "Professional, not stuffy"; and my favorite, a simple black dress that said, "I'm here to party."

Carla sat on the couch when I returned.

"How about this one?" I held up the teal dress.

Her eyes traveled between the dress and my body—a look

I associated with only the most unrepentant of male chauvinists. "Mmmmmm, nice."

You didn't imagine this—she is hot for you. I held up the skintight number.

Carla's eyes almost bulged out of her head. "I don't think so."

I held up the black dress.

She tipped her head to the side. "Could you try it on? Please?"

"Sure." I hung the other dresses toward the middle, not the back, of my closet. Already I could tell that if we were to continue to see each other, dresses, not pants would be the uniform de rigueur.

I slipped into the dress, added a three-strand pearl necklace with matching earrings and a pair of black pumps.

Carla's eyes lit up when I walked into the room. "Can you turn around?" she asked in an unsteady voice.

Go for it. I gave a performance worthy of my Franklin's of Beverly Hills days when I turned around for inspection.

She cleared her throat. "I could get used to this." Carla stood up and offered me her hand. "Shall we go?"

Sometime after 9:30 p.m., we arrived at our hostesses's home in Pasadena. "People are going to be drinking here. Will that be a problem?" she asked as we stood on the doorstep.

"I'll be okay. I still can smoke, can't I?" I fidgeted with my necklace.

"Outside, I think. Neither Marla nor Corinne are smokers." She sounded apologetic.

I didn't care if people thought cigarettes were my crutch. I needed one vice to keep from becoming a born-again member of the House of Purity, where anyone who ate red meat, drove a fast car, or wore anything other than natural fibers was suspect.

Carla's eyes sparkled when she introduced me to everyone in sight: Marla, a Municipal Court Judge and her partner Corrine, Program Director for a local youth program; Pam, a CPA whose firm audited several computer start-up companies, including my employer; Josie, an Associate Professor of Psychology at one of the Cal State Universities; plus a sprinkling of MDs, attorneys, and entrepreneurs. Tall, short, educated, and connected, dressed in Oleg Cassini or REI sportswear, they were a small island of Southern California's lesbian underground.

Carla grinned ear-to-ear as we flitted from couple to couple. "Leah, I'd like you to meet my friend, Bunny LaRue." Her arm around my waist, Carla's posture implied more than "friend." Once again, Carla let her eyes travel up and down my body. It felt nice to be appreciated.

"Leah is an actress," Carla announced. "She's writing a one-woman show."

"Good for you, Leah." These unflaggingly pleasant, well-dressed women all ran together in my head. It had been nearly two years since I'd submerged myself in a large gathering of women and my system was on overload. I twitched from lack of nicotine. I desperately wanted to go outside and light up, but it seemed rude to just leave. "Excuse me," I finally said to Carla and Leah. "I need a cigarette." I disengaged myself from Carla, whose death grip on me since we walked in the door had grown tiresome.

I maneuvered my way through the dining room and into the kitchen. As I was about to open the screen door, I heard someone call out to me.

"Bunny! I haven't seen you in years!"

The voice sounded familiar. I turned around to see an old friend from my drinking days.

Jessie threw her arms around me and kissed me on the cheek. "How long has it been, 10 years?"

"More like a dozen."

"Wait'll I tell Val you're here." She grabbed my hand and dragged me back into the main part of the house. "Val, look who I found."

Our impromptu reunion turned heads in the room. Carla crossed the room and took hold of my arm. "I thought you went outside for a smoke."

"Carla, this is Jessie and Val. I've known them forever. We used to drink together."

"And I mean drink," Jessie added.

"Well, since the seventies, anyway." Val leaned over and kissed me on the cheek.

The color rose in Carla's cheeks. "Yes, we've met before. Did you know Bunny doesn't drink anymore?"

"Neither do we!" Val beamed as she circled Jessie's waist with her arm. "I've been sober for five years, and Jessie's been sober for eight."

"And I've been sober for almost two years."

Carla looked as if her night had been seriously disrupted. I got the impression that I was supposed to be the newly discovered treasure, but Val and Jessie had spoiled the surprise.

Pam walked over and joined our group. "Hitting on Carla's date already, Jessie? I woulda thought you'd wait until Val was outta sight." From the tone of her voice, it was obvious Jessie and Pam knew each other well.

"Everyone hits on Bunny, didn't you know? And Val doesn't care." Jessie shot a glance at her partner, who smiled back.

"How do you and Pam know each other?" Carla asked Jessie.

Pam put her arm around Jessie's shoulder and smiled. "Jessie made partner in our firm about a year ago."

"Congratulations." Carla opened her mouth to say more, but was pulled in another direction by one of the hostesses. "You've got to try the calamari," Corinne said breathlessly. "It's to die for." She grabbed Carla and Pam's hands and whisked them off to the buffet in the dining room. Before disappearing into the next room, Carla turned around and ran her tongue over her lips. There was no mistaking where this evening was heading.

Jessie turned to me. "So what happened between you and Sunshine? I figured you two would be together until the end of time."

I felt the color leave my face. "Unfortunately, the end of time came ahead of schedule."

Val elbowed Jessie in the ribs. "You shouldn't have asked."

"It's okay. A lot of things have happened in the meantime— I quit drinking and changed careers. Grew up, I guess." I looked down at the beige carpeting. "And, I met Carla." I smiled at my old friends and wondered if they could see what was going on inside my heart that minute.

"That's great," Val enthused.

Jessie said nothing.

"I need a cigarette before I explode. Want to join me out- side?" Old friends or not, I had to get out of the house fast.

"I'll come," Jessie volunteered.

"I'll stay inside, thank you. Don't get into any trouble, you two." Val shook her finger at us.

The intensity of the party subsided the minute we step- ped onto the patio. Several women lounged on chairs and chatted amicably. I took a seat with a table full of smokers, thankful I could relax.

"So what's this partner thing?" I asked Jessie.

She laughed. "Good things happen to bad people. But really,

I had to make a choice—either stay in the dead-end accounting job I was at, or get my CPA and get on with my life. I found a niche in Pam's firm and they eventually made me a partner."

The conversation at the table turned to business. I sat back and half-listened to discussions of investments and cruises, weekend cabins and ski trips. These women had the best of all worlds—financial security and the love and support of, if not their partner, their circle of friends.

As I lit another cigarette, I felt someone's hands massage my neck and shoulders.

"Ready to go back inside?" Carla gave me another one of her suggestive glances.

"Let me finish this." I twitched again, but not from lack of nicotine.

Carla pulled up a chair next to me and changed the conversation to house refinancing. I looked at Jessie, who gave me an enigmatic smile. Something is going on here and I don't know what it is.

When Carla and I stood to leave, Jessie pulled me over so she could whisper in my ear, "Don't let her trip you up."

I straightened up, not sure of what she meant.

"Let's keep in touch," Jessie said for all to hear.

"Yeah, sure." Carla and I held hands as we walked back into the house.

"Aren't these women the best?" Carla gushed as we stepped inside. "I'd love to have our own community of just these women."

I could imagine what Sunshine would say to that—predominantly white, upper middle class women who had lost all connection to people who still struggled with race, class, and socioeconomic issues. Carla had a point. There was a feeling of safety being around other likeminded women. Twenty years later it still was "us vs. them," but tonight "us" was a group of educated, moneyed lesbians, a group few people could have predicted two decades ago.

Carla led me to the pantry, where we could be alone. "How are you doing?"

"A little tired. I was hoping to spend some time with you tonight."

"You mean, make our own party?" She pressed me against the shelves of canned goods and kissed me. "I can arrange that. Shall we say our goodbyes?"

"Yeah." Despite her over-protectiveness, her sidelong glances had driven me nuts. I wanted to strip off her cocktail dress and discover the woman beneath.

We left at 11:30. The thirty-minute drive to Carla's house seemed like forever, mostly because Carla kept quizzing me about the party.

"Did you enjoy yourself tonight?" She took my hand.

"Yes. It was nice. Thanks for asking me."

"Aren't those women great?"

"Yes, they're very nice, all of them."

"No one tried to hit on you, did they?" Carla's question sounded strained.

I laughed. "Only Jessie. But you don't have a thing to worry about with her."

Carla frowned, but said nothing.

We turned off the Interstate, passed a shopping mall, and entered a new subdivision. Carla's house sat in a long row of indistinguishable beige homes. I was surprised when we pulled into her driveway. "You have a purple door?"

"It's not purple, it's aubergine. It's my one concession to being gay." She laughed. "Every house on this street looks alike. I needed something to make it easy to find." She fumbled with her keys at the side door. "Can I get you anything?" she asked when we entered the kitchen.

Double scotch. "No thanks. I'm fine. I would like a tour, though."

Like her office, there was little personality in her house—Navajo white walls, oatmeal Berber carpet with a couple of brightly colored rugs scattered about, one bedroom turned into an office, and a guest bathroom that looked like it had never been used. Much to my amazement, she had a loom set up in the formal living room. "What's this?"

"Oh, it's my hobby," she said, embarrassed. "I haven't done any weaving for a while."

"Really?" I looked closely at her latest project, an intricate pattern of maroon and gray threads set on a cream-colored warp. "This is beautiful. Where did you learn this?"

"Art school. A long time ago. I do this when I need to relax." She ran her fingers lightly over the loom.

"You went to art school?"

"Yeah. I started out as an art major. I switched to nursing when I realized I could either be a poor, struggling artist or make a decent living as a nurse."

I looked between her throw rugs and the project that sat half-done on her loom. "You made your rugs, didn't you?"

"Yes," she said, shyly.

It was make-or-break time. "I love a woman with talented fingers."

"Well." She took me by the hand and led me down the hall to her bedroom. "Let's see what these fingers can do." She unzipped my dress, lifted my slip over my head, and pulled my panties off. Her cheeks turned pink as she looked at me. "Oh God."

"I'll take that as a compliment." I turned her around and unzipped her dress, which fell to the floor. Her satin slip looked too inviting. I ran my hands over her shoulders, her breasts, her tummy, and her ass, the satin slip conforming

206

to every curve. I pulled her slip over her head, then unfastened her bra and pulled off her panties. Oh, yeah.

From that moment on, we were like two she-devils locked in concupiscent battle. I pinned her against the wall and explored her mouth with my tongue. Carla strained to get out from under me. She succeeded when she let her body go limp and slid down the wall. As I reached down to help her up, she scooted away and jumped on her bed.

"Come and get me," she taunted.

"My pleasure." I took three long steps and was on top of her in a flash.

Carla seemed more than eager to relieve me of all of my sexual tension. She explored my breasts and neck with her tongue, then caressed my ass with her fingertips. Years of weaving made her fingers deft and I writhed with ecstasy. When her fingers entered my pussy, I came almost immediately. "Don't stop," I begged.

Carla obliged.

Some minutes later, I lay exhausted next to her, my heart racing from an accelerated course in lovemaking. "You think you're quite the stud, don't you?"

"That's Doctor Stud to you." Carla lay back on the bed, a smile plastered from ear to ear.

"Is there anything I can do for you?" I reached over and grazed her nipple with my finger.

She took a sudden breath. "Oh, please."

I wanted to play with her lightly, tease her a bit before I got serious. After our intense connection, she needed something decidedly different. I ran my fingers over her torso, down her legs, along the backs of her knees. I nibbled her ears and kissed her neck and breasts, but avoided her sex all together.

Several minutes of this kind of touching was enough to make her scream, "For God's sake, fuck me!"

With a gracious invitation like that, how could I refuse? I ran my fingers over her pubic mound, until I found her swollen clit. I rubbed it lightly and with each stroke she came closer to the edge. Her body shaking, I entered her pussy and felt my hand swallowed up inside.

She pulled my hair, her body rigid as contraction after contraction radiated from her pussy. Finally she lay still next to me. "Jesus! Is this how it always is with you?" Her body still twitched.

"Call me Stud Bunny." I leaned up on my elbow and smiled down at her.

"God," she said quietly, "I definitely could get used to this."

Between work, school, and Carla, I still managed to go to meetings three, sometimes four times a week. They helped to keep my sanity as well as my sobriety. Within a month after moving to LA, I'd found a meeting where every woman seemed to be actively working on her sobriety, whether she was one hour or eleven years away from a drink. It became my home meeting.

Much to my surprise, Sharon from San Francisco introduced herself as a visitor one Friday evening. After the meeting, we walked outside, where I lit a cig and took a long drag.

"You're still sober? That's great. How long has it been?" Sharon popped a piece of gum into her mouth.

"Almost three years." My guilt-stricken conscience wanted to know how Ella was doing. She, more than anyone, had helped me through those treacherous months of unsteadiness and inertia when I quit drinking. Once again, I promised myself I'd write to Ella. Soon. "How's everyone in The City doing? Darcy? Ella?"

She tilted her head back and looked at me oddly. "Ella? I thought you knew."

"Knew what?"

"Ella died two years ago of lung cancer."

The tightening in my chest cut off my breath. Years of practice caused me to hold my cigarette so it wouldn't burn me as I fell against the building and slid to the ground. Angrily, I flipped the butt into the gutter.

Sharon hovered anxiously above me. "Are you okay? I'm sorry. I thought you knew." She knelt next to me and took me in her arms.

I couldn't think and I couldn't breathe. Tears poured down my cheeks. Oh shit! Oh shit! Ohshitohshitohshitohshitohshitohshit!

Minutes later, when I'd regained some part of my normal self, I staggered to my feet.

"Do you want me to drive you home?" Sharon asked anxiously.

"No. Thanks. I can drive."

"If you don't mind, I'll follow you in my car," she offered.

I shook my head no. Guilt on top of guilt, I didn't want to be responsible for messing up Sharon's life by making her miss whatever function she came here to attend. "I insist." Sharon picked up my purse and headed toward the parking lot.

When I got home, I stared at the horizon, lost in a sea of self-recrimination.

"C'mon." Sharon took me by my elbow and led me inside.

"I'm sorry, Sharon. You probably were here on business. You can leave—I'll be all right."

"I drove here for a trade show I didn't want to go to in the first place. I'd rather be with you. You're not the only woman who was devastated by Ella's death." She rummaged through my refrigerator and brought me a soda.

I sat on the couch and cried.

Sharon held me and explained what happened. "It came on suddenly. She had been in remission for several years. Then, one day she called me and said the tumor had returned and was eating up her lungs. She died three weeks later."

"Why didn't she tell me?"

Sharon shook her head. "She didn't tell anyone. She didn't want to be a burden to anyone. The funeral was nice. Lots of women came, even a few of her old drinking buddies. Some of the women she sponsored spoke about their relationship with her, what a help she had been." Sharon let out a long sigh. "We were all devastated when she died."

I cried myself to sleep that night. When Carla called Saturday morning to confirm our dinner date for that night, I begged off. "Last night, I found out a close friend died. I don't feel like entertaining anyone right now, if you don't mind."

"I know how devastating the death of a friend can be. Why don't I come over and cook dinner for you? At least hold your hand," she offered.

"No, thanks."

"It's no trouble at all."

"An old friend is here and she's taking care of me." I looked across at Sharon, who flipped through the pages of one of my work manuals titled, "Fundamentals of dBase Conversion."

Sharon looked up and smiled.

Sometime late Sunday afternoon, Sharon drove back to

The City. Knowing how fragile I was, Michael picked me up every day for the next week and took me to my AA meetings. I retreated to a place inside myself where I could function like a robot—do the minimum necessary to maintain body and soul. I went to work and meetings. I had no energy for anyone, even Carla, who called me daily.

My grief came in angry spasms of self-hatred for not writing or calling Ella. When I was too emotionally self-battered to hate myself any more, I collapsed face down on the bed and cried my eyes out for the one woman whose love I couldn't touch or manipulate.

A month later, I had repaired to what would be called normal functioning, sans smoking. I focused all of my anger and pain over Ella's death against cigarettes, although I was tempted more times than I can count to break down and buy a pack, light up, and participate in the very ritual that claimed her life. Instead, I went home and cried. Carla backed off during my time of healing. I guess she sensed that I would resist any outright move to sweep in and save me. So I didn't know what to expect when I picked up the phone to call her. "Hi, Carla. It's me."

"Bunny! I hope you're feeling better over the loss of your friend."

"I'm better, thanks." I paused. "I was wondering if maybe we could go out this weekend?"

"I'm sorry, but I have plans to go to the Hollywood Bowl for the Playboy Jazz Festival on Saturday and then on Sunday I'm driving to Santa Barbara."

"Oh." I could hear the disappointment in my voice. What'd you expect? That's she'd drop her plans to be with you?

"But I'm free the following weekend," she offered. "What do you have in mind?"

"I was thinking of going to the Farmer's Market in Temecula, then grab a bite somewhere."

The tone of her voice brightened. "Sounds great! Why don't you call me next week?"

"Okay." I didn't want our conversation to end this quickly. "And Carla ..."

"Yes?"

I blurted it out. "It's good to hear your voice again."

"It's good to hear your voice, too. Call me." The receiver clicked off.

I felt something warm—warm and melting—inside my chest. It was good to get back to life after this last month.

Our trip to Temecula yielded bounty neither of us expected. Besides the home-baked loaves of bread, jars of spiced orange pear butter, and sparkling cider from the Farmer's Market, we got caught up in the everyday moments of living. Our conversation was neither inspired nor sacred. Instead of a quaint out-of-the-way dining experience, we ate hot dogs and nachos covered in liquid yellow glop from a convenience store when we stopped for gas. It was the mundaneness of it all that charmed me. When she got away from all of her high-powered friends, Carla seemed to relax and enjoy non-trendy pursuits. I felt pulled toward her, an island of stability in my life that seemed to have no moorings.

"Would you like to come inside for a bit?" Carla asked when we pulled into her driveway.

It seemed the natural thing to do. We carried in the bread, preserves, and sparkling cider and sat down at her kitchen table. "This day has been just what I needed."

"For me, too." Carla raided her refrigerator and brought out summer sausage, cheese, and butter. She poured the sparkling cider into crystal goblets and sliced the bread, then raised her goblet in a toast. "To good company."

"To good company." I could see myself with Carla, enjoying weekend excursions to Ensenada and Yosemite, participating in all the "guppy" activities that childless gay couples could afford. Not that I wanted to rush into anything just yet. I wanted to experience the non-alcoholic equivalent of being wined and dined, romanced with flowers and silly little gifts. Hadn't I gone long enough without this kind of attention?

Carla gazed at me, her eyes full of passion. She stood up, leaned across the table, and kissed me.

Her offer was not lost on me. This could only lead in one direction. During that month of mourning, I felt no sexual desire whatsoever, but that was now past. I fondled her breasts through her shirt until she moaned. We both wanted it.

Carla took my hand and led me to her bedroom. As she pulled my shirt out of my jeans, she asked, "Would you like to shower?"

"Yeah." I followed Carla into the bathroom and undressed her, then escorted her into the shower. We used half a bottle of lavender-scented body scrub as we caressed each other's backs, asses, thighs, and breasts. I came twice in the shower and still wasn't satisfied. Dripping water and bubbles, we ran from the shower to the bedroom. I threw Carla on the bed, where we made love half the night.

In the morning, while I was still sound asleep, Carla got up and made breakfast—sliced melons, crumpets with spiced orange pear butter, and coffee.

"Your breakfast, Madam." Carla set the tray on the bed next to me.

"Wow. The last time anyone brought breakfast to me in

bed was when I was ten, after I got my tonsils out. My dad kept me supplied with Neapolitan ice cream the whole weekend."

Carla slipped into bed. "Sorry. I'm fresh out of Neapolitan ice cream. This'll have to do."

We spent the morning making love, eating, and sleeping. About one, Carla brought in the Sunday newspaper. As she lay reading the financial section, I flipped through the sports section, world news, weather, and TV sections. Her bedroom floor was covered in advertisements for denture cream, furniture, electronics, brake jobs, potato chips, liquor, and disposable diapers. There was something comfortable about being with Carla—time seemed to stretch out forever.

It was with some sadness when I left that evening. "Thank you. I've had the most wonderful weekend." I wrapped my arms around her. Although it was after eight, I didn't want to get into my car and drive the twenty miles to my apartment.

"I hope that means you'll come again." She brushed my hair back and kissed my neck.

"If you keep doing that, I'll never leave," I murmured.

"Promise?"

Reluctantly, I broke away from her and got into my car. "Thanks again." As I drove down the street, I thought about how nice, how normal it felt to be with her. For years, I felt like I was beating my head against the wall, hoping for a woman who would make my life come together. I watched in my rearview window as Carla stepped inside her front door and let the mini-blinds fall to cover her window. The hallway light shone around the edges of the window, a warm island of life in a sea of indifference.

Chapter 15

Babylon Sisters

My answering machine blinked as if it were possessed when I got home—two calls from an indignant Michael wondering where the hell I was; a hang-up; a wrong number who cursed me because "Phil," whoever "Phil" was, owed him four hundred bucks; and a message from Carla:

"Hey, baby, I want you back, right now!" She laughed. "Call me when you get home, okay?"

I picked up the phone and added Carla's number to my speed-dial memory. "Hi. I got your message." My voice had that elated tone of a woman in lust.

"Thanks for the wonderful weekend. I'd ask you to move in right away, but that would be too forward." She giggled nervously. "You're very special to me."

And you to me, too. "Thank you. I had a great weekend, too. Now I have to call everyone and tell them I didn't die."

"Of course," she said. "I ..." She cut herself off quickly.

"Yes?"

"I think you should make your calls."

That's not was she was going to say. "I'll talk to you soon. Goodnight." I hung up the receiver, walked into the bathroom to wash my face, and looked in the mirror. The woman I saw looked not quite relaxed, like she wanted something more.

It's too soon. It's too soon for me and it's too soon for her. I walked back into the kitchen and speed-dialed Michael. "Hey, bro."

"And just where have you been?" he asked in his superior tone.

"Making friends."

"Friends? Is this the friend who started out as your shrink and now is your, how shall I put this, paramour? Bosom buddy? Girl-toy?"

"Oh, shut up!"

"I knew it!" he crowed.

"Carla and I are dating. We're friends." I never could figure out how Michael knew when I was seeing a new woman.

"Well, don't forget your old friends. I'd like to see you sometime, too."

"Why don't we all go out to dinner next week? You can check her out then." I still relied on Michael for his opinion on my "paramours", as he called them. He knew how easily women fell in love, blinded to the most obvious flaws of their current obsession, the U-Haul charges already on their credit card bill.

Friday night, Michael and his new squeeze Ray, Carla, and I sat at in an elegant restaurant on the water in Long Beach.

"Of course, when Bunny said you were her oldest friend, I just had to meet you," Carla gushed.

Michael smiled. "Bunny's said some nice things about you. She said you'd talked about taking a cruise?"

"We're thinking about the Caribbean. Of course, it would have to be after the tourist season, when everyone's kids are back in school." Carla dabbed at her mouth with her napkin.

"Of course." Michael gave me a significant glance as he sipped from his wineglass.

216

"But then I've always wanted to go to New Orleans for Mardi Gras." Carla took my hand. "Maybe next spring, darling?"

I desperately wanted this meeting between Carla and Michael to work, so I was agreeable to anything. "Sure. Anywhere you like."

Carla burst out in a high-pitched laugh. "You're so sweet. Isn't she the sweetest thing?"

Michael shook his head. "She just knocks me out sometimes."

Carla turned her attention to Ray. "And what do you do?"

"I'm a letter carrier in Bellflower." Ray drained his beer, then signaled the waiter for another.

"Oh. How nice." Carla looked nonplussed, then turned back to Michael. "Are you two going to the gala AIDS fundraiser this month?"

Michael put down his wineglass. "We'd love to, but I've got end-of-the-month reports to get out. Another time, I guess."

Carla sighed dramatically. "Unfortunately I think AIDS fundraisers will be around for years to come. It's a shame." She picked up her menu and flipped through the pages. "This place is famous for its paella. Have you tried it?"

Inwardly I cringed. I couldn't believe how nonchalantly Carla dismissed Michael's condition.

Michael looked grim. "No. It's a little more than my system can handle at the moment."

Ray slugged back his beer.

"Have you seen *Hairspray*?" she asked Ray. "It's a stitch!"

"When it comes out on video," Ray replied. "I've got three kids and my child-support payments are killin' me."

Carla looked pale. "Priorities. Yes."

She monopolized the conversation all evening. Michael politely smiled and nodded through whatever topic she expounded on—the likelihood of a clash between the Israelis and the Palestinians, the current pop-culture infatuation with Teenage Mutant Ninja Turtles, the amusing little swizzle sticks that came with our shrimp cocktails. Even with her high-powered friends, I had never seen Carla try so hard to impress anyone. Everything felt out-of-synch—Carla played lesbian socialite while Ray quietly got bombed. Michael, on the other hand, seemed amused by the whole evening.

"It's been wonderful," Carla said to the boys after dinner. "I'm so glad we finally met. Let's have dinner again, soon."

Michael smiled and extended his hand. "Absolutely. I always like to meet Bunny's friends." He turned to me. "Call me later, okay?" He arched his eyebrow in a way I knew meant business.

"Yeah." Carla struck out big time with Michael.

When we got in my car, Carla turned to me. "Well? How'd I do?"

"Fine. You did just fine." I pulled onto the 710 Freeway and hoped I wouldn't be quizzed all the way home.

"Michael's lovely but that friend of his ..." Carla looked out the window.

"Ray? He was a little drunk, that's all."

"He hardly said anything. And his manners! We were at a four-star restaurant and he orders beer. Beer, for godsakes. He's like some kind of redneck blue-collar worker who's never been to a nice restaurant before."

"He probably can't afford it with three kids."

"Takes all kinds, I guess." Carla settled back into her seat. "I was a little surprised when Michael brought up the cruise."

"Yeah, I guess I mentioned it to him."

"It would be fun, doncha think? Nothing to do but lie in the sun, read, and make love." She squeezed my hand.

"Sounds great. I could use a vacation."

"I'll call tomorrow. What do you think? A week? Two weeks? No," she bit her lip, "I think two weeks would be too much. Where would you like to go? Belize? Cozumel? Rhoda and Ramona took a cruise to St. Croix and they loved it." You like her. She likes you. Relax and let things happen. I tuned Carla out as she chattered on about our impending cruise. I was anxious to call Michael and get his unedited opinion of Carla, but I couldn't call tonight. We had plans for Saturday, a pool-party in San Diego, and Sunday we were supposed to attend the opening of a play that Leah, the actress I'd met at Marla and Corinne's party, had a role in. I hoped that in the months to come, our dating life would be less hectic and we would be able to chill on the weekends and do some of the things I cared about like visit the LA Arboretum or take a drive up to Big Bear.

On Monday morning, I phoned Michael. "How are you doin'?"

"I was about to ask you the same thing. What's the matter with you? Are you so lonely that you'll date Ms. Lesbian California over a real woman? Or are you just horny?"

I felt defensive. "Carla is very nice once you get to know her. She's not just about cruises and galas and swizzle sticks."

"Oh, so you are horny."

"Damn it, Michael, I like her and she likes me."

He sighed. "I'm sure Carla is very nice. She just seems pretentious, that's all. Do what you want to do."

I felt torn. Michael was right, Carla was pretentious at dinner. But there was a softer side to Carla, a side I wanted to get to know better. Maybe middle age was creeping up on me, but I wanted a woman who would be there for me when I needed her. No one was perfect.

219

"Sometimes I wish you and Sunshine were still together. At least you loved her."

Michael's comment caught me off guard. I felt an enormous lump in my throat and my eyes teared up. "Yeah, well, you can't have everything. Look," I added hastily, "I gotta get to work. I'll call you later."

Michael's voice was gentle. "Okay, baby. Take care of yourself."

"Thanks." I hung up the phone as tears cascaded down my face. *Why did he have to bring up Sunshine? She left you for good.*

That afternoon, Carla phoned. "How's my love-machine?" Her voice became soft and sexy. "Come over to my house and I'll give you a piece of candy, little girl."

The blood rushed to my face. Part of me wanted to sit back, assess the situation, then make a semi-rational decision about where our relationship was going. But a larger part of me wanted to throw caution to the wind and immerse myself in a relationship where I could enjoy the company of a woman who seemingly had it all—respectable profession, house in the burbs, and an active non-alcoholic social life.

Michael was right. I was horny.

Over the next four months, Carla orchestrated candlelight dinners when I wasn't at class, flowers that arrived at work with a card signed "Your ardent admirer," and sober weekends in Santa Barbara, San Luis Obispo, and the major theme parks. Our sex life, while not as passionate as our first encounters, cemented a growing bond I felt with her. Work and meetings had consumed too much of my life the past year, so I cut back my shift from ten to eight hours a day and cut my AA meetings to once a week.

After five months, Carla popped the question. "Why don't we live together?"

Yikes! I took a deep breath. "I don't know if I'm ready."

"Why not?" Carla sounded stunned. "I love you and I want to live with you. I've waited all my life to find someone like you—a gorgeous woman who is comfortable with her own lesbianism. This commuter relationship is getting old. I'm tired of stopping at your apartment every time you need to change clothes. I think it's time we made a commitment. Besides, think of the money we'd save."

Carla had a point. My apartment had become a place where I showered or grabbed a bite to eat; my African violets died months ago. Still, part of me wasn't ready to take the big step. For years, I'd lived alone. What if it didn't work out?

I hedged. "I need some time to think about it. I've never lived with a lover before."

"Fine." She threw up her hands. "Take all the time you want. Just remember, most people spend all their lives looking for the kind of relationship we have. What we have doesn't come along every day." She stormed out of the room.

For the next thirty minutes, I sat in her living room and tried to sort out my feelings. When the heavens didn't open with the answer, I called out, "I'm going back to my apartment. Call you tomorrow, okay?"

Carla stood in the hallway between the kitchen and the bedroom while I collected my clothes. Her eyes looked puffy as if she had been crying. I didn't know whether to kiss her on my way out or not. Finally, after an awkward silence, I kissed her.

Carla acted like a puppy that'd been beaten—uncertain, but hopeful. "Think about it, okay?" she whispered.

When I called the next day, she seemed distant. "Still thinking about it?" She didn't bother to hide her sarcasm.

221

"It's not that easy."

"What's not easy? The fact that I love you? Or the fact that the only way our relationship will grow is if we live together. Don't you see? We have it all—a loving relationship and great sex. What more do you want?"

I couldn't articulate my feelings. I felt as if I were drowning in a swamp of confusion, uncertainty, and plain old fear. "Please, I need more time."

"I thought we had something special—something that would last. Maybe I was wrong." She played her "hurt puppy" card again.

"I don't want to stop seeing you. I hoped we could see a movie today."

"I'm sorry, but I've got plans this afternoon. Why don't you call next week?"

Oh God. "Whatever you want."

"No," she said coolly, "it's whatever you want." She hung up the phone.

Women!

Unaccustomed to free weekend afternoons, I switched on the TV while I perused my mail. A talking head announced, "Suzanne Lindstrom, Assistant District Attorney, who was instrumental in the conviction of Buddy Sanderson on charges of assault and battery, is now tapped to prosecute Mr. Sanderson for the murder of his wife. The murder occurred two days after Mr. Sanderson was released from prison. Details at five."

I dropped my mail and stared at the TV. If I hadn't known her from years before, I wouldn't have recognized her now. Suzanne Lindstrom, aka Sunshine Lindstrom, wore her hair to the top of her collar, swept confidently over one ear. Instead of her androgynous, utilitarian wardrobe, she wore an expensive gray suit. Somehow over the inter-

222

vening years she'd managed to get her degree and go to law school. What happened? I spent the rest of the afternoon madly flipping between channels to get the news about Sunshine.

The following Tuesday, I called Carla and hoped two days was enough to make her heart grow fonder. "Would you like to go out to dinner tonight?" As I was the one to walk out, I figured I should make the opening move.

"I'd love to. Of course, you realize this doesn't commit either one of us to anything beyond dinner."

"Of course." I didn't like her sarcasm, but I understood it. Deep down, under her graduate degrees and sophisticated exterior, she felt as overwhelmed by forces beyond her control as anyone.

Carla seemed cool when I picked her up, but after several minutes our conversation regained its former familiarity. We continued to see each other over the next month— movies, dinners, a birthday party for one of her friends. I felt relieved to be with her once again, caught up in the mundane activities of life. She stayed away from the topic of me moving in, probably to keep us both from getting upset.

Rather than feeling relieved by our time out, I felt more distressed. At home, I sat glued to the TV and obsessed over every detail I could find about the Buddy Sanderson case. Bouncing between Carla and the latest news about Sunshine made me crazy. When my work began to suffer, I knew I had to make a decision. Sunshine has moved on. You need to, too.

I showed up at Carla's door with a bouquet of red roses on the night we were supposed to see a movie.

"What are these for?" She looked surprised.

"Why don't you read the card?" My heart was in my throat.

223

She opened the envelope and read aloud, "Roses are red, violets are blue, are you still interested in me living with you?" She threw her arms around my neck and cried. "Oh Bunny, I love you. I promise, you won't regret this." She dragged me into the house, through the kitchen, and into her bedroom, where we ravished each other all night in celebration.

The following morning, Carla came up with an idea for moving that would save both of us a lot of grief: "Let's hire a mover and I'll call some friends to help. We'll make a pizza party out of it."

A month-and-a-half later, I stood waist-deep in boxes in Carla's, now our, home. With the help of Michael, Marla and Corinne, and Jessie and Val, we were done by noon. After the last box was unloaded, we collapsed on the patio to stuff our faces with pizza.

"Congratulations," Michael said. "I hope it all goes well."

"I'm sure it will." I gave Michael my biggest smile. I quashed a faint but persistent voice that repeated, Don't do this, don't do this, don't do this, don't do this. I wasn't about to let cold feet ruin a perfectly good relationship.

When everyone had gone, Carla turned to me. "Why doesn't Michael like me? Doesn't he think I'm good enough for you?"

I hated being Michael and Carla's go-between. I always ended up stretching the truth so neither one of them felt betrayed. "He's like my protective older brother. He doesn't want to see me get hurt."

"Get hurt? How could you possibly get hurt? Doesn't he know I'm madly in love with you?" Carla looked bewildered.

I pulled her to me and kissed her. "Oh, he knows all right. Remember, it's what I think that's important, and I want to be here." Don't do this, don't do this, don't do this, don't do this.

We quickly settled into the lesbian equivalent of marriage. During our "honeymoon," our first six-months of co-habitation, I encouraged Carla to work on her weaving, a passion that consumed her. Interestingly, it was when she was absorbed in warp and woof, color and texture that I loved her most. She lost all track of time and sometimes spent an entire day setting up her loom or choosing a palette of fibers. She even entered some of her pieces in local art shows, with strict instructions for me not to tell any of her friends. Her public persona, that hip and trendy therapist who always showed up at the right events disappeared, and the artist she fought so hard to suppress, blossomed. Our sex life even regained some of its former passion when Carla turned her considerable concentration on me.

At work, there was talk of contracts for a government-sponsored communications network. A complex network was already in place but needed an easier interface. Government contracts equaled bread and butter for many companies and my bosses wanted to hop on the bandwagon. There was even talk of a possible spin-off for commercial enterprises, but nobody put much stock in that idea. Due to my renewed dedication, I was promoted to Team Leader. While Carla spent hours bent over her loom, I studied possible configurations between remote locations. Soon I was consumed with details of networking, file transfer protocols, and interfacing government agencies with incompatible systems.

One Saturday afternoon, Carla poked her head in my office. "That settles it. I'm booking our cruise."

"Great. When?" Deep in the middle of a string of code, I didn't look up.

"Tomorrow if I could. God! You've become obsessed with that computer stuff!"

"I like what I do," I said defensively. "Just look at this," I motioned to the monitor. "I've been working on this for three days and it finally works!"

She let out a long sigh.

Two months later, we walked up the gangplank with several hundred other women primed for fun and sun. Once we settled into our cabin, Carla suggested we take a stroll around the ship. "Would you wear that new swimsuit I bought you?" She ran her eyes up and down my body.

"It's a little skimpy, don't you think? I thought I'd wear it around the pool."

"Don't be a party pooper. We're here to have fun. Besides, I want to see that gorgeous body of yours." She handed me the Lycra swimsuit that left little to the imagination. "Well, put it on."

I pulled on the swimsuit and looked in the mirror. Yikes! One cough would send my boobs spilling out for all to enjoy, and it rode dangerously up my ass. "I'll put some shorts on. I don't want to get kicked off the ship before we've left the dock."

Carla wrinkled her nose. "If you must."

I rummaged through my suitcase until I found a pair of chino shorts that would lend some semblance of dignity.

Our stroll along the Promenade Deck caused heads to turn. "I should've worn a sweater. This is embarrassing." I headed for the staircase that led to our room.

"For godsakes, Bunny, we're here to get some sun. Just relax." Carla smiled and nodded to the other passengers as we made our way into the bowels of the ship.

"If we wanted sun, we could've stayed at home." I unlocked the door to our cabin.

Carla sat on the bed. "Why are you so uptight? You used to get paid for modeling a lot less than what you're wearing now."

How could I explain? "It was different then—I was different." I stopped, not sure if I should continue. "When I was young, I liked ... no, I loved showing off my body. I thought my body was me."

Carla looked confused. "And now you don't think your body is you?"

This is not working. "I'm more than my body. Writing code gives me more personal satisfaction than modeling ever did. My looks are nice, but they're not who I am."

A frown creased her brow. "Only you who can speak from the vantage of former model can afford that piece of enlightenment. The rest of us are always trying to measure up—are we good-looking enough? Are we good enough?"

I had a sinking feeling that had nothing to do with the ship. Carla didn't have a clue about who I was.

In the morning, we hit every on-board activity with a vengeance—shuffleboard, darts, movies, until the afternoon when we sunned by the pool.

"Sweetheart, would you get me some ice water?" Carla held out her glass.

"Sure." I stood up and arranged my swimsuit so my cheeks wouldn't show. I felt the eyes of half of the passengers and all of the crew on me as I walked to the bar.

"Thanks, darling." She smiled lasciviously at me when I handed her the ice water. "Nice ass," she whispered loud enough for everyone within ten feet to hear.

I settled back onto the chaise lounge and hid behind a trashy lesbian novel so I wouldn't have to make eye contact with anyone, male or female, whose hormones I just kicked up.

"Did you know Bunny used to be a model?" she said to a woman on her right who wore sunglasses.

"Really?" A blush spread from the woman's cheeks into her neck. "How nice for both of you."

This is getting old. I'd noticed Ms. Sunglasses the first day by the pool. She gawked at me every time I walked past. On the second day, she chose a lounge chair across from us and today she planted herself next to Carla.

"Will you rub some suntan lotion on me?" Carla handed me the bottle.

I sat up and slathered lotion over Carla. Ms. Sunglasses turned her head slightly to watch. I got the distinct impression that the suntan lotion was a ruse to make Ms. Sunglasses envious.

"Thank you, darling." Carla gave me a big, theatrical kiss.

I was more than ready for this cruise to be over. Besides feeling overexposed, I wondered how Sunshine and the Sanderson trial was going. On the fourth day, I dressed as casually as I could: baggy shorts, oversized T-shirt, and flip-flops.

"Great. You look like a refugee from a thrift store." Carla scowled.

"Just tryin' to be comfortable. That's what vacations are for." I slathered some lotion over myself and curled up with a crossword puzzle. I hoped she wouldn't notice I'd given up socializing on this cruise. I desperately needed a vacation from our vacation.

The last day, I pretended to have a headache. I spent all day in our cabin, packing while Carla said her goodbyes and exchanged addresses and phone numbers with several new friends. Ms. Sunglasses was not one of the chosen few.

"Damn! Coming home is the hardest part." Carla made piles of whites and colored clothes for the laundry. "I'm ready to go again."

"Where do you want to go next year? Rena and Nicole live in New Orleans. They said we could stay with them," I offered.

"We're not putting our lives on hold 'til next year. We're going to start seeing more of our friends." She shut the suitcases and handed them to me. "In fact," Carla grabbed her Day Planner, "I'm going to call Marla and Corrine right now to see if we can all go to Big Bear next weekend."

"I thought you had an art show you wanted to enter next weekend."

Carla shook her head. "I'm through with art shows. While we were on the cruise, I realized that I'd dropped everything for my weaving. Well, I'm not winning anything and I miss our friends. I'm a people person. I'll never make it as a weaver."

I felt deflated at her announcement. "I think you're making a big mistake. Your weaving is good. It's much better than a lot of pieces that win."

"Well, obviously the judges disagree. And you know what? As long as my weaving isn't in style, I might as well pack it in." Carla punched Marla and Corinne's number into the keypad.

I retreated to the living room and flipped on the TV, hoping to catch up on the Sanderson case. After months of wrangling, legal procedures, and extensions of deadlines, the case was about to come to trial. The media, never missing an opportunity to sensationalize a sordid story, lionized Suzanne as the defender of the American Way, as she got her turn at bat to, once and for, all bring justice to the City of Angels. Buddy Sanderson was charged with first-degree murder. A conviction would mean the death penalty.

Carla sat next to me on the couch, brimming with good vibes. "We're set for next weekend. Corinne will ride with us on Friday and Marla will join us Saturday." She frowned at the TV. "What are you watching?"

I tried to sound as casual as possible. "It's the Sanderson

case—you know, the guy who killed his wife. It's coming to trial."

"Bastard." She stood up and kissed me. "I gotta go make some phone calls."

"Sure." I settled back into the couch and wore out the remote, looking for more news about Sunshine.

A month after the cruise, our on-board passions had cooled. As promised, Carla ditched her weaving and over-scheduled our weekends to make up for lost time. I tried to arrange my work to accommodate our newly energized social life, but deadlines prevented me from attending every event she wanted to schedule.

"I'm sorry, but I've got to get this report done this week-end." I looked over the stack of documents I needed to review before Monday and wondered how I'd get everything done even without attending Pam's party.

Carla pouted. "I'm not going without you. People will think we're having problems."

You worry too much about what other people think. "Look—I promise next week we'll take a three-day weekend—drive to Mammoth on Friday, come back on Sunday—rekindle the flame." I gave her my sexiest look.

"Promise?"

I smiled. "Promise."

"Great! I'll call Toni and Adrienne and see if they can join us." Carla hopped off the couch and made a beeline for the phone.

Not what I had in mind, but if it makes her happy, I'm happy. I turned back to my computer.

Often I stayed up after Carla went to bed—to catch the "Late Night Show" I told her. Letterman was funny, but he couldn't hold a candle to Sunshine. I watched in secret, in horror, as Suzanne Lindstrom grew thinner and thinner over the course of the trial. When interviewed, she answered smarmy questions briskly and efficiently, disarming some interviewers and dodging the bullets of others. I wondered how "Suzanne" felt about this whole mess, or if that sensitive woman I'd known as Sunshine had completely disappeared. "Suzanne" now argued as vociferously for the death penalty as Sunshine used to argue against it. My heart ached for her. Where was the Sunshine I used to know? But when I looked in the mirror, the Bunny I knew from Franklin's of Beverly Hills had almost ceased to exist.

One night, while I watched the eleven o'clock news, I looked up to see Carla leaning against the wall, watching me. "You gotta thing for that prosecutor, Suzanne Lindstrom?" she teased.

"Of course not." My voice was too loud.

"She's kind of pushy, if you ask me. But I guess that's what they want in a prosecutor."

"Yeah." I could feel the blood rush to my face.

Carla turned on her heel and left without a word.

Over the next three months, our relationship ran down like a windup toy that sputters to an inglorious end. Acutely aware of our situation, we tackled our problem several times, trying to avert disaster.

"I've made a commitment to this relationship, and I'm not about to leave." I took Carla's hands in mine and tried to comfort her.

Carla looked up, tears staining her cheeks. "I love you so much. You are so much a part of me."

I kissed her. "I think it's time we reconnect." I pulled her up from the couch and led her to our bedroom, where we made tender love that night.

Our lives drifted on—work, frantic weekends, an occasional candlelight dinner. We finally hit that spot which is

231

anathema yet familiar to so many couples—the lesbian deathbed. We lived together like roommates. Why? Inertia. Neither of us wanted to terminate our passionless, yet comfortable life. As long as I didn't have to go to every party we were invited to, I could be pleasant when we did go out. Life, after all, is a series of trade-offs.

An air of electricity surrounded Carla as she walked through the door. She crossed the room and pulled me up from the couch, whereupon she kissed me like we hadn't kissed in months.

"Guess what?" she asked, her eyes aglow.

"What?"

"We just got an invitation to the party of the summer."

"Really? Whose?"

"Geneva Briggs is fêting her girlfriend, Suzanne Lindstrom, for the conviction of Buddy Sanderson. You remember that cute prosecutor in the case, don't you?"

I felt as if I'd been invited to my father's funeral. "Yeah, but I'd rather not go, if you don't mind."

Carla looked at me sharply. "I do mind, as a matter of fact. What's the matter, aren't you feeling well?" She circled me with her arms and smoothed my hair. "It's really important that we go, sweetheart. There will to be so many people I haven't seen in years. And you could wear that new dress you've been saving." She traced her finger down my neck.

"No."

She frowned. "Don't tell me 'No'! You're my partner. I want you there. Jesus, Bunny, everyone who's anyone will be there—the lesbian legal community, the Lesbian News, all the people from the battered women's shelters and domestic violence movement. We have to go!"

In the end, we went to the party. I didn't want to fight her over this, or over anything. Carla wanted to wear me on her arm like some diamond tennis bracelet. After two years, I still wasn't a real person to her.

"Can we take your car?" Carla was pumped for this party, having agonized for two weeks over what to wear and how she was going to do her hair.

This was the real Carla, the Carla I desperately tried to make into my own image of good-hearted therapist who did her best to help people. It wasn't Graduate School that turned her into a conniving social climber; those instincts were there from the beginning. She'd latched onto me when I was wallowing in self-doubt. I set her apart from her friends—Carla with the trophy girlfriend. I was sick of it.

"Yeah, sure." I had major nasty thoughts about her motives, like her Camry wasn't cool enough for this gig, better take the Beemer. Instantly I regretted that thought. Give the woman the benefit of the doubt.

Carla came up behind me and ran her hands down my sides while she watched us in the mirror.

"I'm so lucky to have you." She nuzzled my neck.

I stood there and said nothing.

"You look dynamite in that dress, you know. Every woman in the place will want to take you home."

Every woman except one. I broke free from her grasp and handed her the keys to the Beemer. "Let's get this over with."

Carla talked non-stop as she drove to the party. Talking was her major strategy in life—she talked 'til someone listened, she talked 'til she got her way, she talked 'til she wore the poor sucker down.

Too wrapped up in my own dread, I heard only ten percent of what she said. Maybe if there were enough people at the

233

party, I could disappear into the crowd and not run into Suzanne. Plan B was to give her my hearty congratulations with the same kind of on-camera aplomb that Suzanne exhibited when interviewed. I could do it.

"Where are we going?" I asked when we exited miles before our destination.

"There's a carwash here. I don't want the hottest couple in LA showing up in a dirty car."

Who is this woman sitting next to me? My spirits sank lower.

Carla talked for the next twenty minutes until we reached the San Gabriel Country Club. Sitting like a castle in the foothills, it radiated old-money charm, from its twelve-foot walls to its famous manicured lawns and gardens. The parking lot was full and I could see hundreds of women inside. Maybe Plan A would work.

I excused myself and went to the bar to get a scotch and soda for Carla and a diet something for myself. Carla was right: every A-list Southern California lesbian was here. I smiled and chatted with old friends and acquaintances without ever once engaging my brain. I had been to enough business meetings that masqueraded as social events to know networking when I saw it.

Carla linked her elbow through mine. "C'mon, there's someone I'd like you to meet." We walked through the Grand Ballroom, out the doors, and into the gardens, where a large group of women were congregated.

Like Moses at the Red Sea, we walked straight into the crowd that parted magically at our presence. Suddenly I was standing face to face with Geneva Briggs and the love of her life, Suzanne Lindstrom.

"Geneva!"

"Carla!"

They threw their arms around each other and hugged. Finally, Carla broke away and said, "Geneva, I want you to meet Bunny LaRue, ex-Franklin's of Beverly Hills model and my partner."

I could tell Geneva liked what she saw. She extended her hand. "Bunny, it's a pleasure to meet you." She turned and circled Suzanne's waist with her arm, pulling her close. "Carla and Bunny, I want you to meet Suzanne Lindstrom, woman of the hour and my partner."

We locked eyes. The blood pounding in my ears drowned out the noise of the party. Suzanne was dressed in a rose-colored rayon shirt and tasteful slacks that so many dykes wear when they're trying to look casually elegant. She was thin and pale, but worse than that, there seemed to be no trace of the woman I once knew.

"Hi," she said weakly, holding out her hand.

With tears in my eyes, I let myself shake her hand, holding on for an instant too long. She knew then, without a doubt, that I still longed for her. All the mental preparation was for nothing.

"Congratulations," I managed to say softly.

Suzanne pulled her hand away and avoided my eyes.

"Carla and I were in graduate school together," Geneva explained to Suzanne.

I missed the rest of the conversation. It took every ounce of strength I had not to bolt from the garden. Suzanne looked vulnerable and sad and undone.

"Excuse me," I said, pulling Carla along. "It's been a pleasure meeting you." My heart was breaking and I had to get away from Geneva and Suzanne, the current reigning lesbian legal royalty, before I fell to pieces.

Carla was livid. "Jesus, Bunny, couldn't you be a little less rude?"

At that point, my world stopped making sense.

"Can you get a ride home, Carla? I'm leaving."

"What? Are you crazy? You're not leaving." Carla grabbed me by the wrist and held tight.

"Give me the keys," I demanded.

"If I didn't know you, I'd say you're drunk. No! I'm not going to give you the keys."

"Have it your way. I'm leaving." I broke free from her grasp and walked into the Grand Ballroom. The bartender said the pay phones were behind the atrium off the lobby. I made two calls.

Within minutes, a cab pulled up to the entrance.

"14720 South Highland, please," I said as I climbed in.

"Encino? Off Ventura?"

"That's the place."

"It'll cost 'ya." He looked up into the rearview mirror.

"Drive."

Thirty-five minutes later, I arrived in Encino, where Michael waited outside his door. "What's the matter?" He took one look at my face and hustled me inside. "You look like hell! Tell bro Michael all about it, sweetheart."

I collapsed on the couch in tears. "I just saw Sunshine, Michael. She looked lost and lonely and afraid. And I couldn't do anything. We just stared at each other. God, I wanted to die!"

Michael cradled me in his arms while I cried for what seemed like an hour. He didn't say anything, he just held me.

When I regained a tiny part of myself, I let go another barrage. "So who do I turn to? You! God, Michael, it's so unfair. You're always rescuing me. I bet you had someone over and I ruined all your plans."

"Stop!" he commanded, holding me at arm's length. "You're my family. Of course I'll rescue your sexy ass."

I blushed. "Thanks, Michael."

He pulled me close once more. "What's Carla think about this?"

"I'm leaving Carla. She doesn't know it yet, though. Today I saw the side of her I don't like, which is all of her."

Michael laughed. "Thank you, God! I never could see what you saw in her. She paraded you around like a prize poodle."

"I've missed you so much." We hugged. "I need to find an apartment. Know of any?"

He handed me a tissue. "Let me ask around. In the meantime, do you want to crash here?"

"If that's all right with you and Ray."

"Yeah, it's okay."

The phone rang around eleven the next morning.

"Hello, Carla. Bunny? No, she's not here. Call me when you find her, okay?" Michael hung up the receiver.

I looked up from the Apartment For Rent ads. "Thank you."

"I didn't think you wanted to talk to her. Did you?"

"No. God, no." Although I knew what I was going to do, telling Carla was one detail I hadn't quite figured out.

Michael, Ray, and I watched taped episodes of *One Life To Live* until the doorbell rang, about three.

Ray answered the door. "Bunny? No, I'm afraid she's not here."

"Goddamn it, I know she's here!" Carla pushed past Ray and stormed into the kitchen where we were sitting.

"Carla, good to see you," Michael offered.

"Shut up, Michael!" She turned to me. "What the hell is this all about? You don't come home all night and I'm worried sick that you're lying in the gutter somewhere ..."

"I don't drink anymore." This was still true.

"... dead or worse! Jeez, Bunny, you coulda called! What's wrong with you lately?"

"Carla, it's over between us."

"What?" She looked stunned, like I had knocked the wind out of her.

"I'll leave you two lovebirds alone." Michael tiptoed out of the room.

She sat heavily in the chair. "What do you mean, 'It's over'? Look, I know we haven't been communicating the best lately, and maybe our lives have started drifting apart, but, darling, I love you!" Carla reached for my hands.

I pulled them off the table. "Carla, I don't love you. Sometimes I wonder if I even like you. We can't go on—there's nothing between us anymore. I'm getting my own place. I'm starting over."

Tears welled in her eyes and spilled over her cheeks. It was the first real emotion she'd shown in months. "Bunny, please, you can't ..." she began. "I admit it. I like to show you off. I feel important when I have you next to me."

"You're not important when I'm not next to you?"

"You make me feel whole, like I belong. Like I've arrived."

I couldn't believe what she was saying. "You're whole when you make yourself whole. Your sense of self-worth can't rise and fall on me." Which one of us was the therapist here? I sounded like Ella. When did that happen?

"Please," she begged. "Let's go to couples counseling. I don't want to lose you. Please, Bunny, let's try it again. We can date. We'll start over—take that trip to New Orleans."

"No." Letting her grovel and prolong this scene made it worse and I wanted no part of that. Hard as it was, it was cleaner and quicker than those mindfuck break up–make up–break up games people played. "You need to go." I escorted her to the front door.

"Can I call you?" she asked, hopefully.

"No. Good-bye." I closed the door behind her and slid to the floor, sobbing.

Michael looked at me, amazed. "I didn't think you had it in you."

"I can't play these games anymore. I'm tired of being Carla's, no, anyone's pretty girlfriend. I refuse to be with anyone who can't see beyond what I look like. Comprende?"

Michael nodded. "Comprendo." He smoothed my hair. "When you feel better, we'll go get your car, okay?"

Chapter 16

Hold Me Now

Lost again. Shit! I was no closer to finding what I wanted than when I quit drinking. Now what? I untangled the mass of cables and connectors from a box marked "computer junk." Despite the huge empty feeling in my personal life that alternately whipped me from rage to despair, I reassembled my computer. Computers were no longer my job but my "passion," as Ella would have called it. My employer loved the hours I poured into work. Often I would come in at 9 a.m. and not leave until after 10 p.m. My job was the one stable thing I had left.

Four months into my workaholic schedule, the phone rang one night after 11:30. "Bunny, it's Ray."

My hands turned cold. "What is it? What's wrong?" I heard my voice go up an octave.

"Michael's in the VA hospital with pneumonia." There was a tremor in his voice.

Oh God, no! "When can I see him?" My knuckles turned white on the receiver.

"Visiting hours are from six to eight every night." He sobbed into the phone before collecting himself. "He was doing fine until today. He got up, said he didn't feel well ... couldn't go into work. I took the day off ... had to make sure he was okay." Ray sounded like he was drowning. "I called for an aide car when his fever hit 102. God, Bunny, I'm going crazy!"

"Do you want me to come over?" Although I was collapsing on the inside, I knew I had to pull myself together in order to help.

"It's okay. Some of our friends are here." Ray sounded slightly more in control. "I know he'd love to see you at the hospital."

"I'll be there tomorrow." After I hung up the phone, I collapsed on the couch. This was never supposed to happen. Michael was a fighter. He'd stopped going to bars two years ago when he'd found out he was HIV positive and altered his life so he could work out at the gym and eat all things macrobiotic. He even meditated twice a day, envisioning his body rid of the HIV virus. I clung to the fantasy that he would be the exception, the first man to beat this deadly disease. How could he get sick?

"I'm Michael Sena's sister," I announced to the nurse on duty, the first night I visited.

She gave me a quick glance. "Blond hair, fair skin. His sister. Right." She scribbled something on her chart.

"We had different fathers." There was no way Ms. Officious would keep me from seeing him. I'd tell everyone I was his wife, if necessary.

"Room 303. You'll be happy to see all of your brothers. There's a family reunion going on in there." She nodded her head down the hall, then turned back to her chart.

"Thanks." I expected to see Michael hooked up to IV drips and monitors, the doctors huddled in consultation as they reviewed his chart. My heart was in my throat when I stood outside his room.

Michael sat propped up on pillows, wearing a cheesy

241

tiara, black silk dressing gown, and Groucho Marx glasses—
fuzzy eyebrows and fake nose attached to black plastic
frames. It took a second before I realized that everyone in
the room—Ray, and Sean, a longtime friend of Michael's, all
sported the same glasses. Michael was the king of his
domain, his squires in fawning attendance. "Bunny, come
in." He waved me to his bedside. "We're having a party.
Here, put these on."

"I should've guessed. You've never looked better, handsome." I gave him a kiss on his recently shaved cheek. This
was the Michael I knew and loved, the ex-Marine with a wide
streak of outrageous; the man who knew dying needn't be a
somber affair.

"Thank you, dahling. These ..." Michael was about to say
more, but started to cough, a long, painful series of gut-
wrenching hacks punctuated by shallow gasps for air.

I turned away. I didn't want him to see me cry.

After what seemed like an eternity, his coughs subsided.
"Ohhh, the indignity of it all," he said in a feigned British
accent.

"You need to rest." Ray sat on the bed and wiped
Michael's forehead with a wet washcloth.

"I'm not ready to die yet." Michael sucked in a ragged
breath. "We're here ... to celebrate ... my recent ... recovery ...
from an unfortunate ... bout of pneumonia." He looked
unsettled. "It's too damn ... quiet in here. Would someone ...
please turn on ... the stereo?" Michael coughed for another
minute.

"I made some tapes of your favorite music," Ray offered.
"Anyone care to party?" He looked around at the rest of us.

I nodded.

The tension in the air evaporated when Donna Summer's
"Love To Love You Baby" started to play. Michael sank

farther into his pillows, his exhausted body still struggling for air.

Our party was subdued, quiet conversations about who was doing what, Michael's prognosis for recovery, the latest trends in AIDS research. Michael would rally for several minutes and become the life of the party, only to relapse into another bout of hacking coughs.

Our evening ended too quickly when the nurse came in at 8:15 and told everyone to leave. "He needs his rest. You can see him tomorrow."

"Wait." Michael raised his head from his pillow. "Would you take ... a picture of us?" he said to the nurse.

"Sure." She laid her chart on the nightstand.

Ray produced a camera from Michael's bag and handed it to her.

"Everyone ... put on your glasses. This is ... how I ... want to remember tonight." Michael raised the bed to a sitting position.

Ray sat next to Michael while Sean and I stood around the bed, our Groucho Marx glasses in place.

"Say 'Homosexualitee'," Michael said.

"Homosexualitee," we chimed.

The nurse snapped the picture.

After his discharge, I called Michael every night. It was apparent to anyone who knew him that much of his fire was gone. After two weeks recuperation at home, he went back to work four hours a day, and gradually increased his schedule to six hours.

Fortunately for me, he was not about to stop interfering with my life. "Would you go out and see someone, for Godsakes? Quit waiting for me to die. I'm sure there are some women left out there who'd love to go out with you."

"What happens if you get sick?"

"If I get sick, Ray will call. In the meantime, you're missing out on life. Get out there and meet some women. When's the last time you got laid, anyway?"

Only too well did I know that I hadn't been with any woman in months. In my twenties, I would have seen that as my sexual death knell. Now I looked at dating almost as a chore. "Okay, I'll go out. But remember, I'm only doing this to please you."

Michael laughed with the same gusto I remembered from years before. "Life's a bitch, sweetheart."

Reluctantly, I took Michael's advice and hit the single woman circuit again. Dating sober versus dating when I was drinking seemed so restrained by comparison—no sly glances or raised eyebrows to show interest, no leap to light her cigarette or offer to buy her drinks. No one wanted to jump into anything, commit, then feel the disappointment and embarrassment of having moved too soon. Wiser and warier, we were products of our checkered pasts. Was it just me or did our age and experience make us leery of anything resembling passion? On more than one of my dates, I felt as though we were comparing résumés—intellectual musings on the viability of a proposed union, socially appropriate but no emotional connection. We were bombarded with messages of safe sex—how to, where to, who to. Didn't anyone fuck anymore?

Over the course of many months, I dated a number of artists, office workers, and teachers, plus a couple Goddesses of the Olympic Pantheon. The Goddesses turned out to be my most interesting dates.

Athena was visiting a friend in the same ward where Michael was recovering from another bout of pneumonia. In her Army uniform, she exuded an air of competency and coolness. For three nights, we cruised each other in the hall until we "accidentally" bumped into each other at the coffee machine.

"I couldn't help but notice that you're visiting a friend here," she said, sipping her coffee.

"Yeah. Michael's getting discharged tomorrow." I dropped my change into the machine and punched the buttons.

She frowned. "That's too bad. Not that's he's getting discharged, I mean," she added quickly. "I mean it's a shame for us to meet and not have the opportunity to get to know each other better." She smiled, the embarrassment of her comment coloring her cheeks.

"So what are you doing this weekend?" I volunteered.

"I don't know, but I think it's something with you." She smiled a conqueror's smile.

That Saturday, I narrowly averted World War III. Athena's sense of decorum was offended by the tacky and frivolous entertainment at the local street fair I suggested we visit. That was Tactical Error I on my part. Tactical Error II was when I ordered the vegetarian lasagna for lunch.

"I didn't know you were a vegetarian," she said, nibbling on a kabob.

"I'm not. I don't eat a lot of meat, though." That said, I figured we'd move on to the next topic of conversation.

"They're wrong, you know. It's a scientific fact that you can't get the right kind of protein eating rice and bean sprouts."

"I know lots of vegetarians and they seem to be doing fine." That was Tactical Error III—never disagree with anything she said. Athena expected everyone to take her word as Gospel on all subjects—she was right, end of discussion. I think it stemmed from her childhood as the only child of a career military man who commanded bases all over the world. Yes, Sir! Without a son to follow in his footsteps, General Daddy poured all of his aspirations into Athena, and good artillery commander that she'd always dreamed of being, she obeyed every order to the point of graduating from the War College. Athena never heard a word I said. She preferred to enlighten me with her worldview, which was 90° to the right of Genghis Khan's. Just for fun, I made the briefest mention of Trotskyites (I had no idea who they were; it was a term I heard in my Sunshine days) and watched her go from overbearing to ballistic in seven seconds. We never saw each other again.

Month after month, I watched Michael grow thinner, his life slowly ebbing away. He was with us in spirit—his stories of previous lovers left me laughing so hard I cried; but his body would not repair. He had good nights and an increasing number of bad nights. In and out of the hospital, he barely had time to recuperate from his last illness before another overtook him. When his hospital stays grew longer, I realized with dismay that I'd visited him so often I knew where all the good parking spots were.

I took the elevator to the fourth floor. The nurses at the station smiled when I walked by.

"He's doing better today," Troy, the stocky nurse said. "He'll be glad to see you." I scanned the frontline of the medical unit workers, dedicated men and women who worked tirelessly for their ill patients. I wondered how they did it, day after day, death after death.

Ray sat on a chair next to Michael's bed. "Here's a card from your work: 'We're all pulling for you.'" He held up the card for Michael to see. "Ted writes, 'Get back here soon. I can't stand working with that bitch Denise.' Look, he drew a face with a tongue sticking out." He pointed to the cartoon face.

"Hi, loverboy." I gave Michael a kiss on the top of his head.

Michael worked his mouth but made no sound. He tried to lift his right hand, but it fell back to the bed like a stone. "Let's see who your cards are from." I picked up a veritable bouquet of brightly colored cards from his nightstand. Lovers from years gone by wrote sentiments like "You'll always have the biggest piece of my heart," "Get well soon," and "Get out of bed, you slacker!" A collage of photos covered a large piece of purple construction paper—Michael and Ray at the beach; Michael and a group of his friends dressed in tuxes at an AIDS fundraiser; Michael astride Ray's Harley Davidson Night Train dressed in black leather with the caption "You go, girl!" written underneath. Near the bottom of the collage was the photo from over a year ago—Michael, Sean, Ray, and I in our Groucho Marx glasses, smiling like idiots. Tears came to my eyes as I saw how drastically Michael had aged over the life of the collage—from handsome HIV positive man to his present emaciated state—Karposi Sarcoma covering his face, an IV drip attached to his left arm, his body all but shriveled up. But it was Bruno, Michael's teddy bear—that threadbare, eyeless travesty of a stuffed animal dressed in a white satin evening gown—which made me catch my breath. Michael's arm was draped around Bruno, his oldest friend, faithful to the end.

"Bunny," Michael called faintly.

"Hi, sweetheart. How's it going?" I held his hand.

"Your hair," he said softly.

I brushed back my new hairdo I'd gotten only hours before. Tired of years of long, straight hair that hung irregularly down my back, I had it trimmed so it was all one length. I was thrilled that Michael in his semi-conscious state noticed it.

247

"You look like Hillary Clinton." He closed his eyes.

Hillary Clinton? Before I could reply, Troy, the nurse walked in, carrying a small plastic cup that contained a clear liquid.

"Time for your meds." Troy raised the bed to a sitting position so Michael could sip the liquid. Michael coughed and sputtered, a sound that made Ray and me wince.

Troy stood by impassively until Michael's coughing fit subsided. "No more schnapps for you, Mister. If you can't hold your liquor, you're outta here." He jerked his thumb toward the door.

I pulled my chair close to his bed. "You know, bro, I think Clinton will win in November. Just think, the end of twelve years of Republican rule. Do you realize that a whole generation of kids have gone through school without ever having a Democrat in the White House?"

Michael blinked.

I chattered on and off for two hours while Ray slipped out to get dinner. What Michael heard, I don't know, but when he closed his eyes, I shut up and held his hand.

Looking back, I realized Michael's periods of sleep or unconsciousness had grown longer as the weeks wore on. Over the last year, Michael had been in the hospital eight times, four of them in the last three months. Minute by minute, he was slipping away from us.

At 8 p.m., another nurse came in and changed Michael's IV bag. "Time to go," she urged.

I stood up reluctantly and gave him a kiss. "Sleep well, loverboy. I'll see you tomorrow."

Ray tucked the covers around Michael's sleeping form, then leaned over and kissed him. As he was about to leave, he turned, pulled the covers back, and tucked Bruno next to Michael.

At the elevator, I caught my reflection in a glass panel—red suit, matching pumps, and perfectly coiffed blond hair. He's right. I do look like Hillary Clinton. I made a mental note to give my suit to the local women's shelter and let my hair grow again.

"We won." I produced a Clinton/Gore campaign button from my purse and pinned it to Michael's pajamas.

Michael opened his eyes and smiled weakly at me. "Thank God."

I was elated; Michael hadn't spoken in two days. Ray gave me a high-five, as much in celebration of Michael's words as Clinton's victory. One battle was over, the war yet to be won.

"You can rest easy now. We've got a sympathetic ear in the White House." I held Michael's hand that felt cold and clammy. His other arm was wrapped around Bruno, who now sported a red AIDS ribbon pinned to his white satin evening gown. Michael dozed off, his breathing interrupted by frequent bouts of wheezing and coughing.

I met Artemis on a blind date at a local club, where we celebrated Clinton's victory. She lived on a twelve-acre farm, surrounded by chickens, ducks, cows, dogs, cats, and God only knows what else in Shasta, California. Artemis was the original back-to-earth dyke: jeans, Birks, and flannel shirts, and she drove an '83-4WD Subaru wagon. A midwife by trade, she much preferred her rural lifestyle to the bright lights of LA. Two things stood out about Artemis: she had boobs to rival Dolly Parton's and she could dance. When Artemis took to the dance floor, it seemed like the laws of physics were temporarily suspended. She danced like a maniac or a whirling dervish and infected every woman in the club with some magical tribal power. That magic drew me to her. By the end of the evening, every woman in the club moved to the same ancient rhythms. After dancing five hours straight, we stopped at a late-night eatery to recharge our batteries.

I rubbed my eyes to stay awake. "God, you make me want to pull up stakes and head for Northern California."

Artemis shook her head and smiled. "Trust me, you'd hate farm life."

"How do you know? I can see us getting up, feeding the chickens, me waving to you as you drive off to deliver a baby."

"And what would you be doing at home?" She sipped her coffee.

"I don't know—throwing pots or something."

"There's no cable TV and the only 'art' video at the local video store is Old Yeller. The rest are action films or porn flicks." She shook her head.

"I know, but it's fun to dream."

Artemis mumbled something under her breath that sounded like, "That's what they all say."

She left the following day after bedding down on my couch. "My neighbors are taking care of the animals, so I gotta get back. Besides, I wanna see if Miss Priss has delivered her kittens yet."

How could I compete against Old MacDonald's farm and Miss Priss? I gave Artemis a hug and a kiss on the cheek. "Drop in the next time you're in LA and we'll go dancing."

"Sure." Her eyes twinkled at the mention of dancing.

I reached into my purse to give her my card, but when I turned to hand it to her, she was gone.

♦♦♦

The phone rang one morning as I was about to walk out the door. I picked up the receiver to hear Ray screaming: "The bastards kicked me out! They won't even let me see him!"

"What are you talking about? The hospital kicked you out?" Ray's voice had a murderous edge to it. "Not the hospital. Michael's brother, that prick Larry. The family took me off the list of people allowed to see him. They blacklisted Sean and everyone close to him."

"You've got to be kidding," I said, although I knew Ray was dead serious.

"They said I had no right to see him. Jesus! Where were they when he first got sick? Where were they when I had to change his sheets every night? Where were they when I had to take off time from work to get him to his doctors' appointments? It's so fucking unfair!"

In the back of my mind, I knew the family of origin could come in and throw their biological weight around, but I'd naively thought it wouldn't happen in Michael's case. "Look. I'll go to the hospital and see what's going on. As soon as I find out anything, I'll call you."

"Thanks, Bunny. I'd appreciate it." Ray sounded minutely more in control. "Fucking bastards," he muttered as he hung up the phone.

I made a call to work to let them know I'd be late. As I drove to the hospital, I wondered if I was on a fool's mission. Would Larry bar me from seeing Michael, too? After all, I was just as queer as Ray or Sean.

Over the years, Michael had not grown any closer to his family. He made an obligatory appearance for a few hours every Christmas but otherwise lived his life far from the scrutiny of his bio family. "I don't care how sophisticated they think they've become. They still couldn't handle it," was all he ever said on the topic.

The fact that his family of origin could arbitrarily cut off his family of choice made me crazy. I charged into Michael's room, expecting a knockdown, drag-out fight.

Larry, whom I'd met years before at a July 4th celebration, sat in a chair near Michael's bed, reading the paper. "Hi, you're Bunny, aren't you?"

I glared at Larry. "I want to speak to you outside."

Larry folded his paper and followed me into the hall.

"Ray told me what happened. You can't keep everyone from seeing Michael! They're his friends!" I knew I was shouting.

Larry's eyes narrowed. "They're the goddamned fairies who gave him this disease. And if you're any kind of friend, you'll tell those fucking, disease-ridden queers to stay away."

"Please," I begged. "They've seen him through so much. He needs them."

"Our family made a decision." His tone was flat, final. Larry took a deep breath. "Dr. Conrad said it won't be much longer anyway. It'll be a relief."

For whom? When I saw Michael the day before, he still fought for life, using every treatment known—AZT, massage, mega vitamins. His body, that once beautiful body, lay wasting away at the mercy of the life support systems that beeped and cycled with an artificial rhythm designed to imitate life.

I felt defeated. "Look, I just came to check on Michael before I went to work."

"Well, come on in." Larry led the way back to Michael's room.

I glanced around, suddenly feeling like I was in the wrong room. Everything familiar about Michael was gone. Gone was the collage made by Ray and Sean. On the bedside table where cards and flowers used to arrive daily sat a tall candle with Jesus looking mournfully up at the ceiling, his head crowned with thorns. And something else was missing. "Where's Bruno?"

Larry rolled his eyes. "We pitched it. That thing needed to be burned."

You asshole. You just want him to die! My mind reeled from the steep slope Michael's new arrangements presented—a fast slide into oblivion. There didn't seem to be any more I could do. I gave an unresponsive Michael a kiss on the top of his head and hoped he wasn't aware of the war that centered on him. "Would you at least reconsider your decision?"

Larry shook his head. "Not a chance." He picked up his paper and settled back into his chair. "Thanks for coming, Bunny. I hope you'll come again."

I backed out of the room and ran down the corridor to the nurse's station, where I grabbed Michael's doctor by the sleeve. "They can't really do this, can they? Keep away all of Michael's friends?"

Dr. Conrad looked grim. "Yes. They can. However, contrary to VA policy, I've taken him off antibiotics and AZT, put him on palliative care and a morphine drip. But I didn't tell you that," he added.

"Isn't there anything I can do?"

"Not officially." Dr. Conrad maintained a poker face.

I knew an opening when I heard it. "Come get some coffee with me." I slid my arm through the doctor's and dragged him into the vending machine room.

"So how do we go about this 'unofficially'?"

Dr. Conrad wiped his hand over his face in an expression of either frustration or exhaustion. "The night shift comes on at 11 p.m. I'll leave word for Laurel, the head nurse, to expect you. You bring his friends in after midnight. But you have to make it soon."

Omigod. I knew what he hinted at, but I wanted the facts. "Tell me," I pleaded.

Dr. Conrad looked down at the table. "Michael doesn't have much longer. His weight is under a hundred pounds. There's not enough of him left to fight back. Any time, his body could shut down."

I knew if I dwelled on what Dr. Conrad said I'd collapse. I had to keep moving. "I'll call you this afternoon and tell you when we'll be here."

Dr. Conrad squeezed my hand. "Good."

"He slipped into unconsciousness tonight," Laurel informed us when we arrived that night.

The beads of perspiration stood out on Ray's forehead. "Are we too late?"

She shook her head. "No. Not at all. Just don't expect a response when you talk to him."

We filed silently into the room, like a pack of scared rabbits. Michael lay on his back, a morphine drip attached to his right arm, his eyes closed. His wasted form gave almost no shape to the sheets.

Ray's face was pale. "Can he hear us?"

Laurel pushed Sean up to the bed. "Some people think that the sense of hearing is the last to go. Go ahead," she urged. "Talk to him."

Sean twirled his baseball cap in hands, nervously. "Michael ..." He turned away from the bed. "I can't," he cried.

Ray took the lead. "Hi, honeybuns." He stroked Michael's hand. "Bunny and Sean are here. We came to say we love you." Tears streaked his cheeks. "You're the best, the absolute best. You're the greatest lover and the best friend I've ever had."

Ray swallowed hard. "The petunias you planted outside the front door look great. I'm doin' my best to keep them watered, but god knows you're the one with the green thumb. I know," he continued, "I'm just rambling. But I want you to know that I love you and I'll miss you when you're gone." A small, strangled noise escaped from his throat. "Whenever you need to go, you do it, okay? Don't let anyone push you around. This is your time." Ray let go of Michael's hand and bawled like a baby.

Sean produced a handkerchief and blew his nose. He took a deep breath. "Michael, it's Sean. I just wanted to say 'thank you' for everything. You were always there for me, made sure I had a place to stay when Brian and I broke up, lent me your car when I totaled mine. God ..." he wiped his eyes, "remember when you and I were the 'Disco Divas'? You wore that white feather boa and I came dressed as Bette Midler."

We all laughed as tears ran down our cheeks.

"We've been through a lot together. I just wanted to say, I love you, Michael." Sean put his head on Michael's chest and cried softly.

A sudden tightening in my throat made it impossible to speak. I didn't want to say goodbye. I wanted to pretend that Michael would hang in there another week, another month, another year until they found a cure. Troy said Michael had stopped eating a week ago, so I knew he wouldn't last much longer. I cleared my throat. "Hey, handsome." I leaned down and brushed his face with my hand. It felt waxy. "You're the best brother I never had." My tears dripped onto the sheet. "We did a lot of growing up together—the drinking, the drugs, the sobriety. You made me feel that my life was worth something when I hit bottom. You're the only man I've ever loved, except my dad, of course." What kind of stupid shit is that? "I mean, I love you bro!" I broke down and sobbed. Ray put his arm around my shoulder.

Michael gave no indication that he heard any of our confessions. Gradually, our tears dried and we stood silently around him. For an hour, we watched Michael, each of us immersed in our own thoughts.

"Are you ready?" Laurel finally asked.

Sean nodded.

"Wait." Ray took off his Saint Christopher's medal and hung it around Michael's neck. "Godspeed, Michael." He kissed Michael's cheek.

We filed out of his room, exhausted, tears springing from an endless supply.

"You all did great," Laurel counseled. "I think he knows that you love him. Thanks for coming." She hugged us one by one.

In that intimate space, we felt more connected as a family than all the biological/legal mumbo jumbo the State of California could confer.

Ray turned to me when we got to my car. "Thanks for arranging this, Bunny. Keep us posted, okay?" He wrapped his arms around me and buried his face in my shoulder, the tears streaming down his cheeks.

I nodded. I couldn't speak.

The phone rang insistently as I stepped out of the shower the next morning. I glanced at the clock: 6:57 a.m. With a prickling sense of dread, I picked up the receiver. "Hello?"

"Is this Bunny LaRue?" a man's voice asked.

"Yes."

"This is Larry Sena." He paused. "I'm sorry to say, Michael died at three this morning."

My world stopped at that moment. Although I knew it was coming, his death still was a shock.

Larry continued. "We're having a small funeral on Saturday at Holy Family Church in South Pasadena. Will you come?"

I mumbled my agreement and took down the address of the church.

I didn't go into work that day. Finally I got the courage to call Ray and told him the news. He broke down over the phone, but thanked me for calling. Tears came sporadically, followed by long periods of sitting and staring at the wall. My world revolved around one immutable fact: Michael was dead.

Three days later, I stood on the steps of Holy Family Catholic Church and wondered what to do next. No one I knew was there: not Ray, nor Sean, nor any of the multitude of Michael's friends.

Larry approached me and held out his hand. "Hi, Bunny. Thanks for coming." He escorted me down the aisle to sit in the third row with people who, I supposed, were Michael's extended family. The men eyed me appreciatively; the women, suspiciously. They were an odd mix of traditional old Catholic women dressed in mourning black and their offspring—well dressed, middle-class men and women of Michael's generation.

"Where are all of Michael's friends?" I asked in a whisper.

Larry looked down. "They weren't invited. It wouldn't have looked good."

"Except me?" I was flabbergasted.

"Michael loved you," Larry said uneasily.

My knees gave out and I sat heavily on the pew. Of course! You're Michael's best woman friend—the others were just fags.

One of the women turned and smiled at me.

"He loved all of them," I shot back.

"But you were more like family." Larry pulled at his collar, as beads of sweat formed on his brow.

Family! Their idea of family means blood relative, not those you love and live with.

Michael's short, round Mama, escorted down the aisle by her son Thomas, stopped at the aisle where I sat. "Ai, Madre de Dios!" She took my face in her hands. "Why didn't you marry my son?"

I could see tears streaming down her face under her veil.

The next few hours were the most unreal moments of my life: Michael was a straight boy and I was the woman he should have married. Twenty odd years of being gay, countless male lovers, cause of death AIDS, and still his family pretended he was a happy-go-lucky het who'd never found the right woman. I covered my face with my hands and sobbed, not only for myself or Ray or Sean, but for the funny, gentle, charming man they never knew.

The priest droned on about the Prodigal Son, loaves and fishes, and the glory of God. The only fact he got right was that Michael was a Vietnam vet. Everyone crossed themselves a few dozen times, said the "Hail Mary," then solemnly nodded when the priest mentioned that Michael wished to be remembered with gifts to some Catholic charity. In life, Michael was the most vibrant man I ever knew, but his funeral was a travesty, a cruel joke perpetrated by a Church that denied his very essence. I wondered if anyone in the church noticed that the man whom the priest eulogized never existed.

I desperately wanted to awaken from this nightmare, call Michael, and hear him laugh and carry on about the latest hunk he'd just scored, but the darkness of the service extinguished the last piece of light I carried within. I felt bereft.

258

Michael's mother's words flooded back into my memory: "Chicanos don't have queers."

After the funeral, I drove aimlessly through the back streets of LA. I'm on the edge now. I drove to the first bar I saw, The Valencia Bar and Grille, which might as well have been named "The Last Chance Saloon." It was set back on a small strip mall between a pawnshop and a carpet wholesaler with the word "Cervezas" blazing in garish pink neon above the entrance.

I sat in the parking lot and pondered the meaning of it all. Why Michael? Why me? Jesus Fucking Christ! Where did it all go wrong?

A young mestizo woman eyed me warily from her car two parking places over.

Michael's death still wasn't real to me. The trappings, unfortunately, were very real—the Church, the casket, the flowers, Michael's hysterical mother, and the closet-case priest whose God was as sexless as he was—but Michael dead?

One couple came out of the bar, exchanged something with the young woman in the car, then climbed into their truck and drove off. The woman got out of her car, gave me a dirty look, then disappeared into the bar.

Where did AIDS come from? God's wrath poured out on so many sodomites? An infectious disease that our government swept under the carpet because it singled out gay people? How did anyone cope? Every AIDS victim stripped of their future, wasting away from one horrible opportunistic infection or another—Karposi Sarcoma, Pneumocystis carinii pneumonia, cryptococcus meningitis, idiopathic thrombocytopenic purpura, the list went on and on. No matter how exotic the name, it all added up to one thing— death. Hadn't I been through enough? Hadn't I lost enough people that I loved—Sunshine, Ella, and now Michael? I felt tears burn my eyes. Where was this loving, all-knowing God when everything I had ever loved was wrenched away from me? I put my head down on the steering wheel and cried for everything I had ever lost.

"Are you okay?" A short Hispanic man with tattoos covering his arms knocked at my window, concern written all over his face. The young woman from the car stood outside the entrance to the bar, her arms folded across her chest.

I wiped my face with the back of my hand. "My brother just died."

"Lo siento, I'm sorry. If I can do anything, I'll be in there." He pointed to the bar, then walked inside with the young woman.

The world was dark, deeper, and darker than I had ever known. Getting drunk would only deepen the darkness. I remembered something else Michael once said, "Life is for living and for the living." Some minutes later, I wiped my face, turned my car around, and headed home.

Chapter 17

Constant Craving

During the months I grieved for Michael, I became a robot—a sexless, passionless body that moved silently through each day. I was beyond searching for the meaning of life; I searched for a reason to get out of bed in the morning. Until he was gone, I had no idea how dependent on Michael I was. He never pulled his punches, like the time he reamed me about not writing or calling Ella when I still had the time to do it. On some days, he was my best boyfriend. On other days, he was my best girlfriend. But right now, my best friend was dead and my life felt meaningless.

Val, ever the optimist, called me weekly to entice me back to the land of the living. "I have a friend named Lois. She's an ex-nun who teaches math at one of the alternative high schools."

"Thanks, but I'm not interested."

Val persisted. "She's not anything like Carla."

I sighed. "How did you know that Carla and I wouldn't make it?"

"Carla needs a high-profile girlfriend, or her life isn't complete. She dated a doctor for a while, then one of the attorneys you met at Marla and Corrine's. You're the third client I know of that Carla dated, but you were her biggest trophy. Carla wants the best, as long as it fits with her notion of respectability. I hear she refused to date a wealthy heiress from Atlanta because the woman looked too dyke-y. You were too independent for Carla."

I laughed until I nearly choked: I knew the woman Carla snubbed.

"Hey, you wanna go canoeing with Jessie and me this weekend?" Val used her former cheerleader voice to pump me up.

"Thanks, but I don't feel like socializing. Another time?" I couldn't keep putting Val and Jessie off forever, but I knew the grayness that enveloped me wouldn't dissolve after a couple hours on a lake.

"Then let's go out to dinner next week, okay?"

"Sure." God bless Val and Jessie, they were there for me even when I felt like The Bitch Of The Universe.

I still needed time, time to put my life together, time to grieve for Michael, time to rediscover what life was for. But regardless of how devastated I felt about Michael's death, the bills still had to be paid. I threw myself into my work again. While our product was whiz-bang amazing to some users, I had lost all interest in it. One deadline met, we marched toward the next seven on the horizon—death by adrenaline-laced tedium.

The one thing that did pique my curiousity, however, was the possible commercial aspect of the Internet. It seemed like anyone with half a brain and a 486 computer could surf the web. But my employer didn't see any future in it and I didn't have the physical or emotional energy to pursue it, so I let it drop.

On one of my infrequent appearances at my home meeting one Friday night, I ran into Renee.

After the meeting, she brought me up to date on her work.

"My boss really wants to get into this Internet thing. Do you know of anyone who could make a webpage for Enchanted Gardens? Nothing elaborate, just something simple."

"Yeah. I could."

"Really?" Renee stared at me in disbelief. I thought you did ..." she faltered, "other stuff."

"Code is code. Why don't I come over tomorrow and see what he wants?"

I had a hunch I could make better websites than ninety percent of what was already online. Geeks with bad haircuts who wore plastic pocket protectors and hadn't had a date in ten years cranked them out left and right. They wrote dry copy sans serif, threw in the company logo and snail mail address—finito. I knew what people wanted was colorful pictures and fun links along with their copy—eye candy for the cyber-challenged.

When I arrived at Enchanted Gardens, Renee gave me a quick tour of the nursery. All of those blooming plants, succulents, planter boxes, and bags of peat moss brought back memories of my childhood in Marysville. Unfortunately, none of the LaRue gardening genes passed down to me, so I had to content myself with being an appreciative onlooker—forever a putterer, never a Master Gardener.

Renee gave me four-dozen color photos of penstemon, zinnias, lavender, columbine, three-leaf sumac, a butterfly bush, and my favorite, dianthus. "Here." Renee handed me a brand new copy of the Sunset New Western Garden Book. "You'll probably need this."

I piled into my car with the pictures and my new book and drove home. Between the copy, the pictures, and making sure the links worked, I'd have their website finished in four hours, five hours tops.

The longer I worked on the page, the less satisfied I felt. Their page was on-line at 10:30 p.m. It sat there like an arrangement of silk flowers—moderately attractive but lifeless. By 11:00 p.m., I had changed the fonts twice and still something was missing. What? Unfortunately, this was the page they wanted. At 10 a.m. tomorrow, I'd show them the finished product, collect my money, and be outta there. The clock read 11:22 p.m. Why worry about it any more?

Because you can do better, that's why.

"Shit!" I got up, plugged in the coffeemaker, and sat back down at the computer. I needed a break from Enchanted Gardens and decided to go online to see what other people had put up. After an hour of surfing, two things struck me: it was the commercial aspect of the internet, not the government applications, where the action soon would be. The web was like a huge, blank billboard on which you could advertise anything—flowers, boats, houses, antiques, restaurants, widgets, and photography. Especially photography.

And with my knowledge of writing code, I was in the perfect place to exploit this coming trend.

Sorting through the photographs again, I decided on a bolder approach—more flowers and more color. Now I knew exactly what to make—a virtual garden in which, by clicking on the photos, you'd get growing requirements for each plant. This website would be for all the gardeners like myself, a place where Mr. and Mrs. Blackthumb could learn when to plant, in shade or sun, and how much to water. I grabbed the gardening book and started to work. All kinds of Dianthus thrive in full sun, and in light, fast-draining soil. Zinnias—distinctly hot-weather plants, they do not gain from being planted early. Butterfly Bush—all have some charm, either of flower color or fragrance; sun or light shade, average water.

By 4:11 a.m., everything was in place. I hit Ctrl + S. Nothing happened.

"Don't do this to me!"

My heart was in my throat when I hit Ctrl + S again. Nothing. I hit "Escape." My computer was frozen solid and I had no backup copy.

"Goddamn it!"

Don't waste any more of your time on this. Go to bed. Take them the page they agreed to.

The clock read 4:27 a.m.

"One more time," I said through gritted teeth. I got up, drained the last of the coffee, and started a new pot. When my computer still remained frozen after running all of the diagnostic programs I knew, I shut it down and rebooted. I began again: All kinds of Dianthus thrive in full sun, and in light, fast-draining soil ...

At 5:50 a.m,, I got up and poured myself another cup of coffee. A faint pink glow filled the eastern sky, softly illuminating the Circle K on the corner. Already the street below was filled with early-bird commuters on their way to work. The pink glow gave way to a white light and soon security lights up and down the street blinked out. I turned back to the computer. I'd have just enough time to finish their page, shower, change, and drive to Enchanted Gardens.

"How does it look?" Renee asked anxiously as we walked through the perennials.

"Great. I changed a few things, but I think it looks better."

Renee looked panic stricken. "I put my reputation on the line for you. If you screwed it up, my boss won't pay for it."

Renee was always panicked about something—whether it was her girlfriend of seven years, who she was sure was getting a little on the side; or her house was located right on top of a major fault line; or according to her horoscope, she should have been a brain surgeon.

She stopped abruptly before we entered her boss's office. "It'd better be good."

I sat at the computer and connected to the Web. As we waited for the page to load, her boss walked in.

"Hmmmm," he said, extending his hand, "you don't look like a computer geek. Nolan Hansen. Pleased to meet you." A big bear of a man dressed in overalls and a tie-dyed T-shirt, his graying hair pulled back in a ponytail, he looked like an aging hippie from the 60s. Nolan sat down at the computer and watched the page load. "Wow! This is great!" He and Renee stared at the monitor as the pictures appeared.

I liked Nolan—he radiated good vibes. I could imagine customers walking in, getting greeted by this Deadhead, and knowing right away he could grow anything, legal or otherwise. "Now, click on any of the plants and see what happens."

Nolan clicked on the lavender. Lavandula—All need full sun; loose, fast-draining soil. Little water or fertilizer. "All right! This is cool!"

Renee stared at the screen while Nolan navigated through the pictures and descriptions. She cleared her throat. "Uhhhhh, this isn't exactly what we discussed. I think it's a little overdone." Neo-Luddite that she was, Renee liked to press for smaller and simpler. If it were up to her, microwave ovens wouldn't have turntables.

"This is perfect!" Nolan enthused. "It'll blow the competition right out of the water,"

"Isn't this a little expensive?" Renee wrung her hands. Nolan turned to me. "So what's the damage?"

I took a deep breath. "Here's the deal. I charge you the

same for this page as the other, smaller page. In exchange, I put my name on the bottom as the designer."

"Deal!" Nolan turned back to the monitor and clicked through the links. "Who do I make the check out to?"

"Uhhhhhhhh ..." I didn't have a name for the company, it was just me. Quickly I tried out a couple names in my head. "Future Sites"—sounded like a housing development. "Bunny's Very Kewl Websites"—get real. "Multimedia Ventures"—nice, but distant and corporate. Outside his office, a Bougainvillea in full bloom framed the office door. The pink blooms reminded me of the sky over the Circle K a few hours before. "Sunrise Productions," I said.

"Great. Renee, make out the check to Sunrise Productions." Nolan turned back to his computer screen and clicked on the links like a kid with a new toy.

Three months later, Sunrise Productions had more work than I could handle. Even working weekends, I was behind. I had eight active projects and a backlog of twenty-three emails from companies who begged me to design websites for them, four of which fronted me big bucks to put their projects at the top of the waiting list. Without one iota of remorse, I walked into my day job and gave them a week's notice. There was no turning back.

As a business owner, I needed to look at how to best use what I had, perhaps hire a production person and a part-time bookkeeper. I called Jessie and asked for advice.

Jessie sat back in her chair after she looked at my books. "This is quite an operation. Once we straighten out your cash flow, you'll be in good shape. You've got lots of deductions you're not taking right now, but we can fix that. You're awfully cramped here. Why don't you rent a bigger space? Get some new furniture. And lease a car. Get the car you've always wanted. I don't care how much it costs. When you get tired of it, turn it in and get another. It'll belong to the business and you can write off a good portion of it."

My heart fluttered. "Any car?"

"Yeah." She smiled wickedly. "I can't wait."

An autophile herself, Jessie knew too well my relationship with cars. When she brought home a champagne-colored Jaguar XJS with a rust-colored convertible top, Val flipped and demanded she take it back. After several heated arguments, they compromised on a four-wheel drive SUV that intimidated every other car on the road.

I took the afternoon off and went car shopping.

My love affair with cars, the bane and boon of modern civilization, bloomed again now that my livelihood didn't depend upon them. Any car? A white Mercedes 560 SL with a midnight blue convertible top? My budget couldn't take a hit like that. A sporty Toyota 4Runner for weekend getaways in the mountains? Who was I kidding? There's no way I wanted to go four-wheeling around Mammoth, muckin' in the dirt. Corvette? Why drive a muscle car for stop-and-go driving? I test drove a Chrysler Sebring, Mitsubishi Diamante, Toyota Avalon, and, just for fun, a red 1964 Thunderbird with a white convertible top I found advertised in the Auto Trader. They were lovely and elegant, especially the Thunderbird, but they all lacked some indefinable quality.

My watch read 6:49 p.m. If I didn't find something soon, I'd turn around and go home. On a whim, I pulled into an Acura dealership in Covina. I parked in the visitor's lot and walked past rows of Integras and Legends. A lone red coupé sat in the middle of dark green, blue, silver, and white Legends. V6, 3.2 liter engine, alloy wheels, moon roof, CD player, 6 speed, leather interior—it was love at first sight.

A man, whom I judged to be in his early thirties, approached me. "Looking for a zippy little toy to drive to your aerobics classes?" He offered me his card. "My name is Bill Foster. I can make you a great deal on this car."

Act dumb, sucker him in, then negotiate hard. "Can I take it out for a test drive?"

"Sure." Bill produced the keys from his pocket. "Will your husband be joining us?" He held the driver's door open for me.

I stifled a laugh. "No. He's visiting his mistress tonight."

Bill wisely kept his mouth shut.

Just for fun, I popped the clutch and the car practically jumped out of the parking lot.

"This baby's got a lot of pickup, once you get used to the clutch." Bill wiped his forehead, then fastened his shoulder harness.

We cruised down South Citrus to I-10, screamed down the freeway to Pacific Avenue, meandered up to Baldwin Park, then tested the brakes with stop-and-go driving until we returned to the lot. Yahoo! It drove as good as it looked.

At 7:47, the Bill escorted me into his office. The dealership closed its doors at 8 p.m. By 9:15, the sales manager had taken two phone calls from either his wife or his girlfriend, who demanded to know when he would be home. Bill, frazzled by the dealings, sat tieless on the sidelines and watched the sales manager and I go at it.

By 9:50, I was the proud new lessee of a red 1994 Acura Legend LS Coupe, with a monthly payment of $150.00 less than their first offer. They threw in the floor mats for free.

"It's a steal," Yvonne, my friendly lesbian realtor gushed.

"You're right. $226,000.00 seems like highway robbery to me."

"It's classic 1930s construction. With a little TLC, you could have this place looking like something out of Architectural Digest." Yvonne waved her arm like Vanna White as she pointed to the coved ceilings.

"At this point, I'd settle for something out of the Quik Quarter." I'd been house-hunting for five months and this was the most promising place I'd seen. Thank God, I'd listened to Sunshine and Elizabeth so I had enough money saved to make a substantial down payment on whatever I bought. Tired of apartment living, I decided to take the plunge and establish myself once and for all in my own house, where the length of my stay wasn't subject to the whims of my current girlfriend. Not that I had a girlfriend at this point. In fact, I hadn't had anything even resembling a semi-serious date in well over a year. Voted "Most Likely To Get Laid" in high school, here I was at age forty-three, immersed in my work with no love interest in sight. It was easier this way, no one to look after, no staying up 'til three in the morning to talk things through. Like Queen Elizabeth, I was mistress of my domain, the Virgin Queen. "236 is too much. Offer 195."

Yvonne's eyes glowed as she punched the keypad on her cell phone. "I'll get back to you."

Forty-seven days later, I was the proud owner of an eleven hundred square foot bungalow in the middle of West Hollywood. After a lengthy inspection, I found that structurally the house was sound, but the last time anyone put any money into it was the sixties. My first project was to rip out the orange shag carpet in the small bedroom and get my office up and running. That done, I tackled the cosmetic projects—landscaping, new window coverings, new paint—before embarking on the biggest project of all: remodeling the kitchen. I couldn't walk through it without shuddering.

My utility knife yielded a new wall covering or coat of paint for each decade: genuine stained glass window contact paper, then white paint, pinkish flesh, peach, beige, and the original yellow. Its latest incarnation was mottled gray/green sponge paint, meant to accentuate the avocado appliances. I parked my microwave on the counter, put my dishes on three shelves, and avoided that room whenever possible.

On the positive side, I could say that I had arrived. Finally. Bunny LaRue, former Franklin's of Beverly Hills model, clean and sober, a successful entrepreneur, and now, homeowner. Yet despite all the money and effort I poured into it, the house stubbornly refused to become my home. It was a left-brained house, all lines and angles, color coating and Zen-like simplicity. Yvonne was right. It was like something out of Architectural Digest. When the dust had settled, after the cabinets were installed, the plumbing redone, and the roof patched, I'd throw a housewarming party for all my friends. Maybe they'd bring presents, stuff to hang on the walls, potpourri, little gifties that would transform the place into a warm, livable space. At least, I hoped they would.

My party three months later was a huge success.

"God, Bunny, it's beautiful. You'd never guess you lived here," Jessie said, her mouth full of smoked salmon.

"Thanks." Jessie's unfortunate remark threw the whole affair into perfect perspective: I paid for it, I owned it, but it still wasn't mine. With the remodeling costs, the cleaning service that made the place look spic and span, plus the catered food, I'd spent slightly more than the gross national product of several third world countries on this soirée. For some reason, I expected the joys of home ownership to be more tangible.

Chapter 18

Layla

I think Val used to belong to "Up With People," those grinning, non-religious do-gooders who always felt compelled to cheer everyone up. That's the only explanation I could think of why she constantly pressured me to go out. My life was fine, a little subdued perhaps, and maybe I was working sixteen hours a day in order to keep Sunrise Productions afloat, and while I might not be ecstatically happy, I was far from a spinster schoolteacher whose idea of fun was matching wits with contestants on *Wheel Of Fortune*.

When Val dropped by the house, she insisted that I go to The Dinah. "For godsakes, Bunny, get outta the house! People think you died right after Michael did."

I shot Val a murderous glance.

"I'm sorry, but you know what I mean. Go. Maybe you'll meet some woman who will sweep you off your feet!"

"Yeah, right. Going by myself is not my idea of a good time. All the rooms are probably booked anyhow." Harrumphing was my best defense.

"The Dinah," a veritable Southern California institution, is the social high point for thousand of lesbians from all over the country. One of four LPGA Masters Tournaments, the Nabisco Dinah Shore is held every year at the Mission

Hills Country Club Golf Course in Rancho Mirage, California, and attracts the top women golfers from around the world, their hangers-on and wannabes. Imagine 25,000 lesbians trailing the pros from green to green, then crowding into 7000 hotel rooms at night. Happy hour began after the sun went down. Pool parties, backyard barbecues, wine and cheese parties, beer busts, and elegant dinners as well as four kick ass dance venues where women partied and played 'til the wee hours of the morning.

"I'm staying with five other people in a room designed for four, or I'd invite you to stay in our room. For all practical purposes, I'll be single that weekend."

"What about Jessie?"

"Are you kidding? It's tax season. She's working 78 hours a day. You and I could meet at the Tournament."

I didn't want to succumb that easily. "I've decided to become a curmudgeon and live alone the rest of my life."

"Yeah, right," she said sarcastically. "Bunny, you are too hormonally driven to live alone the rest of your life. Please," she winked suggestively at me, "isn't there any way you'll go?"

I knew her flirting was make-believe. She'd been with Jessie for eighteen years, an eternity by lesbian standards. "Well, there is a woman "

Her eyes lit up. "Yeah? Who?"

"Her name is Tess," I said slowly. "She said she'd be working at the dances both nights."

"Well, there you go!" Val was practically foaming at the mouth.

"I probably should go just to meet her. But I kinda doubt she's my type." My mind started clicking on the possibilities.

"Why not?"

"Tess is a twenty-three-year-old, baby-dyke, computer geek."

"Oh." Val looked deflated, then brightened. "Well, you're a computer geek. You might have something in common after all."

"I am not a computer geek!"

Val snickered. "And what do you mean, you haven't met her?"

"Not up close and personal, anyway." Maybe ...

"Then how ..."

"Like I said, she's a computer geek; a major hacker. She totally fucked up one of my webpages, changed the HTML, then left me a message that read, "Wait 'til you see what else I can do!" She signed it, 'Tess, the Trojan Queen.'"

"But how did she know you're gay? It's not like you advertise that on your websites."

"My guess is that she looked me up in the Valley Business Alliance—you know, the gay and lesbian chamber of commerce—and tracked me down from there."

"Oh."

I continued. "That was only the beginning. From then on, she'd go in and change every new page I was working on; add some clip art, rearrange the text, change the fonts, and sign it 'Tess, the Trojan Queen.' And all of it was password protected!"

The lines on Val's forehead deepened.

"Finally, she sent me an e-mail, asking if I liked her work and would I hire her. She told me she was working all week-end at the dances, and if I was going, to stop by and meet her."

Val looked alarmed. "At The Dinah? Why don't you meet her some place in town?"

"I don't know where she is."

274

"Where she is?" she said slowly.

"She uses different servers. I can't tell if she's my next door neighbor or if she lives in Arizona."

Val gave me a look usually reserved for babies who have urped on mommy's new dress. "You computer people are so weird!"

I hated to think that maybe Val was right.

Weaving through rows of parked cars, we could hear the incessant thump, thump, thump of the disco beat two blocks away. Up ahead we could see a network affiliate news van complete with satellite dish for a direct link.

I spotted Donna, an AA friend, packing a video camera for the network. "Hi, Donna! What's up?"

"Hey, Bunny. We're here to shoot some footage of the go-go girls at the dance."

"Go-go girls?" Val's face brightened in a lecherous grin.

Donna laughed. "Yeah. They're sending me to film it. Figured I wouldn't stand out from the rest of the crowd."

Indeed, she wouldn't. Other than the camera she was carrying, Donna looked like any one of the thousands of women here, her ponytail pulled through her network baseball cap, black tank top, khaki shorts, and sandals.

"Have fun!" Donna waved to us as we passed.

Every step brought us closer to the earsplitting music. We pushed our way through the crowds to the entrance.

"I'm looking for Tess Rinaldi! She's working here tonight!" I shouted at the ticket taker as she circled my wrist with a plastic entrance bracelet.

The ticket taker shrugged. "Don't know her. Ask Security."

The tidal wave of women pushed us into the foyer.

Val gripped my arm. "There's Security!"

A big dyke in a black and gray Security uniform talked into a two-way radio attached to the tab of her shirt.

"Can you tell me where I can find Tess Rinaldi? She's working here tonight!" I shouted.

"Go to Operations. Down the hall, on your left," she shouted back.

"Thanks!" Fearing that if we split up we'd never find each other again, I grabbed Val's hand and dragged her along.

The first door on the left opened to reveal the Operations Room. After I produced my ID and had a long talk with the security guard whose job was to safeguard the many thousands of dollars worth of telecommunications equipment, computers, and cables, she let me in. Several harried-looking staff members comprised Operations. I scanned the room, looking for what I imagined Tess to look like: a vaguely baby faced, slightly overweight girl with shoulder length, mousy brown hair, who wore large, plastic framed glasses. Young. Socially inept. Geek.

I approached a woman sitting at a computer. "Are you Tess Rinaldi?"

"Tess? No, not me!" She giggled. "I think she's out on the floor right now." She looked me up and down in one quick glance.

"How can I find her?"

"I'll take you out there. I gotta go relieve Shirley anyway," said another woman in a Security uniform.

I grabbed Val's hand again and pulled her toward the door. "Thanks."

"Another one looking for Tess." The woman at the computer smirked.

"Damn! That woman has all the luck!" her co-worker said to the computer woman. I assumed they were speaking about me.

We pushed into the sea of women, and sometimes blindly made our way through the seething crowd. Strobe lights blinked on and off, synchronized to the disco beat. The room seemed to have a life of its own.

Following the Security woman through the crowd was no easy task. It took several minutes to get to the dance floor, then longer to get on the dance floor, as we pushed our way into the cavernous room. Up ahead, I could see a bright light spotlighting some almost naked go-go girl. Donna had planted herself ten feet away from a young woman who danced for the camera on top of an eight-foot pedestal. The young woman's head was shaved, à la Sinead O'Connor, and she had multiple tattoos on her shoulder, breasts, arms, and legs. The video camera's spotlight glinted off the dancer's hardware: pierced nose ring, tongue, and belly button ring. She was the hippest, hottest thang The Dinah had to offer—sexy, edgy, and alluring. A crowd, several women deep, formed around the pedestal, their mouths hanging open.

The Security guard poked me in the arm. "There!"

"Where?" I asked, taking my eyes off the dancer for one second.

"There! Up there!" She pointed at the young woman dancing on the pedestal.

Oh my God! Still holding onto Val's hand, I stared at Tess Rinaldi, grrl techno-geek. *Well, LaRue, you wanted someone hip and totally now.*

Val squeezed my hand. "Nice employee ya got there, Bunny!" She laughed so hard tears ran down her face.

There was nothing to do but watch Tess dance. All eyes within fifty feet of the pedestal seemed glued to her. The title of a new TV show flashed through my mind: "Lesbians—The Next Generation."

"Never in a millions years would I do something like that!"

"Oh, puhleeze, Bunny! If you were her age, you'd be doing the same thing!" Val collapsed on me, laughing hysterically. She wiped her eyes. "I don't know whether I'd want to take her home and get her some new clothes, or take her home and fuck her!"

I started laughing. "Maybe take her home, get her some new clothes, then fuck her!"

Val and I held onto each other and watched Tess dance for the next fifteen minutes. Finally a slow song came on, and Tess climbed down from her pedestal.

The crowd mobbed her. She pushed her way through her admirers, some who stuffed tens and twenties in her g-string. I grabbed Val's hand and pushed through the crowd after her. When we caught up with her at the North exit, she stepped outside, where a dozen drooling women offered her a smoke.

"Hey! Don't bug the entertainer!" A security guard stepped between Tess and her admirers, shooing us all back inside.

I waved at Tess from the fringes. "Tess! It's me! Bunny LaRue!"

Tess looked up, the sweat glistening off her body. "Bunny! Yeah! C'mere!" She waved distractedly at me.

I gave the security guard my winningest smile. "I know her!"

"Yeah, yeah, everybody knows her." The security guard was not impressed.

"Hi, Bunny. Glad you could come." Tess offered her hand.

"You are one hell of a dancer, Tess!" God! I sounded like some breathless young woman with a schoolgirl crush.

"Yeah. Thanks." She took a long drag on her cigarette. "Hey! I was wondering, could I crash at your place tonight? Otherwise, I was going to sleep in a friend's car."

She can sleep on the couch, no big deal. "Uh, yeah, sure."

"Cool! Meetcha after the dance, say 2:10?"

"Yeah. Fine. See ya then!" I pushed my way back into the building.

"That was quick! So is she going to work for you?"

"I dunno. She asked me if she could crash at my place tonight. I said yes."

Val raised her eyebrow. "You're letting some baby dyke you don't even know spend the night with you?" Her quizzical expression was replaced by a more familiar, lecherous grin. "Or is it because she's so damn sexy and you haven't had any for a while, LaRue?"

"Oh, shut up! I'm doin' the kid a favor! If that's all right by Mother Superior Val." I stretched to my full height and looked down at her.

"A long while," Val muttered and walked back toward the dance floor.

At 2:10, Tess sat on a low brick planter box in front of the East Entrance with a butch little number in tow. She had changed into what I guessed was her usual attire: baggy jeans that rode dangerously low on her hips, no bra under a man's white undershirt, Doc Martens, and baseball cap turned backward. "Hi, Bunny! This is Cori, my girlfriend. You don't mind if she spends the night, too, do ya?"

Val clapped her hand over her mouth and turned away, her shoulders shaking with laughter.

"Uh, sure, that's fine. Let's go." I grabbed Val's hand and dragged her behind me once again.

We piled into my car and rearranged the backseat to accommodate my two new passengers and their duffle bags.

Val absentmindedly played with my hair on the drive to

her hotel. As she got out of the car, she turned to Tess and Cori. "Nice to meet both of you! Have fun!"

"I'll pick you up for breakfast at nine." Damn her! Val was enjoying this soap opera way too much for my comfort.

Tess disengaged herself from Cori and got into the front seat. Cori glared at me in the mirror from the backseat. "When do you want to get together and talk about my job?"

"I was hoping this weekend."

"Yeah, but I got a bunch of things I want to show you. Could we do it next week at your office?"

"Okay. Sure." I was tired and wanted to go to bed. At forty-four, I wasn't used to staying up 'til nearly 3:00 a.m. anymore.

As we walked toward my room, a mother-in-law cottage adjacent to a million-dollar house that belonged to one of my clients, Tess took me aside. "You're not going to hit on me, are you? I just hate it when you old dykes hit on me."

I stared at Tess, almost unable to comprehend what she said. This sexy young babe, brash, full of herself, the center of everyone's attention; God, how she reminded me of someone I knew years ago. "No. I'm not going to hit on you."

"Good." She seemed pleased. "C'mon Cori, hurry up!" Tess wrapped her arms around her girlfriend and gave her a kiss. "You Hot Mama! We've got some lovin' to do!" She ran her hands up and down Cori's sides.

It didn't take a rocket scientist to see where this was heading.

When we got to the cottage, I excused myself and undressed in the bathroom, making sure they had plenty of time to get under the covers. When I emerged, Tess and Cori were stacked like sardines on the living room couch, kissing, the bedspread half covering their naked bodies.

"Take the bedroom," I offered. "I insist." Let them have the bed, I just want to sleep!

"Thanks, Bunny." Those were the first two words Cori had spoken since we were introduced. Smiling, Cori kicked off the bedspread, stood up, and held her hand out to Tess. I gasped when I saw Cori's naked body, her toned muscles, her firm breasts, nipples erect. I was glad I'd brought my "Simpson's" sleep shirt to sleep in. My body was nowhere near the condition hers was in. I climbed onto the couch, covered myself with the bedspread, and rolled over to face the back of the couch. As soon as my head hit the pillow, I was gone.

I woke with a start to hear a woman screaming, "Yes! Yes! Yes!"

It was Tess. They've been up all night! How do they do it? I lay there awake for what seemed like forever, listening to their cries and moans through the bedroom door. You brought this on yourself, LaRue. As they gave no indication of stopping, or even slowing down, I pulled the bedspread over my head, hoping to muffle the sounds of their pleasure.

When I came to, the clock read 8:35 a.m. Tess and Cori were gone, along with their duffle bags. I was supposed to meet Val for breakfast in twenty-five minutes. Her hotel was fifteen minutes away, so I had ten minutes to shower and get dressed.

"Where are the kids?" Val asked brightly, when I walked into the lobby, twenty minutes late.

"I don't know. I'm not their mother!"

"A little testy this morning, aren't we? Kids keep you up all night?" Val didn't bother to conceal her amusement.

"They fucked all night long! I remember looking at my watch at 5:30. They were still going at it!"

Val burst out laughing. "Remember when we used to do

that? Work all day, party all night, then go home and fuck our brains out? Not with you, of course," she added.

"Awwww." I took her hand and kissed it. "You'll always be my first runner-up, Val," I teased. Val and our almost affair went back to our drinking days when we met at a Halloween party. Val came dressed as Princess Leia of Star Wars and I came dressed as Honey West. Val won first runner-up; I didn't even place. Val, Jessie, Sunshine, and I partied together off and on for the next couple of years until I moved to The City. With our long-standing history, the good, the bad, and the ugly, we had enough sense to know that our relationship would forever remain platonic.

"You look beat!" Val said over breakfast.

"I know. At least I could have gotten some of the bennies associated with looking this tired, but I didn't even get that!" I laughed. "You know, I'm going to watch the tournament, then drive home today. I can't handle another dance."

"Really?" Val looked surprised. "You know, I miss Jessie. Mind if I catch a ride home with you tonight?"

"Sure. That way, if I get tired, you can drive, okay?"

Val and I drove to the Mission Hills Country Club, where the tournament was in its third day. We joined the gallery of one of the golfers who stood at eight over par; not close enough to place in the money, but a good, well-liked player.

By the thirteenth hole, my butt was dragging. "I'm going into the Clubhouse to sit out the rest of today. You go ahead."

"Let's go now," Val urged.

"No. You keep watching. I'll sit in the lobby and watch the girls."

"Bunny, let's go home. Now!" She grabbed my hand and pulled me behind her.

Although it was 2:30 on Saturday afternoon, the I-10 was

bumper to bumper, guaranteeing a three-hour drive home at best.

"You drive." I handed Val my car keys. "I'm going to catch a few." I sat on the passenger side and tilted the seat back so I could stretch out.

"What about Tess and Cori? Did they leave you a note or anything?"

"Nah. I know Tess. She'll get a hold of me when she wants to." I settled into the seat and pulled a straw hat from the backseat over my eyes. According to Val, five minutes later I was in la-la land.

At 10:00 a.m. the following Tuesday, Tess walked in, carrying two twenty-ounce coffees and a paper bag that smelled of something deliciously decadent.

"Hi, Bunny. I figured you didn't have breakfast this morning, so I brought you some." She set the bag and coffees on the table.

How did she know? "Thanks, Tess." The bag yielded freshly baked pastries, that unbeatable combination of artery-clogging butter, bleached white flour, and white death sugar. I might die from this stuff, but what a way to go. I stuffed some of the still warm, cream cheese-filled danish into my mouth. "This is heavenly. Where'd you get this?"

"Cori made them. She's going to cooking school to become a chef."

"Really? Maybe I should hire her. I can't cook, but I can create webpages." I licked the sticky frosting off my fingers and took another bite.

Tess shrugged. "Hire me and you get us both. She loves to cook. She'll probably send enough lunch for both of us."

"Have a seat." I indicated my desk where my new computer sat.

She slid into my chair and looked over the All Saints AIDS Hospice page I was working on. "It's kinda boring. Why don't you add some rainbows? Better yet, how 'bout some angels? Angels are big right now."

Already I could tell that Tess would need some reigning in, or she'd put Lee Iaccoca in a grass skirt, inviting mainlanders to see Hawaii, or Newt Gingrich inviting everyone to "come on down" to the Atlanta Gay Pride Festival.

She opened files that had nothing to do with my work in progress. "You don't mind do you? I wanna see what you got."

I bit my tongue. "No." I wanted to watch her work, see exactly how much she knew. If necessary, I could restore the files after she left. Fifteen minutes later, Tess had finished reconfiguring my registry, reset my color, and given me her lecture on the necessity of antivirus software.

"You download files from some sites and you're guaranteed to get viruses with them."

"Yeah? Like where?" I'd run across an occasional virus from downloading files, but places guaranteed to come with viruses?

"Porn sites."

"Porn sites?"

"Yeah," she shrugged. "Hackers know guys go in and download X-rated pictures, so they attach their viruses to these pictures and poof! Their computers are toast."

"How do you know this? Never mind, I don't want to know." I sat back and munched another danish while Tess the Trojan Queen worked. Within minutes, I realized she wasn't good, she was a computer genius.

"Where did you learn all this?"

"My dad, mostly. He's owns one of the software companies in Silicon Valley, or at least he did two months ago. I hear some mega-corporation is trying to buy him out."

"Oh." Of course, that's where I knew the name. Hal Rinaldi, Tess's father, just signed a deal with a rival software company for a new language he'd written, rumored to be the Next Big Thing in cyberspace. And at my desk sat the heir apparent to this fortune.

"So how come you don't live at home?"

"Fuck!" Tess momentarily slumped in her chair, then sat back up. "Because my dad's an asshole." Her voice quivered. "He kicked me out when I was sixteen because, as he put it, 'Italians don't have queers. No fuckin' dyke is living under my roof.' " She shut her eyes to keep the tears that suddenly appeared from spilling onto her cheeks.

"What happened?"

"Everything was cool. I was Daddy's little girl until I was, I don't know, fourteen. You know, good grades, private schools, shit like that. My parents freaked when I told them I was gay. I mean, here they are, like major Republicans and their daughter is a fuckin' lesbo. He told me to get the hell outta the house when I brought my first girlfriend home. So I've been living on my own ever since."

I didn't know what to say.

"I lived with some older girls, one was eighteen and the other was twenty-one. They took care of me." She allowed the hint of a smile to cross her lips. "They taught me a lot."

Don't go there, Bunny. I nodded to the computer. "So, show me some of your stuff."

Tess took the bait and soon we were surfing some of the larger sites, discussing online databases, the latest encryption techniques, and the prospect of having Internet access in every home by 2000. After an hour, Tess began to fidget.

"If you need to smoke, go outside and do it."

Tess leapt up from her chair, grabbed her bag, and headed out the door.

"Those things'll kill ya," I called after her.

"Yeah, I know." The door slammed behind her.

Tess was more than adequate for the job. In fact, Tess would probably have more technical know-how than me in a year. At the rate new technologies and languages were coming online, there was no way I could keep on top of everything website design demanded. Conceivably, I could sell and design them and Tess could create them 24/7. Besides, who else would hire her? Tess was too innovative to work in a large, faceless corporation like I had worked for. All people would see would be a shaved, tattooed, in-your-face baby dyke, who hadn't yet acquired the necessary social skills to massage the most liberal customer. Relegated to data entry positions, mailroom runner, or Assistant to the Assistant, she'd be bored in a week, smoke dope on her lunch break, then tell her boss to go to hell. All of those brains wasted because no one could see beyond her looks.

I wanted to give Tess a chance to put her considerable talents to work, help her through those awkward years between nineteen and twenty-nine when want collided with reality, get her beyond the stage of reacting without a viable alternative in mind. I'd hire her if—and this was a big if—she'd go to school to get the necessary background in informational systems and writing whatever new code was up and coming.

Tess slid back into the chair, looking considerably more relaxed. She beat me to the punch. "So you gonna hire me, or what?"

You're hiring yourself a pain in the neck here. "You're hired on one condition. You're going to school to take classes so you know the network management side of the house as well as website production."

"Big fuckin' deal. I can do network stuff in my sleep," she bragged.

"I'll pay for your classes."

Her eyes widened. "Really? You'd do that for me?" She quickly tamed the excited little girl and slouched into her "I'm-too-cool" persona again. "Yeah. That'll work. When do I start?"

I looked at my watch. "You started at 10 this morning. Better get to work. We have eleven sites we're working on right now."

Something like a bolt of electricity shot through her. She sat straight up and took control of my computer. "What do you want me to work on first?"

"We're doing a site for 'LA Wings,' an air charter service that does sightseeing flights over Southern California. And when you get a minute, go online a find me a new computer. I can see I've lost mine."

Tess grinned broadly. "Sure thing, boss."

I sat behind Tess on a folding chair and drew up a plan: I'd go out during the day and get new accounts while Tess produced the pages I designed. At night, while Tess was in school, I'd make revisions and do the billing. From now on, there'd be no bosses who didn't have a clue, no groping hands by male co-workers who counted on bureaucracy to kill any sexual harassment complaints, and no gossiping by women whose unresolved sexuality issues made them freak out over the prospect of having to work with a lesbian. For better or for worse, I had a company to run.

Chapter 19

Something To Talk About

If success were rain to a parched desert, then five months later I was Noah, building an ark that was already afloat.

The phone rang at 8:10. "Sunrise Productions," I answered.

"Hi, Bunny."

The speaker paused for maybe two heartbeats, but in those two heartbeats my entire universe came to a screeching halt.

"It's Sue Lindstrom." She paused again.

"Sue," was all I could manage to say. Oh. My. God.

"I'm sorry for calling you like this." She took a deep breath. "I, uh, was wondering, if maybe ..." Her voice trailed off.

I could feel her tension through the phone line. Whatever was up, I could tell this phone call was costing her dearly. About a thousand things ran through my head right then, not all of them charitable. My stomach clenched when I realized this could be as simple as Sunshine—Sue wanting a website. But if that were the case, why ask me? There were lots of good web designers out there. OK, not as good as me, but there were plenty of people who would be more than happy to take her money.

"Maybe what?" I asked softly.

"Would you have dinner with me? At your convenience, of course," she added quickly.

I was flabbergasted. "Like a date?"

"Well, yes ... no. I don't know. What I really wanted was to see how you're doing."

I felt like I'd fallen into an alternative reality, like Alice Through The Looking Glass. "When?"

"Saturday night?"

Her choice of days brought me back to terra firma. I didn't even need to check my calendar. "I'm right in the middle of a huge project that's got me booked through Saturday. What about the following Saturday?"

"Oh, okay." I could hear the disappointment in her voice. "Next Saturday would be great. I want to take you to Girard's if that's okay." She sounded happier, or maybe it was relieved.

"Sure. I'd love to go to Girard's. Why don't you come to my house at 7?" I hung up the phone after I gave her my address, my heart beating furiously. Dammit! For years, I'd dreamed of this moment, when Sunshine called me up and asked me out. But now that we had a date, I almost felt sick. It had been eighteen years since we'd broken up and a lot had happened in the meantime. What was it that fortune had said from years ago? Be care of what you ask for—you might get it? I realized I'd finally attained that magical place I'd hoped for, when I had put Sunshine behind me.

And I'd just made plans with her for dinner.

Thank God I had Gray's Electrical website to work on! "How's the database coming?" I called to Tess.

"Errrrr," she growled. My little computer genius was getting a run for her money with this project.

I walked to her desk and stared at the screen. "Where are you?"

"Here. " She pointed to a short string of code. "It's like it's not reading the 'Find' command. Stupid fucking thing, " she muttered.

"When all else fails, read the manual. Let me look it up." I walked back to my office and grabbed one of my references books. I found the answer quickly and got Tess working on the next problem. The cursor on my monitor blinked at me, but my mind was elsewhere. You have a date with Sunshine in ten days. Do you know what you're doing?

The phone rang about noon when I was halfway through the Sunday Times. I'd gotten up at ten that morning to reward myself for the number of hours I'd put in that week. Tess and I had fought with Gray's website Wednesday, Thursday, and Friday, until we finally made the damn thing work and put it to bed about 11, Saturday night.

"What's up?" Val said. "Wanna come over for dinner and cards tonight?"

"Tell her it's my fifteenth anniversary of being sober," I heard Jessie say in the background

"I'd love to. What time? And by the way, I have news."

"We're eating at 6:30." Val eagerly took the bait. "What do you mean news? What kind of news?"

"Tell you when I get there." I hung up the phone. This was an unexpected pleasure. My impending date with Sunshine had rattled around in the back of my mind for the last couple of days and I still hadn't decided if I was happy or just anxious. I knew Jessie and Val would have an opinion about it.

I wracked my brain for an idea for a congratulations gift. I settled on a pot of red and yellow tulips from Todd, my gay neighborhood florist. At six, I pulled up to their house. I handed Jessie the tulips and kissed her on the cheek. "Happy sobriety."

"Thanks. How did you know tulips were my favorite?"

I didn't know that. I blurted out the first thing that came to mind. "They're a harbinger of spring, a time of renewal. I thought it fit the occasion."

"You are too sweet." She positively glowed.

"I'm starved. What's for dinner?" I asked, walking toward the kitchen.

"I hate you!" she said. "You can eat anything and still stay skinny while I just look at food and get fat."

"Well, not anything," I protested. "Besides, I love you just the way you are."

"God! If I had a nickel for every time someone said that to me, I could retire right now," Jessie groused.

Val snickered from out on the patio. " We're having hamburgers. Can you bring out the buns?"

I grabbed the bag of buns and joined Val on the patio.

"So, what's the news?" Val asked as she flipped the burgers.

"I'm having dinner with Sue next Saturday," I said as casually as possible.

"Sue who?" Val asked.

"Oh God, Bunny, no!" Jessie said as she joined us. "Please tell me you're not going out with Sue Lindstrom."

"Well, yeah." I had expected a reaction from Jessie, but not quite this strong a reaction.

"Who's Sue Lindstrom?" Val looked between Jessie and me. "You mean Sunshine? You're going out with Sunshine? That's terrific!" Val grinned from ear to ear.

There they were, my two oldest friends, taking opposite positions on my love life, just as they did on everything. Maybe that was the secret to their relationship—they could disagree vehemently on a subject and still come together as a couple.

291

"Okay, so tell all the prurient details." Val's dark eyes shone.

Jessie shook her head in disgust.

"She called me Wednesday and asked me out. I had to put her off until next Saturday because of a deadline I had with one of my clients."

"I think you oughta go for it. God, Bunny, how long have you loved her? Twenty years?"

Jessie pried the lid off the potato salad. "It's not like you're a twenty-two year old chickie anymore, Bunny. Screw this one up and you've pretty much screwed yourself for the rest of your life."

"But how do you feel?" Val was practically dancing with delight. Matchmaker that she was, Val loved a good falling-in-love story.

"I dunno. I'm happy with my life right now. I've been so involved with my work that romance has been the last thing on my mind. But you're right. Do I want to jeopardize my hard-earned, sane life for something that might feel good for a little while? What happens if it all falls apart?"

"Atta girl!" Jessie patted my hand.

Val frowned. "But what about love?"

Jessie turned to her partner, a condescending smile on her face. "Sometimes being an adult trumps the feel-good side of life. Look at her! Bunny's happy and she's got her life together." She turned to me. "I vote you give her the old heave-ho."

Val folded her arms across her chest. "I'm sorry, my love, but you are wrong. Life should be lived from the heart, not the head."

"Right. Tell that to the tax man."

Val leveled her gaze at her partner. "Yes, Miss Head-Of-The-Mormon-Youth-Group-Who-Was-Engaged-To-Be-

Married-When-She-Was-Eighteen. And how many children were you planning on having? Six, or was it eight? Look where you'd be now if you hadn't followed your heart."

"Touché." Jesse gave a mock bow to her partner. "Okay, so there's something to be said for living from the heart."

"And amazingly, you turned out halfway decent." Val ruffled her partner's hair. She winked at me in triumph. "Dinner is served."

Over dinner and cards that evening, we stuck to the less volatile subject of how the Republicans had taken over the Senate.

"They want to balance the budget," Jessie said, her Republican background showing.

"They're a bunch of selfish crooks," countered Val.

It became apparent as the night wore on that neither Jessie nor Val would give up their position on politics or my love life. Jessie still championed her idea of thinking this through sanely, although she couldn't refute Val's argument that she hadn't followed her own advice. And Val thought the important things in life should be ruled by the heart.

With a sense of trepidation, I knew I'd have to decide this one on my own.

At exactly 7 p.m., a car pulled up to the curb and Sunshine emerged. When I opened the door, we stared at each other for a second before she blurted out, "It's good to see you."

"It's nice to see you, too. Come in." Don't do anything rash. Don't hug her.

She crossed the threshold and glanced at my living room, which I had dusted that afternoon.

"Would you like a quick tour of my house, Sunshine? Jeez, I'm sorry. I don't know what to call you." Good going, LaRue.

"That's okay. I go by Sue now. Most people don't want an attorney named 'Sunshine,' and after I left the DA's Office I didn't want to be known as 'Suzanne' anymore, so I settled on 'Sue.' Just so you know, " she looked up at me, "I left 'Sunshine' a long time ago. God," she muttered, "sometimes I feel like I've lived several lifetimes with all the changes I've been through."

Wow. I rephrased my invitation. "Would you like a tour of my house, Sue?"

She smiled at me. "Sure."

After a brief tour, which did not include my office, Sue turned to me. "Your house is very nice. Very tasteful."

Tasteful? Something in her voice told me she was thinking something else. "Very tasteful, but ..."

"It's beautiful. Not what I pictured for you, that's all." She looked away.

What's wrong with my house? "No, I'd really like to know what you think is wrong with this house."

Sue looked incredibly uncomfortable. "There's nothing wrong with it," she began. "It's like those model homes you see on a Tour of Homes. It's pretty, but you can't imagine someone actually living there. You know, the carpets might get stained or God forbid, you left a dirty dish on the counter. Real people have messy lives. As beautiful as it is, your house looks more like a museum and people don't live in museums."

A museum? I looked around and realized she was right. My house was perfect; there wasn't a dirty dish in sight. And my office was the one room I didn't let anyone see because it was too cluttered. "Would you like to see my office?"

Sue shrugged noncommittally.

I opened the door and stepped over the manuals and stacks of catalogs sitting on the floor. A half-eaten container of fries sat on top of an In-N-Out sack in front of my monitor. My waste basket was filled with empty diet Coke cans, styrofoam containers, and last Sunday's LA Times. On the window ledge sat a variegated philodendron, the one plant I'd managed to keep alive since I moved in. This was where I lived when I wasn't at work or sleeping. Sue was right. The rest of my house was for show, not for living in.

"Yeah!" Sue brightened. "This is more like it."

"You're the first person I've ever shown this room to in its natural state."

"Why? Because it's messy?"

I nodded.

"Why should it be perfect? People aren't perfect."

"Damn! And here I hoped you thought I was perfect."

Sue smiled wanly.

I had ventured a little joke. It fell flat. "Ready to go?"

"Sure."

As we got into her car she said, "You know about my career choices and name changes. Why don't you tell me what you've been up to?" She spoke with a candor I found refreshing. I was glad to see that part of her hadn't changed.

"Well, the biggest thing is that I quit drinking."

Sue was about to pull out into traffic when she swiveled around in her seat to face me. "Seriously? That's fantastic. I never told you at the time, but I always worried about your drinking. I shoulda said something."

I laughed. "It wouldn't have done any good. I had to bottom out before I quit. It probably woulda been something else for us to fight about."

"You always were stubborn."

I laughed. "Like you weren't?"

She ignored my comment and pulled out into the street. "So how's your Dad?"

295

I smiled. "He's fine. He retired a few years ago after he sold his two plus acres to a developer and made a bundle. Now he lives in a retirement community where there are twenty available women to every man. He's got himself a little harem. He fixes their squeaky doors and hangs pictures for them and they fuss over him and make him meals." I smiled at the thought of all of those little old ladies laughing and tee-heeing, putting on their best when he came to visit. "Plus he quit drinking a few years after I did. He said if I could do it, he could do it, too. Believe it or not, he's an AA sponsor," I laughed. "Who'da thunk it?"

"That's great. Speaking of drinking, I heard that you moved to San Francisco after we broke up. Was that before or after you quit?"

"Before. The City was like one gigantic, non-stop party. Too bad I had to work all the time," I added. I wondered how much I should tell her. I decided not to regale her with tales of my exes. "I got a job selling auto parts, which kept me out of town most weekends."

"Auto parts?" she asked incredulously.

"Yeah. In fact, selling auto parts is what made me able to start my own business and buy a house. Remember when you put me on a budget and made me save some money? Well, I did the same thing, except on a bigger scale. I admit it. You did have some good ideas."

A small smile spread across her face as she slowed for a stoplight. "What about now? Like, how's Michael?"

"Michael?" I turned to her, aghast. "I thought you knew."

"What?" Concern was written all over her face.

A huge lump formed in my throat and I was barely able to say, "Michael died of AIDS four years ago, right after Clinton was inaugurated." Try as I might, I couldn't stop the tears that appeared instantly at the mention of his name.

"Oh God, Bunny. I'm so sorry." She reached for me just as the light turned green. "Damn!" She gunned her car through the intersection and turned abruptly into a one-way alley going the wrong way. "Here." She handed me a tissue.

Don't complicate matters. Keep Michael to yourself and out of this equation. "Thanks. I'll be fine." I took the tissue and wiped my eyes. "Let's go."

"How did you get reservations here on such short notice?" Looking around, I could see why Girard's was on everyone's see-and-be-seen list. Located right off Santa Monica Boulevard in Beverly Hills, the location alone was designed to keep tourists from stepping foot inside. A menu posted in an unobtrusive niche reminded the middle-class that if they could afford to eat here, they couldn't do it often. A garden salad was $22 and the entrées started at $46.

"Reservations for Lindstrom," Sue said to a pretty, dark-haired woman at the reception desk.

"Please follow me." The woman gave us a curious glance, then led us farther into the restaurant.

"We could have gone somewhere less expensive. We didn't have to come here," I said after we were seated.

Sue shrugged. "Emile Girard is a client of mine. He owes me big time." She did not elaborate.

A pony-tailed waiter appeared from the shadows and handed us menus. "Good evening. We've got some fabulous specials tonight, including freshly caught rainbow trout ..."

Sue wore an open-necked teal silk blouse with a simple silver necklace that complemented her graying hair. Her charcoal gray slacks looked like they were from Nordstroms. Her entire personae had changed from no-nonsense politically correct dyke to elegantly understated lawyer who knew

297

clothing was yet another weapon with which to wage the war.

"... with baby choy sum topped with a caramelized mandarin orange chutney-filled bouillabaisse over medallions of chipotle smoked bison and tarot root purée, all by our CIA trained executive chef."

"CIA?" That's the only part I heard.

"Culinary Institute of America," Sue explained.

"Or we have a cheeseburger if you prefer." The waiter registered no emotion whatsoever, but I got the feeling he was mocking me.

I glanced quickly at the menu. "I'll have the scallops."

"I'll have the filet mignon." Sue handed her menu back to the waiter.

"Very good." The waiter bowed to us and disappeared.

"You're not a vegetarian any more?"

Sue shook her head. "No. During law school, I never had time to cook, so I got used to Chinese takeout. One thing led to another and pretty soon I was eating everything I'd sworn off over the years."

"Really?" New name, new food, new clothes. This is not the same woman you knew years ago.

Our pony-tailed waiter swooped in with our salads and an offer of fresh ground pepper. As we ate our salads, the question that had puzzled me for years popped out: "So how did you go from being a lesbian/feminist/separatist/socialist—that's socialist with a small 's'—to an Assistant DA?" I chuckled at my own joke.

Sue looked down at her lap and shook her head. "Okay. I'm busted." She pushed her hair over her ear. "My sister, Samantha, got beat up by her boyfriend—broken nose, black eye, typical shit. Her boyfriend won her back with flowers and promises to get counseling. Then he beat her up again. The cops chalked it up to a family dispute." She took a deep breath. "I knew the guy was a dangerous, violent asshole, so I decided to go to college and on to law school, where I could do some real good and put those battering creeps behind bars. The Domestic Violence unit at the DA's office had an opening after I graduated, so I charged in, ready to kick ass. Well, you heard about the Sanderson case. I prosecuted Buddy Sanderson for beating up his wife and won my first conviction."

"Scallops," the waiter set my plate down, "and for you, the filet mignon. Can I get you anything else?"

"I'm good," I said.

Sue shook her head. She did not speak for a minute, as if weighing what she should say and what she shouldn't. She picked at her food.

"It felt good. No, it felt fantastic. There I was, lesbian activist turned avenging assistant DA. Finally I was doing what I had always wanted to do, make the bad guys pay for their crimes. I loved my job and took every opportunity to improve. My boss took note of it and assigned me to more complicated cases. I was the rising star of the DA's office. I schmoozed all the right people until I scored the biggest coup of all, getting promoted to the Murder Squad."

Her hand tightened around her water glass. "Then Buddy Sanderson killed his wife. In a marketing move calculated to generate a ton of favorable publicity, the DA decided to make me the face of the State of California and assigned me as lead prosecutor for the case. What should have been the high point of my career nearly did me in."

"You mean the whole capital punishment thing when you were opposed to it all those years?" I remembered how gaunt Sue had looked at the end of the trial. Something had been eating at her.

"Yeah. I had so much emotionally invested in seeing Buddy Sanderson put to death that I couldn't separate my desire for justice from my desire for revenge. And I hate to say this," she looked down at the table, "but revenge won out.

"Weeks later, when I still wasn't sleeping, I came to the realization that I'd given everything and I had nothing left for myself. It was my lesbian activist days all over again. That's when I knew I had to get out—out of the DA's Office and out of my relationship with Geneva. I needed to start my own practice and choose my own cases. Being top dog was killing me."

"I take it that was after your party," I said, trying to sound sympathetic.

Her cheeks flushed red. "The party was the icing on the cake." Her eyes teared up. "It was too much when I saw you there. And when I held your hand too long, I knew I was still in love with you."

What? I was so stunned I couldn't speak. And to my astonishment, she kept going.

"At the end, when you volunteered to quit Franklin's, I was such a self-righteous prig that your offer wasn't good enough for me. If I'd had any brains at all, I would have seen that when couples are faced with problems, they solve them together. Years later in the DA's office, I had to deal with problems that made our issues look like a mosquito bite by comparison. I loved you dearly, but I threw you away because you wouldn't conform to what I wanted.

"I'm sorry, but I had to tell you. It was bound to come out sooner or later." She looked away.

I didn't want to even think about what she had just said. I was back in Alice Through The Looking Glass reality again.

"I'm sure I've overwhelmed you with my confession

tonight. Once I get an idea in my head, it's hard for me to let go. I guess this evening is over." Sue signaled the waiter for the check.

I nodded. Once again, I was speechless.

We drove the 15 minutes to my house in silence.

"Thank you," she said, as I got out of her car. "Seeing how I've totally blown tonight, I won't presume to call you again. If by some miracle you want to call me, here's my home number." She reached into her purse, pulled out a business card, and scribbled her number on it.

"Thanks for dinner," I managed to say before she drove off. I noted distractedly when I looked at her number that we shared the same area code.

This must be a dream. I lay awake that night, replaying her confession in a never-ending loop. "And when I held your hand too long, I knew I was still in love with you and when I held your hand too long, I knew I was still in love with you and when I held your hand too long, I knew I was still in love with you..."

That night I dreamed about Sue's water glass breaking in her fist, not small pieces of harmless safety glass, but huge shards of broken glass raining down on me and blood everywhere.

In the morning, I was still faced with her confession from the night before: Sue was in love with me. What was I going to do with that information? Thank God I didn't have to go into work today. Try as I might, the Sunday paper couldn't keep my interest. My thoughts kept coming back to Sue and our date last night. I reread her business card: Sue Lindstrom, Attorney, Specializing in Family Law. I knew Family Law meant child custody and divorce proceedings, highly charged emotional situations. That fit. Sue, once a fighter, always a fighter.

God! In my head I'd always imagined it so differently, like there'd be this immediate, intense connection, when we'd both cry and declare our love for each other and I'd bring her home and we'd talk about saving the world for days on end and make love for weeks on end and Michael would tease us and we'd grill steaks on the barbeque, and we'd still be young and pretty.

And alive.

At 45, I had another 30 or 40 years to go, but I was definitely past midpoint. But 30 or 40 years is a long time to be single. Up to the point when she dropped her bomb on me, things had gone well. Rather than shut the door completely on the possibility of Sue and I together, I wanted to give it another try in a short, manageable chunk of time. Afterward, I'd walk away and see how it felt. One day at a time.

I picked up the phone and dialed her number. "Hi, Sue. How would you like to go out for coffee Wednesday?"

Chapter 20

Everybody Hurts

With a prickling sense of anticipation, I walked through the front door of Haute Caffe. Sue sat buried in an overstuffed chair, reading the LA Weekly, when I sat down across from her. "What a cool place. Let's get our coffee." We walked to the counter together.

I discovered this place soon after buying my house and kept coming back for its funky atmosphere, good coffee drinks, and baked goods. On the many days I had nothing to eat in my house, I came here for a super caffeinated breakfast. The mismatched chairs, scruffy wooden tables, and local art on the walls was a better choice for our meeting than one of those sharp-looking corporate coffeehouses that seemed to be on every block these days. We were, by far, the oldest patrons in the place.

"Hey, Bunny." Nicki, the young, lesbian barista greeted me warmly. "Double iced mocha and a brownie?"

I nodded.

"And how about your friend?"

"Iced cappuccino and a snickerdoodle for me." Sue grinned like a little kid. "Do you know how hard it is to find snickerdoodles?"

"Go sit down," Nicki said. "I'll bring them right over."

Minutes later, Sue was happily munching on her snicker-doodle and I was getting my chocolate fix for the day.

"I have to tell you, I was more than a little surprised when you called Sunday. I figured I'd never hear from you again." She brushed the crumbs off her fingers onto her plate.

"I'm just full of surprises," I teased.

"You always were," she shot back. "So tell me more about how you went from selling auto parts to designing websites. I don't see the connection at all." She sipped her cappuccino and gave a little shiver of delight.

Another convert to Haute Caffe, I could already tell. "There isn't any connection. I looked for a career with growth potential while I still sold auto parts, and realized that computers were the wave of the future. Because I knew nothing about writing code, my company sent me to school so I could learn it. I'd still be working on databases if a friend from AA hadn't asked me if I knew someone who could design a website for her company. The rest, as they say, is history." I motioned to Nicki. "Another round for us." I could see this was going to be my dinner tonight.

"Thanks." Sue sipped her cappuccino. "You know, what you haven't mentioned are any girlfriends. I heard about Carla from both Geneva and Marla. I bet you'd never guess they both had the same opinion of her—she was smart but insecure, always on the lookout for a pretty girlfriend to wear on her arm."

I nearly choked on my mocha. "Yep. That about sums her up." Sue knew all she needed to know about Carla. I wasn't about to give her any more. "There were others, but nobody I couldn't live without."

Sue tilted her head and smiled. "I'd forgotten that about you. You never said anything bad about anyone. That's one of the reasons I loved you."

I'd never viewed discretion as a badge of honor, I'd always seen it as a survival skill. Why burn your bridges when there was no need to?

"Okay, now you know my past. What did you do after we broke up?"

Sue chuckled. "I channeled all of my anger and energy into various causes. By this time, we were—"

I interrupted. "Who's 'we'?"

"Angie, Phyllis, and Connie."

"Oh, you mean the Righteous Sisters. And don't forget Evelyn."

"No, not Evelyn. Shortly after we broke up, Evelyn's grandmother died and left her a huge fortune."

"Evelyn?" I looked at her in disbelief.

"Yeah, Evelyn. I was vaguely aware that she came from money, but I was too busy with my causes to think about it. Later I found out that she had been going through her post-adolescent rebellious stage with us, the whole Karl Marx and the separatist thing. It was this big liberal guilt trip for her, and once she got the cash she was outta there."

"Evelyn?"

"Yeah." She chuckled. "I hear she's big in the Log Cabin Republicans now."

I bit my tongue. Evelyn?

"Anyway, I got more and more into my causes—union organizing and a whole host of women's issues. And because I knew that you could sleep with any woman you wanted, I wanted to prove to everyone that I could, too. I was this radical dyke whose politics and sexuality were way out there, see? To this day, I don't remember all of their names. I'm not proud of that." Her cheeks colored red.

I had a hard time picturing the naïve little Lutheran girl I'd known sleeping around.

She continued. "But I wasn't satisfied with these mostly one-night stands. I reasoned that these women weren't the 'right' kind of lesbian, so I narrowed my search to only separatists whose politics were the same as mine."

Oh. My. God. I could almost hear fingernails scraping across an emotional blackboard.

"But that didn't satisfy me, either. I chalked it up to having too many ideological differences with these so-called separatist women. I wanted a woman who was ideologically pure, one who had the correct beliefs about feminism and the evils of corporate America, one who believed exactly as I did." She paused. "And I found her."

My mouth dropped open. "You did?"

"Yeah." Sue played with her spoon. "Her name was Anna Benton. We clicked immediately. We shared the same beliefs and held the same righteous anger. Together we were going to change the world."

She sighed, then sipped her cappuccino before she continued. "Our first project was WIDSOWA, the 1981 Women's Interracial Dialog on the State of Women's Affairs, a week long conference to lay out the agenda for women's issues in America. Surely you heard of if?" She looked up at me.

"No," I said sheepishly.

"I can't imagine why not." She laughed derisively. "We spent six months organizing it. We expected hundreds of women from all over the country to attend. Fifty-eight women showed up, and thirty-two of us were involved one way or another in making the conference happen. I was joking when I asked if you'd heard about it."

"Oh."

"Double mocha and a brownie, and another cappuccino and a snickerdoodle." Nicki set our order on the table. "I'm starting a tab for you, Bunny."

Sue took a bite of her cookie. "Mmmmm. We're definitely coming back here." When she was finished, she licked her fingers.

"On the first day of the conference, my mom called and said my dad had been admitted to Swedish Hospital in Seattle with a 'cardiac incident.' I flew out the next day after begging off on my responsibilities. That pissed off everyone except a couple women who helped me book my flight, God bless them.

"When I got to the hospital, my dad was bitching about everything—how he couldn't afford to take time off from work, how this was costing him a fortune, how Jimmy Carter had ruined the country and goddammit they should have kicked his sissy ass out of office sooner and why the hell were the Mariners in the crapper again?" Sue pounded her fist on the table, imitating her father.

"That musta been hard on you."

"Not just me, the whole family. I stayed as long as I could, but when he started in on me I figured he was getting better, so I flew back to LA."

"You don't do things in a small way, do you?" I teased.

"Oh, it gets better." Sue turned her head from side to side until I heard her neck crack. "When I came back to LA, I found they had canceled the last three days of the conference because so few women had shown up. I walked through the door to find a huge fight over whose fault it was the conference had bombed. Everyone was accusing each other of not putting this issue or that issue on the agenda. Talk about a feeding frenzy! These were well-meaning women, but they needed a scapegoat and anyone who didn't agree with them completely became the enemy."

She took another sip of her drink. "Anna accused me of bailing out the moment she needed me most. And get this, she wanted to start planning the next year's conference with me immediately." Sue rested her chin on her hands. "Between the conference and my dad, I was totally burned out. I mean totally. That's when I had an epiphany—I had turned into my father. I was just like him, angry about everything. The only difference was that he was angry at the 'damned liberals' while I was angry at the 'ruling Establishment.'"

She tensed her muscles, then relaxed. "That's also when I realized I was dating myself. Anna and I had the same hair style, we dressed the same, we ate the same food."

"You fucked the same," I added.

"No," she shook her head, "we'd stopped fucking altogether. We were both too exhausted from everything we were doing. When I told Anna that I needed time for myself, she accused me of being selfish and putting my own petty bourgeois needs before the very real needs of all women."

"Yikes! That was harsh. What did you say to her?"

"I told her to fuck off."

"In so many words?"

"Yes."

A small smile began at the corners of her mouth and soon we were both laughing hysterically, the tears running down our faces.

"God! It's good to talk to you," Sue said, wiping the tears from her face.

"Yeah. It's nice." Two good dates doesn't equal marital bliss, LaRue.

Sue looked at her watch. "I gotta go. How would you like to meet here a week from today?"

And three dates doesn't equal happily ever after. I stalled for a second.

Quit being so judgmental. "That would be nice."

"Great! Meet you at 5:30?"

I took a deep breath. "Sure."

When I got home, I headed for my bedroom and collapsed on the bed. Okay, so the date went well. But give her a while and she'll start in on the fact that you make money from companies that aren't gay friendly, ecologically friendly, or have ties to Big Republican Business.

No, that's what Sunshine, the lesbian feminist separatist socialist with a small 's' would have done. As far as I could see, Sue wasn't rigidly married to any ideology, except maybe to do some good in this world. Sue really had mellowed.

I reviewed what I knew so far:

1. Sue professed to love me;

2. my entire universe had been turned upside down by her unexpected appearance;

3. I found her to be warm and charming, not unlike the Sunshine I had known years before; and

4. after two dates, I still wasn't sure how I felt.

My Thursday morning meeting with Strong's TVs and Appliances lasted an hour longer than I'd anticipated. Consequently, when I walked in the door I was more than a little anxious about the time I'd lost.

"You have two calls." Tess handed me two slips of paper. "The California Floral Association wants a website that looks just like Enchanted Gardens, and that trade rag, Southern California Online, called to see if you'll do an interview."

"An interview? What for?"

A smile spread across Tess's face. "Sunrise Productions has been named Southern California Online's 'Best Website Designer.'"

"You're kidding."

"Nope. They want to send an editor over to interview you." Tess paused. "Hey, boss, now that we've hit the big times, can I have tomorrow off? Cori and I are going to celebrate."

"You know what this means, don't you? From now on, everybody is going to want Sunrise Productions to create their websites, which means working overtime and hiring another production person. You can't even make it to work on time as it is now, so no, you can't take tomorrow off."

Tess brightened at the mention of the word "overtime." "I could use the money. Cori's birthday's coming up and I want to buy her one of those cool KitchenAid mixers. And if you're looking to hire someone, I know a guy named Michael. He's good."

I winced at the mention of that name. "Okay. Tell him to call me." I shut the door to my office and sat down in my chair. There was so much to do and now, an interview? I switched on my computer and brought up my calendar. Two more appointments today, plus I had to look over Tess's work on both the amusement park and the jewelry manufacturer websites. She was getting better. At least, she'd stopped putting rainbows on everyone's page in order to make some kind of lesbian "statement." As far as I could tell, her activism extended to having a "Lesbian Avengers" bumper sticker on Cori's car and wearing a rainbow neck-lace. She said it set her apart from her boring hetero friends, as if her shaved head and multiple piercing were no clue.

"Excuse me." Tess stuck her head in my office a half hour later. "There's a delivery for you." She smiled like the Cheshire Cat.

"So sign for it." Just what I need, another interruption.

"I think you should come out here." She held the door open for me, still grinning.

Irritated, I got up and walked into Tess's area. On her desk sat the largest arrangement of red roses I'd ever seen. Omigod.

"There's a card for you."

I reached into the arrangement and pulled out the card.

"Bunny's got a girlfriend, Bunny's got a girlfriend," Tess sang.

"Oh, shut up!" I could tell my face was as red as the roses.

"There's twenty-four of them. I counted. So what's the card say?"

Not only was she late all the time, she was nosey too. I cleared my throat to keep my voice from shaking. "I'm looking forward to coffee next Wednesday. Thanks a bunch. S."

"Wow. So who's the babe? Whoever it is, sounds like she's after your ass." Tess smirked.

It seemed senseless to deny the obvious.

Before I could answer, she asked, "So, you gonna call her, or what?"

"Don't you have a project you should be working on?"

"Bunny's got a girlfriend, Bunny's got a girlfriend," Tess sang as she sat back down at her computer.

I picked up the bouquet and carried it into my office, then closed the door. I didn't want Tess to witness what might be my meltdown.

Now what am I going to do? I stared at the roses, hoping the answer to my dilemma would appear in the red blossoms. I knew it wasn't by accident that red roses symbolized love—delicate flowers that opened over time to reveal their full beauty, red for passion, atop thorny stems—beauty and passion mixed with pain. Without the thorns, the flowers would be pretty, but not memorable. And the thorns by

311

themselves? Who but the most masochistic of lovers would want only pain?

Certainly our relationship had been passionate and beautiful at times. It absolutely had been painful. I hesitated a second before I picked up the phone and dialed her number. "Hi, Sue. Thanks for the roses, they're beautiful. I'm looking forward to coffee next Wednesday, too."

Chapter 21

As

Sue was sitting at a table, flipping through the LA Times, when I walked in. She stood up like she wanted to hug me, but thought better of it and sat back down. "Hi, Bunny. It's good to see you."

She seemed slightly distant, but I didn't give it much thought. Maybe she'd had a difficult client today.

I, on the other hand, was feeling lucky. Today I'd snagged the City of Los Angeles Department of Public Works, aka the Bureau of Sanitation, as a client. This afternoon, I'd toyed with the idea of a new motto for them: No shit.

"The usual, Bunny?" Nicki asked.

"Nah, I wanna try your white chocolate mocha."

"Over ice?"

"Nope. I'm feeling adventurous today. Make it hot."

Nicki rolled her eyes.

When I returned to the table, Sue was reading the Real Estate section. She folded, then unfolded, then folded the paper again, set it down, and drummed her fingers on the table. She wasn't the nervous type, so whatever was on her mind had to be important.

"I ... I wasn't quite honest with you at Girard's," she said before I'd even sat down.

Oh no! This can't be good. I set my large steaming white chocolate mocha on the table and slid into the seat across from her. "What do you mean?"

She hesitated. "I didn't tell you about the most important thing that's happened to me since we broke up." Her knuckles were white around her drink. I remembered my dream of broken glass and blood.

"Do you remember years ago when I said I wanted kids?"

I nodded.

"Well, twice now I've tried to get pregnant. I'm going to try it one more time. If it doesn't work this time, I'm going to start adoption proceedings."

It took me a moment to process what she said. "You'd make a great mom, Sue." She wouldn't be a great mom, she'd be a wonderful mom, an exemplary mom, a Mother-of-the-Year mom. Then it struck me.

"Ummm," I began. "What if ... what if you have a boy?" Sue was statistically more likely to have a boy than a girl, I knew, and given her history of not liking men, I wondered how she would handle raising a son. "Or are you going to do a sex selection thing so you get a girl?"

Sue's face colored bright red and she looked down. "Oh, you mean my separatist stage? I was pretty naïve back then. I thought everything was either good or bad, good being women's stuff and bad being anything to do with men. Then I met some men who were thoughtful, intelligent, and abhorred everything I railed against—violence against women, racism, and unbridled greed.

"And I found some women, more than I ever dreamed, to be shallow, vain, and incredibly selfish. I finally came to the conclusion that there's good and bad in everyone. Including myself," she added quietly.

"That's quite an insight. One some people never come to." And quite an admission!

"Yet you seemed to know that." She looked at me, puzzled. "When did you figure that out?"

"I dunno. High school. Certainly when I modeled for Franklin's. Some of the models were really nice, like Gloria who became a nurse or Betty who I heard got her Master's degree and now works with autistic kids.

"But I also knew some of them were petty and self-centered and took advantage of their looks. You don't have to be an ethics professor to figure out that a person's looks or wealth or education doesn't make them a good person any more that it makes them a bad person."

"Or gender," Sue added, smiling. "I could've saved myself a lot of grief if I'd learned that sooner." Sue looked serious again. "I kinda got off track there. Bunny, I'm going to have kids one way or another. I don't care whether it's a boy or a girl."

"How does that work? I mean, how'd you do it?"

Sue settled into her chair. "A year after I started my own practice, I tried intrauterine insemination. I charted my fertility cycle to the minute, did all the things they recommended to boost my chances of getting pregnant, and for some reason, it didn't work.

"Several months later, I tried again. I used a home pregnancy test two weeks later and voílà, I was pregnant." She waved her hand for effect.

"My first trimester went fine, but into my fifth month, I started cramping badly." Her voice sounded choked. "A couple of days later, I miscarried." She put her hand over her face as she struggled to maintain her composure.

"I went into a huge depression after I lost the baby. It was like thunder and black lightening crashing all around me and I couldn't find my way out of it. I had to scale back my practice to fifteen hours a week. That didn't pay the mortgage, so I got two roommates to help out. Pretty soon my roommates started getting on my nerves, so I kicked them out. Marla finally suggested I see a shrink."

"And did that help?"

"Yeah. The woman told me the truth, which I didn't want to hear. She said that she could prescribe an antidepressant that probably wouldn't work because I had to grieve over losing my baby." Sue wiped away tears with the back of her hand.

I knew better than to interrupt, so I said nothing.

"I cried for months. And she was right, I had to go through the darkness by myself." She wiped her eyes with a napkin. "I don't think I'll ever get over it." Sue was silent for a minute. "She did suggest one thing, though."

"What was that?"

"She said to remember a time in my life when I felt the most alive, and see if maybe I could gain some solace by recreating whatever it was that made me happy."

"So did you do that?"

"Yeah. And she was right. It did help."

Part of me desperately wanted to think the happiest time of her life had been with me, but then I remembered how we'd fought at the end and how painful that time had been, probably for both of us. "So what time was that?" I asked with great trepidation.

Sue looked at me with an odd expression, but said nothing.

"Well ..." I prompted.

She leaned on the table, her arms folded. "Don't you get it? It was when I was with you!"

316

Omigod. Take me now, Jesus. "Me? As I recall, you were pretty pissed off at me when we broke up."

"Of course I was. That's because no one had ever stirred such deep feelings in me, both happy and angry. I was never more alive than when I was with you."

She took my hand in hers and waited several moments before she said, "Bunny, I love you and I want to spend the rest of my life with you."

All of a sudden, it got very hot in the room and I knew it didn't have anything to do with my white chocolate mocha. "Is this a proposal?"

"Yes, but I'm not dumb enough to think that just because I love you means that you feel the same. You may or may not be interested in raising kids with me, but that's a major part of the deal. For that matter," she said, "you may not be interested in being with me at all. But I wanted to be up front with you so you'd have all the facts going in. Okay?"

No shit.

Sue took a deep breath before continuing. "It was the memory of us being together that got me through those black months. You always seemed able to keep your balance when it came to things you loved. Now I look back on all the causes I worked on and think I was always going off the deep end. I remember the days and weeks and months of working on projects and planning my next move and never taking time for myself. You were able to take me away from my meetings and my committees. You made sure I had time for myself. I couldn't do it by myself. I felt too guilty that I was an educated white woman who couldn't stop the world in its headlong rush to destruction." She took my hand in hers. "You balanced me, Bunny."

I could feel the blood rush to my face and my heart racing. What now, LaRue?

"Look, you probably need some time to think about it. But I also want you to know that I will chase you down to the ends of the earth if I have to." She looked fierce, an in-love kind of fierce, not a stalker kind of fierce. Her face softened. "There's always only been one woman for me, and that woman is you."

My hand wasn't steady as I raised my cup to my lips. From behind me, I heard a woman scream, "David, sit down!" then something hit me from behind and I spilled my drink all over my lap. "Shit!" I jumped up from the table and grabbed a napkin to wipe up the scalding hot coffee.

"I'm sorry, I'm so sorry. I'll pay for your dry cleaning," said a young woman who looked to be no more than twenty-four. She pointed to a boy who looked to be about six, "My son has ADHD and he can't sit still."

Indeed, the little terror now was pressed up against the pastry case, leaving sticky finger and nose prints wherever he touched.

"Are you okay?" Sue looked up at me from the floor, where she was kneeling, wiping the remnants of the drink from my pants.

Shit, this hurts! "I'll be fine. Thanks for the offer," I said to his mother. "I need to go home and change."

Sue stood up and followed me out to my car. "I'll drive you home if you like."

I shook my head. "That's all right." I slid into the driver's seat and lowered my window.

"Bunny, I know you're afraid I'll walk away from you again. But I promise you that isn't going to happen. I love you and I want to spend the rest of my life with you."

"With kids."

"With kids and a dog and an aquarium and piano recitals

and soccer practice. I want you there with me, to share all of it."

I said nothing.

She looked into my eyes for a minute before she said, "I know you'll make the right choice."

I wasn't so sure.

I stripped off my pants when I got home and examined the damage. It looked to be a second-degree burn, not bad enough to scar but tender for a couple days. I limped to the kitchen and rummaged in the freezer for my comfort food, a Fudgesicle, which I applied to my burn before I tore off the wrapper and ate it.

This was the sum total of what I knew: Sue loved me and promised fidelity and forever. Sue's life would include children, with or without me.

The only kid experience I had was growing up without brothers or sisters for me to tease and torment. The only contact I had with my family had been my dad's mother, who with her brother Alan and his "roommate" Randall, ran a speakeasy in Sacramento during the 1920s. And Dad refused to speak of my mother except for once in a maudlin moment he described her as "Aphrodite, the woman who broke my heart." My family was far from "normal," whatever that was. What kind of parent would I be? I didn't know.

I wondered what Michael would say. Something on the order of "so many women, so little time," no doubt. Or would he? He'd embraced life, which included AIDS, until the very end. "At least you loved her," he'd said. Would he have been disappointed if I just walked away?

What was love, anyway? Carla once had described it as "swimming in an ocean of endorphins." Yeah, I swam and I almost drowned. If straight folks, who had the backing of society and the Church, had a divorce rate of 50%, how could gay people, who often had no more than a cobbled together social/legal structure and sometimes not even that, be expected to stay together forever? The odds were against us. How many long-term lesbian or gay couples did I know? Jessie and Val. And Frank and Bernie, two old queens who had been together since Anita Bryant went on her crusade against queers in the 1970s.

What would my life be with Sue? PTA meetings and an extra-large capacity washer/dryer. Considering our occupations took up huge chunks of our lives, would we even see each other beyond a "Bye, honey. Don't forget to pick up milk?" Not to mention, I'd have to learn how to cook something other than microwave meals, soup, and grilled cheese sandwiches.

What would Ella say? "What do you want?" I had agonized over whether I wanted to see Sue when she invited me to Girard's, then again when we went out for coffee. For that matter, I'd agonized over Sue for most of my adult life. That couldn't be a good sign. Worse than that, after everything that had transpired over the last twenty years, I knew I was in love with her again.

The only sane thing for me to do was to walk away from Sue. Once and for all.

What did I want?

My leg hurt and my brain was on overload. How could I possibly live with a woman who, just thinking about her, made me crazy?

Epilogue

Day Planner—Monday, May 12, 1997

8 a.m.Mtg w/Animal Humane Society—see Geri
10 a.m. Go to bank
11:30–1 p.m. Gay & Lesbian Chamber of Commerce
luncheon @ Mama's Diner
2 p.m.Talk to Tess about showing up late for work
4 p.m. Fertility Clinic w/ Sue

Bywater Books

GREETINGS FROM JAMAICA, WISH YOU WERE QUEER

Mari SanGiovanni

Marie Santora has always known her Italian family is a little crazy, but when she inherits her grandmother's estate, they now have a million more reasons to act nuts.

Marie plans her escape. She'll give her family a parting gift and then move to Hollywood to chase her dream of writing film scripts. But with millions at stake, it will take more than a free vacation to Jamaica to get the erratic Santora family to toe the line. And the timing couldn't be worse when her hot pursuit changes from screenplay to foreplay.

Climb aboard this hilarious rollercoaster ride where Marie is left wishing "out" was the new "in," and where every lounge chair is a hot seat when the Santora family ventures this close to the equator. The island of Jamaica just may not be big enough …

Greetings from Jamaica, Wish You Were Queer
*is a runner-up for the first annual
Bywater Prize for Fiction.*

Paperback Original ◆ ISBN 978-1-932859-30-0 ◆ $13.95

Bywater Books

BABIES, BIKES & BROADS
The Third Cat Rising Novel

Cynn Chadwick

Cat Hood doesn't want to go home. She has a new life and a new love in Scotland. But her brother, Will, has been widowed and left with two small children. So there's no choice for Cat now. She must return to Galway, North Carolina, the place she left when love got lost.

But it looks like love wants to get found all over again. When Cat gets back, she comes face-to-face with Janey, the lover who betrayed her all those years ago. And with only the slender thread of a phone line to bridge the gulf between America and Scotland, Cat can't help fearing a new betrayal.

As Cat helps her brother to rebuild his life, she starts to see that her own needs attention. That maybe it's time to acknowledge this is her home. That maybe it's time to leave behind the pain of the past.

And maybe it's time to get over Janey. If she can ...

Babies, Bikes & Broads *is a runner-up for the fourth annual Bywater Prize for Fiction.*

Paperback Original ◆ ISBN 978-1-932859-62-1 ◆ $14.95

Bywater Books represents the coming of age of lesbian fiction. We're committed to bringing the best of contemporary lesbian writing to a discerning readership. Our editorial team is dedicated to finding and developing outstanding voices who deliver stories you won't want to put down. That's why we sponsor the annual Bywater Prize. We love good books, just like you do.

For more information about Bywater Books and the annual Bywater Prize for Fiction, please visit our website.

www.bywaterbooks.com